F

KB

NO CONTROL

When his mouth trailed down her throat to explore the pulsing hollow of her shoulder, Barbara fought through the haze of wild sensation.

"What are you doing here, Jock?" Her voice wavered, in traitorous betrayal of the havoc he was wreaking on her self-control.

"What the hell kind of question is that?" The warmth of his laughing breath caressed her sensitive skin. He lifted his head long enough to let the tawny gold of his eyes hold her mesmerized. Then his mouth came down near her lips, his breath mingling with hers as he answered amusedly, "I live here, of course."

from "Southern Nights"

BOOK YOUR PLACE ON OUR WEBSITE AND MAKE THE READING CONNECTION!

We've created a customized website just for our very special readers, where you can get the inside scoop on everything that's going on with Zebra, Pinnacle and Kensington books.

When you come online, you'll have the exciting opportunity to:

- View covers of upcoming books
- Read sample chapters
- Learn about our future publishing schedule (listed by publication month *and author*)
- Find out when your favorite authors will be visiting a city near you
- Search for and order backlist books from our online catalog
- Check out author bios and background information
- Send e-mail to your favorite authors
- Meet the Kensington staff online
- Join us in weekly chats with authors, readers and other guests
- Get writing guidelines
- AND MUCH MORE!

**Visit our website at
http://www.kensingtonbooks.com**

Stealing Kisses

JANET DAILEY

ZEBRA BOOKS
Kensington Publishing Corp.
www.kensingtonbooks.com

ZEBRA BOOKS are published by

Kensington Publishing Corp.
850 Third Avenue
New York, NY 10022

All Kensington titles, imprints, and distributed lines are available
at special quantity discounts for bulk purchases for sales promotion, premiums, fund-raising, educational, or institutional use.

Special book excerpts or customized printings can also be created to fit specific needs. For details, write or phone the office
of the Kensington Special Sales Manager: Attn.: Special Sales
Department. Kensington Publishing Corp., 850 Third Avenue,
New York, NY 10022. Phone: 1-800-221-2647.

Zebra and the Z logo Reg. U.S. Pat. & TM Off.

ISBN-13: 978-1-4201-0304-5
ISBN-10: 1-4201-0304-0

First Printing: July 2008
10 9 8 7 6 5 4 3 2 1

Printed in the United States of America

Contents

SOUTHERN NIGHTS

Chapter One

The traffic thinned out once they were north of Miami, and Todd Gaynor relaxed behind the wheel. He reached over and gave Barbara's arm a friendly pat. Then his hand rumpled the short curls of her silky black hair.

His caresses were affectionate, she thought with a small inward sigh. But not passionate. Still, considering what had happened months ago, before she met him, it was just as well. Barbara had been madly in love with another man and thought it was for real. It hadn't lasted.

After that, she'd decided to make reasonable choices about guys. Everything about Todd fit the checklist. He was a grandmother's dream: reliable, pragmatic, not too bad-looking, and he never made a move without asking if it was okay with her.

Okay, she wasn't going to get swept off her feet again, but she could get carried over a threshold. He was already hinting at making "this" permanent.

Barbara glanced his way and managed to smile. So far "this" didn't involve sex. Kisses, yes. Holding hands, yes. Looking at rings, yes. Rings in the inexpensive tray, rings with mock diamonds that were a reasonable choice in terms of cost. He had even looked deep into her eyes and discussed the tax benefits of filing as a couple.

Some women would feel lucky to be in your shoes, she told herself, feeling a little unhappy.

Todd took his eyes from the highway long enough to glance at her. "Tired?"

"Mmm." It was a soft, negative sound. Through half-closed lashes Barbara saw the late afternoon sunlight glinting off the waters of Lake Okeechobee.

"Nervous?" Todd's voice was calm. He just wasn't a particularly emotional guy.

"A little," she admitted. It was difficult to be too nervous around him. She told herself that Todd was her rock. With him she felt safe and protected, not dangling on the edge of a precipice about to take a nasty fall. He had a way of making sure that most things went smoothly—even something as potentially daunting as meeting his family.

"In love?"

Just for a moment, the inflection of his voice made her heart flutter in reaction to the memory of another man's voice. Looking out the window at nothing in particular, Barbara forced the sensation to go away.

"Yes," she answered. Her voice sounded loud to her ears, as if she was attempting to deny the unwanted memory.

"I'm in love, too."

By his definition of it, maybe he was. It seemed rude to argue. She ought to count her blessings.

"Are you?" It wasn't that easy for Barbara to match his light, bantering tone.

"Yes. With a very nice lady who has big blue eyes and a wonderful personality."

Which sounded like a runner-up in a beauty pageant. She didn't exactly feel special, but she knew that he meant well. "I hope she makes you very happy." Her hand sought his and their fingers interlaced. It was a gesture oddly reminiscent of another time, and another man's hand entwined possessively with hers. A shudder trembled through her.

"Are you cold?" Todd was instantly attentive. "I could turn the air conditioner down."

"No, I'm fine," she insisted, and tilted her head back against his arm to gaze at his face. "Sometimes it seems that I've known you all my life instead of just four weeks."

"It's been awesome," he said.

Not the word she would pick. But if that was how he saw this relationship, she didn't feel up to arguing about it. He just wasn't the kind of guy who got riled up or lost his temper or let emotions take over, anyway. She felt a poignant throb of memory and swallowed hard.

"Well, things happened fast," she said carefully. "Sometimes I wish—" Shoot. There was a catch in her voice.

"What?"

"I wish I had met you first."

He slid her a look before letting his attention return to the highway. "Do you want to talk about him?" It was a considerate question.

A long silence followed his question. Barbara was barely aware of it as her gaze ran over his profile.

Funny how he reminded her sometimes of Jock. So did other guys, of course—Jock stayed on her mind and she still tended to see him coming down the street when it really wasn't him at all.

But Todd's hair and eyes were plain brown, not shot through with gold from being outdoors. At thirty-one, he lacked the character lines that had etched Jock's eyes and mouth. Nor did he possess that potent brand of sexuality that had taken Barbara's breath away the first time she saw Jock on the beach. She had only to close her eyes to remember the hard feel of his body against hers and the undermining caress of his sure hands.

"What's there to talk about?" A bitter hurt that Barbara had thought was behind her crept into her voice. "He dropped me like a rock."

It was no good to claim that only her pride had suffered. And she couldn't claim that he had taken advantage of her. She'd gone into the affair with her eyes wide open, never dreaming it would last less than a few weeks. For her, loving Jock was everything. Until it was suddenly over, she wouldn't have been able to say how long she'd loved him, only that she did, and she'd wanted it to last forever.

Jock's huskily seductive voice echoed in her head, saying the words she'd heard six months before. "I'm not any good at small talk, honey. I want to make love to you." The forthright statement had thrilled her. Jock Malloy had only been saying what was on her mind whenever he was within touching distance.

"Todd, did I tell you that he once asked me to go with him when he left?" It was a short, mocking question, laced with yearning that she hadn't gone. She had thought many times about that offer, and also her reaction to it. She flashed Todd a brittle smile. "I nearly agreed. I was so tempted . . . But I kept thinking about my job, and my apartment. Can you imagine the mess I would have been in if I had gone with him, and he'd gotten tired of me and dumped me between here and Texas or wherever his ranch was—if he had one?"

Details hadn't mattered at the time. She'd known Jock was vacationing in Miami, and that the beach house where he was staying belonged to a friend. Stupidly, she had thought that it was the real deal, forever after, hearts on fire, and all that. She'd had no idea that it would come to an abrupt end when he left. Jock was a man who knew how to make the loving last, but he didn't look back when he was done with her. *Later, alligator.* He hadn't said that, but his interest had been just about that casual, when all was said and done. She was so positive it would continue that she had never bothered to ask him the usual questions.

Talking—well, serious talking—hadn't seemed necessary. No, Jock was more about margaritas at sunset, and making her laugh for hours, and wild, soul-satisfying sex.

She doubted she would ever experience that again. Of course, Todd had probably put sex on one of his lists—he liked to keep lists—but Barbara knew without even asking that getting physical wasn't a priority for him. Jock's very male amorousness had been unmistakable from the second their eyes had met. But it's over, she told herself angrily. Over means *over.* Afterward Barbara had been glad she didn't know a whole lot of details about him other than his name and, vaguely, what he did. Something about a cattle ranch—he'd mentioned it once.

"But you didn't go with him," Todd pointed out, moving into the right lane to let a white-haired driver zoom past on his left.

"No." A sudden, almost desperate sigh broke from her. "Why am I telling you all this?"

"Confession is supposed to be good for the soul." He kept his eyes fixed on the road ahead.

"I . . . can't." She looked out the window of the luxury sedan again, feeling a little depressed by the sameness of the landscape. Other than the bare bones of her story, Barbara had never fleshed out the affair to Todd. Even now he wasn't asking her to, only offering a willing ear to listen. Her refusal to confide in him didn't produce a reaction.

Taking out a map from the glove compartment, Barbara unfolded it and pretended to study it. "So where am I going?"

Good question in more ways than one.

Todd exhaled and drummed his fingers on the steering wheel. "I told you before we left. You can check it on the GPS system." He switched it on and a soft but robotic female voice gave the distance to their destination.

"I love this thing," he said. "She never gets lost and she never gets excited." He cast a glance at Barbara, who was absent-mindedly trying to stick the map back where she got it. "And she never folds up a map like that. Would you mind doing it right?"

Barbara took it out again and folded the map in neat sections. "How's that?"

"Better. Thanks."

She smoothed it against her thigh, regretting the

crinkles she'd unintentionally put into it. But she didn't see why he had to get snippy about a map when he had an expensive GPS gizmo. And a radar detector that he didn't need because he usually drove at least five miles under the speed limit.

She wondered why he'd thrown caution to the winds when it came to her. A question nagged at her and at last she asked it. "Why haven't you ever asked about him, Todd? His name? How we met? What happened?" Her sideways glance was wary, apprehension shimmering in the blue depths of her eyes.

"Because I know that someday you'll trust me enough to tell me the whole story," he answered without hesitation.

"I do trust you." Barbara glanced down at the folded map in her hands. She'd agreed to meet his parents and it was early in the relationship for that.

"All right. That's important. You can't love somebody you can't trust."

"Well, yeah." Trust was a tough word. So was love. Good guy that Todd was, he had promised to keep her heart safe. It had been shattered when she met him, but she was hoping her heart would be whole again. He did things by the book, so it should all work out. Sometimes she wasn't sure that she appreciated him enough. "But doesn't it bother you that there was someone else before you came?"

"No. A woman doesn't reach the age of twenty-five without, you know, being experienced. I accepted that when I met you." He seemed thoughtful.

Barbara considered the implications of that remark, then looked at his hands on the steering wheel. One at ten o'clock, one at two o'clock. Their touch didn't make her skin tingle, but she didn't trust that sensation anymore. His comment prompted a fleeting curiosity to voice itself.

"What about your heart? Has it ever been bruised and battered, Todd?" She found it hard to believe. His face was so smooth and calm. There were no shadows of tormented longing and heartbroken grief in his eyes. Which was probably a good thing.

"A half a dozen times, at least." It came out like a joke.

"Be serious," Barbara insisted.

"I am. It's difficult to judge past emotional involvements since I met you. From this perspective, they all seem like infatuations. Does that answer your question?" He briefly arched an eyebrow in her direction, his brown eyes warm with amused indulgence.

"Yes, I suppose it does." She didn't have that perspective.

"Besides, if you had met me first, maybe you wouldn't have noticed me," Todd said.

"That isn't true," Barbara protested quickly. "You're a really nice guy, Todd. And you're nice-looking. Any woman would notice you." Unless Jock Malloy was around, a naughty little voice qualified her statement.

As if reading her mind, Todd followed his thought one step further. "Or maybe I would have lost you to him." Barbara was thankful he didn't give her a chance to respond to that remark, because she didn't know what she could say to that distinct possibility. "The 'maybes' don't have anything to do with the present or the way it happened. There isn't any reason to say 'what if.'"

"Yes, there is," she said in a sober voice. "What if I had never met you? You have been so good *to* me and *for* me, and *with* me"—she emphasized the little words carefully—"that sometimes I wonder what I did to deserve someone like you. You're just so understanding and patient."

"When I first met you, you reminded me of a stray kitten I once found that someone had dumped on the highway," Todd mused. "You were so scared and frightened . . . not that you let it show." He darted her a glance. "No, you arched your back and hissed at me, pretending you weren't scared or frightened. How many times did you turn me down before I finally persuaded you to go on a date with me?"

"At least twelve." Barbara remembered his gentle coaxing. "Although I don't know why you bothered," she sighed.

Letting go of her hand, Todd reached up and flipped down the sun visor on her side. The mirror on the back side of the visor reflected her image, midnight black hair framing an oval face, brilliant blue eyes outlined by long, sooty lashes, and delicate features that were enhanced by a golden Florida tan.

"That woman in the mirror should answer your questions," he said. "When I first met her, there were dark circles under her eyes and a sad smile. You needed affection more than you needed love, you know."

A passing thought crossed her mind that love had given her the dark circles and sad smile in the first place. Barbara didn't mention it, but she couldn't keep the pain of remembering what she had lost from flickering across her expression.

"I promised I wouldn't rush you into marriage, Barbara, and I won't. We'll have a long engagement, an old-fashioned courtship period where I can shower you with presents and flowers and love poems." A bantering note in his voice seemed to tease his own romanticism and make her smile with him. Still and all, she felt guilty for not feeling more enthusiastic about it.

"And then," he went on, "we can have a big church wedding, which will make my mother happy, and a Caribbean honeymoon, which will make me happy. You'll like my mother," he added unexpectedly.

"I hope she'll like me," was the automatic response.

"She will," Todd assured her. "I wish we'd had more time together for ourselves. I wouldn't have suggested spending our vacations with my family if either one of us could arrange to take them later this year. But these two weeks are the only slack time the hotel has before the Easter crunch hits, then summer tourists. My manager takes his vacation in the fall and—"

"The airline wouldn't let me rearrange my schedule unless I gave up my vacation for this year," Barbara said. She worked the reservation counter at the airport, after two years as a flight attendant with the same company. "It's just coincidence that we have the same vacation time now."

"Could be a sign," he smiled. "And I want you to get to know my family. I want you to think of them as yours."

"You haven't told me very much about your family, besides that your mom's a widow, and your brother," she began, and Todd picked up the conversation from that point.

"There's just my mother and brother, but we've always been very close. Maybe three is a magic number. My mother, Lillian, is a great lady. Gentle, warm and loving."

"You must take after her," Barbara said politely.

"I don't know. My dad was a pretty great guy, too. Mom said he was the softest touch in town. When any charity in Miami needed to raise money, they stopped at his hotel first. He couldn't say no to anyone in trouble. If he had, he'd probably have been a multimillionaire when he died. Not that he left us broke." Todd laughed at the thought.

Only recently had Barbara even realized that she was involved with a relatively wealthy man. The hotel Todd owned and operated was one of the most popular resorts on the oceanfront strip. The income from it could have enabled him to do nothing at all, but Todd had chosen to work. He was frugal by nature, except for this car.

"What about Sandoval?" she asked, referring to the citrus farm that was their destination. "Is that where you grew up?"

"No. We did spend time there. J.R. liked it but I'm not much of a country boy. I prefer city life, like my dad," Todd admitted.

Looking at him, Barbara was glad. She was beginning to prefer his good grooming and cared-for skin to the rugged look of an outdoorsman. It would have been an unwanted reminder of a man browned from hours in the sun. Like hers, Todd's light tan came from lazing by a pool or on an ocean beach.

"J.R. is your brother?" she asked for confirmation.

"My older brother, yes. It's a good thing Sandoval belongs to him. That life fits him like a glove. I should warn you about J.R.," Todd added after a second's consideration.

"Warn me?" Her blue eyes sent him a quizzical glance as a little shiver of fear danced down her spine.

Todd met her look with a smile. "He's going to hit on you."

"But why? I—I'm—whatever the next step before fiancée is." She remembered the inexpensive tray of rings that she'd politely passed up. If she had one of those on her left hand, she'd be safe. "Todd, he wouldn't—" She tried to stammer out an astonished protest, but Todd laughed out loud.

"In the first place, J.R. has a roving eye. He invariably locates the most beautiful woman in every crowd," he began his explanation. "And women automatically go wild over him. Which was something he discovered early on. Knowing J.R., he might have a couple of reasons to hit on you. One would be to test you—to see if his brother's girlfriend is really sincere."

"Gee, he sounds like a prince," Barbara said wryly. "And the second?" she prompted when Todd paused.

"The second reason?" He lifted his shoulders in an expressive shrug. "The second reason would probably be for the sheer hell of it."

"What am I supposed to do when he tries something?" She couldn't keep the edge of challenge out of her voice.

"I can't tell you what to do." There was an underlying chuckle in his voice. "All I can do is warn you in advance that it's coming. I trust you to know how to handle him, Barbara."

Slightly reassured by his confidence in her, she still had to ask, "I take it your brother isn't married?"

"J.R. is the original swamp fox. He's too wily and experienced to get caught. His problem is he's always had his pick. Anything that was out of his reach, he regarded as sour grapes. When it comes right down to it, J.R. has a take-them-or-leave-them approach. Mostly he takes them and then leaves them. He thinks marriage is a trap." Todd grinned.

"Do you?" Barbara asked.

The smile disappeared from his mouth. "No. I was being a smart-aleck. But people say things like that about my brother. They aren't really fair to him. I think he would like to have a wife and children, if he could ever find the right one. He needs someone like you—someone he can protect and cherish." He sighed. "J.R.'s just had too many eager applicants for the position. He tends to view them all with a jaundiced eye."

"You really care a lot about your brother, don't you?" Barbara realized with a vague sense of shock. From Todd's description, the two seemed to be polar opposites.

"I used to hero-worship him. I still do. J.R.'s someone to look up to," Todd insisted. "You'll know what I mean when you meet him."

She relaxed a little. There was no reason to disbelieve what he said. If his brother was half as nice as Todd was, Barbara knew she would like him.

"What have you told your family about me?" she asked curiously.

"Nothing."

"Really?" She sat up straighter and turned to look at him.

A lazy smile tugged at the corners of his mouth. "Knowing my mother, if I told her I was bringing my girlfriend home with me, she'd connect the dots all the way to future bride. Then she'd invite everyone at the place over to the house for a champagne party. I don't think you're prepared for that kind of a welcome. It's too soon for us yet. So I just told her I was bringing a friend. That way you can have a few quiet days to get acquainted before she asks if you want an engagement party." He slowed the car and turned off the highway onto a narrow lane where he stopped in front of a gate. "We are now on Sandoval land."

Barbara glanced at the plain wooden gate painted white. A small sign on the top rail stated: *Sandoval Ranch. Private Property. No Trespassing.*

"That isn't very welcoming," she remarked.

"The main entrance is a few miles up the road yet," Todd explained. "This is a shortcut to the house, as well as a scenic drive through the orchards. Wait here while I open the gate." He switched off the air conditioning and rolled down the car windows before climbing out of the car to open the gate.

The tangy fragrance of oranges drifted on the warm air that filled the artificially cooled interior of the car. Precise, orderly rows of dwarf trees flanked the narrow dirt road beyond the gate Todd opened. As he drove the car through and stopped to close the gate, Barbara had a closer look at the fruit hanging from the tree limbs.

"Valencia," Todd identified the variety. "There are probably more Valencia orange groves on the property than any other. They're excellent juice oranges. My mother uses them in fruit salads and dessert cups. They start to ripen in March so they'll be picking these soon."

"For a city boy, you know a lot about oranges," Barbara teased.

"Isn't every Florida native supposed to be an expert on oranges?" he countered.

"Not this one," she admitted. "I've driven past a lot of orange groves and stopped at fruit stands to buy the local product, but what I know about citrus fruit wouldn't fill a page."

Todd drove slowly along the narrow lane. "We'll try to correct that while you are here."

"Look." Barbara pointed at the tree on the driver's side. "Isn't that an orange blossom on the same limb with an orange?"

"Yes. You are about to receive your first lecture on citrus fruit."

Barbara groaned, but in fun.

"Oranges and grapefruit take a full twelve months to mature, unlike apples and other fruit that mature in three or four months. Therefore, you have ripened fruit and blossoms on the tree at the same time—this year's crop and next year's."

"Interesting." After seeing the first blossom, Barbara spotted more white petals sprinkled through the green leaves of the trees, contrasting with the orange globes of fruit. The car rolled slowly past the arrow-straight rows of trees that seemed to stretch endlessly.

"Oranges and grapefruit won't ripen once they are picked like other fruit. So they can't be picked when they are green and shipped. They have to be tree ripened," Todd explained.

"I didn't know that, either." Barbara laughed at her own ignorance. "I mean, 'tree-ripened' is always on the juice cartons as a selling point. But they don't say it's a given for every single orange in the orchard."

"Tomorrow I'll arrange to take you on a complete tour of the citrus groves and make up for your neglected education. How would you like that?"

"I'd love it."

As they rounded a turn, the groves of fruit trees were replaced by hayfields. Ahead Barbara could see white rail fences and green grass beyond the purple blossoms of clover. In the lush pastures, sunlight glistened on the sleek coats of grazing horses. A spindly-legged foal stood next to its mother, close to the fence.

"You raise horses?" Barbara asked in surprise.

"Yeah, thoroughbreds for racing. Didn't I mention that?"

"No, you didn't," she said with amusement, and looked again to the pastures. "Aren't they beautiful."

"Do you ride?"

"Every chance I get—which isn't many." A wistful note crept into her voice.

"There are more than enough horses here. You can ride a different one every day if you want," Todd offered.

"This place is beginning to sound like paradise."

"Glad you think so. We are going to be marooned here for two weeks," Todd said.

"I'm not going to mind." The roofs of the stables were coming into sight, white, gleaming buildings that matched the white rail fences.

"I'm not going to mind, either, not when I'm spending that much time with you. I'll probably be so busy looking at you that I won't even miss the bright lights," he concluded, warming her with a look.

Despite the fact that he was driving, Barbara leaned to kiss him. It was a spontaneous gesture, the first kiss she had initiated between them, even if it was just a peck on the cheek. Once she had been much bolder, but then it had been another man's mouth she sought.

Todd let the car slow to a crawl, the only response he could make to her unexpected action. She liked the softness of his skin, and the thought of his lips tasting hers. Sometimes really kissing him was pretty nice and their mutual tenderness sent a contented glow flowing through her veins. He promised a different kind of satisfaction, one less dangerous and soul-destroying.

"I think I love you," she whispered, her lips feathering over his ear.

He seemed to hesitate. Then he got a better grip on the steering wheel and concentrated on driving again. She settled back down. The ardent light in his brown eyes said her declaration had gotten to him somehow, but common sense had taken control.

"Then you'd better let me see where I'm going before we run into something," he suggested.

"You're right," she conceded and leaned her head against the head rest, not wanting to go farther. The seatbelt prevented her from doing much anyway. Todd chuckled and drew her glance. "Why are you laughing?"

"You look like a kitten again. But not so scared."

"I'm not," Barbara admitted to that much. "I feel pretty good about my life at the moment."

He seemed to know that no reply was expected from him, although his hand tightened on the wheel. From the tree-shaded pastures of green grass, past the white boards of the stables, the narrow lane led toward a lawn that boasted big oaks. Rising in the midst of the treetops was a red-tiled roof. The narrow lane connected with the black asphalt of the main road to the house.

As Todd turned onto the main road, the Spanish moss draped from the branches kept the house from view. Her eyes widened when the gray-green curtain wafted apart in the breeze. A massive two-story home rose in front of her, the dull red tile of the roof complimented by the natural color of the stucco walls. The dramatic arches and balconies reminded her of traditional Spanish design. Arched exterior walls led into a courtyard with a splashing fountain, and more arches led to the main entrance. Black wrought iron, scrolled like lace, lined the balconies on the upper floor, covered by arched frames.

"Are you going to sit in the car and admire the place, or should we go inside?" Todd said.

Overwhelmed by the magnificence of the house, Barbara hadn't realized Todd had stopped the car and turned off the engine. She gave a guilty start of surprise at his question. "You should have warned me it was so impressive, Todd."

"I think I had probably forgotten until I saw it through your eyes," he said and climbed out of the car to walk around and open her door. "But it's just a house, Barbara. Four walls and a roof."

It was more than four walls and a roof, but Barbara didn't argue the point. For all its old-world grandeur, the house wasn't intimidating. A riot of bougainvillea crowded the walls of the courtyard where the water playing in the fountain made a happy sound. The noise of their footsteps on the tiled walkway didn't seem like an intrusion as they entered the courtyard. More greenery hung from suspended pots while a profusion of colorful blossoms spilled from stone urns. Beyond another archway, Barbara saw the blue water of a swimming pool. But it was to the huge carved doors that Todd guided her.

The door opened into a tiled foyer. A second, glass-doored entrance into the foyer came from the porch on the pool side of the house. The carved balustrade of an open staircase curved gracefully from the foyer to the second floor. A glazed archway opened into the living room. Todd paused inside this spacious room.

"Would you mind waiting here?" he asked. "Mom's probably in the kitchen and I don't think she would thank me if I took you back there when she might be arguing with the cook."

"I don't mind waiting here." Since Todd hadn't told his mom he was bringing his new significant other, the announcement might come as a shock. Barbara thought it was better if she wasn't around when Mrs. Gaynor and her son got through the family small talk and did a little catching up.

"Are you thirsty? I'll bring us back something to drink if you are," he offered.

"I'd like that," she nodded.

He started toward the archway into the dining room with its heavy Spanish-designed furniture, then stopped and came back to kiss her lightly on the mouth. "Don't go running off. My mother will love you."

Strangely, Barbara discovered she didn't feel nervous about meeting his mother. Maybe the warm, comfortable atmosphere of the house had reassured her somehow. She glanced around the spacious living room with its white walls, arched windows and fireplace. The cheery rugs on the tiled floor and the abundant pillows on the sofa softened from the rigidity of the Spanish furniture. The impression was one of solidity and relaxed comfort.

The place really was paradise. And she felt very much at home there.

Chapter Two

A door slammed in the foyer, glass rattling in the pane toward the poolside entrance. Barbara turned toward the archway at the sound of long strides on the tiled floor, made by someone wearing boots. A tall, broad-shouldered man entered the living room, faded denims hugging narrow hips and muscled thighs. The dusty and sweat-stained shirt had once been white, just as the wide-brimmed Stetson on the man's head had once been brown. The shadowing brim of that hat hid his features until some unconscious movement from Barbara betrayed her presence. He looked right at her.

A shock wave trembled through her at the sight of the hard, male features toughened by the sun. His tawny eyes flicked over her.

Oh, no. It couldn't be. Her imagination was playing some cruel trick on her, she thought frantically. The hat came off, sailed by a hand to land on a chair. Brown hair was streaked with gold, the handiwork of the sun. The action was followed by the white flash of a smile. His rough-hewn features exuded male sexuality.

"Jock?" The name was forced past the lump of disbelief that gripped her throat.

"Well, look who's here. So you changed your mind and decided to accept my invitation after all." That low, drawling voice ran over her like a caress. "It took you long enough."

It was a dream. Barbara was convinced it had to be. But he was walking toward her. Jock hadn't been specific—his only invitation had been to come with him. Not much later he had let her know it was all over between them. So he wouldn't be saying something like that. But what on earth was he doing here, in this house?

He had the audacity to sweep her into his arms and press her slender frame to the hard contours of his body. The pleasurable weight of his mouth on hers made her tip her head back while he kissed her with a hungry force that was nonetheless passionate. Her fingers were splayed across his shoulders, feeling the ripple of flexing muscles through the damp, thin cotton of his shirt.

The dominating quality of his embrace pierced her numbed senses and filled her with a dangerous excitement. The wild emotions his touch evoked were undermining defenses Barbara had vowed would never be breached again. Yet the mastery of his kiss was awfully hard to resist. Her own hunger didn't help. The skillful prowess of his hands was awakening her all over again to his desires and making them her own. When his mouth trailed down her throat to explore the pulsing hollow of her shoulder, Barbara fought through the haze of wild sensation.

"What are you doing here, Jock?" Her voice wavered, betraying the havoc he was wreaking on her self-control.

"What the hell kind of question is that?" The warmth of his laughing breath caressed her sensitive skin. He lifted his head long enough to let the tawny gold of his eyes hold her mesmerized. Then his mouth came down near her lips, his breath mingling with hers as he answered amusedly, "I live here, of course."

And then the hot languor of his kiss melted her again. The sensation was pleasurable but terrifying. The dizzying loss of control hadn't frightened her before, until he'd dumped her and depression struck. Todd had helped her out of that black pit. It was his voice that interrupted what Jock was doing. "Mom sent me out with the drinks. She'll—" His voice stopped in midsentence.

The muscled chest beneath Barbara's hands expanded in a deep breath as Jock lifted his mouth from its possession of hers and sent an impatient glance beyond her. The gold-flecked eyes returned quickly to her face, roaming her passion-dazed features with lazy pleasure.

"Your timing's off, little brother," Jock said in an indolent way, never letting his gaze stray from her upturned face. "Go away and arrange to arrive about an hour from now. Better make it two hours." He added a few more words that were meant only for Barbara. "It's been a long time. Too long."

The spell he'd cast shattered into bits. His arrogant presumption that she would instantly return to him, no questions asked, was the spark her pride needed. Todd's presence in the room gave Barbara the strength to retaliate. In one motion, she pushed out of his arms and struck. The palm of her hand connected with stinging force against a lean, hollowed cheek. His stunned look was immediately replaced with an intense focus on her. There was anger in his eyes, but it was intuitively and instantly clear to her that he would rather die than return the slap or hurt her in any other way. All the same, sensing she had roused something wild in him, Barbara cautiously began to back toward Todd.

Todd's low laughter dissipated a little of the tension. "I told you that you would know how to handle J.R. when the time came." The firm clasp of his hand was on her shoulder. Barbara turned into it, seeking the protection and safety of Todd's nearness. "Although I have to admit I didn't expect anything to happen so soon. Guess you're losing your touch, J.R. I don't think you expected to get slapped."

Barbara risked a glance at Jock. A hand was rubbing his cheek where she had slapped him. There was a wary glitter in his eyes, as if he was trying to assess this puzzling situation, too. She didn't understand why Todd kept calling him J.R. How could Jock be his brother?

"Should I bother with formal introductions?" Todd was still finding amusement in the situation. "Or are you just going to congratulate me for finding such a beautiful girl?"

"Are the two of you engaged or something?" If Todd didn't hear the deadly quiet note in Jock's voice, Barbara did.

"We don't have the ring yet. Isn't that right, Barbara?" Todd's voice prompted her to back him up.

"No, not yet." Which was the truth. Her left hand

was stiffly resistant to the orders sent along her motor nerves. At last it was lifted to show her bare fingers to Jock's piercing gaze.

"Okay. But you two are more than just pals, obviously. Happened kinda suddenly, didn't it, Todd?" There was a measure of challenge in Jock's calm comment.

"We only met a month ago," Todd admitted and smiled at Barbara, not apparently noticing her troubled expression. "But I copied a page from your book, J.R. I didn't waste any time once I found her."

"I don't understand," Barbara finally voiced her confusion. "You two are brothers, yet with different—"

"Half brothers," Jock interrupted. "Same mother, different fathers. Didn't Todd mention that?" The edges of his mouth curved up in a not very polite smile. It relayed his discovery that he now realized she'd had no idea that she would find him here.

"No, he didn't," she said, flustered by the situation she was trapped in.

"By the way, Todd is the only one who calls me J.R. To everyone else I'm Jock."

"Jock Malloy," she said in an almost inaudible voice. Barbara didn't know why she'd whispered his whole name—she told herself a second later that she would have to be incredibly careful about if and when she told the truth.

Fortunately, Todd didn't seem to have heard.

The last thing she wanted Todd to guess was that Jock had been the man with whom she'd had that disastrous affair. She knew it. And Jock knew it. Poor Todd was the only one who didn't. How long could she keep it a secret from Todd? How long before Jock told him?

"I'm a Malloy," Jock said blandly. "He's a Gaynor."
He nodded toward his brother.

"I see." She swallowed hard, thankful in a way that
he'd covered her slip. "I'm Barbara Haynes." She
pressed her fingertips to her temples. "And I think I
have a headache."

"You do?" Todd asked with concern.

"Kind of. Not too bad." Actually it was a terrible,
throbbing one that clawed at her temples. "It's probably from the trip," she lied. "I used to get carsick as a
child."

"Why don't you sit down, Barbara?" Todd suggested and attentively guided her to the sofa and its
many plump pillows. As she sat down, his hand happened to rest on the straining muscles of her neck.
"Wow, you're tense . . . all strung out like a wire."

"Nerves, I guess." Under the scrutiny of Jock's
tawny eyes, Barbara knew she would never relax, but
for Todd's sake she tried to appear that way.

"She needs a rubdown, Todd. A good massage
would work wonders." Jock's look was deliberately
suggestive of other, more intimate times despite the
bland tone he used.

"Yeah, well, I can take care of that," Todd said.
"Hands off, bro." He seemed to be joking but Barbara picked up on the undercurrent between him
and Jock.

Barbara protested when Todd took a step toward
the couch where she sat. "It really isn't necessary. An
aspirin would work just as well."

"Jock, there's a bottle in the medicine cabinet,"
suggested Todd.

"I have some in my purse." Barbara had something
stronger, in fact. Just dealing with Jock's sudden reap-

pearance was going to take more than one little aspirin. His nearness reminded Barbara of sensations
she would rather forget.

When Jock handed the straw purse to her, Barbara
only had to see his hands to remember how expertly
they aroused her and how intimately they knew her.
"Thank you." She offered him the polite phrase and
lifted her gaze to his face.

The clean, decisive outline of his mouth arrested
her attention. Its latent sensuality made her remember even more: how those lips had discovered all the
special places that stimulated her the most. Heat
flamed her skin as Barbara hurriedly bent her head to
look for the bottle of anti-anxiety pills in her purse.

"Hope you find what you're looking for," Jock said.

A hole to crawl into and hide was what she wanted,
but she found the bottle in a few more seconds.
Prying off the safety cap, she took out two tablets in
her palm. Todd was offering her a tall, iced glass.

"Mom fixed an orange smoothie and left the
blender jar in the fridge ready to go. It's nice and
thick, unless you prefer water," he said.

"No, this is fine." She washed down the tablets with
the fresh citrus drink. "Where is your mother?" In a nervous gesture, Barbara raked her fingernails through the
dark curls near her ear, ostensibly fluffing her hair, and
reached for her purse again.

"She wanted a few minutes to freshen up before
she met you," Todd explained.

A plump pillow was offered next. She didn't need
to look to know whose hand owned those strong,
sun-browned fingers, so capable and adept at love-
making.

"Put this at the back of your neck and try to relax," Jock murmured.

"Don't mind if I do." Barbara didn't even attempt a refusal, not able to keep the breathlessness out of her voice. She took the pillow from him.

"Comfortable?" The way he said the very ordinary word caused a rush of heat in her cheeks.

"Yes." She arranged the pillow just so, remembering how it had been to lie beside him and see his handsome head resting on a very different pillow. Her imagination helped to fill in a few more sensual details. Her darkened blue eyes made a furtive glance at his face, ricocheting away when she found his gaze centered on her mouth. The click of heels on the tiled floor heralded the arrival of Todd's mother and gave Barbara an excellent excuse to think of something else entirely. She put the pillow to one side and started to get up.

"I'm sorry I took so long, but Todd didn't catch me at my best." A tall, pretty woman entered the living room, her dark hair liberally streaked with gray. Her warm smile and all her attention were directed strictly at Barbara. Alert brown eyes swept her in silent appraisal. Apparently she was dissatisfied with the result. "Oh, hello. When Todd mentioned he was bringing a friend, I thought . . . well, it doesn't matter what I thought."

Barbara rose from the sofa automatically at the woman's approach, with Todd standing at her side. But it was Jock, leaning back in his chair looking relaxed, with lazy amusement gleaming in his eyes, who made the introduction.

"Mom, meet Barbara Haynes."

"How do you do, Mrs. Gaynor." Her greeting

sounded stiff, but the woman was so like Todd that Barbara wanted to cry with relief.

"Call me Lillian, please," the woman corrected, putting them on a first-name basis immediately. "And I'll call you Barbara. Welcome to Sandoval."

"Thank you. I'm really happy to be here."

Brown eyes sparkled when they glanced at Todd. "She's very beautiful."

"Don't sound so surprised, Mom." He laughed and slid a hand around Barbara's waist.

"You'll have to forgive me, Barbara, if I'm at a loss for words. Your visit is a bit of a surprise. Todd hasn't even mentioned you so I didn't have any inkling that he was serious about anyone." Realizing that she was making everyone stand because of her, Lillian Gaynor insisted, "Please, sit down." She took a chair close to the sofa. "How long have you known each other? How did you meet?"

"We bumped into each other a month ago, literally," Todd answered, draping an arm along the sofa back behind Barbara. "She walked into my car at the airport as I was backing out of a parking space."

"Were you hurt, Barbara?"

"No."

"I took one look at her and insisted that I had to see her home safely," Todd said with a wink. "After a whole lot of arguing and persuading I finally convinced her to go out with me. She didn't have a very high opinion of men at the time or—"

Barbara felt a pair of gold-brown eyes narrow on her and quickly interrupted. "Todd," she cautioned. She had escaped the affair with Jock with a few shreds of her pride intact. She didn't want Todd unintentionally taking that away from her.

Todd hesitated, then smiled. "Or it wouldn't have taken me so long." He changed what he had been about to say and an awkward silence fell for a few beats.

"Well, then," Lillian said soothingly and Barbara hoped the questions were over. "I don't want to pry. You'll tell me more when there's more to tell, right."

"Not yet. Give us time, Mom," Todd said affectionately.

"I don't suppose there's any need to rush, not in this day and age," Jock said. Nobody misinterpreted his innuendo. While Barbara reddened under his knowing regard, Todd flashed him a silencing look.

It was Lillian who reprimanded him. "Instead of being so cynical, Jock, you should be following Todd's example."

"I would," he stated. "But I don't think Todd would share his girl with me."

A wild sensation ran through Barbara, a direct reaction to his suggestion. Jock was just too masculine and magnetic for her not to react. It was going to take some doing to resist his attractiveness.

"Damn right I wouldn't share her, mate," Todd declared, taking Jock's remark as a joke.

"Mate?" A quizzical brow lifted in Jock's lean face. "Where did you pick that up? Is there a convention of Australians at the hotel?"

"A charter group," Todd admitted with a chuckle. "They all checked out this morning."

Todd may have missed the electric undercurrents sizzling in the air between Jock and Barbara, but Lillian Gaynor didn't. She sent Barbara a troubled look, sensing how much her oldest son's presence unnerved her guest without knowing why.

"Jock, don't you think you should shower and change?" Lillian suggested.

Jock seemed completely unconcerned by his sweaty and dusty appearance. It only heightened that rough charm. But he dutifully rose and retrieved his Stetson from the chair.

"I'll see you later," he said in parting, and Barbara had the distinct impression the general remark was meant only for her.

Coming from the open stairwell, she heard the firm, hard clump of his work-scuffed boots on the steps, deliberate and unhurried. Barbara knew she was being granted only a temporary respite from his company, not nearly enough time to find a safe course out of this tangled situation.

"Did Todd offer you the cold drinks I fixed?" Lillian asked, then noticed the frosted glass on the side table near Barbara. "I see that he did."

"It's delicious." Barbara picked up the glass to sip the frosty cold mixture. "What's in it?"

"Fresh orange juice, yogurt and honey. It tastes much better than the ingredients sound," the woman laughed, but the conversation had been successfully diverted to a lighter topic. After several minutes it naturally progressed to the suggestion by Lillian, "Let me show you which room you'll have, Barbara. I imagine you'll want to unpack and freshen up before dinner."

"Yes, I would. Thank you," she agreed quickly, grabbing at the offer to be alone even for a short time.

"I saw Arthur outside a few minutes ago, watering the flowers. He can help you with the luggage, Todd."

"All right."

While Todd exited the house through the heavy cypress doors, Barbara followed Lillian Gaynor up the open staircase to the second floor. Gleaming hardwood floors were a rich contrast to the continuation of white textured walls. The carved balustrade encircled the open stairwell, marking the boundaries of the wide hall. All the bedrooms opened onto the hall. Barbara wondered desperately which bedroom belonged to Jock, insisting to herself that it was only self-defense that made her wonder.

"I think you'll like this room," Lillian was saying as she walked to a carved door to the right of the three-tiered staircase. "It's reserved for special guests since it boasts a private bath and a private balcony. You are definitely a special guest, Barbara."

"Unique" would have been a more fitting description, Barbara thought with irony. She doubted that Lillian Gaynor would be quite so welcoming if she knew her special guest had had an affair with one of her sons and was practically engaged to marry the other.

The room was a stunning combination of turquoise and white with the dark wood of the furniture for contrast. It was sparsely furnished, which kept the heavy Mediterranean pieces from seeming oppressive or taking away from its natural spaciousness. A velvet spread of deep turquoise blue covered a large, four-poster bed with a carved headboard. The same turquoise color was repeated in the Persian rug on the floor, and again in the upholstery of the love seat. A double set of doors opened into a huge closet and a second door led to a mosaic-tiled bath with ornate Moorish fixtures. Beyond glass-paned doors was the private balcony, complete with black wrought-iron furniture spilling over with brightly flowered blue cushions.

"It's fabulous," Barbara said.

"I'm glad you like it." The sound of footsteps on the stairs turned Lillian toward the door. "Here's Todd with your luggage. I'll leave you to unpack."

As she left the room, Todd walked in, juggling Barbara's three suitcases. "Where do you want them?"

"Just set them by the bed. Thanks."

When his hands were free, he came back to put them around her. "How do you like my mom?"

"She's so much like you, how could I help but love her?" Barbara admitted, sliding her fingers along the lapel of his summer jacket, and watching them instead of looking into Todd's face.

Sensing an aloofness that was emotional if not precisely physical, Todd curved a hand under her chin and lifted it, a concerned frown on his face.

"What's the matter, Barbara? Is something wrong?"

"No. Nothing," she insisted, but she couldn't keep the coolness out of her answer. She simply couldn't be comfortable in Todd's embrace, not when he didn't know about Jock.

"Is it J.R.?" Todd could so easily read her thoughts. "You aren't still upset about his behavior, are you? Don't let him bother you."

"Do I bother you?" Jock's mocking voice came from the doorway, causing Barbara to move out of Todd's arms with a guilty start. His tawny eyes were laughing at her, because he knew very well that he bothered her—and why. He was leaning indolently against the frame, his arms crossed in front of him. The faded denims and dirty shirt were gone, replaced by a sensuously crisp silk shirt, open at the throat, and desert-brown pants.

"So this is the room my mother gave you." His gaze swept the room somewhat curiously, as if it had been a long time since he'd been inside it. "A nice big double bed." His gaze lingered on it before sliding to Barbara. "More than big enough for two."

"Come on, J.R. Skip the suggestive remarks. You're beginning to bother me." Todd spoke without anger or indignation.

"It's okay, Todd." The words rushed out in the low breath Barbara exhaled. "I'm not a saint."

"You aren't a sinner, either." Now Todd was frowning at her.

"Let me know one way or another when you figure it out," Jock declared with a twisted smile. Unfolding his arms, he straightened from the door frame. "Dinner is at seven. Sundowners on the veranda anytime before that. Come down whenever you're ready."

It was the first time Barbara had heard that authority in his voice. It came very naturally. She realized Jock could command as well as seduce. She had known him only as a lover, and knew very little about him as a man.

"That doesn't give us much time, does it?" Todd murmured.

"No." Although she didn't have any idea what time it was.

"I'll stop by to see if you're ready before I go down," he promised and kissed her lightly on the cheek before he left the room.

It was an hour later when Todd knocked on her door. In that time Barbara had unpacked, showered and put on a blue-flowered dress. The soft material fell in natural folds that didn't show off too much, but she liked the way it swirled around her legs. Todd complimented her appearance, but Barbara couldn't take any pleasure in his approval. Together they made their way down the stairs and out onto the covered veranda at the side of the pool.

"Are you all settled in?" Lillian rose from a white wrought-iron chair to greet them, but Jock barely glanced their way from his position by the drink cart.

"Yes, thank you," Barbara nodded.

"If you're acting as bartender, J.R., I'll have a Scotch," Todd ordered.

"It's being splashed on ice right now." Jock tipped the bottle of liquor to pour it over the ice cubes in a squat glass. "What about you, Barbara? Want a girl drink or would you rather get stoned with me?"

"Now, Jock," Lillian admonished him.

"Rum and Coke, please," Barbara ordered.

"I have to apologize for my son," Lillian said somewhat ruefully. "Jock has been hard to get along with lately. He's been very moody these last few months."

"Some people claim there is a woman to blame," Jock said, passing out their drinks. "Here you go. Rum and Coke. Scotch for you, Todd."

"A woman?" Todd joked. "More than likely, it's women—in the plural."

Through her downcast lashes, Barbara darted Jock a puzzled glance. Two phrases kept echoing in her mind. *Moody these last few months . . . a woman to blame.* Maybe she'd had more of an effect on him than she'd thought. Not that it would do her any good at the moment.

"To happiness. Now and in the future." Lillian lifted her glass in a toast to Todd and Barbara.

As the three sipped their drinks, Barbara noticed that Jock didn't take part in the toast. His cocktail glass was still sitting on the drink cart, conveniently out of reach. He took his time returning to claim it. Even then, he remained apart from them, aloof from the small family circle, and silent. His silence made Barbara equally uncomfortable as his remarks had earlier. His silence, and those watchful eyes . . .

Chapter Three

The cook, a quiet Cuban woman named Antonia, removed the bowls that had contained a spicy, chilled gazpacho. Her presence brought a slight pause in the conversation.

"Where do your parents live, Barbara?" Lillian asked, sitting at the end of the table as hostess while Jock sat at the head.

"They're no longer living. They were killed in an air crash five years ago," she explained quietly.

"Five years ago," Todd repeated sitting opposite her. "I didn't realize that. You were still a flight attendant then."

"Yes."

"Is that when you asked to be transferred?"

"No. I continued flying for almost a year, until I got the shakes," Barbara admitted. "I started to believe that what goes up must come down."

"You became afraid of flying," Jock concluded.

"In a way. But I can quote you all the statistics that prove flying is much safer than highway driving." She smiled in self-mockery.

"But the skies are getting crowded," Lillian insisted.

"Not as crowded as the streets. When an airliner goes down with two hundred people aboard, that's news. And it's flashed all over the world. But two hundred cars can crash with two hundred people in one day and it isn't spectacular enough to be reported. Now if one car with two hundred people in it crashed, that would be a different story," she said.

"If you're convinced flying is safe, why are you afraid?" Jock asked.

"Fear isn't always rational," she answered with a shrug. "Just about everyone who flies—pilots, flight attendants, navigators—deals with it now and then. Normally they have a lot of air miles logged, more than I did. It goes away. I just transferred before mine did."

"Your parents' accident was probably a contributing factor," Lillian said thoughtfully.

"Possibly. I know the schedule, the jet lag, the layovers in strange cities were all getting to me. After my parents died I began wanting a home again—not a room where I slept between flights. I wanted to have a place of my own, somewhere that I belonged." *And someone to belong to,* she could have added.

"You don't have any other family?" Lillian asked with a gently sympathetic look.

"No." Barbara shook her head, black curls moving with a silken gleam.

"You can borrow mine," Todd said, and glanced at his brother. "Such as it is."

For the life of her, Barbara couldn't think of a suitable reply to Todd's statement. Luckily, his mother spoke up to prevent what would have been an awkward silence.

"You happen to be a welcome addition to this family, Barbara. I liked you on sight," she told her. "When I first saw you, I had the craziest feeling that I'd known you all my life."

Shock drained the color from Barbara's face. Those were the same words Jock had said when they'd first met, moments after he'd walked up to her on the beach. Two seconds later he was kissing her. Her hand jerked in reaction to Lillian's comment, knocking the water goblet over and spilling the contents on the white linen tablecloth. Ice water dripped on her lap, wakening Barbara to what she had done.

"Oh, my gosh!" she breathed in sharply, but Lillian had already righted the glass and Todd was mopping up the water with his linen napkin. "I'm sorry."

"It was only water," Lillian assured her. "Did I say something to upset you?"

"No. That is . . ." Barbara slid a furtive look at Jock. Was he pale beneath his tan, or was it her imagination? "Someone else said that same thing to me once and—I'm sorry I spilled the water."

"It will dry," the older woman insisted.

"Especially in this heat," Todd volunteered and shifted the topic of conversation to a discussion of the weather.

Somehow Barbara managed to get through dinner and the coffee in the living room afterward. Not until ten o'clock could she safely excuse herself without raising any eyebrows. It was a relatively chaste good-night kiss she gave Todd in the foyer before climbing the stairs to her room.

Bruised. She'd known that word described the condition of her heart during the drive here. After seeing Jock again, Barbara knew it wasn't accurate. He had walked all over her heart, stomped it into the ground. The pain was still there, and very real.

There had been other times, before she met Jock, when she had imagined herself in love. First there had been an infatuation with her high school sweetheart, but it had never matured. Shortly after she became a flight attendant she had been pursued relentlessly by a handsome married pilot. She had been flattered by his ardent attention, but it was amazing how quickly his interest lagged when she was transferred to ground operations. Her pride was bruised by that, but not her heart, because she had never let herself be serious about him. After that it had been a football player. She nearly fell for him until she found out he was romancing another girl at the same time he was supposedly dating only her.

Those were disappointments, bruises, but none of them could be considered heartbreak. Deep emotions had to be involved for that. And that, in a breathtakingly short space of time, was what Jock had aroused. Barbara was scared, because she knew he could do it again. She didn't want to be taken to those heights attained by that love. She wanted to be safe, with both feet on the ground. It was that old irrational fear of falling again.

Barbara changed quickly into her pajamas and switched off the light, surrounding herself with darkness. The heavy four-poster swallowed her up. Barbara wondered if she could sleep.

She was lying on her stomach, the bed covers partially kicked off, when a hand at the small of her back gently shook her awake. Mumbling an incoherent protest, Barbara resisted the attempt. She was having a wonderful dream and she didn't want it to end yet.

But the hand was insistent and a familiar, husky voice added to its efforts. "Come on, lazybones. You would sleep until noon if I let you."

Rolling onto her side, Barbara arched her back in a feline way to keep in contact with the caressing hand. Her lashes lifted sleepily. A tiny smile of contentment touched her lips as her dream came to life at the sight of the man sitting on the side of her bed.

"Mmm, Jock." She ran a hand up the sleeve of his shirt to his shoulder. "How come you're dressed already? I thought we were going snorkeling . . . or was it skin diving today?"

Her fingers curled around the column of his neck to pull him down. Her sleepy senses were unaware of the glint in his eyes. It was the strong, mobile mouth that claimed all her interest before it came down in tender possession of her lips. Pleasure rose within her in a shower of bliss-filled sensations. Jock lifted her until her head and shoulders were resting on the plump pillow.

Both of her arms now circled him to let her hands glide over his strong, well-muscled back. A sexual fire seared through her veins with a glorious heat. It spread through her nerves, making them come alive to his nearness. When he dragged his mouth from hers and lifted his head, her hands came to the front of his chest.

Her eyes were slow to open as she sighed his name with longing. "Jock . . ."

"That was six months ago, honey," his voice

mocked her. "This morning you're scheduled to tour the citrus groves with Todd. Remember him?"

The beautiful dream popped like the fragile bubble it had been. Hands that had been thrilling to the solid rhythm of his heartbeat now stiffened to keep him at bay. A stifled gasp of dismay became choked in her throat as Barbara woke all the way up. "What are you doing here?" she cried, pummeling him. "This isn't funny!"

He only shrugged.

Barbara sat up, looking around wildly. "Where's Todd?"

"Waiting for you at the sorting and grading sheds." With amusement Jock watched the abrupt change in her attitude, from drowsy passion to fiery indignation in one lightning move. "I knew you'd take advantage of the chance to sleep late, so I promised to take you to him before noon."

"Get out of this bedroom!" she said in hoarse anger. Then another thought occurred to her. "What if your mother walks in here?"

"Don't worry about it. She isn't here." The slashing lines on either side of his mouth deepened in an arrogant smile. His gaze lowered to make a leisurely survey of the upper half of her body. "I didn't realize long-legged pajamas could be so provocative."

The top half of her pajamas consisted of pink lace, suspended by spaghetti straps and secured by silk ribbons tied in two bows between her breasts. The long bottoms were pink silk with a wide band of see-through pink lace down the outside seam. But Jock's interest was directed at the pink ribbons tied in small bows. A trailing end of one ribbon was trapped between his fingertips, his knuckles brushing the flimsy lace covering a swelling breast.

"You always did enjoy making love in the mornings, didn't you?" he mused and untied the bow with hardly any effort.

"Don't." The one-word protest was all her breathlessness would permit.

"That isn't what you said a minute ago." The second bow was undone with equal ease.

"Stop it, Jock." Her resistance was weakening despite the empty warning.

"Or what will you do?" With her breasts no longer confined by the lacy fragment of her top, his hand slipped beneath the material to mold his rough palm to the firm roundness of her breast, a thumb rubbing the sensitized peak. His lowering weight forced her elbows to bend as his warm breath teased her lips. "Whisper for help?" There was silent laughter in his murmured question.

Barbara turned her face into the pillow, fighting the melting weakness that wanted her to relax under his caress. Not having her lips to possess didn't bother him. He nuzzled the sensitive hollow below her ear and nibbled at the delicate cord in her neck. Excited tingles danced over her skin in direct response. Barbara felt desire stirring and knew she had to stop him before she was overwhelmed by this inner upheaval.

She used his own words to do it. "Your brother's waiting for me. Remember him?"

His caressing hands became clumsy, abandoning her delectable curves to accidentally tangle his fingers in the lace material as they gripped the soft flesh of her arms. She was half lifted off the pillow by him. His gleaming gaze was impossible to turn away from.

"You were mine before you ever became his." Ever so gently, Jock let her fall onto the pillow. Barbara frantically sought to cover herself with the thin lace top, but he was already pushing himself from the bed to stalk to the door.

He didn't have a right to do what he'd just done and her pride demanded retaliation. "Get out of my room and stay out of it!" Barbara ordered.

"Whatever you say." Jock was barely controlling his temper. "Looks like you might be the next lady of the house."

"Lillian—" Barbara attempted a defensive argument.

"My mother likes you a lot. And Todd obviously thinks you're the best thing that ever happened to him." The volume of his voice was reduced to a growl. "Which leaves me. The odd man out. I don't have to like it, but . . . what else can I do, Barbara?" A muscle worked convulsively in his jaw as he held his anger in check. "Be downstairs in fifteen minutes. We'll be riding to the sheds, so dress accordingly."

With that clipped command, Jock pivoted to stride to the door. In desperation, Barbara grabbed the spare pillow and threw it at the closing door. It bounced harmlessly off onto the floor. Her eyes burned with tears.

I won't cry, she told herself fiercely. *I won't shed one more tear for you, Jock Malloy.*

It took a lot of cold water from the bathroom faucet to splash away the scorching tears stinging her eyes. As much as Barbara would have liked to ignore it, there had been a measure of authority in his command to be downstairs in fifteen minutes. If she wasn't, Jock was just as apt to come up and bring her down himself. That, and the knowledge that he was taking her to meet Todd, who was her only line of defense at the moment, made Barbara dress quickly in blue jeans, a T-shirt and boots. She was out of breath from hurrying by the time she reached the bottom of the stairs.

Pausing, she realized Jock hadn't said where he would be. She took a chance and tried the veranda. He was standing in the shadows, a shoulder leaned against an arch, a hand running tiredly over his jaw and throat. That impression of tiredness vanished in total alertness when he saw her. Barbara walked toward him, tilting her chin in challenge.

"I'm ready," she said.

"There's orange juice, coffee and muffins on the table." He was curt with her as he motioned to the glass-topped table of wrought iron behind him.

"No eggs or bacon?" She said it just to be difficult. Her normal appetite was stolen.

"You slept late," Jock reminded her. "So you have a choice of dawdling over breakfast and spoiling the lunch Ramon's wife will be fixing for you and Todd, or—"

"Who is Ramon?" Barbara interrupted as she walked to the table to pour fresh-squeezed orange juice from the pitcher into a glass.

"One of my foremen. He's in charge of the fruit shipments. His house was practically a second home to Todd and me when we were younger." He was making an effort to sound civil.

It only irritated Barbara. "This Ramon works for you? He isn't family?"

"A lot of people around here work for me. Before that, they worked for my father. Before that, his father," he snapped. "That makes everyone on Sandoval land family—by loyalty if not by blood."

"You have a little feudal empire here, don't you?" she goaded. "With you the lord and master."

After throwing her a glowering look, Jock turned away.

"That was uncalled for," she admitted. "I'm sorry, Jock. I don't know why I said it. I . . . suppose I wanted to make you angry . . . to pay you back."

"Forget it." He coldly dismissed her apology, pricking her pride once again. She stared at her glass of juice, wanting to throw it in his face. "What'll it be? Breakfast or lunch?"

"Lunch." She forced herself to swallow the orange juice, then set the empty glass on the table. Her blue glance still held a shimmer of resentment at the way he had brushed away her apology. "I'm ready."

"No coffee or muffin?" An eyebrow arched sharply to match the metallic edge of his look.

"No." She'd choke on it. "You said we would be riding."

"Mike is bringing the horses now." His announcement sent her glance to the treed lawn beyond the pool. A man was approaching the house leading two saddled horses, a blaze-faced chestnut and a gray. "Do you have a hat? The noonday sun can be fierce."

"No, I don't." While she was looking at the horses Jock had moved with that animal quietness she had forgotten he possessed. He had already put on his hat and was pulling it low on his forehead.

"I didn't think you would. Here's one of my mother's." The hat in his hand was cream-colored with a flat crown and brim. "See if it fits." He handed it to her and waited.

Under his watchful eyes, Barbara set it on her head. It fit snugly over her black curls and made them softly frame her face. She pushed away the ones that tickled her temple and forehead, tucking them under the hatband. Finished, she turned for his inspection. "How's that?" Her head was thrown back in challenge.

His gaze didn't stop with the hat. It continued downward to roam over the curves of her breasts against the thin knit fabric of her T-shirt. Barbara sucked in her breath in reaction to the stripping touch of his eyes on her stomach and waist, over her hips and down narrow-legged jeans.

"I brought the horses, Jock," a man called, snapping the invisible thread that had bound Jock's gaze to her.

Without a word to her, Jock turned and walked to the end of the veranda where the grass grew to the edge of the tile. The big, muscled gray horse whickered at the sight of him, pricking its ears in his direction. Barbara was slow to follow Jock, not recovering as quickly as he had. The man holding the reins of the two horses was about her age and height, with a fresh, open face and candid blue eyes that didn't attempt to hide the admiration in his look when he saw her up close. Although Barbara couldn't see Jock's face, he had obviously noticed the man's interested look.

"This is Mike Turbot. Barbara Haynes." Jock made the introductions with indifference. "Give her Sebring," he commanded and took the reins of the gray. "While she's here the chestnut will be hers, but I don't want her riding alone."

"Yes, sir." The wrangler flashed Jock a puzzled look

as if he wasn't used to a tone of voice like that coming from him. "Here you are, Barbara." Mike Turbot passed Barbara the reins and held the chestnut's bridle while cupping a hand under her elbow to help her into the saddle, Jock was already on the big gray, stepping into the stirrup and swinging into the saddle all in one fluid motion.

"Thank you, Mike." Because of Jock's rudeness, her smile at him was a little warmer than it might have been.

"Anytime." He smiled and touched the curved point of his hat brim.

Jock had already reined the gray gelding away from the veranda to walk it across the thick carpet of lawn. Barbara's chestnut mount was more lightly built. It whirled gracefully at a touch of the rein on its sleek neck and glided after the horse and rider in a smooth, effortless walk. Spirited but well-trained, the horse was a joy to ride, but the tight-lipped profile of the man riding beside her kept Barbara from expressing her enthusiasm.

The pace was kept to a walk as they crossed the lawn rather than have the metal shoes of the horses dig out clumps of lush grass. Twice Barbara had to dodge a draping curtain of Spanish moss that bearded the massive oak trees shading the lawn. A white paddock gate stood open and the gray horse went through it at a trot. With a touch of the heel, Barbara's chestnut picked up the pace too.

When Todd had mentioned riding to her, she'd looked forward to the opportunity with pleasure, but Jock's grim silence was turning it into an ordeal. She was too conscious of his rough-hewn features set in unyielding lines to enjoy the feel of the horse beneath her.

A barbed-wire fence blocked their way. Without dismounting, Jock maneuvered the gray horse close to a gate Barbara hadn't noticed and unhooked it, fastening it again after they had both gone through the opening.

As they started out again, Barbara couldn't stand the silence any longer. "I didn't know you were Todd's brother. Believe me, if I had, I never would have come here." Her voice trembled with the vibrant force of her conflicting emotions. "You gave me the impression you owned a ranch—I actually thought you were Texan, if you can believe that, and I—"

"I do own a ranch," Jock interrupted smoothly, not bothering to look at her.

"Your definition of a ranch and mine don't coincide. I wasn't thinking of orange groves and racehorses." There was a faint edge to her response. "A ranch to me means cattle—"

"That isn't a water buffalo." With a nod of his head, he directed her attention to his right.

A big Brahma bull stood in the shade of a tree, his massive humpbacked shape concealed until that moment by the mottled brown of his coat and the shadows of the thick limbs overhead. The bull twitched a drooping ear at a buzzing insect, his curved horns turning as his small dark eyes watched them ride by.

"Okay, so you run a few cattle." Barbara shrugged her shoulders in a vague dismissal.

"Over fifty thousand head, counting stock cattle and feeder steers," Jock informed her with a cool glance. "More than likely there are a couple thousand head running wild in the swamp that should be carrying the Sandoval brand."

Her mouth dropped open mentally, if not physically. With new awareness, her eyes encompassed the wild pasture they were riding through. It seemed to go on forever.

"How big is this place?" she murmured.

"It covers around two hundred and twenty thousand acres, a thousand of it in citrus trees and five hundred for the thoroughbreds. The rest is all cattle. I have about seventy-five people working for me. This operation is small compared to the Deseret Ranch or the Lykes Brothers. Surprised?" he asked.

Barbara couldn't deny it. "I didn't know there were ranches this large in Florida."

"There have been ranches in Florida, and cowboys, before the first white man ever discovered there were tumbleweeds in Texas. Ponce de León brought the first boatload of Andalusian cattle here in 1521. The shoot-outs, the lynchings, the rowdy saloons were all romanticized in Westerns, but it happened here first." His gaze skimmed her face. "Driving cattle through palmettos, fighting cougars and malaria fever and swamps that would suck up a full-grown steer didn't appeal to the Zane Greys and Remingtons who built the myth of the cowboy."

"Florida is oranges, Disney World and Miami Beach, not cowboys." Barbara's image of her native state was being rapidly reevaluated.

"Cow hunters or cracker cowboys, that's what they were usually called. Cow hunters because so much of this land was unfenced that they had to hunt through high grasses, swamps and cypress forests for the cows. Cracker cowboy comes from the rawhide whips they carried"—Jock's hand touched the side of his saddle and Barbara noticed the coiled whip tied there—"and the cracking sound the whip made. You could be hear it for miles when the cowboys were rounding up cattle. The three things a cowboy needed then he still needs today: a good horse, a whip and a good cow dog."

"And Sandoval Ranch is yours." Barbara looked at him. She had been aware of the strength in him, but now she saw how heavy the burden he carried really was. Yet it seemed to rest easily on his broad shoulders.

"Yes." In that single word was a wealth of pride and possession, understated and simple.

Barbara remembered his earlier reference to his inheritance of the land. "It's been in your family for generations."

"In the Malloy family, yes. My father left it to me when he died, just as Todd's father left him the hotel on that expensive strip of sand."

The reference to Todd brought silence. The ground beneath their horses became marshy and Jock angled the gray gelding toward a raised strip of land. It was a dike to hold back the seeping waters of a cypress pond. As Barbara rode the chestnut along the crest, her gaze wandered over the raw, wild beauty of the exposed and tangled roots of the cypress giants. Primitive and unspoiled, the landscape was no different from what it had been a hundred or two hundred years ago.

Where the pasture ground became firm again, Jock reined his mount down the sloping side of the dike. Barbara followed, her saddle shifting slightly beneath her. It affected her balance for only an instant, but Jock noticed it and reined his horse to a stop.

"I'll tighten the cinch," he said, swinging out of his saddle and forcing Barbara to do the same.

She stepped to one side as he flipped her stirrup across the saddle seat to tighten the girth. He did what needed doing without hesitation, she thought. And he looked after his own.

Chapter Four

His head was bent to the task, his masculine profile seeming sculpted out of teakwood, hard-grained and strong. Barbara watched him, her hand absently stroking the silken hip of the chestnut gelding. She was reminded unwillingly of Jock's tautly muscled flesh. Sunlight glistened in the brown hair curling near the collar of his shirt. The impulse was strong to run her fingers through its sensuous thickness. She rolled her hand into a fist to resist the temptation.

"I take it you didn't tell Todd about me." He sent her a fierce look as swift as a lightning shaft.

Barbara stiffened defensively. "He knows there was another man, but I never told him who."

"Why?" Jock let the stirrup fall and turned to face her, resting an arm on the cantle.

"Why should I?" she said. "We're going out, that's all."

"Really," Jock said evenly.

"Okay, Todd and I are talking about more than that, but nothing's definite. And he doesn't have the right to know the name, date and place of every man I've ever gone out with. Todd knows I've . . . been with another man in the last year, but he doesn't expect a graphic description of who, what and where. And I don't expect him to tell me about the women he's been with."

"The circumstances have changed. Or hadn't you noticed?" His low voice was dry with challenge.

"How could I know you would turn out to be Todd's brother?" Barbara replied sharply, all her raw tension surfacing. "He kept referring to you as J.R. and he never said anything about different fathers and last names. The way he talked about this place, I thought it was a citrus farm. And you—you never said anything about having a brother. I can't remember you mentioning anything about your family. You were always too busy—" The rest of the sentence got stuck in her throat.

But Jock finished it. "Making love to you."

"Yes," she snapped, unnerved by the way he was studying her with narrowed eyes.

"Are you sleeping with Todd?" he asked bluntly.

"No!" Barbara immediately wished she had told Jock it was none of his business. Instead she had to defend her answer. "I'm not so impulsive anymore. Racing into a relationship or a man's bed just isn't smart."

"No, it isn't." Jock straightened away from her saddle and Barbara took it as an indication he expected her to mount.

She wanted to be back in the saddle with the solidness of the chestnut beneath her instead of legs that were trembling. But when she took the step forward to mount, his arm crossed in front of her to block the movement. Barbara found herself enclosed in a trap. She leaned away from any contact with his hard, lean frame and closer to the saddled horse.

"I don't think you have the right to ask me a lot of personal questions, Jock."

"No? I would hate to be put in a position where I would have to beat up my own brother for taking what was mine."

"I'm not yours." Her denial was breathless, the wary blue of her eyes darting over the complacent expression on his rugged face, a face that was much too close.

"I wish you were, though." His hand touched her shoulder, then glided to her throat to stroke the underside of her chin with his thumb. Her pulse surged and fluttered madly at the caress. "Am I allowed to wish?"

"Stop pretending that I was anything more to you than a fling!" she protested stridently, needing to remind herself as much as him of the fact.

"Was that what it was?" Jock grinned and gave her a bad-boy wink.

She choked. "What does it matter how many? It was just a way to pass the time."

"A very pleasurable way."

"No." Which was an outright lie that challenged him.

When Barbara realized his intentions, her hands came up to ward him off, but it was already too late. His mouth was on hers, his hand cupped to her neck and his thumb under her chin to prevent her from eluding his searching kiss.

Her hands strained against his chest to keep his body at a distance, but it took more effort to ignore the pleasant sensation of male sinew and bone beneath her fingers. When the hard point of his tongue probed the tightly closed line of her lips, a response quivered through her. Barbara fought it and his seductive insistence.

"Open your mouth," he growled against her lips. His breath was warm and sensual, and it muddled her already hazy thinking. "Open it, honey."

"No." She said it, but her body didn't listen and neither did he. She had to experience the compelling sweetness of his erotic kiss.

It just about burned up her paper-thin control. His arms went around her to gather her close and Barbara melted into his embrace. She was riding a shooting star, arching high in the heavens, and she didn't care when it might come down. Jock's hands had slid beneath her T-shirt to explore her skin.

A hand slipped inside the waistband of her denims to the hollow of her spine and arched her to his thrusting hips. Her fingers became hungry for the hair-roughened texture of the skin beneath his shirt and forced their way inside to let springy chest hairs tickle her sensitive palms.

The fiery comet she was riding was climbing too high. The crash to earth and reality would be too devastating. Barbara had to get off. She dragged her lips from his and shuddered as his mouth scorched her jaw and throat.

"It's over between us, Jock," she insisted in a whisper. "Why can't you let it go? Why can't you forget?"

"Can you forget?" he demanded, a rough edge to his low voice. "Can you forget what it's like to have my hands on you? To feel my kisses on all over your bare skin? Can you?"

Barbara groaned in answer because she couldn't

forget. The tender, wild memories lived with her, as intimate as their affair had been. She had survived its ending, but she'd had no intention of reviving it. Her eyes were tightly closed, trying to shut him out. But Jock would have none of it.

"Look at me!" he commanded. "You want me the same way I want you. Look at me and deny that's the truth."

She forced her eyes to open, taking in his golden gaze, then the well-cut mouth still warm from her lips, and then down to the rumpled and unbuttoned front of his shirt. She had done that, opened his shirt herself to touch him as intimately as he'd touched her. Barbara couldn't deny the truth. She could easily abandon her pride and self-respect in his embrace. So she clung to the one good thing that had happened to her.

"I think I love Todd," she whispered. Todd, whose gentleness had helped her feel like a human being again. Todd, who made her feel safe and protected, not threatened by emotions she couldn't control. No, he didn't inspire this kind of crazy passion in her, but she couldn't have everything.

His mouth tightened. The grip of his fingers gradually relaxed until Barbara was standing alone and he was stepping away.

"It isn't going to work, Barbara." He left her to walk to his horse.

For an instant she couldn't fathom his statement. Then its meaning struck her and she reached for the saddle horn to stay steady on her feet.

"You are going to tell Todd, aren't you?" she said.

"I'm not a nameless nonentity who went in and out of your life." Jock's back was to her as he looped the reins over the gray's neck before mounting. "If you don't tell Todd about our affair, I will. We may have had different fathers, but he is my brother. Nothing's ever come between us before . . . not until now. If you two stay together, I'll never be able to look at you without remembering what went on between us. Todd deserves to know why I'll be avoiding him in the future."

The tiny hope that Jock might keep their previous relationship a secret died a cold death. In her heart Barbara knew Todd had to be told. It was only fair. Jock was braver than she was and he had essentially issued an ultimatum. If she didn't tell him, he would.

She climbed into the saddle and gave the chestnut its head. It followed the gray gelding when Jock started it forward. Her shoulders sagged under the weight of her decision. She didn't notice the pastures of high grass give way to orderly rows of fruit trees. When her horse stopped in front of a metal building, Barbara heard the murmur of voices and the hum of machinery.

"Where's Todd?" It was Jock who asked the question, and Barbara turned in her saddle to see him talking to an elderly man.

"Here he comes." The man gestured to the yawning door of the building.

Todd was walking toward her, all smiles and gladness. "I was beginning to wonder what had happened to you."

He reached up to span her waist with his hands and lift her from the saddle. Barbara was too numbed to refuse his assistance. Her wide, troubled eyes searched his face as he set her on the ground. When Todd bent his head to kiss her, the gray horse snorted, and Barbara remembered Jock's presence. Before Todd's mouth brushed hers, she turned away.

"I'm sorry I'm late," she apologized. "I overslept."

"You needed the rest." But his brown eyes narrowed to study the lines of stress in her face. Todd smoothly concealed the look when he lifted his gaze to Jock. "Thanks for bringing her over here, J.R."

"Don't thank me, Todd. You might regret it." Jock's answer was terse, its message a mystery to his brother but not to Barbara. "I'll see you later at the house." He jabbed a heel into the gray's belly and the horse bounded forward into a canter.

Barbara slid a glance at Todd's puzzled expression as he watched Jock ride away. She wished that he didn't have to know the truth, that things could be the way they were before the two of them had arrived at the ranch.

"Come on. I'll show you around the shed." He was smiling again when he looked at her.

Gathering the threads of her courage, Barbara shook her head to refuse the invitation. "Not now. There's something I have to tell you first."

"Can it wait?" Todd asked with a quizzical expression. "Ramon is free now to guide you through the place, but he's busy later. We're having lunch with Ramon and his family."

"Yes, Jock mentioned that," she admitted and took a breath to continue her explanation.

"You'll like Ramon. He's like an uncle to J.R. and me. We slept as many nights at his place as we did at the ranch house when we were kids—"

"Todd," she broke in impatiently. "Please, I have to talk to you?"

"You make it sound urgent."

"It is. I . . . I'm sorry about Ramon, but this isn't going to be easy and I don't want to put it off." She might not find the courage to tell him if she had to wait.

"Okay." His caressing hand was absently rubbing her spine but it didn't have the power to provoke a searing response. His touch was pleasurably sane. "Let me introduce you to Ramon, then we'll go walk in the grove."

Ramon Morales was the elderly man Jock had questioned. His dark eyes were intelligent and the smile he gave Barbara was warm. On another occasion she would have enjoyed meeting him, but now she was too tense to show more than polite courtesy to him.

"I'm sorry, but something's come up that Barbara needs to talk to me about," Todd explained. "I'm sure she would have learned much more from you, but I'll take her through the operation later."

"You will come to lunch?" Ramon asked.

"Of course," Todd insisted, but Barbara wondered if he would want to after he heard what she had to say.

After apologizing again for keeping Ramon from his work, Todd promised to meet him at his house. Barbara's stomach was churning as they walked away from the man toward the trees. The air was heavily scented with oranges, weighted down by the hot sun. A faint breeze stirred the green leaves of the orange trees. Barbara would have continued walking, but once they were out of sight of the sheds, Todd stopped.

"Okay. Explain. What's on your mind?" he asked gently.

She moved a step beyond him before halting. Her

nervous hand reached to trace the round circumference of an orange. "The man I had an affair with—"

"That's in the past, Barbara," Todd interrupted. "I thought we had agreed to forget about it."

"You don't understand," she breathed in agitation. "That man was Jock."

The truth was out and she suddenly couldn't breathe. Unwillingly Barbara turned to see the look of stunned shock and disbelief on his face.

"There must be a mistake," he murmured.

"I wish there was," Barbara replied in a stark voice. "I didn't know he was your brother. I never connected Jock Malloy with the brother you called J.R. I assumed you had the same last names. If I had known—" What was the use? She hadn't known. Now it was too late.

"But you didn't." His hand covered hers while his brown eyes searched her face. "Do you still love him, Barbara?"

"I—" She shook her head mutely, unable to answer that question. The conflict of her heart and mind must have been expressed in her eyes, because Todd wrapped her in his arms and held her tight, resting his chin on the top of her black curls. "He was going to bring it up," she mumbled into his shirt. "I had to tell you before Jock did."

"How does he feel about you?"

"He still wants me." The admission came out in a bitter laugh.

"And you?"

"Oh, he might think he can still make me want him." It was a self-deprecating answer, exposing her shame. It brought a sob to her throat, but she took a deep breath and forced it down. As much as she wanted the comfort of Todd's arms, she couldn't in good conscience accept it. She firmly pushed away from his chest. "I can't stay here, Todd. I have to leave."

"No. You're wrong. You have to stay and you have to face him," he insisted. "Hiding won't do any good. After a bad fall, you have to get back on the horse."

"But not the same horse!" Barbara protested.

"Sorry. That was an unfortunate metaphor."

She nodded.

"What happened, Barbara? Between you and J.R., I mean. You said he didn't want you around anymore. I know my brother can be harsh at times, but not totally insensitive." He frowned.

"In his way, I suppose he let me down easy. Jock just didn't know how far I had to fall," she said, trying to laugh but not succeeding very well. It hadn't been funny. Even in retrospect, it wasn't now. "After he'd asked me to come with him to his ranch—Sandoval, as it turns out—I refused for all the reasons I've already told you. Later on that same day, I went into the bedroom and found him packing to leave . . ."

Barbara could remember it all so clearly, walking into the bedroom, seeing him folding his shirts so neatly and laying them in the suitcase. A intense love for him had seared her. She had walked up behind him and wound her arms around his middle to hug his back. Jock had stopped packing to half turn. Barbara had ducked under his raised arm to be held in his embrace. Instead of kissing her as she had expected, he had locked his hands behind her back for a moment and looked down at her. Then, if he had repeated his previous invitation, she would have accepted in a flash.

"Hey, lover," she'd whispered.

Jock had unwound her arms from around him and held her hands in front of him. For the rest of her life, she would hear his words of rejection. "Don't call me that. Not any more. It's time we became friends."

Her heart had begun to shatter then and there. Somehow she had managed to force out a husky laugh and pull her hands from his loose hold to turn away. Jock hadn't attempted to stop her. She had been overwhelmed with love for him and all he wanted was to be friends.

Barbara couldn't remember now exactly how she had responded. Something to the effect that she couldn't, just couldn't. Not with someone like him, so why not just make it a clean goodbye? It was fun while it lasted, but it was over.

The rest had been a blur of pain. Jock had mentioned calling her the next time he was in Miami, but Barbara wasn't going to become a name and phone number in his little black book or his BlackBerry. So she said, "Don't call me, I'll call you." A trite phrase, but she had meant it.

All of that she explained to Todd in considerably less detail. "I never meant to come between you and Jock. Please believe that," Barbara concluded.

"I do," Todd assured her.

"Jock was right about one thing, though," Barbara sighed. "You can't marry me. How could you face him knowing that he and I—"

"No. Don't think about me," he interrupted, catching her chin and lifting her face to his. "Could you face him as my wife?"

"I thought I could. But now . . . I'm not sure."

"We have never been lovers, Barbara. Perhaps if we—"

But she suddenly jerked away from his hand. She knew what Todd was about to suggest and she couldn't. If he made love to her now, she knew she would compare him to Jock. She knew she would come away from it dissatisfied and wanting. Before she had thought it was the commitment she was afraid of, but now she realized she had avoided intimacy with Todd because she instinctively knew the passion wouldn't be there. Without love, sex would be simply a physical act.

Didn't she love Todd? She needed him desperately. She needed his kindness, his gentleness, but did she love him? The emotion he aroused in her was tame compared to the wild glory of Jock's caresses. Barbara doubled her hands into fists. She cared enough about Todd to learn to love him. Maybe not the way she loved Jock, but she didn't want to be that crazy about anyone again. It hurt too much.

"It's too soon, Todd," Barbara protested brokenly.

He caught her by the arms and held her when she tried to turn away. "I've never asked you to do anything for me, but I'm asking now. I want you to stay here for these two weeks and get my brother out of your system once and for all."

"What if I don't, Todd?" She voiced the fear that was so strong within her.

"Then we can break up," he said flatly. "Think of it as a test. In the meantime we'll carry on as usual. Which includes lunch with Ramon and his wife."

"Todd . . ." Her dark head made an uncertain movement.

"Two weeks isn't a lifetime."

But it will seem like it, she thought. "No, of course, it isn't," she agreed for his benefit.

"Come on. We'll walk over to Ramon's house. It isn't far from here." He put an arm around her shoulders and started walking back the way they had come.

Ramon Morales and his wife Connie were a warm, friendly couple who welcomed Barbara into their home as if she was already a member of the family. She could well understand why Todd and Jock regarded it as their second home. The couple naturally regarded her as Todd's girlfriend and regaled both of them with tales from his childhood. It was inevitable that Jock's name would be included in the stories.

After lunch, Barbara volunteered to help the older woman wash the dishes while Todd and Ramon walked out to the groves behind the simple wooden structure. The warmth of the kitchen made Barbara feel at home, less of an intruder.

"You're lucky, Barbara." Connie Morales rinsed a plate under a faucet. "Todd is a very understanding guy."

"Yes, I think so, too," she agreed, ignoring the twinge of guilt she experienced.

"Two brothers couldn't be more different than Jock and Todd. When they were boys, it was like night and day. Jock never learned to share his toys. What was his was his," she declared with a raised eyebrow for emphasis, "and woe to those who tried to play with something that belonged to him. But Todd gave his toys away. He had the softest heart. Stray animals found their way to his doorstep. If they were hurt, Todd took them to Jock and—"

"To Jock?" Barbara interrupted with surprise.

"Oh, yes, he has healing hands. Todd found the hurt animals, Jock cured them, and Todd loved them. All except once," the woman remembered with a pause. "Jock accidentally backed the car over a puppy one time. He set its broken leg and took it home with him. It's the only dog I've ever known that was allowed to sleep in the house. It had a rug at the foot of Jock's bed. The two were almost inseparable until the dog finally died of old age."

"When was that?" she asked curiously.

"It must be almost four years ago now. When Blue died—that was the dog's name, a blue heeler—Jock wouldn't take another dog with him when he went out to check cattle. As far as I know, he still doesn't. I never really thought about it until this moment." Connie Morales paused in her dishwashing to look at Barbara.

"Todd always had a menagerie of pets around him with love enough for all, but Jock had only one." With an unconcerned shrug, she returned to her washing. "As I said, they were as different as night and day. And still are."

Totally different. Barbara couldn't agree with the woman more. It showed in other ways, too. Todd loved the hotel business, constantly meeting new faces, the atmosphere changing with each convention. The variety, the whirl, the social life were important elements in his life. And Jock ran this immense ranch like a small country, acting as a caretaker of the land and its people. He followed the deep-seated tradition of the soil.

Barbara wasn't certain she wanted to learn this much about either man. In two weeks she might have to walk away from both of them. Enough time to carry a lifetime of poignant memories away with her. She wished she hadn't agreed to stay, but Todd had asked so little from her and had given so much. She felt guilty all over again for not appreciating him more and faulting him for being what he was: calm and unexciting.

After the dishes were washed, Todd came in and Barbara said goodbye to the couple and promised to see them again before she left. She got through the tour of the sorting and shipping sheds. When Todd explained about the different grading of fruit, she appeared to listen, but her mind was miles away. If Todd noticed her lack of attention, he didn't comment on it.

Her chestnut horse and a mahogany bay were tied outside the sheds when they completed the tour. The route Todd took her on back to the house was different from the way Jock had brought her. It was longer, more scenic, abundant with wildlife and colorful birds stalking marshland pools. With Todd, Barbara was able to relax. When she was with Jock, she was never sure when the world would explode around her.

Chapter Five

As Barbara descended the stairs to the first landing, she met Lillian Gaynor on the way up. She hadn't seen Todd and Jock's mother all day. Lillian hadn't been in the house when she and Todd had finally returned. Barbara had gone directly to her room and taken a leisurely bath to soak away the horsey smell and dress for dinner.

"You look lovely, Barbara." Lillian paused on the stairway to admire the accordion-pleated caftan of tussah silk.

"Thank you." The caftan was a little dramatic, but it fit her mood.

"I understand from Jock that you've had a busy day—lunch with Ramon, a tour of the citrus operation and a horseback ride," Lillian remarked with a broad smile.

"Yes, I have." Barbara didn't have to ask when Lillian had seen Jock. She'd heard him come upstairs an hour before and the rush of water running in a shower. And she had recognized the sound of his footsteps when he'd left his room to go downstairs. She expected that he was out on the veranda now.

"I hope you like Connie. She's a dear friend, and like a second mother to my sons," Lillian explained.

"Both Connie and Ramon made me feel like one of the family already," Barbara admitted.

"They do seem like family, don't they? John and Ramon were like brothers. John was Jock's father, John Randolph Malloy," Lillian explained. "Ramon provided me with a strong shoulder to lean on when I lost John so suddenly. And Connie . . . well, she simply took over running the house and looking after Jock until I could handle it again."

"I can imagine."

"Goodness, what am I thinking about, keeping you talking on the stairs like this," Lillian admonished herself with a laugh. "Here comes Todd downstairs and I haven't even made it to my room yet. You will all have a head start on me if I don't hurry."

"Hello, Mom. Are you coming or going?" Todd stopped on the step behind Barbara, casually resting a hand on her shoulder.

"Going," she laughed. "I'll see you two on the veranda in about twenty minutes. Save me a drink."

"We will," Todd promised. As his mother passed him to climb the last flight of stairs to the second floor, Barbara started to proceed down them. Todd's hand tightened on her shoulder to stop her. She glanced back at him in surprised question. His dark head bent to nuzzle her neck. "You smell delectable, honey."

Honey? He'd never used any term of endearment before, Barbara thought with a start. She could hardly object to it, being his girlfriend and talking about their future, quote-unquote, together. So why did it make her uneasy?

"I found some perfumed bath salts," she said, to explain the scent that clung to her skin. "I got a little carried away."

"It's very provocative," Todd murmured. "But so are you."

His mouth teased her mouth with a feather kiss, but her lips didn't tremble in response. Barbara felt almost guilty at that. Todd had always been affectionate, but never as loverlike as this.

The irony of the twist in circumstances suddenly struck Barbara. One brother, who was her friend, wanted to become her lover and maybe even her husband. The other brother, who had been her passionate lover, had wanted to become her friend. There was humor in that somewhere. It was a pity she couldn't find it.

It was impossible for Todd not to sense her lack of interest in his attempted caress. Concealing a sigh, he lifted his head and flashed her a forgiving smile. Then he was releasing her shoulder so she could continue down the steps while he followed.

"Have I told you how beautiful you look?" His hand curved possessively around her waist when they reached the foyer.

"No, but my ego would love to hear it." She needed some bolstering, she thought, as she turned toward the veranda doors.

"You do look beautiful. And if I'm lying, may I turn into a frog," Todd vowed and made a muted croaking sound in his throat.

Barbara laughed, as she was supposed to do. Todd reached in front of her to open the veranda door and

Barbara walked through, a smile remaining on her face as a result of his well-meaning joke. It started to fade when she felt the scrutiny of Jock's tawny eyes. She had the feeling she was facing a predatory beast about to spring on her at any second. Todd's arm was around her waist again, protecting her from even an imaginary attack. When she looked up at him, the smile came back, born by the feeling of relief and safety.

"Isn't it a rule of the house, J.R., that the first one at the drink cart has to play bartender?" Todd's gaze pointedly noted the fact that Jock was standing in front of the cart with a drink in his hand.

On the surface Jock appeared relaxed and at ease, enjoying an early-evening cocktail while a slowly setting sun left a crimson stain in the sky. His hair shone after his shower, its rich chestnut gold thickness unruly in a sensual sort of way. Unlike Todd, Jock didn't bother with a light jacket. The brown silk shirt was unbuttoned at the throat with the sleeves rolled up to expose tanned forearms. Jeans molded his masculine length, his feet slightly apart in a stance that suggested command and readiness. He was always ready for something. Barbara sensed a lot of tightly coiled energy waiting to be released.

"Your drinks are fixed. Scotch and water. Rum and Coke." Ice clinked against the sides of the glass in his hand as Jock swung it toward the drink cart to indicate the filled glasses on the tray.

"Now that is service," Todd declared.

"I heard Barbara laugh and knew you were coming." Jock explained his foreknowledge with a measured look at her.

"Thank you. It was a thoughtful gesture." A response

seemed to be expected from her so Barbara gave a courteous one.

The humid, balmy air suddenly felt very warm and heavy. Her breathing seemed labored even if it didn't show. The closeness of the atmosphere reminded Barbara of the way it felt before an approaching storm front moved in, oppressive, sticky and much too still.

Jock didn't move out of the way as she walked with Todd to the decorative wrought-iron cart. The intimidation of his presence was strong. She wished she had armor to shield her from his piercing eyes, their force not affected by the thick veil of masculine lashes. Picking up her drink, Barbara turned and got the full impact of his gaze.

Her head moved back in protective defiance. "Stop looking at me that way, Jock. Todd knows. I told him," she said stiffly.

He made a quick scan of her features, then swept down to her left hand as if he expected to see a diamond glittering there. Then he looked swiftly to Todd. Cool and alert, Jock took a sip from the drink in his hand.

"How did you take the news, little brother?"

"It didn't change anything." Todd only shrugged. "Whatever there was between you and Barbara happened six months ago. It's in the past and had nothing to do with today."

Jock gave her a mirthless smile. "You must have told him one hell of a story, honey," he jeered.

"I told him the truth," Barbara retorted, stung by his insinuation.

"I know all about it," Todd confirmed her statement.

"When you met and the time you spent together. You gave her a pretty raw deal, but it's over."

Jock tipped his head at an angle to study her through half-closed eyes. "Did I?" Within that drawling comment there was something hot and biting. "Is that what you told him?"

"I'm sure it's a matter of definition and point of view." Her fingers tightened around the glass, its chill matching the one inside her. She stared into the dark surface of the liquid rather than continue to hold Jock's gaze. She knew the exact second his eyes left her. That tingling sensation of danger went away.

"She belongs to me, Todd. I want her back," Jock stated.

Just like that. As if she were some object two little boys were squabbling over. Her head came up with a start, indignant fire glittering in her blue eyes. But neither man took any notice of her.

"You couldn't keep her so you lost her," Todd said. "Now it's a case of finders keepers. Your prior claim doesn't mean anything anymore. I found her. And I'm not going to let her go."

"This isn't a game!" Barbara protested angrily. "You aren't going to play tug-of-war with me. Neither of you!"

"Stay out of this!" Jock ordered her.

"No!"

"Barbara's right," Todd sided with her. "You can't have her back because she isn't mine to give. It's her choice to make."

He looked up when he heard his mother calling from the house, then looked at Barbara. "Do you mind if I—"

"Go ahead," she said. "I think your brother can manage to behave himself for a few minutes."

Todd left, but not before he squeezed her hand and shot an I-dare-you look at his big brother. Jock waited a little while before he spoke. He was obviously seething. "I have an idea. Why don't you kick him to the curb now and save some time?" Jock said.

"How incredibly arrogant!" she hissed. "What makes you think I would prefer you?"

Jock turned to confront her squarely and bring himself within a foot of her. That powerful magnetic aura that surrounded him sucked Barbara into its force field, trapping her as securely as if he'd taken her into his arms. The warm, clean smell of him was almost too much, combined with the dangerous virility that heightened all her senses whether she wanted it to or not.

"You don't really want me to answer that question, do you, honey?" His low voice was a husky caress. "You don't want me to remind you of that first time we made love. Afterward you had bright, beautiful tears in your eyes because it had been so wonderful. Todd doesn't need to know that we once made love outside with only the stars of a soft, southern night for company."

"That's enough." It was a gasping plea for him to stop seducing her with memories. The wild yearning to be possessed by him again was throbbing through her veins and she couldn't let it take control.

A tigerish gleam of satisfaction glowed in his eyes. He had accomplished his objective—to make her cry out for mercy because he still had the power to make her want him without even having to touch her. All Jock had to do was make love to her in his mind, promise her with his eyes and tease her with his voice and she was trembling with searing desire.

They both were quiet as they heard Todd's returning footsteps. How much had he overheard?

Todd put an arm around Barbara and pulled her out of the invisible circle of Jock's attraction. "Did I miss anything?"

"No," said Jock.

Todd looked from his brother to Barbara. "Let me guess. She doesn't want you."

"She hasn't said—"

Todd interrupted him. "So don't bring up memories of an affair she wants to forget."

"I'm not convinced that she wants to. And neither is she," Jock replied.

Barbara shivered, but Todd's arm absorbed the action. "We still have to leave it up to her. But I think reason will prevail." He got in a dig of his own. "I look forward to seeing you in a tux. I want you to be best man at our wedding, dude."

"You have to be out of your mind!" was the astonished and angry retort Jock issued.

"You'll have a year to get used to the idea," Todd countered and Barbara marveled at his calm. "You are my brother. I wouldn't want anyone else."

"That's not an invitation, that's an insult," Jock growled.

"Call it whatever you like."

"If you think I'm going to stand beside you while she walks down the aisle—" Jock's mouth snapped shut on the sentence. Then he took a deep breath. "If she does marry you, you can be sure I'll have urgent business elsewhere on your wedding day, no matter what date you set. I'll never be able to accept her as a sister-in-law, Todd. Understand that now."

There was no reply from Todd as Jock's warning hung heavy in the air. The spiked fronds of a leaf on the palm tree by the pool made a rustling sound, stirred by the first breath of the evening breeze. The door to the veranda opened and Lillian Gaynor walked through to join them.

The smile didn't leave her face as she walked toward them, but Barbara noticed the sudden alertness that leaped into her eyes. Her glance darted between her sons.

"I have the feeling I'm entering a combat zone," she declared in a lighthearted tone. "Are you two arguing about something? Todd, fix me a planter's punch."

"Sure, mom." Todd's hand reassuringly squeezed Barbara's shoulder before he took his arm away to walk to the drink cart.

"Well?" Lillian said expectantly. "Is someone going to tell me what's going on or am I just going to listen to all this lovely silence?" She continued to smile, a maternal indulgence in the expression.

"When we were children, you always managed to settle our disputes. Maybe you can handle this one," Jock said.

"Okay. I'll give it a whirl," Lillian said.

"It's complicated," Jock warned her.

"Try me," Lillian said.

Her older son drew in his breath before he began. "I knew Barbara before Todd did. And I'm not willing to give up my prior claim to her."

It was obviously the last thing that Lillian would have thought her sons would be quarreling about. Her startled gaze flew immediately to Barbara. "You and Jock met each other before this weekend?" she asked.

"Yes, but he doesn't have any prior claim to me," Barbara insisted. "We said goodbye several months ago."

"Several months ago?" Lillian echoed and turned to look at Jock with curious, questioning eyes.

"Here's your punch, Mom." Todd handed her a tall glass, frosty on the outside. "No, Barbara didn't realize J.R. was my brother until she came here. That's why no one has mentioned any of this before. She told me today, afraid it might make a difference. But it doesn't to me."

"You're wrong, Todd," Jock said. "Because I'm going to take her back."

"Barbara isn't a toy or a doll, Jock," his mother admonished.

"Which is just as well because now you can't insist that I share her with Todd." His mouth twisted wryly into a smile.

"I think it's the other way around," Lillian said. "Barbara and Todd are very close. About to be engaged, unless I miss my guess."

"No, I don't think so," Jock replied with complacent certainty. "I'll win her back. I have an edge over Todd in that I know a few of her weaknesses. All I have to do is take advantage of them." He lifted his glass in Barbara's direction, a toast of silent promise to carry out what he'd said. There was a mercurial rise in her pulse.

"You can try, Jock," Barbara said, furious with him all over again.

"And I thought I would throw a party after the riding competition Thursday night," Lillian sighed, glancing at Jock. "If you and Todd are going to be at each other's throats, perhaps I should postpone it until you two settle your, ah, difference of opinion."

Diplomatically Lillian didn't indicate which one of her sons she thought would win or which she supported. She didn't even suggest that Todd's relationship with Barbara might be in jeopardy. Barbara admired her tact.

"Don't worry, Mom. We aren't going to come to blows over this," Todd assured her.

"Don't be too sure about that, little brother." Jock took a sip of his drink and didn't glance at Todd before or after his remark. He kept his attention focused on the drink in his hand.

"Like I said," Todd replied, "this is Barbara's decision. She won't make it on the outcome of any fight between us."

"My practical, sensible brother," Jock declared cynically. "Sometimes I'm amazed that we're related."

"That's because you're so intense, Jock," his mother declared. "You can be much too single-minded at times."

"That's why I always win," Jock pointed out. "Because I never let anything stand in my way. So go ahead with your plans for a Thursday night celebration. We need an excuse for a party. It might just as well be that. Any objections?" He directed the question to Barbara.

"A hundred," she said in irritation. "But go ahead with the party. No one listens to what I have to say anyway."

"Maybe that's because you don't say what you're really feeling," Jock suggested.

"How do you know what I'm feeling?" Barbara asked hotly. "You can't crawl inside my body!"

The look in his eyes told her that he'd like to do just that.

"Jock." His mother's tone said he had gone too far.

Then two quick blasts of a horn interrupted them. It was followed immediately by a slamming door and the sound of someone hurrying across the courtyard to the veranda arches. Everyone turned as the young wrangler, Mike Turbot, came into view.

"Jock, we've got a mare down. We called the vet a half an hour ago and he should be arriving any minute. She had a stillborn foal and she's starting to hemorrhage. Sunny said for me to get you right away." While Mike was rushing out his urgent message, Jock was already setting his glass down and letting his long strides take him across the veranda toward Mike and the courtyard.

"Don't wait dinner for me," Jock tossed over his shoulder as he followed the wrangler to the pickup truck waiting in front of the house, its engine still running.

When Jock didn't return to the house for dinner, Lillian had Antonia, the cook, fix sandwiches and hot coffee and sent her to the foaling barn with them. "Jock will forget to eat otherwise," Lillian explained.

A little after ten o'clock, Todd suggested that they take a stroll in the moonlight and Barbara agreed. It was peaceful outside, the air holding the day's warmth. The moss-draped trees cast ghostly shadows in the light of a full moon. The Milky Way was a white gossamer ribbon of stars trailing across a midnight-blue sky. All was quiet as Barbara wandered beneath the oaks of the back lawn, her hand in Todd's.

But her gaze kept straying to the buildings of the horse stables, white shapes in the night. Jock hadn't come back yet, and she couldn't help wondering how much longer he'd be. The realization drew a sigh. Even when he was out of her sight, he wasn't out of her mind.

"Tired?" Todd asked.

"Yes, a little," she replied because she didn't want to admit the real cause for it.

"Would you want to go inside or stay up for a while?"

"I think I'd rather go inside to bed, if you don't mind." Barbara didn't want Todd to suspect or even think that she wanted to wait up for Jock. It was far better to pretend exhaustion.

"I don't mind," Todd insisted and turned toward the arches of the veranda. "It's been a tiring day—in one form or another." His lips brushed the springing waves of her black hair. "Do you feel more relaxed after our walk?"

"Yes, very much so," she agreed.

As they neared the veranda, Barbara saw a small red light glowing in the shadow of an arch. It puzzled her until she caught the aromatic scent of burning to-bacco and realized it was the red tip of a cigarette. Jock was on the veranda and her heart skipped a beat.

She stole a glance at Todd to see if he had noticed it, but he gave no sign. With the aid of the faint glow from the cigarette, she was just barely able to make out Jock's outline in the shadowy darkness of the arch. He was leaning a shoulder against the inside wall of the arch, gazing out into the night, although Barbara couldn't be sure if he was looking at them.

It was through another archway that they stepped onto the tiled veranda floor. Jock straightened, and the movement attracted Todd's gaze. He hesitated, then stopped, his hand closing tighter around Barbara's.

"How did it go with the mare, J.R.?" Todd inquired.

An interior light in the house spilled through the windows to dimly illuminate the veranda. It was just enough to permit Barbara to see the smears and stains on Jock's light-colored trousers and notice wisps of straw clinging to his clothes. He had a glass in his hand, a short, fat one. Jock didn't immediately respond to Todd's question. With a flick of a forefinger he tossed the cigarette into the night's darkness, and swirled the dark liquid in the glass before downing it in one impatient swallow.

"The mare died twenty minutes ago," he announced flatly.

"That's too bad," Todd offered in sympathy.

"I'm sorry, Jock," Barbara said softly.

It was to her that Jock responded. "Are you?"

Even in the semidarkness his slanted, mocking smile was clear enough.

"Yes." Her answer came back quickly, provoked by his skepticism.

He faced her, an invisible force seeming to reach across the distance for her. "Then come comfort me."

For a charged second Barbara nearly succumbed to the temptation of his unexpected request. All her nerves were poised for the command to accept and glide across the space to him.

At the last second, she couldn't do it. She pulled her hand free of Todd's and managed only a choked good-night before her desperate flight. She raced into the house and up the stairs to her room. Then she heard Todd following and went into the private bathroom and turned on the sink faucet so she wouldn't hear his knock on her door.

Coward, she called herself, but she didn't have the courage to face Todd. Even after he'd gone to his own room, Barbara let the water run to cover the sound of the dry sobs wracking her chest. But no tears fell.

The next morning, a knock at her bedroom door was followed by Todd's voice asking, "Are you ready yet?"

"Almost!" Barbara shouted back her answer so it could be heard through the closed door and wiped at the streak of cinnamon lipstick that had strayed outside the curve of her lip. "Will I need a hat for church?"

"No. I'll meet you downstairs," he called.

"I'll be there in just a couple of minutes," she promised and heard his footsteps on the hardwood floor as he moved away from her door toward the staircase.

After running a brush through her black hair, she fluffed the thick, long curls with her fingers and stepped back to inspect her reflection. The summer linen suit made a startling contrast to the black of her hair and brought out the vivid blue of her eyes. Yet its trim cut had a subdued elegance that seemed right for attending the local church.

Satisfied with her appearance, Barbara turned away from the mirror and walked into her bedroom for the purse that matched her heeled sandals. Since Todd was already downstairs and waiting, she didn't linger and hurried into the hallway that surrounded the open stairwell. She had reached the first landing when she heard Lillian's voice in the foyer below.

"Aren't you coming to church with us, Jock?" she asked. Barbara paused, not wanting to encounter Jock yet.

"I can't."

"It's Sunday. Do you have to work on the Sabbath?" his mother protested.

"Somebody forgot to tell Mother Nature this is a day of rest," Jock said wearily. "Another mare is foaling. I'm on my way to the barn as soon as I change clothes."

Barbara realized waiting had been useless. She wasn't going to be able to avoid Jock since he was on his way upstairs. She started down the steps and met him halfway.

"Good morning." His gold-flecked eyes quickly skimmed over her.

"Good morning," she murmured, trying to keep her gaze downcast without succeeding.

Jock deliberately blocked her path, forcing her to stop. Her pulse started beating rapidly in her throat. He noticed it and a smile twitched at his mouth.

"Say a prayer for me, will you, honey?" His fingertips touched her cheek, his thumb brushing her lips in a fleeting caress that was there, then gone, as he unexpectedly moved out of her way and continued up the stairs.

Having braced herself for who knew what, it took her a second to realize he had left. Yet brief as the meeting had been, he had his usual effect on her.

Barbara continued down the stairs, encased in a warm feeling she couldn't shake.

The small community church was an unpretentious building of wood with stained-glass windows only in the area of the altar. The pews were old, made of hand-hewn polished cypress wood. The floor, too, was of hard cypress wood, except for a worn, carpeted runner down the center aisle. The church was hushed inside, a place of worship. No one used it for gossiping conversation, although Barbara noticed that Lillian Gaynor received many nods and smiles. She was obviously a familiar member of the congregation and well liked. The service was a simple one, the sermon short and filled with a message of God's love.

After the doxology, the minister stood at the door. The exodus from the church was slow. Todd spotted a childhood friend and excused himself to go say hello. Barbara lingered with Lillian at the back of the line.

"This is a little old church, not nearly as grand as the ones in Miami," Lillian admitted, "but I prefer it."

"So do I," Barbara agreed.

"Jock's father and I were married here three weeks to the day after we'd met. It would have been sooner, but the minister was ill. J.R.—my husband—was furious about that." Lillian smiled and Barbara could tell by her expression that she was recalling happy memories. "His name was John Randolph Malloy, but everyone called him J.R. That's where Todd gets his nickname for Jock. When he was a toddler he heard people referring to Jock as J.R.'s son and just picked it up," she explained. "But my first husband was quite a man. Once we'd met, he hardly gave me a chance to catch my breath. I never had time to say no, yes or maybe. Not that I wanted to, mind you," she laughed softly.

And Barbara understood the feeling. That's the way it had happened to her with Jock. He had taken her up on cloud nine, three east of the Milky Way, and she hadn't wanted to come down ever. But he had finally pushed her off.

"Sebastian and I were married in Miami, too. Todd's father," she added in explanation. "It was a fancy affair with an enormous reception afterward. Sebastian thought I'd missed out on that excitement of a big wedding." Her gaze strayed to the altar and Barbara had the impression the simplicity of Lillian's first wedding to Jock's father was a more precious memory. As if concerned that she had sounded partial, Lillian added, "Todd's father made me very happy. He was very good to me."

"Knowing Todd, I'm sure he was," Barbara murmured, understanding clearly that Lillian had not been swept off her feet by him as she had by her first husband. Barbara couldn't help drawing parallel comparisons between her reactions to Todd and Jock, and Lillian's to her two husbands, their fathers.

Todd rejoined them and the subject was immediately changed. "I mentioned the engagement party on Thursday to Frank. He said he would come."

"That's wonderful," Lillian smiled.

"What is this riding competition you were talking about?" Barbara asked.

"It's a weekly get-together for the ranch hands. They compete between themselves in jackpot roping and riding," Lillian explained. "A limited version of a private rodeo, strictly for our own benefit and pleasure. The cowboys get to show off their skills and have some fun. I think you'll enjoy it."

"I'm sure I will," Barbara said.

Chapter Six

When they returned to the house after church, Jock wasn't anywhere around. The three of them had Sunday dinner without him. That afternoon Todd and Barbara walked to the foaling barns. Jock wasn't there, but they saw the mare and her hours-old foal, all legs and head.

Sunday seemed to set a precedent. With a ranch the size of Sandoval there was always something happening, something needing to be done, and a major or minor crisis cropping up that demanded Jock's presence. Except in the evenings, Barbara saw very little of him.

It was Todd who took her riding and introduced her to some of the foremen and their families who lived on the property. He showed her around and kept her entertained. This two-week vacation seemed to be going just the way they had planned it before she arrived and found Jock in residence.

Sunday, Monday and Tuesday passed without incident. Jock's determination seemed to have dissolved. Since that meeting on the stairs, Barbara hadn't spoken to him alone. And in the evenings he had made no attempt to maneuver her out of Todd's company.

She was . . . disappointed, Barbara realized. She had wanted Jock to pursue her and attempt to win her back. Not that she was admitting that she wanted him to succeed. Blowing out her breath, Barbara struck out across the pool in a vigorous crawl. When her outstretched hand touched the concrete side, she stopped to catch her breath, holding onto the edge while she pushed the wet black curls out of her face.

"Who are you racing against?" Todd laughed.

Barbara looked up in surprise. He stood near the side, fully clothed. "I thought you were going to change into your swim trunks and join me. Or do you intend to come in like that?"

"No such luck. Mom has this long list of things she absolutely has to have for the party tomorrow night and I was deputized to fill it. Instead of swimming, do you want to go into town with me?" he asked.

Barbara hesitated. It was a hot, sticky day, which was why she'd opted to swim after lunch. The prospect of leaving the cool water of the pool to ride into town and walk up and down store aisles did not appeal to her.

"I'd rather stay here."

"I don't blame you." Bending down, Todd cupped the back of her head with his hand and pulled her halfway to meet his descending mouth. His kiss was hard and long—passionate if she had been so inclined to respond. Barbara simply couldn't fake that desire, so she settled for not resisting his. Todd didn't appear disappointed by the kiss when he straightened. "I won't be gone long."

"Hurry back."

He disappeared through the arches into the court-yard. A few minutes later she heard a car going down the private lane. She splashed and lazed around in the pool for a while longer until she finally got tired of it and climbed out. She wiped droplets from her skin with a long, thick beach towel, then laid it over a lounge chair and stretched out on it to let the hot sun dry her bikini and evaporate the dampness on her skin. Donning a pair of sunglasses, Barbara picked up the novel she'd brought along and began reading.

The exercise and the hot sun made her drowsy, and the book really wasn't holding her interest. Giving up, Barbara set the book aside and removed her sunglasses to slip them under the chair out of the sun. She rolled onto her stomach and curved an arm under her head for a pillow. The sun's rays were warm and relaxing and she dozed.

"Didn't anybody ever tell you that you shouldn't sleep in the sun?" Jock's drawling voice wakened her.

She was instantly on the defensive. "I wasn't sleeping." Barbara opened her eyes and was dazzled by the white smile. So very male, with an I-could-eat-you-up intensity. "I was just . . ." she faltered for an explanation.

"Sleeping," Jock supplied knowingly.

He was too devilishly attractive in that mood. Barbara turned her head to face away from him and keep from being at all disturbed by his blatantly sensual attractiveness. She even made her voice sound irritated.

"So what if I was sleeping?" Her words were half-mumbled because her cheek was resting on her wrist. She closed her eyes tightly, pretending to ignore him.

"Then you should reapply sunblock," he said.

Something cold squirted in a squiggly line down her backbone. Barbara yelped at the shock and started to rise, but Jock's hand pushed her back down into her former position. He began smearing the sunblock over her back.

"I really don't need it," Barbara protested. "I'm going back into the pool in a few minutes and it'll all wash off." She tried to lever halfway up with her elbows.

"It's waterproof."

"But—" she began.

"Just be quiet and enjoy it." The weight of his hand between her shoulder blades pressed her back down.

It would be much too easy to enjoy it. His hands were gliding over her shoulders and spine with intimate ease. It wasn't just the sun that was warming her flesh. Jock sat down on the edge of the lounge chair and Barbara inched her hip away from the contact with him.

"Don't you have a ranch to run?" she demanded when his hand wandered down to the hollow of her spine, sending crazy, curling sensations all the way down to her toes. "Shouldn't you be off somewhere working?"

"I have been. But I discovered I was hungry and realized I didn't have lunch. Didn't you miss me?" he taunted and began rubbing the lotion on the skin of her waist and hipbones.

"No, I didn't," Barbara lied, and struggled to appear unmoved by his stimulating massage.

"I was on my way to the house to rob the refrigerator when I saw you sleeping in the sun with all that bare skin exposed, shiny and golden. You look very tasty lying here. Maybe I should eat you." His mouth opened on her shoulder bone to rake his teeth over its sensitive skin in a sensual bite. Barbara gasped at how great it felt and missed feeling his fingers unfasten the back hook of her bikini bra. As soon as she was aware the sudden looseness around her chest, she realized what he had done.

"What are you doing?" she demanded angrily and twisted her hands behind her back to try to refasten it. But while she was doing that, Jock untied the knot at the back of her neck, freeing the top completely.

A sound of exasperation came from her throat, tinged with a little panic. All the while his hands kept moving and rubbing, purposely interfering with her attempts to refasten the top. Barbara finally gave up the struggle.

"Why did you do that?" Barbara hissed, her voice wavering from her sheer helplessness.

"This sunblock lotion leaves stains," he reasoned in an amused tone. "I didn't want to ruin your bikini."

"How thoughtful of you," she murmured sarcastically.

"I thought it was," Jock agreed.

Without the thin straps to get in the way, his hands were free to roam every inch of her back. The lotion lubricated her flesh so his hands could glide smoothly and sensuously over her. His strong fingers kneaded the taut cords at the base of her neck, rubbing out the tension. Then, working from the base of her spine, his thumbs followed the rippling line of her backbone up to her shoulders where his hands smoothed out to her arms. On the way back to her spine, his hands made a firm exploration of the sides of her rib cage, fingertips brushing the swelling curve of her breasts.

Her fingers curled into the beach towel, crumpling the terry-cloth material into her palms. The teasing brush on her breasts was deliberate. It was meant to get a reaction from her. She steeled herself not to let it show that his intimate touch bothered her, not to take the bait, to pretend that she was indifferent. But each time Jock became bolder and bolder, his fingers exploring more of the full curve.

"Will you stop it?" Barbara choked on the whispered demand.

"Stop what?" Jock bent to nibble at her shoulder, sending excited goose bumps over her skin.

At the same time, his hands made a bolder foray, curving to the underside of her breasts. "Stop doing that," she ordered.

"Do you mean this?" His hand slid again toward her breast and Barbara tried to knock it away with her arm.

"Yes!" she hissed, her arm missing altogether.

"Don't you like it?" With an ease that revealed his muscled strength, Jock simply turned her over. The unfastened bikini top ended up beneath her. In panic, Barbara grabbed at his forearms, hard bone and sinew beneath her fingers.

"What are you doing? Someone could see us from the house," Barbara protested in wild desperation. The almost physical touch of his eyes made a slow inspection of her.

"No one can see you unless I move," he pointed out lazily. Which was true. His broad shoulders shielded her from the view of anyone in the house. "Do you want me to move?"

"Yes . . . no," she said quickly.

She didn't know what she wanted him to do, so Jock did what he wanted. "You have a beautiful body, honey, and these—wow." He cupped one in his hand. "So ripe and firm and gold, they remind me of grapefruit."

"That's just weird. And you just crossed a line."

"I don't care." As he bent toward her, Barbara turned her face aside, but Jock didn't seem interested in pursuing her lips, preferring instead the exposed curve of her throat. She moaned at the erotic teasing of his warm breath in her ear as his teeth made love nips on her lobe.

"Jock, stop it," she pleaded. "What if Todd comes back?"

"Is he gone?" he murmured against her neck and worked his way down her throat.

"You know he is," Barbara whispered, trying to be angry, but too many other delirious sensations were crowding in, especially when his mouth continued its downward path and he rolled his tongue around a rosy nipple.

"Actually, I didn't give him a thought." Jock kissed the other one to treat them equally and Barbara found that her fingers were digging into the hard flesh of his back, holding him instead of fighting him. Lifting his head, he studied her flushed and aroused face. His gaze lingered on her parted lips, knowing they wanted his kiss. He lowered his mouth closer to tantalize them. "Do you know what Todd would do if he found us like this?"

"No." She didn't want to think about it. She couldn't think about it with his mouth brushing softly against the outline of her lips.

"Eventually he'd forgive me." There was derision in his murmured answer. "He would be understanding toward you because you can't help yourself, and he'd have to forgive me because I'm not in control of myself around you." Jock seemed to take great pleasure in teasing her with near kisses. "Do you know what I would do if I found you like this with Todd?"

"No."

"I'd rather not say." His voice was a deep, rumbling growl. "Because you're mine. I won't share you with anyone, not even my own brother."

He took her mouth with fierce possession, claiming her as if he wanted to make her his own forever. Barbara was swept away by the force of his intense passion, her senses spinning under the brilliant fury of his kiss. With an exultant moan she surrendered to the wild desire that only Jock could kindle. An arm slipped beneath her to crush her to him, trying to absorb her body into his own. The embrace seemed utterly natural and deeply emotional.

An elemental hunger took over both of them as his mouth began to devour her lips, sampling their softness and tasting their honeyed response. No longer needing to hold her captive, his hands began caressing her again, enjoying the texture of skin made silky by his tender treatment of it, and her feminine roundness and sweet curves. Her own hands were moving over him with joyous familiarity, glorying in the hard muscles of his arms and back, tangling her fingers in his thick hair.

When his mouth moved from hers to explore her cheek and the soft sweep of her lashes, Barbara felt his labored breathing, the fiery warmth of his disturbed breath against her skin. She had aroused him fully, and it was a heady knowledge.

"Does Todd make you feel like this?" Jock lifted his head long enough to let his dark gold eyes blaze possessively over her face. "Do you even let him hold you his arms?"

"No," Barbara admitted. His chin and jaw rubbed against her cheek, the faint stubble of a beard sensually scraping at her skin, as his mouth moved against her temple.

"I want you," he declared huskily. "It doesn't matter whether it's in the glare of broad daylight or after midnight."

The mention of Todd's name had returned a thread of sanity to her overwhelmed mind. "I don't think so. Not really," she said with a bitter, soft laugh. "You just don't want anyone else to have me."

"That isn't true," Jock dismissed her statement. His hand came up to hold her face. "You want me to make love to you, so don't deny it."

"You're right." There was an ache in her throat that made speech difficult. "But all you have to offer is sex, Jock. I know it's going to be super-hot and passionate for as long as it lasts, but—"

His jaw hardened. "If it's all we can have, then I'll be satisfied with that." His mouth came down to claim hers, but she avoided it.

"It isn't enough for me." Barbara felt the heat of tears in her eyes and willed them not to fall. "At least Todd cares about me as a person."

For an instant Jock was motionless. But Barbara could feel the seething anger inside him. She steeled herself.

"Big deal. Todd brought you home. Yes, he cares

about you. He'll care just as much for the stray he
brings home next month or next year. If he lost you
tomorrow, he wouldn't hurt for long. There are too
many strays for him to find and he has enough love
for them all." His low voice was laced with scorn.

Barbara guessed that Jock was probably right. It
wasn't that Todd's affection was shallow. It was genuine, but easily transferred to the next lost soul that
came along.

"At least Todd knows what love means," she argued
bravely.

"And you think I don't?" The gleam in his tawny
eyes was contemptuous.

"That's right." Barbara choked on the whisper.

"You don't know how wrong you are. He'll never
satisfy you."

"But he'll make me happier than you can," she retorted in a small, tight voice. "That's the point behind
all this, isn't it?"

Jock glared at her for another long minute before
he levered away and straightened from the lounge
chair, turning his back to her. Miserable with love for
him, Barbara watched his fingers coil around the
back of his neck. She crossed her arms in front of
her to cover herself and hug the pain throbbing
inside. As if picking up her silent movement, Jock
sliced a glance over his shoulder.

"Better tie yourself up in knots again," he snapped.
He flicked a dangling strap over her shoulder.

His anger stung and Barbara rolled away from him
onto her stomach. Her fingers were all thumbs as she
tried to fit the top to her breasts and fasten the hook
behind her back. Jock was watching her and she

sensed his impatience with her fumbling efforts. Suddenly his hands were pushing hers out of the way.

"I can do it," she protested against the torture of his touch. Her eyes burned with tears, the heat scorching them dry before they could fall.

"Just shut up." Cold and impersonal, he fastened the back hook and pushed her head down to tie the straps. Barbara didn't make a sound. When he was done, Jock stood up to look down at her, but she didn't move. "We aren't finished, you and I. Not yet."

It was a warning. Barbara didn't mistake it for anything else as his long strides carried him away from the pool toward the house.

Pushing out of the chair, she walked to the edge of the pool and dove into the cool water. She swam the length of the pool, releasing the frustrated energy born of unsatisfied desires. The ache in the pit of her stomach went away, but not the pain in her heart. It wouldn't be soothed so easily.

There were no drinks before dinner on the veranda that Thursday since dinner was served early. The meal was a light snack to leave room for the food and drinks that would be served at the party after the ranch's riding competition. Barbara lingered at the table, nibbling at a sectioned orange until Jock left the house.

"You're awfully quiet, Barbara," Lillian commented. "What are you thinking about?"

"I . . . was just trying to decide whether I should wear pants or a dress tonight," she lied. She had no taste for the juicy flesh of the orange and set it aside.

"That depends," Todd said, "on whether you want

to ride over to the arena or take a car. Which would you like to do?"

"I think I'd rather ride." Barbara opted for the transportation that would demand the least amount of conversation.

"Then you'd better go change so we can start out," he suggested, "while I arrange to have the horses saddled and brought to the house."

In her room, Barbara put on a pair of bone-colored denims and a blue madras blouse. When she came downstairs Todd was waiting for her. He, too, had changed into more rugged clothing for the ride. The horses were outside. It was an older man who handed Barbara the reins to the blaze-faced chestnut.

"Where's Mike?" she asked Todd after they had mounted and started the horses down the lane.

"He's at the arena already, I imagine."

The rhythmic gait of the horse beneath her and Todd's easy company were letting Barbara relax. "How long will this last—the competition, I mean?"

"Until the sun goes down. Eight, eight-thirty."

"Is it like a rodeo?" she asked.

"Do you mean bucking broncos and bull riding?" Todd smiled. "No. It's mostly roping and cutting cattle. Once in a while there's a young horse and the boys will take their turns on it, but that's an exception rather than the rule."

There was a confusion of trucks and horse trailers when they arrived at the arena grounds. Horses and riders were milling about, some in the arena and others weaving through the congestion of parked vehicles and people. Most of the men that worked on Sandoval were married. Their wives and families had come along with them to watch the competition.

Since there weren't any bleachers to sit in, many of the women had brought folding lawn chairs to set outside the white-railed fence of the arena, close to the end where the chutes were.

Their arrival didn't go unnoticed. As Todd led the way to the trailer where they were going to leave their horses tied, greetings were called out all along the way. A few of the people Barbara had already met, but most of them she hadn't seen, so there was a constant stream of introductions as she and Todd rode their horses to the trailer and walked back to the arena fence.

"Do you have the feeling you've just run the gauntlet?" Todd laughed softly, putting an arm around her waist as they both leaned on the top rail.

"Yes," she admitted. At the far end of the arena, she saw a muscled, iron-gray horse that she instantly recognized as Jock's. He was sitting casually in the saddle, talking to another cowboy. "Will Jock be competing in any of the events tonight?" Barbara asked, trying to sound casual even though her heart was knocking against her ribs.

"No, he hasn't been riding in them for the last few years. Usually he takes part in the judging."

"Why hasn't he been riding?" curiosity made her ask.

"Because he was winning all the time," Todd grinned. "Well, not all of the time," he conceded, "but a lot. J.R. is competitive and he loves to win. Being the owner, he didn't think it was right so he quit riding."

"I see," she murmured, but she was thinking about that reference to Jock as a competitor and his desire to win. Jock had warned her that he hadn't given up.

Barbara glanced at him again. She was running out of defensive moves. Being with Todd wasn't enough, although she still felt safe when she was with him.

"They're clearing the arena," Todd observed. "It looks like they're going to start with calf roping first."

The horses and riders began filing out of the arena through the gate near where Todd and Barbara were standing. A hefty-sized calf was prodded along the chutes while the first roper backed his horse into the box beside the chute. Jock and another rider stayed in the arena to judge and time the event.

It was impossible for Barbara to watch each of the contestants without being aware of the rider on the big gray horse. When the calf roping was over, Mike Turbot had won the event. The fact that it was someone she knew made it more interesting to Barbara.

"Congratulations, Mike," she called to him when he rode past.

"Thanks." He reined his horse to a stop and modestly insisted, "Half the guys out there could beat me."

"But they didn't," Barbara pointed out.

"Yeah, well," Mike shrugged, looking pleased, "all these events are based on what a cowboy and his horse do on a ranch. Like roping a calf for branding and in this next event, cutting a steer out from a herd. Those are things you've got to do every day."

"You are good at it."

"So are the others. You should see them in action for real. As a matter of fact, they're going to be rounding up the spring calves over in the Crosstimber section. Have Jock take you over there one day to watch. It's interesting if you've never seen one before," Mike suggested.

"I'll bet it would be." But Barbara doubted that she would ask Jock.

Mike glanced toward the arena and edged his horse toward the fence. "Hey, Jock!" he called him to the fence.

Jock trotted the gray toward the fence. Barbara felt his gaze touch her and flick to Todd before centering on Mike. "What is it, Mike?" he asked with seeming casualness.

"Vince dislocated his shoulder and can't ride in the team roping with me," Mike explained.

Barbara felt a twinge of relief that he hadn't suggested Jock take her to see the roundup. "I wondered if you would be my partner."

"I'll see if I can't get someone to take over as timer for me on that event," Jock agreed after a brief hesitation.

"Great. Let me know," Mike nodded.

"I will." Jock let his gaze slide to Barbara. "Are you enjoying yourself?"

"Yes." She felt wary.

Todd spoke up. "Mike was just mentioning that you'd be rounding up calves over at Crosstimber."

"Yes, starting Monday," Jock admitted.

"I think Barbara would find it fascinating to watch," Todd explained.

"Okay." Jock gave her a considering look, his mouth twitching in what might have been a dry smile. "You could come on Tuesday. Would that be all right?"

"If it's all right with Todd." Barbara shrugged.

"Tuesday will be fine," Todd agreed. "You'd like to go, wouldn't you, Barbara?"

"Of course," she said, because it was expected of her.

"Hey, Jock!" The other man who had been acting as judge with him waved to him. "They're ready to start the cutting competition."

"See you later." The encompassing phrase was issued before Jock wheeled the gray horse away from the rail.

Chapter Seven

Before the team roping started, Jock rode out of the arena and another man took his place to judge the event. As she realized that he would be competing, Barbara's interest in the event was increased. When the first team of two ropers entered the arena, she turned to Todd.

"What's the purpose of this event? I mean, what is its practical use in ranching?" she questioned. "Why would a cowboy have to rope a full-grown steer? Obviously it would already have been branded as a calf."

"Generally it's done to treat an injured or sick animal. Sometimes it's referred to as heading and heeling because one rider ropes the horns or the cow's head and the second rider catches the hind feet in his loop. The steer is stretched between them till he goes down so he can be treated," Todd explained.

"Ouch," she said, feeling sympathy for all parties involved.

The first pair of ropers in the event ended up with no time when the second roper failed to catch the hind legs. "It's tricky," was Todd's comment.

When Mike Turbot and Jock rode into the arena,
Barbara could feel the change in the atmosphere.
There was more than ordinary interest from the on-
lookers who worked for the man about to compete.
The big gray horse seemed aware of the change, too.
It sidestepped into the arena, almost galloping in
place, its neck arched, the embodiment of speed and
power waiting to be released.

The steer was in the chute. Jock backed the gray
into the boxed opening on the right of the chute and
Mike put his horse in the left. The chute gate sprang
up, releasing the steer. The animal had a length's
head start before the two riders bounded after it.
Within two strides, Mike was swinging his lariat and
tossing it over the steer's horns. He dallied the rope
around his saddle horn, turning his horse and pulling
the steer around to offer the hindquarters to Jock's
rope. His loop snaked low to the ground and was
jerked tight above the steer's hind hooves. In the blink
of an eye the steer was on the ground, the ropes taut
on either side. The time was lightning fast.

There was no applause as the two men rode out of
the arena. A couple of people shouted their approval. But there was a look Barbara noticed in the
eyes of the cowboys, a gleam of respect when they
glanced at their boss.

"Great job. You've done it again, J.R." There wasn't
a trace of envy in Todd's voice as he congratulated
his brother. "I'll make a side bet with you that you
just posted the winning time."

"I won't bet," Jock said, but his inner satisfaction
was written on his face. The gray horse tossed its
head, snorting as it paused near Todd and Barbara.

Mike stopped alongside him. "You had that loop

around the steer's hind feet before I even had it turned properly. That was good roping, boss."

"Give some credit to Ghost." Jock patted the arched neck of his horse. "He put me in position to make the throw."

"Yeah, and you trained him," Mike said with a wry shake of his head. "A good horse just makes a good cowboy look even better."

The praise seemed to tighten Jock's features. Barbara sensed he didn't like it whether it was earned or not. It made him uncomfortable, because of his position as owner, she supposed. Jock's finger touched his hat before he pivoted the gray horse toward the collection of horse trailers.

Another team of ropers entered the arena and Barbara turned absently to watch them. But her mind was on the man astride the gray. Even when she was determined not to think about him, she did.

Before the event was over, Todd asked, "Did you want to ride the horses back? I can borrow Ramon's truck if you want to go back to the house and change before everyone arrives for the party."

She frowned. "What about the horses?"

"We can send them back in one of the horse trailers. Mike will look after them. If we ride them, it will take longer."

He seemed to think that was a concern. Barbara wasn't looking forward all that eagerly to Lillian's party in honor of the two of them. She didn't object to being late, but obviously Todd did.

"Maybe you should ask Ramon if we could use his truck," she said.

"Wait here while I find him." He pressed a kiss to her temple before leaving.

Barbara turned back to watch the rest of the team-roping event. Mike and Jock were the winners when all the times were in. Todd still hadn't come back for her when the next event started. When Mike rode by, Barbara stopped him.

"Have you seen Todd?"

"Yeah, he was over by Ramon's pickup." Mike pointed. "It's that blue one behind the red and white horse trailer."

"I see it. Thanks." She started off toward it.

She had to zigzag around trucks and trailers, dodging horses and riders along the way. It was an obstacle course, she decided, when she stopped to let one horse pass in front of her while another walked behind her. Intent on avoiding what was ahead of her, Barbara didn't notice the gray horse approaching from behind.

"Todd is looking for you," Jock announced, causing Barbara to start in surprise.

"Where is he?" Her glance ricocheted from him to search the crowd of faces. "He went to borrow Ramon's truck so we could leave and I—" The gray horse was maneuvered in front of her to block her path.

"Hop on and I'll take you to him." Jock stretched an arm down to help her swing into the saddle behind him.

She didn't want to be that close to the man. "No, thanks. I'll walk. Just tell me where Todd is."

"He's over by Ramon's truck, but it will be easier—and safer—to ride. There are a lot of horses and hooves to dodge."

But Barbara ignored his suggestion and ducked under the muscled neck of the gray horse to continue in the direction of the blue pickup. She had taken three steps when an arm hooked her waist and she was scooped off the ground. Barbara struggled as Jock sat her on the front of the saddle.

"Put me down!" she ordered, unaware of how loud her voice was until she heard two cowboys chuckling.

"Got trouble, boss?" one called.

Barbara crimsoned, flashing a resentful glance at Jock's face, too close to her own. His arm circled her waist so tightly that her shoulder was wedged against the unyielding wall of his chest. There was a smile on his mouth but not in his eyes.

"How about this, boys?" he responded to their comment. "I come riding up on an almost white horse and plan to carry off a beautiful lady into the night—and this is what happens."

"Just take me to Todd," she hissed.

"I said I would," Jock reminded her in a voice as low as hers had been.

She felt the gray horse bunch its muscled hindquarters at the touch of Jock's heel. It gave a little jump forward before a check of the reins slowed it to a quick-stepping walk. Barbara held herself rigid in Jock's tight hold. But she wasn't in a position to balance and had to rely on his support to keep her on the horse. She forced her gaze to the front, looking for Todd, but with each breath she took, her senses were filled with the scent of Jock, spicy and male. She almost didn't see Todd standing beside the blue truck.

"There you are." Todd walked forward when Jock stopped the horse and lifted Barbara from the saddle. "Thanks, J.R."

"See you at the house." The silent promise of that statement was in the look he let linger on Barbara before turning the big gray gelding away from the truck.

Barbara tried to pretend that the look held no significance and turned to Todd. "What was the problem?"

"What problem?" His expression was blank.

"I waited for you, but you didn't come back."

"No, I sent J.R. to get you. It's a lot safer to get through this jam of horses and trailers on horseback. Weren't you at the gate when he found you?" Todd asked.

"No, I'd come looking for you. I didn't realize you'd sent Jock for me," Barbara said with a trace of irritation.

Todd opened the passenger door of the truck cab for her. "Why? Does it matter?"

"Well, yeah," she said impatiently.

"He hasn't been bothering you lately, has he?" Todd frowned.

Only when you aren't around. But she didn't say that. "I just wish you hadn't sent him, that's all," she repeated.

Todd walked around the front of the truck and slid behind the wheel. "You might as well get used to his being around, Barbara," he said firmly. "You'll see a lot of him at Sandoval."

"Not as if I have a choice," she murmured. "He does like to have his way."

"Have his way about what?"

"Never mind." Barbara shrugged, not wanting to continue the conversation, and Todd let it drop.

The truck made the drive to the main house seem relatively short. The sky was lit up by a lingering sunset when Todd stopped in front of the hacienda-style building. Climbing out of the cab, Barbara hurried into the courtyard. Through the arched openings leading to the veranda she saw Lillian Gaynor setting a platter on a buffet table that had been set up to hold the food. The woman glanced up at the sound of Barbara's footsteps in the courtyard.

"You're back. How was the competition? Did you enjoy it?"

"Yes, it was fun," Barbara replied. "I'm going upstairs to wash off this arena dust and change clothes, then I'll be down to help you."

"Don't rush. Antonia and I have just about everything done. Besides, this is an informal party. A guest shouldn't have to worry about all the refreshments. So take your time," Lillian insisted, then added, "Oh, dress casually. Most everyone will come as they are from the arena."

"Okay. Thanks for the warning." Barbara hurried toward the double-door entrance to the foyer and its stairwell.

While she was in her room washing and changing, she heard the sounds of trucks and cars driving up, doors slamming, and a multitude of voices congregating on the veranda. Taking Lillian's advice, Barbara changed into a simple white peasant blouse and a wraparound skirt of red cotton.

The party seemed to be in full swing when she stepped onto the veranda. Built-in speakers piped music outside from the entertainment center in the house. The guests were all talking and laughing with either a plate of food in their hands or a beer. Todd appeared almost instantly at her side to take her in hand.

"Are you hungry?" He led her toward the buffet

table, mounded with platters of sandwiches, cheeses, fruits, hot hors d'oeuvres and chips.

"Not very." She shook her head.

"Want something to drink? We have a couple of kegs of beer and some punch. I have to warn you somebody spiked the punch very generously. You have been warned," he chuckled.

"No iced tea, I suppose," Barbara said with a mock sigh.

"Hey, this is supposed to be a celebration," he chided her playfully. "Some punch for the lady," he ordered and Barbara found a glass cup being placed in her hand. Todd bent toward her and whispered again, "Be careful."

She took a tentative sip and felt the fire in her throat. "Gah. That is strong," she agreed, unable to stop a coughing protest.

"You can carry it around with you all night. No one will notice if you don't drink it." Todd grinned and linked his arm in hers. "Come on. I think we'd better circulate. This is a friendly group. I don't know what you've heard about cowboys, but this bunch loves to dance. Most of them are pretty good so you won't have to worry about smashed toes."

Todd's information was correct on all counts. It was a very friendly and open crowd. Barbara found it easy to talk and laugh with them. No one noticed that all she did was moisten her lips with the potent drink in her glass cup without the level of liquid ever dropping much. Mike Turbot was the first to come up and ask her to dance. When she proved to be a willing partner, it seemed to break the ice and she was inundated with invitations.

Slow dances, fast dances and the in-between tempos—

she danced them all. Her partners were young cowboys, old ones and middle-aged. Barbara was half-convinced that every man at the party was determined to dance with Todd's new girlfriend. It became impossible to refuse anyone for fear of offending him. Besides, Barbara couldn't remember the last time she had danced so much, and she was having fun.

The song ended and she thanked her partner, a young, fresh-faced cowboy whose name she couldn't remember. As she paused for a breath while the record changed, a hand tapped her shoulder. Barbara turned with a start, half expecting to find Jock confronting her. She had seen him on the fringes of several groups all evening but so far hadn't encountered him.

"Ramon," she laughed in relief.

"If the next song is a slow one, may I have this dance?" he asked with a formal little bow. "I don't have the stamina anymore for the faster songs."

"I'd be delighted," Barbara agreed with a slight curtsy.

A hand gripped the curve of her waist from behind. "Sorry, Ramon," Jock said without apology. "But I've got dibs on the lady. This dance is mine." He was already turning her into his arms as he spoke.

"Oh, but—" Barbara tried to protest, looking frantically over her shoulder at Ramon.

"It is all right. I will wait until later," he assured her and turned away.

With that excuse gone, Barbara had to seek hurriedly for another. At the same time, she made the discovery that Jock had both arms around her waist, his large hands splayed over the small of her back. She had no place for her own hands but his chest, and the lower half of her body was being molded to his.

"I'd really rather sit this dance out," she said nervously, staring at the buttons on his shirt.

"Would you? Why?" His drawling tone indicated that he knew the reason: he was getting to her.

"I'm tired. I've been dancing practically every time. I'd like to catch my breath." It sounded reasonable to Barbara.

"You were willing enough to dance when Ramon asked you," Jock reminded her, knowing it was a vital point she had overlooked in her search for an excuse. "Since you're tired, we won't move around too much. Feel free to lean on me if your feet hurt."

"No, thank you." The stilted little refusal sounded ridiculous even to her own ears, almost prudish.

The way their bodies were swaying together, so exactly in unison with each other and the tempo of the slow music, made her even more nervous. She flattened her hands against his chest, trying to wedge more space between them, but her action only curved her hips more fully against the muscles in his thighs. Although they were barely moving, Barbara discovered that they were in the more shadowed area of the veranda, away from the lanterns strung near the buffet tables. She stopped straining away from his chest since it only made her more tense. The warmth of his breath stirred her hair.

"With all that creamy skin in view, I'm surprised somebody hasn't taken a bite out of you," Jock murmured and bent his head toward a bare shoulder. "How could they resist?"

Barbara wiggled in protest, but she couldn't stop him from nibbling at the base of her neck. "Not everyone is a cannibal like you, Jock." She tried to sound angry, but it was difficult with a quiver of excitement racing over her skin.

"They don't know what they're missing." His firm lips formed the words against her neck, as he continued his exploration with bold unconcern.

"Jock, stop it." Barbara squirmed uncomfortably, liking what he was doing and afraid of it at the same time. "Somebody might see you. What would they think?"

"That I'm having myself a very good time," he laughed softly against her skin. "And they wouldn't be wrong. But keep pretending to struggle and they'll think you are just trying to avoid an embarrassing scene."

He nipped at her earlobe and Barbara shuddered against him. "Don't do this, please."

With a sudden turn, Jock maneuvered her behind an arch where curious eyes couldn't see them. He leaned against the concrete support, pulled her hard into his arms and covered her lips with a very amorous kiss. It happened so fast Barbara had no warning and her response was purely instinctive. Her hands glided around his neck while he pressed himself against her. For several moments, a mutual and highly sensual insanity claimed them both, but Barbara was thrilled by it.

Until Lillian's voice gasped, "Jock, what are you doing?"

The demand ripped the kiss apart. Too shaken to move, Barbara hid her reddening face in Jock's shadow, averted from the gentle woman she had grown to like. Her fingers were slow to unclasp themselves from around his neck, like a child's hands inching away from a cookie jar. She was flooded with guilt.

"You missed the point, Mom," Jock said, drawing a deep breath. "What is Barbara doing to stop me?"

That was the last straw. Barbara was so stunned by his self-serving question that she just stood there, needing Jock to set her away from him and leave, which he did. She stood defenseless in front of his mother, too ashamed to speak and too embarrassed to move. The weighted silence stretched for several seconds. Then Lillian stepped toward her and curved a hand around Barbara's bare shoulders, which had only moments ago been warmed by Jock's mouth.

"Come with me, dear," Lillian murmured. "We both need a few moments to collect ourselves."

"Thank you. Yes." Her voice was shaking as badly as her nerves were. She couldn't have faced that happy, laughing crowd just on the other side of the arch.

Lillian guided her through a side entrance into the house, away from the noise of the party. Once the doors were shut and they were alone, the woman's brown eyes made a quick inspection of Barbara's pale face.

"Would you like a drink? A brandy, perhaps?" she suggested.

"No. No, thank you," Barbara refused with a quick shake of her head. She moistened her lips nervously, knowing there were going to be questions.

"I'm sure this isn't any of my business," Lillian began with a sigh. "But as a mother to both Todd and Jock, I can't exactly be called a disinterested party."

"I know. I'm sorry." Barbara swallowed.

"I understood that you and Jock had met before.

But I had the impression that you were no longer interested in him. That obviously isn't the case, is it?"

"I—" Barbara stopped and admitted, "No, it's not."

"Are you in love with Todd? Or Jock?"

"Both." Barbara realized that answer demanded more of an explanation. "In different ways. Todd makes me feel so safe and protected. Jock takes me to the edge of the world." She rubbed her arms, fighting a chill.

"Hmm. How well did you know Jock?" Lillian phrased the question delicately.

Barbara took a deep breath and released it in a sigh. "Very well."

There was a long pause before Lillian asked, "What happened between you?"

"It just didn't work out." The last thing Barbara wanted to do was go into that long story again. She felt the sting of tears in her eyes. "But he isn't going to make me cry again. I'm not going to let him," she protested in a voice that sounded amazingly calm and rational.

"How much of this have you told Todd?"

"All of it. He's aware that I never really resolved things with Jock." Barbara didn't want to tell his mother that he had done all the resolving when he told her it was over and they had to be friends. "It's a complicated situation. Todd suggested that I take these two weeks to make up my mind. So far I haven't been very successful at treating Jock like a brother." She smiled bitterly.

"Barbara, you're not even engaged to Todd. You two are just . . . together. But even an engagement is meant to be a sort of trial period."

"What would you do, Lillian?" Barbara lifted her gaze, her blue eyes shadowed with uncertainty.

"That isn't a fair question." The older woman laughed briefly in surprise. "I hope that I would do what I felt in my heart was right."

"Yes, of course." Barbara turned away, a little disheartened.

"That isn't an adequate answer, I know," Lillian murmured. "It must be very difficult for you. But I really am in the middle here. I don't think I can be all that impartial or even give you more specific advice."

"You've been very understanding as it is." Barbara meant that very sincerely. "I doubt I made a very good impression, considering my behavior tonight."

"I was young once," Lillian reminded her. "It may be hard to believe, but it's true." Her brown eyes held a gently twinkling light.

Barbara smiled. "I find it very easy to believe, because you are still very young in many ways."

"Now you've made an excellent impression." Lillian laughed with a soft warmth.

"I meant it," Barbara insisted, not wanting Jock and Todd's mother to think she was attempting to flatter her. "I didn't say it just to—"

"I know you didn't," Lillian assured her quickly. "If you feel up to it, we should return to the party. People do talk."

Barbara wished there was a way she didn't have to return at all, which, of course, was impossible. Thanks to the older woman's quiet understanding, her nerves were in better shape, although she wasn't certain how much her shattered poise could withstand.

"Yes. Todd will be wondering where I am," she agreed with the suggestion.

Exiting the house through the veranda doors, Barbara was immediately enveloped in the noise of the party. The music and laughing voices hammered at her ears. Lillian paused beside her while Barbara searched the crowd of faces. Someone called to Lillian and she excused herself to resume her duties as hostess. At almost the same moment, Barbara saw Todd separate himself from a small group and walk toward her.

"I've been looking for you," he said gently and took her hand to pull her to his side. "The last time I saw you, you were dancing with J.R. Then you just disappeared. Where were you? Powdering your nose?" He kissed the side of her hair, nestling her inside the crook of his arm.

Todd offered her the perfect excuse, but honesty wouldn't permit her to take it. "Your mother and I were talking." She paused for a beat. "She rescued me from Jock."

He was still for an instant, every muscle tensed. Barbara lifted her gaze to his face and found him staring at a distant point. She glanced in the same direction.

Jock was standing by the punch bowl, looking back at the two of them. His hard gaze seemed to click off as he turned his head and a muscle flexed in his cheek from a sudden clenching of his jaw. Then he was downing the contents of a glass and turning to ladle more punch into it.

"Let's dance." Todd didn't give her a chance to refuse as he escorted her to the area of the veranda where other couples were swaying to the music coming from the sound system.

Held close in his arms, Barbara felt genuinely protected. Todd's undemanding embrace was a haven for her stormy emotions. She relaxed under his comforting hold, no longer needing to be on her guard.

"Is he getting to you?" Todd murmured near her ear.

Barbara released a long sigh. "Jock always could. I think you made a mistake when you brought a stray like me home, Todd."

"Mmm." He made the negative sound against her hair. "I couldn't let you keep wandering around so lost and alone. You need someone to look after you."

Was that what really true? It had been once. And Barbara had often thought she just wanted someone to care about her. Now she wasn't so sure. Her glance strayed to the punch bowl. Jock was still there, the glass cup in his hand, watching them again.

Chapter Eight

Around midnight the party began to wear itself out. A few had already gone home. Although the rest still lingered, their voices were subdued and the music quieter. They had separated into groups without much mingling going on between them. Barbara knew the party was on the verge of breaking up, and she was glad.

"Mom had the coffee and tea brought out. Would you like some?" Todd asked.

Barbara glanced to see Lillian setting a coffee service on the buffet table. For once, Jock wasn't in the vicinity of the punch bowl, a place he had haunted since their dance. She looked back at Todd, her bulwark that evening.

"Sure, coffee would be great," she agreed and he led her to the table.

As Todd started to pour them each a cup of coffee, Ramon and Connie Morales approached them. "We are leaving now," Ramon announced. "We wished to say goodbye."

"I'm glad you came, both of you." Barbara's smile

was as warm as she could make it. It had been a rather odd evening.

"We enjoyed ourselves," Connie declared.

"We never did have our dance, did we, Ramon?" Barbara remembered.

"You did not seem in the mood to dance later," he replied. Did his dark gaze linger on her a little too wisely before he turned to Todd? "Barbara is a lovely woman. You must be proud of her, Todd."

"I am," he stated.

"Hey, little brother." With animal quietness, Jock appeared at her side. His hand hooked her waist to pull her against him. "You're right. Barbara is really something." There was a possessive ring in his voice that carried over the veranda, silencing conversations.

The hard imprint of his length burned down her side. The onslaught of heat made her weak and shaky inside, but the awareness of curious eyes watching gave Barbara the strength to struggle. She pushed at him.

"You're making a scene, Jock," she protested.

"So what? Do you think they haven't noticed that I haven't been able to take my eyes off you all evening? Or the way you kept looking for me?" he asked.

The questions bordered on outrageous. His warm breath washed her face with a potent mixture of fruit and alcohol. "You're drunk," Barbara accused him. It was a hopeless attempt to negate his statement but she had to try.

"Am I?" Keeping an arm around her, Jock looked into her eyes. "Well, it takes the edge off. Whatever works, right?"

Barbara couldn't reply. His behavior was completely out of line, but no one spoke up.

Jock went on, "If I were stone-cold sober, I'd keep right on thinking about you—"

"Get a grip, J.R." Stepping forward, Todd laid an controlling hand on his brother's forearm.

In a shrugging movement, Jock released her and attempted to knock away Todd's restraining hand, but his swinging arm accidentally struck Todd's chin, drawing a muffled sound of surprise and pain. Todd rubbed his chin, a stunned frown creasing his forehead as he stared at Jock.

"Todd, I—" Jock's ragged voice seemed to come from some deep place within him.

"It's all right. It was just an accident," Todd said quietly.

Fighting for self-control, Jock stared at him for another second before turning away and leaving the veranda with long, reaching strides. Barbara watched Jock enter the house, slamming the glass-paned door so that it rattled. Todd moved to her side.

"Are you all right?" She looked up, feeling guilty about what had happened.

"It didn't hurt," Todd insisted, taking his hand away from his chin. "Not that much. It just surprised me, that's all."

Barbara suddenly remembered the presence of Ramon and Connie Morales. She turned, wanting wholeheartedly to offer an apology. "I'm sorry this happened."

"It was inevitable," Ramon responded, smiling gently. "It is sad when two brothers fall in love with the same woman."

Love? Barbara questioned that in her mind, but she said nothing.

"Don't feel badly," Connie offered. "Everyone regrets that this happened, including Jock. It's best forgotten."

"Yes," Ramon agreed. "This time we will say good-night."

The departure of the older couple began a general exodus of the other guests. Barbara stayed at Todd's side to bid them all good-night, but she was just as anxious to leave the veranda as they were.

When they were alone, Todd put an arm around her and suggested, "We never did have our coffee. Would you like that cup now? We can sit down and unwind for a while. In one way or another, it's been a trying evening. You could do with some relaxing."

"I think I'll pass on the coffee," Barbara refused. "I'd rather go to my room. I—"

"You don't have to explain," Todd interrupted and kissed the corner of her mouth. "You'd rather be alone. I can understand that."

"Some celebration. Your girlfriend is running off to hide the instant the last guest leaves," Barbara sighed. "Maybe we should call this whole thing off, Todd. This can't be the way you wanted it."

"It isn't, but I have a lot of patience. Good night." He gave her an affectionate push toward the glass-paned doors.

"Aren't you coming?" Barbara paused.

"Not right away." He shook his head and moved to the buffet table.

Barbara watched him pour a cup of coffee from the insulated service, then turned to enter the house. Passing through the informal family room, she walked into the hall that led to the foyer. It took her past the door to a small den. Usually the door was closed. This time it was standing open. Her gaze was drawn into the room.

Jock was reclining in a wooden-armed chair, his long legs stretched out in front of him. An empty glass was in his hand, and his hair was rumpled as if by raking fingers. While Barbara watched, Jock turned away from the door to reach for something on a table beside him.

As he faced forward in the chair, she saw a whiskey bottle in his hand. He started to tip the bottle to fill the glass; then an unpleasant smile pulled at his mouth. Instead of filling the glass, Jock set it aside and took a swig straight from the bottle.

Not conscious of making a sound, Barbara nonetheless became the object of his slicing gaze. His features seemed to harden into bronze, smooth and emotionless. Uncoiling from the chair, he strode toward the door, and Barbara took a step backward. His mouth tightened as he reached out and slammed the door shut in her face.

Shaken, she turned away to move to the stairwell in the foyer. His action made her feel all the more to blame for what had happened that night. Sleeping wasn't easy.

It was past midmorning when Barbara came down the stairs. Her few hours of sleep hadn't left her feeling rested. The party was a reasonable excuse for having slept so late, but Barbara knew Todd had probably been up earlier—and Jock, too. Everyone in the household except herself. Which meant if she had breakfast, it would be alone. Sighing, she turned into the living room, using it as a shortcut to the dining room where she knew a pot of coffee would be warming.

As she started toward the archway, she heard Jock's voice raised in anger. "I'm too old to be slapped on the hand. Just stay out of it!" Lillian murmured a response that Barbara couldn't hear, but Jock's reply was plain. "I don't need you to tell me what's right and proper."

"Then for God's sake quit shouting!" Lillian retorted.

Barbara hesitated a minute. When she heard the door leading from the dining room to the kitchen open and close, she presumed Jock had left and she started forward again. At least she would be able to have a cup of coffee with Lillian.

As she rounded the archway, Barbara saw Jock, not Lillian, seated at the table. His elbows were resting on the polished surface, his forehead cradled in his hands. He was wearing the same clothes he'd had on the previous night. Which indicated to Barbara that he'd slept in them, probably passing out in the den.

The hand that had been shielding his eyes came down to circle a tall glass on the table in front of him. His gaze swept up to Barbara. "Quit hovering in the doorway," he grumbled. "Come in and have your breakfast. That's what you were going to do, wasn't it?"

"I thought Lillian was here." Barbara hesitated a fraction of a second longer before entering the room and walking to the coffee service.

"She's in the kitchen." Jock didn't move from his position. His mouth twitched cynically as Barbara walked to the table with her coffee. "You'll have to settle for my company." The chair leg scraped the tile floor as she pulled it out, and Jock winced. "Be a little more quiet, please."

"Hung over?" Barbara commented a trifle maliciously.

"That's putting it mildly," he sighed.

"What's that?" She glanced at the glass in front of him. It looked something like tomato juice, but the liquid was much too frothy.

"A little of the hair of the dog that bit me." He took a swallow from it and grimaced. "It's a concoction of Antonia's. I don't know what's in it, and I think I'm better off not knowing. It works, which is what counts."

Sitting opposite him, Barbara didn't find Jock quite so dangerous this morning, despite his obvious bad temper. "Did you just get up?"

"I came to a few minutes ago, which is what you were really asking." She heard the scrape of day-old bristle as he rubbed his cheek.

"So that's why you're so touchy this morning." Barbara discovered that she was gloating a bit over his physical suffering. She had gone through enough mental agony over him to find satisfaction in it. "Didn't the booze help you forget?"

The question drew his sharp glance, brown eyes shot with glittering sparks of gold. "It helped me forget I accidentally hit my own brother." Jock took a big swallow from the glass while Barbara uncomfortably studied the steam rising from her hot coffee. "Todd has already forgiven me for that." His voice was laced with cold amusement.

"It was an accident. You didn't intend to hit him," she murmured.

"No, I didn't intend to, but if it had been reversed,

I would have slugged him on general principle. But not Todd." Jock paused, drawing a deep breath. "He's forgotten. And thanks to my old friend Jack Daniels, so have I."

Barbara sipped at her coffee, blue eyes studying him over the rim of her cup. Strong, sun-browned fingers were massaging a point in the center of his forehead. She suspected that his head was pounding with a thousand sledgehammers. He had to be feeling very rocky.

"Drinking doesn't solve anything, Jock," she commented.

"No, it didn't put you out of my mind," he agreed, lifting his gaze to lock it to hers.

Barbara broke free of his gaze to clutch the handle of her coffee cup more tightly. "Then maybe you shouldn't drink so much," she suggested.

"More lectures?" His tone was sardonic. "This must be my morning for them. First my mother, now you."

She recalled his voice raised in anger at Lillian before she had entered the dining room. "She has a right to speak her mind. And obviously she's concerned."

"Oh, she wasn't lecturing me on drinking," Jock corrected her. "She was accusing me of taking unfair advantage of a previous relationship with you."

Her nerves tingled at the static electricity that suddenly seemed to fill the air. Her gaze roamed the table, looking everywhere but at him. Trying to hide her sudden discomposure, Barbara took another sip of her coffee.

"Well, you are." She forced out the calm answer.

"You don't have to like it." His voice was low, almost seductive. "But the way you respond tells me you do."

It was impossible to deny his statement, especially when the husky caress of his voice was unnerving her. But Barbara couldn't permit the remark to stand unchallenged.

"People can like something that's no good for them," she said, flicking him a wary look. "And I can't deny that you and I have, you know, chemistry." A nice, scientific word for passion, she thought. "But what happened between us didn't last very long and it's not going to happen again. I don't think we should make a habit of being together."

His gaze roamed over her face, pensive and measuring. "No? You have me hooked, honey."

That was a heady thought, one that made her reel with the possibilities of tomorrow. But it was an illusion, a mirage. Jock sounded so convincing, but Barbara wasn't as impulsive as she used to be.

"Six months, Jock," she reminded him. "You went six months without me. And I can't see that you suffered much. You can get along without me just fine."

"What makes you think I have?"

"It's obvious, isn't it?" Barbara countered. He hadn't made a single attempt to contact her in all that time. He'd never be able to convince her that she meant as much to him as he was attempting to claim. "When we said goodbye, it was final. And I found out that I got along without you very well. So did you. Let's keep it that way."

Her control was splintering. Barbara knew she had to escape before he came up with some new argument to undermine her. She pushed her chair away from the table.

"If you'll excuse me, I'm going out to the kitchen to persuade Antonia to fix me some breakfast."

"You and Todd don't belong together," Jock announced.

Barbara paused at the door to the kitchen. "That is my decision to make, not yours."

"Then I'm going to do my damnedest to be sure you make the right one." His parting shot followed her through the door.

During the next two days Jock didn't make any overt attempt to act on his warning. In fact, he seemed to make it a point to stay well clear of her. Barbara wondered whether he was engaging in psychological warfare, letting her fret and stew over what his next move might be. And she did a lot of mental pacing.

Sunday brought another visit to the rural church the family regularly attended. This time Jock went with them. Barbara found herself sandwiched between Jock and Todd, with Lillian sitting on the other side of Jock. The church pews were crowded, making contact with Jock impossible to avoid. Her shoulder was pressed to his until he finally lifted his arm to rest it behind her on the back of the pew. It was a possessive move that disconcerted Barbara because it appeared to link her with him instead of Todd. Yet Jock rarely looked at her, although she stole several wary glances at his profile and glanced the hands that held the hymnbook.

By the time the service was over, her whole body was stiff from being held so tensely. As they filed out of the church, Jock walked with his mother and Barbara finally felt as if she'd been given some breathing room as she left on Todd's arm.

On the way to the car, Lillian asked, "Will you be here for Easter, Todd?"

"I'm afraid not," he answered over his shoulder. "You know that's one of the hotel's busiest times."

"Oh, of course. I thought, though, because of Barbara, you might arrange to have the weekend off," she explained.

"It's a great idea, but it won't work." Todd opened the rear passenger door and helped Barbara into the backseat while Jock assisted his mother into the front passenger seat.

Lillian turned to look at the couple sitting behind her. "Did you know, Barbara, that Florida was named after Easter?"

"No. I was under the impression it was the Spanish word for flower." She was grateful for something random to talk about.

"You're right. But when Juan Ponce de León landed near St. Augustine, it was Easter, the time of the Feast of Flowers, or Pascua Florida as the Spanish called it."

"How interesting," Barbara murmured as Jock slid behind the wheel and turned the key in the ignition.

"Speaking of feasts," Todd said, "I hope Antonia has dinner ready for us."

"Yeah. I'm hungry," Jock said. Barbara glanced at the mirror in the center of the windshield and saw the reflection of Jock's eyes, tawny and watchful. Her pulse skittered madly as he shifted the car into gear, remembering vividly the times his lips had devoured hers.

Fighting the attraction was useless, Barbara thought, averting her gaze to stare out the side window. She didn't have a single defense against his look or his touch. She had won a few minor skirmishes in the past, but the battle for her heart had been lost. Todd's hand closed over hers in silent reassurance. Barbara pushed the realization to the back of her mind, not wanting to make the decision it demanded.

"How about a swim this afternoon?" Todd suggested.

"All right," Barbara agreed, wishing she could sound a little more enthusiastic.

"How about you, J.R.? Want to join us?" he asked.

"Nah. I'll make myself scarce this afternoon."

Jock kept his word and left the house soon after Sunday dinner. The evening he spent in the den, busy with paperwork. He was absent from the house all day Monday. Although she didn't ask, Barbara guessed he was at the Crosstimber unit of the ranch where they were starting a cattle roundup.

Lillian, Todd and Barbara had gathered on the veranda, minus Jock, for predinner cocktails. As Todd walked to the drink cart to get more ice, Lillian glanced at her watch.

"I had better tell Antonia to postpone dinner another twenty minutes. If Jock isn't here by then, we'll eat without him," she sighed. "Excuse me."

"Of course." Barbara smiled as the woman moved toward the house doors.

"Would you like some more Coke?" Todd asked. "How about rum in it?"

She glanced at her half-empty glass of lime and Coke. For some reason she hadn't wanted any liquor that evening. A quenched thirst hadn't changed that feeling.

"Just plain Coke, thanks." Barbara handed him the glass to be refilled.

As he poured the soft drink, they heard the phone ring. Todd paused to listen. It stopped after the second ring and he finished filling her glass, adding a fresh twist of lime to float with the cubes.

"Todd?" Lillian came to the paned doors as he returned the glass to Barbara. "It's your hotel manager. Apparently something's come up—he didn't say what the problem was."

"I'll take it in the den." He walked swiftly toward the door.

Alone, Barbara took her drink and wandered to the edge of the veranda. The slanted rays of the sun glinted off the surface of the swimming pool, while the fanning leaves of the potted palms around the deck swayed in a gentle breeze. Her gaze turned to the lawn, the Spanish oaks and the distant white stables beyond, unconsciously looking for Jock.

He came through the trees with long, slow strides. Her perceptions heightened as they always did around him and Barbara sensed his tiredness. When he came closer she saw it etched in his face, feathered out from his eyes and drawn around his mouth. Sweat made the rugged denims and cotton shirt cling to his muscled frame, the material streaked with dirt here and there.

When he saw her, his expression didn't change. His swift pace didn't either and soon Jock was close to her. Barbara couldn't stop looking at him.

"We were about to give up on you," she said by way of a greeting.

As the distance lessened from feet to inches, she expected some kind of response from him, one of his usual mocking rejoinders. The last thing she anticipated was the hands that gripped her shoulders and pulled her forward while his mouth descended to seize her lips. Miraculously she avoided spilling the drink in her hand as her body strained closer to his, her back arching. She was engulfed in the heat of his body, overwhelmed by his earthy smell of male sweat, mingled with horse and leather.

Lingering, Jock kissed her lips, seizing the lower one between his teeth and lovingly nibbling at it. His hand drifted down to her waist to keep her hips molded to his while his other hand slid up her arm to the drink she held.

"You don't know how many times I've imagined you waiting for me after a long, hard day, with a drink in your hand." Jock lifted his head, taking the glass from her unresisting fingers. "What's this? Rum and Coke?" Before she answered, he drank from it. Barbara looked at the working of his throat as he swallowed and the moisture on his mouth when he took the glass away.

"Just Coke and lime," she told him after he'd already discovered it on his own.

"No rum tonight?" The sheer sexuality of his roaming look had Barbara searching for the breath she lost.

"No, I didn't feel like it." She was suddenly aware of how easily she'd gone into his arms and surrendered to his kiss. She hadn't even challenged his right to do it.

"Good," Jock said. "I'm not in the mood for forgetting tonight."

As he drained the contents of her glass, Barbara extricated herself from his embrace. His mention of forgetting made her remember his comment about imagining her waiting for him. Free of his arms, she finally reacted to it. "Whatever. Just don't try to sweet-talk me tonight, Jock."

"Huh?" He lifted a bemused brow and walked to the drink cart to refill the glass.

"It's nothing but sweet talk. Or a lie," Barbara retorted. "I mean, what you said about imagining me waiting for you with a cold drink."

"What makes you think so?" Jock fixed two glasses instead of one. "It may have been a while ago, but I did ask you to come here with me. Or had you forgotten?"

"I hadn't forgotten. I refused to come with you and I've never regretted that decision." She'd been close to crushed when he'd dropped her after their brief time together. She would never have endured the tearing agony of a breakup after they'd spent months together.

The veranda door opened and Todd walked out. "I guess I couldn't expect to have two full weeks off without business intruding," he apologized to her.

"Was it serious?" Barbara asked and would have gone to his side except Jock was managing to get in her way.

"The chef walked out and the kitchen is in an uproar. It's nothing new. Claude does this about every two months." Todd's attitude dismissed it as a trifling matter. Glancing at Jock, he said, "We were just about to eat without you."

"So Barbara mentioned. Is this your drink?" Jock motioned to the one sitting on the drink cart.

"Yes." Todd walked over to get it. "Had a rough day, did you?"

"A long one," Jock conceded. "Do you and Barbara

still want to come over to the Crosstimber unit tomorrow?"

"Sure." But Todd cast a questioning look at Barbara for her affirmation.

"Yes," she agreed.

"Then we'll leave in the morning at eight," Jock announced and arched a knowing glance at her. "Can you get up that early?"

"I can," she insisted with an irritated snap.

"Jock, you're home!" Lillian spotted him the instant she stepped onto the patio. "I've just had Antonia keep dinner warm for another twenty minutes."

"Good. I'll have time to shower and change first." Taking his glass, he started toward the doors. "If you'll all excuse me."

"Gladly," Lillian laughed. "You smell like a sweaty horse."

"Be warned," Jock said to Todd and Barbara. "That's what it'll be like tomorrow out there."

"I think we can take it," Todd assured him.

"That's right. I'd forgotten. You are going over to watch the roundup tomorrow, aren't you?" Lillian declared. "Jock is right. It's a hot, smelly job. But I think you'll find the operation interesting."

While she was speaking, Jock entered the house. Barbara wasn't positive that it would be wise to see Jock in his environment. It might feed tomorrow's regrets. But it was too late. She was committed to go and she didn't want to explain to Todd why she was getting cold feet.

Chapter Nine

A few minutes after eight o'clock, Barbara walked out of the house with Todd. She started across the courtyard, expecting to see Jock waiting with their horses. Instead a pickup truck and horse trailer were parked in the driveway. Inside the horse van, she could see three saddled horses.

"Aren't we riding the horses there?" she asked Todd.

"No. It's too far. Half the time would be spent riding there. It's easier and quicker to track the horses where they are needed and ride from that point," he explained.

"I guess I'm forgetting how large this ranch is," Barbara admitted.

When they approached the truck, Jock didn't bother to get out. His arm was resting atop the open window of the track, his other hand on the steering wheel. His alert gaze ran over Barbara, noting the hat she had borrowed from Lillian.

"Awake?" he asked pleasantly.

"Wide awake," she insisted.

If she wasn't before, she certainly was now as she realized she would be expected to sit in the middle between the two men. The cab of the pickup was not all that wide. There wasn't a chance she could avoid contact with Jock.

Todd opened the door to the passenger side of the truck and stepped aside for her to climb in. "Would you mind if I sat by the window?" Barbara asked.

"Don't you think it's safe to sit beside me?" Jock taunted before Todd could answer.

"I prefer the outside. Unless you drive so recklessly that the door will fly open and I'll be thrown out," she countered.

"She has you there, J.R.!" Todd laughed.

"It doesn't matter to me where either one of you sits, but you'd better make up your minds. We aren't going to sit here all day." Jock turned the ignition key and the engine rumbled to life.

"You can sit by the window and benefit from all the fresh air," Todd volunteered and climbed into the cab, sliding to the middle of the seat.

"Thanks." Barbara hopped in beside him, barely managing to slam the door shut before Jock put the truck in gear.

Away from the house, Jock turned onto one of the many dirt roads that crisscrossed the ranch, interconnecting the vast sections. Of necessity, he drove at a moderate speed because of the horses in the trailer behind them. The only breeze was generated by the draft the truck made slicing through the still, muggy air. The noise of the engine and the air rushing in kept conversation at a minimum, and Barbara didn't take part in what there was of it.

Forty minutes from the house, they approached a

place where other trucks and trailers were parked on a wide spot in the road. Jock slowed the truck and maneuvered it and the trailer among the others. Despite all the vehicles, there was no one around as Barbara climbed out of the cab, followed by Todd. Beyond the barbed-wire fence and its gate was a long meadow of tall grass, but there wasn't a sign of a horse and rider or a cow.

Barbara walked to the back of the trailer where Jock was unloading the horses. "Where is everyone?"

"Out there." With a nod of his head, he gestured toward the field as he backed the blaze-faced chestnut out of the van, tossing the reins to Barbara. "They've been here since a little after daybreak. We'll catch up with them."

After checking the cinch, Barbara mounted, sitting astride her horse while Todd stepped into the saddle on his bay. Jock was the last to mount after closing the tailgate of the trailer. The big gray horse sidled up to the fence gate and tossed its head eagerly as Jock unlatched the gate and gave it a push. Barbara and Todd rode their horses through and waited until he had shut it.

With an open field before them, the horses needed no second urging to break into a canter. The trucks and trailers soon became distant objects on the horizon, scarcely discernible. It seemed to Barbara that they were escaping the present and riding into the past where the creak of saddle leather and the thud of horses' hooves dominated a much more rural world.

The land rolled and dipped, undulating like a sea of grass. Here and there, trees poked at the blue sky with a thicker cluster of woods ahead. A distinctive cracking sound could be heard, a sound like a whip. Barbara smiled, guessing they soon would be joining the cowboys, remembering the information Jock had given her about the bull whips some of the men carried. When Jock angled toward the sound, she knew she was right.

Then Barbara saw them, first the dark hides of bunched cattle, then three riders. There were thirty or so cows with an apparently equal number of calves. As they rode closer, she noticed the dark blue gray dogs trotting near the cattle, racing up now and then to nip at any that showed an inclination to stray. One rider separated himself from the others and rode out to meet the group.

Jock reined in the gray. "Hello, Clint. How's it going?"

"You know how it is." The big, stocky man shrugged. "With cows, it's hide-and-seek. Hello, Todd." He leaned forward to shake hands. "Sorry I missed your party the other night."

"That's all right. It's good to see you again, Clint." Todd smiled and motioned to Barbara. "This is my girlfriend, Barbara Haynes. Jock's foreman, Clint Darby."

"Pleased to meet you, Miss Haynes." He tipped his hat to her, dark hair pressed flat beneath the hatband.

"Same here." She nodded back in acknowledgement.

"Jock tells me you're getting your first look at a roundup," the foreman stated.

"Yes, that's right."

"You'll find most of the excitement is over where Al, Rick, Jessie and Bob are working the trees," he explained and glanced at Jock. "We're moving this bunch to the pens."

"We'll see you there later on." Jock lifted his hand in a half salute and reined the gray horse away. His backward glance indicated Todd and Barbara were to follow him.

With a wave to the foreman, they turned their horses after the iron-gray horse. Cutting behind the herd, they rode toward the stand of trees growing thickly along the edge of the meadow. Dark outlines of horses and riders moved in a backdrop of dark trunks. The riders were working close to the fence line, driving what animals they found toward the open field.

Most of the cows and their calves moved in the direction the cowboys herded them, but occasionally one would object. Barbara was surprised by the swiftness and agility of the placid-looking animals. A wayward cow would dodge, cut and feint, changing speeds and directions with an ease surprising for its size and weight. When it was unable to elude the cowboy, it would turn and plod like an elephant.

"We'll keep the cows bunched in the open for the boys," Jock stated.

The cows and calves were already ambling along in the right direction. The sun threw the shade of the trees onto the grass. Walking in their shadows, Barbara soon became aware of the oppressive subtropical climate, the muggy heat baking into her. This far inland, there was no sea breeze from the Atlantic or the Gulf of Mexico.

She felt the sweat gathering between her shoulder blades and under her arms, rivulets running from her collarbone down between her breasts. She

longed to trot her horse and stir the air, but she kept
it at a walking pace behind the slow-moving cattle,
driving them on to a destination only Jock knew. Barbara wiped at the sweat on her neck and shook it
from her fingers.

"It's hot work," commented Jock, observing her
action.

"I'm not complaining," she said.

"If it was any hotter out here, you could fry eggs,"
Todd remarked.

"That's an original comment," she said, smiling at
him.

"Sorry. My brains are fried too."

Jock signaled to the riders flushing out the cattle
in the trees. Three rode out to take their place, a
fourth remaining at his work. With a wave of his
hand, Jock motioned for Todd and Barbara to come
with him. The chestnut broke into a trot and Barbara
felt the blessed stirring of still air.

"Just give your horse its head when you see a cow.
It'll know what to do," Jock instructed.

Fanning out, the three worked their way among
the trees. Jock and the fourth cowboy worked the
cows they found. An old black cow appeared to
submit to Jock's herding into the open without com-
plaint. But the instant it was past Barbara, it whirled
on a dime and attempted to race through the riders
back to the trees. The chestnut whirled to give chase
with no command from Barbara. She kept her balance, gripping the saddle horn and hugging her legs
tight to the stirrup leather.

When the agile horse blocked it from slipping
through, the cow changed direction and raced for
the open field. Barbara raced after it, hearing the

thudding of galloping hooves following her. She spared a lightning glance over her shoulder to see Jock in pursuit of the cow as well, the big gray horse looking like it was stretched out flat.

In the open meadow, the cow began a wide circle to get back to the trees. The air whipped at Barbara's face, billowing her blouse behind her. She didn't take her eyes from the cow's black hide, trusting her horse to avoid any holes or ruts in the thick grass. When she turned the cow away from the trees, there was a wild, exhilarating feeling of success. Jock was at her side to keep it heading in the right direction. When the cow broke into a run, it was to join the small bunch.

Slowing the chestnut, Barbara leaned forward to pat its sweating neck. The wild ride had left her breathless and elated. She laughed from the sheer stimulation of the experience.

"That was exciting!" Her eyes sparkled and danced.

"You have the makings of a real cow hunter if you stay around awhile longer." The flashing white of Jock's smile was warm and vital, sharing her enthusiasm for the ride and unmarred by cynicism or mockery.

Danger signals went off. Jock's potent charm tugged painfully at her heartstrings. But she had given in to it before and paid the price. She resisted its magnetic pull, turning away, her own smile fading into nothing.

"Mmm. But I'm not staying longer. Todd and I are leaving at the end of the week." Barbara deliberately coupled her name with Todd's in her reminder.

His hand reached out to grip the reins ahead of

her hold and check her mount. "You won't admit it yet, will you?" Jock demanded. "You still won't see that Todd isn't for you."

"No," she retorted. "But even if he isn't, I'm sure about one thing—neither are you!" She jammed her heels into the chestnut's sides and sent it leaping free of Jock's restraining grip.

Once loose, Barbara didn't attempt to outrace the superior speed of the gray horse, but slowed her mount to a sedate canter. She rode toward the trees to rejoin Todd. When Jock drew alongside, she didn't alter her course and he didn't attempt to side-track her.

"Still in one piece after that hair-raising ride?" Todd joked when she reined in beside him, seeking the protection of his company.

"Where were you?" Barbara forced a casual smile on her face. "I thought you'd come, too."

"Are you kidding?" he laughed. "You can go racing at that breakneck speed, but I know my limitations."

"It was fun." It had been, even if the confrontation with Jock wasn't.

"But not my kind of fun," Todd replied without apology and smiled.

After combing that section of fence line and woods, they had banded together a small herd of cows and calves. They drove them to the working pens, near the road where all the trucks and trailers were parked. The noontime break was almost upon them.

Going home for lunch was impractical for the cow-boys, considering the distances involved on the ranch. A meal of hot stew and sandwiches was served out of the back of a pickup truck along with gallons of black coffee. There was also an insulated keg of cold water.

"Drink plenty of it," Jock advised, "to replace what you lost out there in the sun." His gaze raked Barbara, noting the way sweat had plastered her blouse to her curves. "Even though coffee is liquid, it isn't as effective as plain water."

Unnerved by his penetrating look, her reply was cool. Even without his advice, Barbara would have known to visit the water keg to slake her parched throat. She said as much, and he added another comment to remind her that the possibility of heatstroke was not something to take lightly. So she drank plenty of water as she had been ordered.

Todd picked out a place in the shade where they could eat their lunch. Jock didn't join them, having his meal with the men. It was a scene permeated with the noise of bawling calves and male voices, and the smell of animal sweat and another, faintly obnoxious odor.

Finished with his meal, Todd leaned against a tree trunk with a contented sigh. Barbara removed her hat and ran her fingers through her long black curls to let the air reach her damp scalp. She glanced at the group of cowboys, standing around drinking coffee before returning to their work.

Jock was among them, standing tall and widelegged. He easily stood out in the group of men, although he dressed no differently. It had always been that way, but Barbara had assumed it was his strikingly masculine good looks. Studying him, she realized it was his easy air of command: authority was bred into every bone. He got noticed and he didn't have to shout to make himself heard. People automatically listened when he spoke.

"This is what J.R. loves to do," Todd remarked. "It's a good thing this ranch is his. All this rugged outdoor life isn't for me. Give me a penthouse suite with an ocean view and deluxe room service anytime. What about you?" His gaze slid with absent curiosity to Barbara.

"Oh, you know. I want fur pajamas and diamond-studded cellphones as much as the next girl—no, I'm kidding." She laughed at Todd's startled expression. "My needs are pretty simpler, but I like my comfort," she admitted. "So does Jock, I guess, in his way."

"He's in his element here."

Barbara couldn't have agreed more. Jock embraced the challenge of running this vast holding, of dealing with the vagaries of nature and its whims. While Todd's position as hotel owner was comparable in power and prestige to Jock's, he didn't have to deal with wild weather, ornery cows, or anything that would get his hands dirty.

Trying to compare the two brothers was impossible. An apple couldn't be likened to an orange. Barbara sighed and drank more water. It was probably just as well there weren't many similarities between them. She wouldn't want to look at Todd and imagine Jock.

The groaning creak of saddle leather signaled that the men were riding out. Barbara looked up as Jock approached their shaded spot. The touch of his gold-brown eyes had her whole body tensing.

"Do you want a closer look at the operation from this end, after the cows have been rounded up?" He directed his question at her.

Barbara realized that Todd was probably familiar with all of this. "Yes, I would like that." Picking up her hat, she pushed to her feet and glanced at Todd, expecting him to do the same.

Instead, he settled more comfortably in his position against the tree. "You go ahead. What breeze we have is blowing away from me toward the pens. I'd just as soon leave the stench over there," he smiled.

"Ready?" Jock prompted.

Barbara hesitated, but she could hardly refuse to go with him now. Besides, she was interested in seeing it even if Todd wasn't.

"Sure," she agreed and started forward, carrying her hat.

Jock matched his stride with the length of hers to walk at her side as they crossed the grassy space to the iron pens fenced with pipe. Activity had already begun inside, animals milling as a horse and rider entered their midst, cowboys moving about within the confines and outside of it. Barbara paused at the horizontal bars.

"Once they're inside the working pens, we separate the calves from the cows," Jock explained.

It wasn't a situation that pleased the cow or the calf. The horse and rider didn't give either an option and Barbara was reminded of the cutting-horse competition she had watched at the arena. There, it had been an exhibition of skill. Here, that skill was being put to practical use as the calves were cut out and herded into a narrow corral. The bawling cries of the confused and frightened calves were answered by the frantic lowing of their mothers.

"From the calf corral"—Jock walked toward it and Barbara followed him—"the calves are put into that chute one at a time. The chute is called a turn-over because once a calf is locked inside, the chute turns over to make an operating table." Barbara watched the procedure as he explained it. "The calf is inoculated, dehorned with those pincers and receives an identifying earmark; the bull calves are castrated, and all are branded."

The branding iron was typical of the ones she'd seen in Western movies. In this case, there was a scrolled S at the end of the iron rod, the Sandoval brand she had noticed on the hips of the cows. Instead of the traditional campfire heating the iron to a red-hot color, a butane torch was used. She heard the iron sizzle as it was pushed on the calf's hip and smelled the acrid stench of burning hair and hide. She half turned away from the unpleasant smell.

She told herself not to be too squeamish. Just because she got meat in a plastic tray at the supermarket didn't mean it hadn't been raised somewhere like this.

Once branded, the calf was released to return to its mother and the next calf was loaded into the chute. Jock spoke again. "With the turnover we can handle an average of fifty calves an hour. When we had to rope them and stretch them out on the ground, we were lucky to do that many in half a day. Thanks to the chute, it's an efficient operation with less wear and tear on the calves and the men. It's known as progress"—his gaze rested on her face and his voice lowered in volume and tone—"which is something you and I aren't making."

Barbara stiffened at the unexpected injection of a personal reference. "We aren't making any progress because I'm here with Todd," she said in defiance and continued to stare at the calf corral.

"You aren't in love with him," Jock replied. The handle of a rawhide whip was laid against her cheek to turn her to face him. "You couldn't be in love with him and respond the way you do to me. And you do respond, Barbara. Your pulse beats so fast in your throat when I kiss you . . . the same way it's doing now." His gaze flicked pointedly to the hollow of her throat. "And the way you sigh when I'm loving you—do you know what you sound like? Guess not."

"I don't deny it." How could she? But Barbara managed to keep the rising tide of emotion in check, despite the seductive quality in his voice. "Sex was always good between us. But you're very, very good at arousing a woman, and I know good and well that I'm not the first woman to respond like that to you. Your technique is excellent."

Her reply made him impatient. She could see it in the thinning line of his mouth. Jock wasn't touching her, except with that rawhide-wrapped handle of the whip, but he stood so close she could feel his body heat.

"Point taken. No, you're not the only woman who said she liked my technique, as you call it," he said thinly.

That stung. She was just one of many, part of a stable he kept around for his amusement. But she wasn't going to be available to him every time he snapped his fingers.

"When we split up, you suggested that we might become friends. At the time, I refused because I didn't have any intention of ever seeing you again," Barbara declared in a taut, strained voice. "But since

I'm now your brother's girlfriend, it might be the practical solution. It was your idea. Maybe you should consider it again."

Turning on her heel, she walked away from him. She had taken less than a half a dozen steps when something made a swooshing sound in the air near her and a strap began wrapping itself around her waist. It took a second to realize it was his whip, coiling around her so expertly it didn't hurt.

With it wrapped tightly around her waist, Jock pulled her toward him while walking to meet her, not allowing any slack in the whip. She could see the anger flaming in his brown eyes, but she was angry, too.

"You enjoy making a scene, don't you, Jock?"

"Don't walk away from me, Barbara," he said under his breath. "Don't ever walk away from me again."

"Or else what, Jock?" she taunted him. "What will you do?" She didn't feel the least bit afraid of him. If he wanted to play dominating games, he wasn't going to win.

His hard features were grim. "Don't push me, woman," Jock warned huskily and released the tension on the whip so that it fell loose from her waist.

There was a rawness to his look that made Barbara turn away. Jock didn't try to stop her this time when she started toward the tree Todd was sitting beneath. He had dozed off, wakening when she slumped to the ground beside him. Barbara began to think Todd was like the three monkeys. He never seemed to see, hear or say anything wrong.

Todd noted her pale face and commented, "The

smell of those pens gets to you, doesn't it? Now you know why I didn't go over there."

"Yes," she murmured.

"Want to ride? Get some fresh air after all that stench of burning hide?" He straightened from the tree, flexing his shoulders.

"Why not?" Barbara sure as hell didn't want to stay in Jock's vicinity.

It was late afternoon before Jock found them and suggested they should load the horses up to start for the house. As they rode to the horse trailer, his eyes kept seeking hers, but Barbara avoided them. For some reason she felt vulnerable and didn't know why. Again she sat on the outside by the window, using Todd as a buffer and keeping out of the conversation.

Chapter Ten

Barbara lay in her bed, unable to sleep. After the previous day's riding and the restless night before, she had expected to succumb to exhaustion tonight. Instead, her thoughts kept twisting and turning in her mind.

Rolling over, she looked at her watch on the bedside table. In the dim moonlight glowing through the balcony doors, she saw it was after midnight. Giving up, Barbara tossed the bed covers aside and climbed out of the bed. The softness of the night called her to the balcony.

The air was so warm that Barbara didn't bother with the robe lying on the foot of her bed. She pushed open the doors to her private balcony and stepped outside. A crescent moon seemed to look down on her with a half-closed sleepy eye. Barbara sighed in envy and wandered to the iron-lace railing.

Stars littered the velvet black sky and a faint breeze whispered in the moss-draped trees. The balcony overlooked the rear lawn on the opposite side of the house from the veranda. A night bird sang somewhere in the trees and Barbara tried to see the feathered creature sharing the night with her.

She leaned over the iron railing, staring at the thick branches. Her side vision caught a flicker of movement in the trees, but when she tried to focus on it, she saw nothing. It was so dark within the shadows of those trees that it was unlikely she could distinguish any shape.

Barbara didn't hear the bird again and guessed it had flown away. She wished she could fly away with it, soar into the dark, cloudless sky and lose herself in the shimmer of stars. Straightening, she wandered along the balcony's edge, trailing a hand along the railing, around an arching pillar onto the railing again stopping at the corner. Half sitting on the narrow iron rail, she leaned a shoulder against a concrete arch and let the peaceful serenity of the night soothe her troubled mind.

Once Barbara thought she heard a movement inside the house, but all the rooms were dark, except for the small lamp by her bed. She chalked it up to her imagination. After a while she drifted into a reverie on abstract things: the immensity of the universe and the minuscule importance of one person on the planet. From far away came a sound that should have been familiar to her, but her concentration didn't permit it to register.

The sound of a footfall on the balcony did. Barbara straightened in alarm at the dark figure of the intruder, her heart leaping into her throat. It beat all the more wildly when she recognized Jock.

"How did you get out here?" she demanded in shock. "Why are you here?"

"I saw the light on. I knocked at the door. When

you didn't answer, I came in to make sure you were all right," Jock explained, moving toward her in an easy way.

Barbara turned back to the night, gripping the railing with both her hands. "I'm all right, so you can leave."

He ignored that. "Couldn't sleep?" He stopped when he was less than two feet from her.

"No."

"Neither could I." Jock paused, but she didn't offer a reply. "The truth is I didn't see your light on. I was out walking and saw you on the balcony. Unfortunately, there aren't any trellises or vines to climb so I didn't get to be a romance hero. I used the stairs."

"Why bother? I don't want your company," Barbara retorted, her heart telling her that was a lie.

"Don't you?" He let his hand glide over her shoulder, bared by the slender strap of her pajama top.

With a shrug Barbara eluded his caressing touch, frantically wishing for the robe she had left on the bed. The moon and starlight had silvered her skin. The lateness of the hour suggested far too many possibilities.

"Will you please leave?" she hissed desperately. "What if someone wakes up and finds you in my bedroom at this hour?"

"With your sexy pajamas on and the bed all rumpled. Yeah." Jock grinned, then got a little more serious. "Don't worry. Everyone is sound asleep except us. They aren't likely to wake up unless you make a lot of noise."

"If you don't leave, I'll start screaming," she threatened.

"No, you won't," he chuckled softly. "You don't

want my mother or Todd to find me in here 'at this hour.'" He stressed the phrase with mocking emphasis. "Why do you suppose you and I are the only ones who can't sleep?"

"I really don't know and I don't care." Barbara tried to sound emphatic, but his voice was so velvety that it took the starch out of her reply.

"Do you think it might be this soft southern night?" Jock mused.

This time when his hands touched her, they curved onto both her shoulders. Barbara was trapped—on one side by the railing, on a second by the corner of the balcony, and on the other two sides Jock could easily block her way.

"Jock, leave me alone . . . please." Her whispered plea was heartfelt but her body quivered in uncontrollable reaction to the caress of his hands.

"That isn't what you want." His head bent to her neck, his mouth trailing a lazy fire along the nape. "You want the same thing I do, honey. Why keep fighting it?"

"Don't." Barbara tipped her head back to stop the dangerously sensual teasing of his mouth on her skin.

Jock simply transferred his attentions to the exposed curve of her neck and shoulder while his hands slid down her rib cage to cross in front of her stomach. A sensual warmth spread through her limbs as he pulled her back against his hard length.

Cupping a hipbone in one hand, Jock slid his other hand beneath the lace pajama top to seek the ripe fullness of a breast. The male outline of his aroused need was imprinted on her hips, kindling an answering ache within her.

"Todd isn't the man for you," Jock murmured into her ear, sending shivers of wild ecstasy over her flesh. "Why won't you admit it? You want me to make love to you as much as I want to."

Barbara fought the insidious demand of her senses in the only way she could find. "If that isn't an example of a macho male mentality, nothing is." Her voice was laced with sarcasm. "You think all you have to do is hold your body against mine and I'll agree to anything."

"Sounds about right," he said confidently.

To prove his point, his fingers teased one nipple while the hand on her hipbone moved to make slow, sensuous forays over her belly. Giving in for a glorious second, Barbara relaxed against him. Jock half turned to let the corner pillar of the balcony support him. When she made a move toward him, his arms loosened to permit it.

Barbara took the opportunity to twist out of his embrace. Jock started to straighten, then waited as her weak legs took her no farther away from him than just out of arm's length.

"Come here, honey," he invited.

"Why won't you leave me alone?" Barbara protested in a voice that wasn't as strong as she wanted it to be.

"I'm not leaving you alone until you say you'll give me a fighting chance." He pushed from the pillar to claim her.

In agitation, Barbara spun away and half ran to the glass-paned doors leading to her bedroom. Soon enough she was inside the bedroom, but Jock was behind her.

"To do what?" She was standing by the bedside table within the circle of the lamplight before she realized that he could see her naked outline right through her pajamas.

"To hold you, for starters." Smiling lazily, he came toward her and reached out to take her shoulders. "This is where you belong." He curved her trembling body inside the circle of his arms.

Her soft curves fitted themselves to his male shape all too easily. Before she could escape it, his mouth covered hers in a long, drugging kiss. Her fingers curled into the material of his shirt sleeves as she clung tenaciously to an invisible link with sanity.

When he let her up for air, Barbara seized on that link. "We shouldn't be doing this. We shouldn't even be in the same house together," she told him in a fierce, breathless voice.

Jock lifted his head to gaze at her with an incredulous and angry frown. "Well, we are. You can't expect me to leave you alone now. It's not as if you and Todd are engaged."

"Granted, I'm not wearing a diamond ring. We never got that far." She strained against his hold, bending her head to avoid his eyes. "Come on, Jock. Don't you understand that this is crazy?"

He stroked her black hair and the soothing sensuality of it made her drop her head back. He purred into her ear, "You don't want me to leave."

"Yes, I do," she whispered.

"Oh yeah? You say one thing, but your body tells me something different. You really do want me to make love to you," he insisted.

"I want you to go," Barbara declared on a choked sob. "You have to. No matter what either of us wants."

His hands slipped to her shoulders, fingers caressing

the bare flesh. "What are you trying to do to me?" Jock demanded harshly.

"I'm trying to make you do the right thing and behave, even though there isn't any ring on my finger. Now leave me alone!" Her voice broke on the last word.

Her anguished blue eyes watched the indecision warring in his expression. Barbara knew if Jock persisted, she couldn't deny him. At last he pushed her away from him and she stumbled backward onto the bed.

"Okay. This time, I'll leave," he agreed angrily. "But it isn't what you really want and you'll never make me believe otherwise."

"Then go." She was losing her control. She could feel the sobs building like a volcano before an eruption. She didn't know how much longer she could hold back the torrent of tears.

"Thanks to you, we are both going to spend a frustrated, miserable night alone when we could have had each other," he growled.

Right. As if. In his mother's house, with his brother not far away? That would never, ever happen. When he continued to stand in the same place, Barbara challenged in desperation, "Are you going to leave or not?"

"I'm going!" Jock strode to the door, yanking it open. He paused to look back at her. "Sleep well!" And he slammed the door shut with a vengeance.

The dam burst and Barbara grabbed for the pillow to smother her sobs. She had sworn she would never cry over Jock again, but she was. There wasn't anything she could do to stop it.

Minutes couldn't measure the time she cried. When the sobbing finally subsided, she ached all over. She lay there hurting with a pain that was physical and mental.

Barbara didn't know how long she lay there staring at the shadows on the ceiling. Sleep wouldn't come to ease her torment. Turning her head on the pillow, she glanced at the bedside table and her watch, still lying in the pool of light.

Dawn would soon come and it seemed to her that it would be the hour of reckoning. At least Jock had forced her to make one right decision. She knew she could never marry Todd. Jock would always stand in the way of whatever happiness Todd might have been able to give her. Barbara realized the affection she had felt for Todd had never truly been the right kind. She had needed him so desperately as a friend that she had been willing to do without love—the kind of love she craved, anyway.

All-consuming. Passionate. Almost irrational. It was no mystery why she'd never been able to accept Todd as a lover. It would probably be a very long time before she could ever accept any man in that role—because of Jock. He had taken so much from her that she had little left to give.

There was no reason to continue this farce. She would explain everything to Todd in the morning, which wasn't more than a couple of hours away. Barbara rolled back to stare at the ceiling again. She faced another realization. There was no more reason to linger here at the ranch. Remaining in Jock's company was inviting disaster. She couldn't risk it.

A second time, she crawled out of bed. This time it was to drag her suitcases out of the closet and begin emptying drawers and hangers to pack her clothes.

She wasn't going to let anyone talk her out of it, not anyone . . . and especially not Jock.

From her balcony Barbara watched the sun rise. She heard Jock go downstairs; she recognized his firm tread on the stairs. A little while later Barbara heard Lillian stirring, then the shower running in the room next to hers—Todd's room. At about the same time that she heard Todd leave his room, she saw Jock walking toward the stables. It was the last time she would see him. Barbara knew this image of him would be forever branded on her memory. She watched until Jock was out of sight, then left the balcony.

Her suitcases were stacked neatly by the door. She paused to pick up her watch from the bedside table and continued to the hall. Todd was halfway down the stairs when she started down.

"Todd!" she called to him to wait.

"You're up early this morning," he commented, stopping in the foyer. He surveyed her nice clothes with surprise, as if he'd expected to see her in something a lot more casual. "You're really dressed up too. Are you planning on going somewhere?"

"Yes." Barbara halted on the last step to look at him, wondering where to begin.

"Hey?" Todd frowned, his hand reaching out to trace her cheekbone. "Where did those circles under your eyes come from? Didn't you sleep last night?"

"Not much," she admitted.

"Why not?" He studied her face, his frown deepening.

"Because—because I can't be with you, Todd. On

any terms. I realized that last night. So I'm heading home," Barbara explained.

"Huh?" He took a moment to process that, then cleared his throat. "Did I say or do anything to—"

"No. I'm sorry, Todd," she apologized with genuine sincerity. "I feel like I led you on."

"You didn't," he said flatly.

She thought with a flash of guilt that she'd just been going through the motions of a relationship with him. They'd never really connected, emotionally or physically. It wasn't a crime for a man to be cautious and calm—but he'd never made her heart sing and he never would. Deep down inside, she'd known that Todd Gaynor wasn't the one.

"Barbara, you can't—"

"What we had was nice for a while. But it never was more than just . . . nice. And I shouldn't have let you talk me into staying here when I found out Jock was your brother."

"It doesn't matter about J.R.," he protested. "I wanted you to stay because I loved you. Maybe I had something to prove to my big brother," he added reluctantly. "That did enter into it."

"Todd, it doesn't matter now. Just understand that I never meant to hurt you. Please believe me. You've been so good to me that I wish things were different." Her blue eyes were wide and troubled. "I know what it's like and I don't want to hurt you."

Todd took a deep breath, then clenched and unclenched his hands. "What you are trying to say, very gently, is that you don't love me, isn't it?"

"Not the way I should. Not the way you deserve," Barbara admitted. "I'm sorry."

"It's J.R., isn't it? You're still in love with him," he

guessed. The corners of his mouth were pulled down with a grim wryness.

"I didn't want it to be that way."

"I can't really say that I'm surprised." Todd's expression was resigned. "I think I suspected it was going to turn out like this when you told me who J.R. really was."

"I wish we had both known before we came here."

"Don't look so glum." He curved an arm around her shoulder and brought her down the last step. "If we had known, we wouldn't have come and we would have always wondered whether you were really over him. Now we know definitely that you aren't." Todd looked searchingly into her eyes. "Does J.R. know about this?"

"Yes," she whispered, nodding. It was a comforting arm that was around her. Right now, she needed Todd's undemanding solace although she was no longer entitled to it, by her thinking. "What I just told you doesn't change anything with Jock," Barbara clarified that point quickly.

"So what comes next?"

"I want to leave, Todd—today—this morning." With each pause, she went a step further in stating her objective.

He held her away from his side to look at her. "But you don't have to be at work until Monday. You still have four days left of your vacation. There's no reason for you to go back yet."

"Yes, there is," Barbara insisted. "We aren't engaged, Todd, and I can't pretend we're going to be."

"You're my guest," he pointed out. "A friend instead of a girlfriend."

"I can't stay, Todd. Not with Jock here." She finally offered the real reason.

"No, I suppose not," he sighed.

"Just because I want to go back is no reason for you to cut your vacation short. If you drive me into town, I can catch a bus," Barbara offered.

"What? No way. I brought you here. I'll take you back," Todd promised.

"All my luggage is packed. I have it sitting in my room by the door," she explained.

"You really are determined to leave this morning, aren't you?" he laughed. "What did you do? Stay up all night packing once you'd made up your mind?"

"Yes," Barbara admitted, his laughter drawing a faint smile.

"If I hadn't agreed to take you—or drive you into town, you would have walked, wouldn't you?"

"Maybe. The sooner I get away from here, the better off I'll be," she declared.

Todd studied her thoughtfully. "Aren't you going to tell J.R. goodbye? Does he know you're leaving?"

"No. And I don't want to see him. We said our goodbyes six months ago. I don't want to go through it again." A cold chill quivered through her shoulders and Todd pulled her close to his side, rubbing her arm as if to warm her.

"I won't try to change your mind. If you don't want to see him before you go, I'm not going to argue. But knowing my brother, he isn't going to be too happy about it when he finds out," he said.

"It doesn't matter whether he likes it or not. That's the way it's going to be," Barbara stated decisively, more so than she felt.

"There's one thing I want clear between us. I know

we aren't engaged, and we're not going to be, but I'd like to go on seeing you occasionally." He gave her a wry smile, reading her thoughts. "I'm not going to try to put a ring on your finger. It's just that I like being with you and I wouldn't want that to stop because of this."

"When I get back to Miami"—Barbara paused, taking her time to finish the difficult sentence—"I'm going to ask the airline for a transfer."

"Where?" Todd frowned.

"I don't care, just as long as it's far away from Florida," she added tightly.

"No, I'm not going to sit quietly by while you do that." Todd shook his head. "I don't like the idea of your being alone, Barbara."

"Don't you see, Todd," Barbara reasoned, "the last time you helped me through this. You taught me I could make it. This time I have to do it on my own."

"Maybe not, but—" He stopped whatever his next argument was going to be and smiled. "We'll talk about this later. I'll get your luggage out to the car while you pour us some coffee and juice."

"Yes, and I want to say goodbye to your mother . . . and explain," she agreed.

"You do that." Todd kissed her on the cheek, his lips lingering a little longer than necessary before he let her go to climb the stairs.

Barbara watched him take the first flight and remembered what Jock had said. Todd would get over losing her. He always had enough love left for the next person. She should take lessons from him in how to do that, she thought as she turned from the stairs.

Crossing through the living room, she entered the

dining room. Lillian Gaynor was seated at the table, sipping at her morning coffee. She smiled in surprise when Barbara walked in. "You're up early this morning," Lillian declared.

Was that so unusual that everyone commented on it, Barbara wondered. She hadn't thought she'd slept very late while she was there.

"Yes, I am." Barbara glanced at her watch, noticing for the first time that it was a little before seven, which actually was early for her.

"Coffee? You look very nice, by the way. Are you and Todd going somewhere?" She asked the questions while she offered Barbara a cup of coffee.

"Actually . . . Todd is driving me back to Miami. I'm leaving this morning," Barbara announced.

"So soon?" Lillian stopped in the act of filling a cup. "I thought you were staying until this weekend?"

"Um, change of plans. You see, Todd and I—well, we decided to be friends again." She met the older woman's look and tried to appear more calm and in total control than she felt.

"Oh. I understand—at least I think I do. When did this happen?" Lillian was still trying to take it all in.

"This morning. I talked to Todd just a few minutes ago," Barbara explained.

"Where is he?" Lillian glanced toward the archway.

"He's putting my luggage in the car."

"What did Jock have to say?"

"Nothing. He doesn't know I'm leaving," Barbara admitted and took the cup she was offered.

"He doesn't know?" Lillian repeated. "Aren't you going to tell him goodbye?"

"No. There's no point," she answered, shrugging.

"But surely—"

"I didn't choose either of your sons. They both know it," Barbara replied. Jock just didn't happen to fully believe it, and she didn't want to get caught in the trap of trying to convince him. "Todd asked me to have some coffee and juice ready for him."

Lillian began pouring another cup. "You're leaving right away?"

"Yes. It will be more comfortable driving if we go before the sun is too hot." She pretended that was the reason.

Todd came striding into the dining room. "That didn't take long. Is that my coffee?" He glanced at the cup his mother was filling.

"Yes. Barbara has just told me she's leaving. Were you planning to leave without something to eat?" Lillian protested.

"We'll stop for a bite along the way," Todd shrugged.

"Nonsense." Lillian dismissed that immediately. "There are Danish pastries in the kitchen. At least have a nibble on one before you leave."

"I'm not really hungry," Barbara protested.

"It doesn't pay to argue with my mom," Todd said. "She'll get her own way. She always does."

"Todd is right," Lillian agreed with him.

"Okay. Bring on the Danish," he said to his mother.

"I won't be a minute," she promised and rose from the table to go to the kitchen.

"Pour me some orange juice, will you, Barbara?" Todd requested.

She poured him a glass and one for herself. It had seemed petty to argue about breakfast, but even that small delay made her nervous. Sitting in the chair next to Todd's, she set his glass in front of him and drank from hers.

Chapter Eleven

At Lillian's insistence, Barbara double-checked her room to make sure she hadn't left anything behind. There was nothing in the room that belonged to her, except some memories that she knew would follow.

Todd and his mother were waiting in the foyer as she descended the steps. Barbara felt awkward when the older woman came forward to hug her goodbye. There was apprehension in Lillian's brown eyes when she stepped back.

"Goodbye, dear. I would have liked to have you stay longer," she said. "But if you feel you can't . . . well, then that's how it has to be."

"Goodbye, Lillian." Barbara didn't want to say more. The situation was incredibly awkward as it was.

"Ready?" Todd opened one of the double doors for her. "I'll be back sometime late this afternoon, Mom."

"All right."

Barbara paused in the courtyard to look back and wave at Lillian before Todd stepped out and closed the door. He walked to her side. Guilt made her say again, "You don't have to drive me back, Todd." He took her arm as they passed the fountain in the courtyard. The sound of the falling water reminded Barbara of tears. Todd's car was parked in front. He reached ahead of her to open the passenger door.

"What's this all about, Todd?" Jock's voice demanded.

Barbara whirled to see him stalking from the veranda through the courtyard toward them. She looked back at Todd as if to accuse him. *How could you?* Her mind had already leaped to the conclusion that Todd had let his brother know she was leaving.

"Antonia came to the stable with a message from mom, but I think she got it mixed up. Antonia said something about Barbara leaving," Jock continued, evidently not seeing her standing on the other side of the car door until he had emerged from the courtyard.

So Lillian had sent the message, not Todd. Barbara realized she should have known better. Either way the damage was done. Jock's piercing eyes were narrowing on her. Awareness was sinking in that the message had been accurate.

"It's true," Barbara said. "I am leaving."

"Without letting me know? Without even a goodbye?"

"How many times do we have to say it?" she countered.

"You've told me a lot of things, and your actions have told me a lot more. You aren't leaving, Barbara," Jock stated.

"Leave me alone, Jock. Just let me go." She turned to slide onto the car seat. "If it isn't too much to ask."

"Not this time." His hand took her arm in an

I-mean-it grip. "I'm not letting you go. We're going to talk this out."

"No." Barbara strained against his hand and appealed to Todd. "Todd, I want to leave."

"You aren't going anywhere unless I say so." Jock didn't give his younger brother a chance to reply. "I can have a man at every gate within minutes. You couldn't leave Sandoval land without being stopped. You are going to talk to me."

"I'm not your prisoner!"

Jock held up his hands. "No, you're not. Sorry. I went too far with that one."

"You sure as hell did." She glowered at him, then looked over at Todd. He hadn't exactly rushed to her defense.

"You might as well talk to him, Barbara," Todd said quietly. "You don't have to, but if you could . . . for my sake, I guess."

"Why? Is your he-man brother going to give you a black eye if I don't?"

Jock, to his credit, looked deeply ashamed. "No, Barbara. I just lost it for a minute there. Again, I'm sorry. I sincerely am."

She flashed Jock a mutinous look to conceal the pain inside. "All right then. But I don't like feeling as if I don't have any choice."

"Just talk to me," Jock said. "It would be the right thing to do. That's all I can say."

His sun-browned features were set in hard lines as he let her walk ahead of him toward the house. This was a development Barbara hadn't expected and she took advantage of the few minutes without conversation to prepare her defenses, meager as they were. In the house Jock directed her to the small, wood-paneled den and closed the door.

"Why are you leaving?" he demanded, squaring himself so she faced him.

"Because there isn't any reason to stay," she retorted stiffly, keeping the inner tremors out of her voice.

"I want you to stay. Isn't that a reason?"

"Not a good enough one." Her gaze wavered under the blazing force of his.

The answer got a growl out of him, an actual growl. "Not good enough? You drive me half out of my mind and it isn't good enough," Jock muttered. "Isn't it obvious how much I want you? I do nothing but think about you day and night—"

"Stop it!" She cut across his words with an angry protest. "Six months, Jock! You never gave me a thought for six months! I didn't get so much as a phone call or an e-mail or a postcard from you! Don't try to make me believe that you were tied up in knots all this time! You never even tried to reach me!"

"No, I didn't!" he shouted. "I'm not in the habit of going begging to a woman to ask her to love me."

"I'm sure you don't have to. You can get all the women you want with a snap of your fingers, so leave me alone!" Barbara cried in agitation.

"But I want you!"

"To be what? Your friend? Or your lover?" She hurled at him the words that had wounded her so deeply. "You can't make up your mind, can you? If I stay, how long will it be before you suggest we be friends again? Three days? Four?"

"Friends?" Jock frowned. "You're damned right I want you to be my friend. I want a woman who's more than a lover. I want a *wife*. I want someone who will be at my side, not just in my bed!"

The one single word in the middle of all that dissolved of Barbara's hurt anger. It seemed like a shining light, flickering uncertainly to guide her through the darkness. She stared at him, fearful—hopeful. "A wife?" she repeated in a breathy murmur.

"Yeah," Jock snapped. "I want you to be my wife."

"You . . . never said anything about that before," Barbara whispered, waiting for him to blow out the light that was burning brighter with each second.

"I didn't?" The hardness began leaving his chiseled features. "I took it for granted—"

With a sobbing cry of joy, Barbara wrapped her arms around him to hug him tightly. She bit at her lip, wanting to laugh and cry at the same time as she cherished this moment.

"Honey?" He cupped her face in his hands and lifted it so he could see the happiness brimming in her eyes. "What did you think I was proposing? I love you. Of course I want you to be my wife."

"Of course, he says." Laughter bubbled in her throat. "When you asked me to come with you to the ranch and I refused, I thought you just wanted me for my . . . loving companionship. So to speak."

"Nothing wrong with that." He kissed her cheek. "But I wanted you to meet my mother, to see our home, where our children will live, and the ranch. Most of all, I wanted us to have time to get to know each other," Jock explained in a husky voice. "You have to admit the few short days we were together, we never got out of bed."

"Yes, we did. To watch the sunset on the beach. And pick up Chinese takeout. And—"

"Go back to bed and start all over again," he said with a happy sigh.

"It was great. But I thought that was all you wanted this time too," she breathed. "And I nearly accepted. I would have if you had asked me again, because I realized that I loved you so much I didn't care."

"Imagine how I felt when I suggested we get acquainted and you told me, in no uncertain terms, that you didn't want to get better acquainted with me?" Jock countered, able to smile at the thought now. "Here was the woman I wanted for my wife—and all she wanted was a carefree weekend in bed with no strings. She didn't sound like a likely candidate for motherhood, not of my children."

Barbara shook her head. She'd gotten it wrong, so wrong, for reasons that were going to take a while to sort out. But for now she had him right where she wanted him: in her arms.

"Jock—when you suggested we be friends instead of lovers, I thought you were letting me down easy—that you were tired of me."

"Tired of you? Never, baby!" Bending his head, he found her mouth and kissed her with a deep hunger that had her heart spinning. "You're mine. All mine."

"Oh, Jock . . ."

She didn't say more. She couldn't, not the way he was continuing to kiss and caress her.

"And now you and I have some catching up to do." He swept her up in his arms.

"Are you carrying me off to bed? I don't think so—not with your mother and Todd out there." She didn't struggle against him, though.

"No. Not yet. This is just a trial run." He held her

tightly and turned around in a dizzyingly fast circle, making her breathless.

"F-for what?" she laughed.

"I have to practice carrying you over the threshold, don't I? Are you ready?"

"Yes!" Barbara wrapped her arms around his neck and kissed him madly.

ONE OF THE BOYS

Chapter One

Two small round tables were shoved close together in the dimly lighted hotel lounge. There was hardly an inch of surface that wasn't covered with drinks, ashtrays, pretzel dishes and candle-burning globes. Almost a dozen chairs were crowded around the two tables, all of them occupied by men, except one.

Petra Wallis was the sole female in the group, but she was accustomed to that. At five foot nine she was as tall as most of them. Despite her khaki top and camo-print pants, there was nothing masculine about her. The unisex clothes hugged her slim, willowy frame and the neutral colors served as a contrast to the long wheat-blond hair pulled away from her face and secured with a gold clasp at the back crown of her head. The length of it fell straight down her back in a shimmering silk curtain.

She'd been blessed with flawless skin and strong, straight features. Her jaw line slanted cleanly to her pointed chin. Her mouth was wide with a sensually full lower lip, her nose straight with the faintest suggestion of an upward tilt at the tip. And her sea-green eyes had a naturally thick fringe of dark brown lashes.

Pet, as her co-workers liked to call her, had often been told she was model material, but she wasn't interested in being in front of the camera. She preferred being behind it.

In the confusion of several conversations and jokes punctuated with laughter, Pet made herself heard. "Have any of you seen the inside of Charlie's van?" Her easygoing question was answered by a couple of chuckles. Charlie Sutton, who was sitting across from her, grinned.

"You rode down here with Charlie, didn't you, Pet?" one of the men prompted.

"Sure did. Although after I climbed in that thing, I wondered whether I was asking for trouble or Charlie was asking for a slap in the face." Her laughter was mellow. "The van looks so innocent on the outside."

"Did you pimp it up the way you wanted to, Charlie?" one of the other men asked.

"Almost," he shrugged. There was a gleam in his brown eyes. "There are still a couple of things I want to add."

"I can't think what they'd be!" Pet retorted, rolling her eyes for the benefit of the others. "He says he uses it to go camping. Ha. That van is totally over the top. I'm talking silver shag carpeting on the floor, walls and ceiling. And a great big bed with a black fake-fur spread. Plus a built-in bar."

"Okay, okay." Charlie had to concede the point but Petra wasn't ready to stop.

"HDTV," she went on. "Hidden speakers connected to an iPod dock. A flick of a switch and you get a smooth groove going to make love by. There's even a compact fridge and freezer to supply ice for drinks."

"You shoulda put those mirror tiles on the ceiling, Charlie," someone suggested.

"What does the wife think about it, pal?" another person teased.

"Sandy loves it," Charlie insisted. "We can slip away for a weekend and have all the comforts of a motel room without the cost."

"We get the point. It was worth every penny." Lon Baxter rose halfway from his chair next to Pet's, and reached for one of the glasses of beer on the table.

"Whoops! That's mine, Lon." Pet rescued her drink and put another glass in his hand. "This is yours."

"How can you tell?" He looked skeptically at the half-empty glass of beer she had substituted for the fuller one.

"Unless you've started wearing lipstick, this has to be mine." She laughingly showed him the peach-colored imprint on the rim of the glass.

"In this light I don't see how you can see any-thing." He groped, pretending to be blind and "dis-covered" her bare forearm. "Hey, what's this?"

Setting his glass down, he took advantage of the fact that Pet was still holding hers. He turned in his chair to get closer to her while his other hand slid across her stomach, stopping on her rib cage just below the swelling curve of a breast.

"It may be dark, Lon," Pet smiled sweetly, "but I know exactly where your hands are. And if your left hand moves one more inch, you're going to get an elbow in the throat."

The warning was issued with deliberate casualness,

but it was no less sincere because of it. Conscious of the others observing this little byplay, she knew she had to put Lon firmly in his place without making an issue of it.

Lon Baxter was one of the few single men in the camera crew. Young and good-looking, he tried to get next to anything female, convinced he was irresistible. Pet was willing to admit that she thought he was cute, but she had learned a long time ago to stay clear of any romantic entanglements with her fellow workers if she wanted their respect.

Lon she would have avoided under any circumstances. She doubted he had a faithful bone in his body. But there had been a couple of guys she wouldn't have minded dating from time to time. She'd tried mixing her social life with work a couple of times, but the involvement invariably caused friction on the job. Since then she had made it a rule to date only men who didn't work in television.

With an exaggerated sigh of regret Lon withdrew his hand and sat back in his chair, reaching for his beer. His retreat was noted by the others with a few taunting chuckles.

"Shot down again, huh, Lon?"

He winked. "Yeah, but I'm alive to pursue her another day."

Pet didn't believed for one minute that he had given up.

"Why don't you put the poor guy out of his misery, Pet, and let him catch you once?" Charlie suggested, knowing exactly what her opinion of Lon Baxter was.

"I know what my competition's going to be in these next couple of weeks," she replied, not taking offense at the ribbing. "I'm not in Ruby Gale's league."

"Nah, you're better looking," said Charlie. "Ruby's only a whaddyacallit—a pop-tart."

"She's paying our bills," Pet said, laughing. Taping the pop-tart singer turned sex goddess was next on their job roster. She went on, "Lon won't even notice me after he's spent a day looking at her through his camera."

"Here's to Ruby Gale. Better than Fergie-slash-Avril-slash-Kelly Clarkson." Andy Turner, the fourth cameraman in the production crew, lifted his glass in an acidly cynical toast to the star of the television special they were assigned to. "What a combination. Enough to make me squint."

"Just so long as you can focus the lens," Pet spoke up.

"Ruby is a major talent!" One of the sound technicians spoke up in the singing star's defense. "Think she'd mind if I asked for her autograph? My wife and I downloaded every one of her songs for free."

"I wouldn't ask her for anything until the special is all done," Andy advised. "She's a real diva. Not to mention a shrieking bitch when she doesn't get her way."

"The voice of experience," someone said. "You worked with her, right?"

"Yeah, on an awards special a couple years ago," he replied. "All she had was one song and an award to present, maybe five minutes of the entire show, but it turned into total chaos. Demands, tantrums—name it. I've seen my share of temperamental performers, but Ruby Gale is the pits. This isn't going to be a picnic."

"Dane can handle her," a lighting technician insisted.

An odd smile touched the corners of Pet's mouth. "Oh, right. Dane Kingston, the big man himself, is going to be here. I understand this production is going to carry his personal stamp as both producer and director."

One of the gaffers shot her a questioning look. "I thought Sid Lawrence was the director."

"He's just the assistant director," Andy retorted. "When you're Ruby Gale, you can demand number one and get it."

"Dane will to be on hand to protect his investment," Charlie suggested. "After all, this special is costing him a hefty chunk of dough. He'll make sure it stays within the budget and comes in on time."

"And I'll bet he makes millions out of it," someone remarked enviously from the adjoining table.

"Makes sense that he'd want to protect his interests," Pet said. "Which are money and Ruby Gale."

"What do you mean?" Joe Wiles, one of the lighting technicians and the grandfather of the group, frowned at her comment.

"Dane Kingston and Ruby Gale are a hot item, according to the gossip columnists. Perez Hilton says they're having a totally torrid affair. And what Gawker says can't be repeated in front of a little boy." She nodded at Lon and the others hooted.

Ignoring the slight to his dignity, Lon waved her sarcasm away. "Some say he wined and dined her just to get her to sign to do this special," he remarked.

"She's a really talented performer, but if she's the bitch you say she is, Andy"—Pet took a handful of salted snack mix while sliding a look at the sandy-haired cameraman and nibbled a little of it—"then it seems to me that she and Dane Kingston are perfectly mated."

"What do you have against Dane?" Andy laughed. "I wouldn't wish Ruby Gale on my mother-in-law, let alone someone like Dane. Besides, I always thought women went for him. At least, my wife tells me he's hot. And I've always been convinced that she knows a good thing when she sees it—she did marry me."

The joking boast drew the expected round of guffaws and heckling from the group. The conversation could have been easily shifted to another topic, but the mere mention of Dane Kingston had set Pet's teeth on edge. She knew the tension wouldn't ease until she had vented a little, veiling her dislike so the rest of the crew wouldn't guess how deeply it ran.

"Hey, Dane Kingston can be charming if he wants to be." She nibbled a little more mix and dumped the rest into a small dish on the table. She had to quit eating junk food. She was going to quit. Soon. Okay, not now. She snuck another bit of the mix.

"Let's hope he uses all his powers of persuasion to charm our sexy star into performing without her usual temper tantrums," Andy suggested dryly. "Otherwise we'll be in for a miserable time."

"Who says we won't with Dane Kingston?" Pet countered in a low voice.

"What did Dane Kingston ever do to you?" Charlie asked, subjecting her to his narrowed scrutiny. "I always heard he was an all right guy."

"Dane Kingston?" She arched one eyebrow, refusing to join the admiration society. Just because Dane was a man like them was no reason for her to like him automatically.

"Did you have a run-in with him or something?" Charlie frowned.

"Haven't you heard the story about Dane and Pet?" Lon Baxter leaned forward, smiling broadly.

Only a few members of the group nodded. The rest either shook their heads or admitted their lack of knowledge—and they were all curious. The ones who knew Pet were well aware that she couldn't be pushed around, but she was also easygoing and fun to work with. Since she obviously had some kind of grudge against the producer, Dane Kingston, they were interested to know why.

"I don't remember you ever working on a production directly supervised by Dane," Andy commented.

"I haven't," Pet admitted.

"No, but remember that variety series Dane produced last year?" Lon was eager to tell the story. "Pet worked on it. The very last show of the package ran into a lot of problems and delays. Everything went wrong. It was way over budget and it wasn't a sure thing that it would be finished in time to make the airdate deadline. When the word finally filtered up through the ranks and reached Dane, he took action immediately and heads began to roll."

"I remember hearing about that," someone agreed. "He threw out the director and a half a dozen others in charge, and finished the last show himself."

"That's what happened," Lon agreed. "Of course, at the time there were a lot of rumors that he was coming to see what was wrong, but he didn't let anybody know when he would arrive. One minute we were talking about him, and the next minute he was there. It was hot that day, really hot. The air condi-

ONE OF THE BOYS

tioner was broken, wasn't it?" He glanced at Pet, a little vague on that point.

"It was making too much noise and they had to shut it off," she explained indifferently.

"That's right," he said. "Anyway, he walks in and what's the first thing he sees? Our Pet in a pair of white shorts and a sexy red tank top, between takes and getting lined up for the next shot. Evidently nobody thought to tell Dane that we had a woman on the camera crew, because he immediately assumed she was somebody's girlfriend. He lost his temper and began chewing her out—and everyone else, too—for messing around with an expensive piece of equipment. Did you know who he was, Pet?" Lon paused in his story to ask.

"No. And I didn't particularly care," she retorted.

"That's for sure!" he laughed. "Nobody wanted to interrupt him to explain who she was, for fear he'd start yelling at them. So finally Pet just shouted at him to shut up. It got so quiet in that place you could have heard a flea scratch. Then Pet began reciting her résumé and wound up telling him that it was idiots like him who didn't know their rear end from a hole in the ground that were causing all the problems on the show, and suggested he should take a long hike."

There was laughter, but it was generally subdued. The glances that were directed at her, for the most part, held respect and admiration for the way she had stood up for herself. Yet she was fully aware that her defense had been dictated solely by the instinct of self-preservation. She had felt intimidated, overpowered and dominated by the angry guy who'd confronted her.

"What was Dane's reaction to that?" Joe Wiles was smiling.

"I thought he was going to knock her on her backside," Lon remembered with an amused shake of his head. "He gave her an ultimatum. Either she collected a week's pay and went on down the road, or she changed out of the shorts and top into something that reminded him less of a hooker."

"What did you do, Pet?" The question came from one of the younger men sitting in the shadows of the other table.

"I'm still working for Kingston Productions, so obviously I changed my clothes."

"Sounds like an honest mistake to me," Andy remarked after giving the story his thoughtful consideration. "You aren't still mad at Dane because of it?"

Pet had encountered alpha men before and usually dismissed their egotism with a shrug. But Dane Kingston's treatment of her was not something she could forgive and forget.

"Dane Kingston is an overbearing you-know-what," she declared.

"Pet!" Charlie tried to shush her with a silencing frown.

"No, I'm going to say what I think. I don't like him, I've never liked him and I never will like him," she stated forcefully. "If he was here I'd say it to his face."

"Then maybe you should turn around," an icy voice suggested.

A cold chill ran down her spine. Pet turned her head slowly, her gaze stopping when it found the buckle of a belt thrust through the loops of the well-worn jeans on the man standing behind her chair. Traveling by inches, her gaze made the long climb up his clothed body, subtracting the shirt that covered his muscled torso and huskily built shoulders, and moving beyond the tanned column of his neck and the drawn line of his mouth finally to reach the smoldering brown of his eyes.

Her pulse thundered in her ears, reacting to the male aggression of his presence. Pet's seated position intensified the impression that he was towering over her. Perhaps if she hadn't felt so threatened she would have acknowledged that he was a ruggedly sexy man. His dark hair was thick and full, inclined to curl while seeking its own style and order. The sheer force of his personality was enough to make her erect barriers of defense, rather than be absorbed by him.

"Well, hello. Haven't you heard the old saying that eavesdroppers never hear good about themselves, Mr. Kingston?" Her voice was tight with the effort to oppose him.

The atmosphere around the two tables became so thick a knife could have sliced it. Someone coughed nervously while Lon shifted uneasily in the chair beside Pet. She continued to wage a silent battle of wills with Dane Kingston, refusing to be the first one to lower her gaze, but with each second it was becoming increasingly difficult to meet the iron steadiness of his eyes.

Andy cleared his throat. "Er—care for a beer, Mr. Kingston? We can squeeze another chair in here."

"Petra Wallis can give me hers," Dane challenged, a mocking glint in his dark eyes. "I'm sure she's tired by now and ready to get some rest."

"Sorry to disappoint you, but I'm not tired—and I have no intention of giving you my chair," she

defied him. "Besides, I haven't finished mine." She
turned to pick up her glass as an excuse to look away
from him.

"Here, you can have my chair, Mr. Kingston." Someone down the way started to rise.

"Don't bother, I'm not staying," Dane said. "I only
came by to remind you that we'll start setting up the
equipment at six o'clock tomorrow morning. You'd
better be thinking about breaking the party up and
getting some sleep."

His statement was met with a few grumbles and
self-pitying moans, but the advice was generally taken
good-naturedly. By all but Pet, who felt she was capable of knowing how much sleep she needed without
being told when she should go to bed.

"Good night." Dane included everyone in the
group before he turned to leave. "Don't forget, I
expect you to be bright-eyed and bushy-tailed in the
morning—or you'll wish you were."

"Right, boss."

"Sure."

"Good night."

The replies crowded on top of each other, drown-
ing themselves out. Relief drifted through Pet now
that Dane Kingston's unwelcome presence was about
to be removed. She sipped at her beer, but it had
grown flat and tepid.

"I feel like I'm in a dormitory again, complete with
curfew," she muttered to no one in particular. "Do
you suppose he's going to do a bed check and make
sure we're all tucked in for the night?"

"Would you like me to tuck you in, Miss Wallis?" his
voice came back to mock her.

She jerked around to find he was only a couple of

steps away from the table, clearly close enough to have heard her complain. She could have screamed in frustration, but managed to restrain her anger.

"No, thank you." She had to grit her teeth when she spoke.

"If you change your mind, let me know," Dane said deliberately, but his eyes were cold.

This time Pet watched him walk out of the lounge so she wouldn't put her foot in her mouth again. When she turned back to the table, the others eyed her, not wanting to ask if she'd lost her mind or something. There was a definite possibility that they were right.

"You're asking for trouble," Charlie murmured the warning.

"He rubs me the wrong way," Pet declared with a discouraged sigh.

"We noticed," was the dry response.

Dane's appearance had the desired effect of breaking up the gathering. After he had left, gradual stirring began. Drinks were finished and a few cigarettes snubbed out in the ashtrays. Production crews were good at finding the few places on earth that still allowed indoor smoking. Chair legs scraped the floor as they were pushed back to allow their occupants to stand. Although she hated to think she was obeying Dane Kingston's instructions to have an early night, Pet followed along with the group as they left the lounge for their rooms.

"It must be nice to have a room all to yourself, Pet," Charlie remarked. "You don't know how lucky you are. I have to bunk with Andy and he snores like a freight train."

"Wait until you have to share a bathroom with

Lon!" Joe laughed. "It takes him an hour to comb his hair in the morning."

At the end of the hotel corridor, Pet turned to the left while the others started right. "This is where I leave you guys. Good night."

"Where are you going?" Lon stopped, although the others wished her goodnight and continued on to their rooms.

"My room is over there," she explained, waving the keycard she had taken from her shoulder bag.

"How come you're down that way when all the rest of us are down this way?" he frowned.

She lifted her shoulders in an indifferent shrug. "Maybe because I have a single room." The question had crossed her mind when she had arrived, but it hadn't seemed important. It didn't now.

"Good night, Lon." She turned to walk down her corridor, the silken straightness of her long blond hair swinging softly over her back.

"Wait a minute, I'll walk with you." He hurried to catch up with her. Nearly the same height as Pet, Lon had the advantage of only an inch. As he curved an arm around her waist, his smile promised all sorts of pleasures.

"I can take care of myself, Lon." She firmly removed his hand from her waist. "I don't need to be escorted. I won't get lost."

"I just wanted to be sure you got there safely." He seemed annoyed that she had misunderstood his interest.

"I'll tuck myself into bed. Good night, Lon," Pet repeated, and let her long legs carry her swiftly away from him.

He paused indecisively before he retreated. Halfway

down the hall, Pet reached her room. The keycard worked and the tiny light flashed green but the lever-style doorknob didn't cooperate. She had to wrestle with it before she could open the door.

The single room was small. The bed was a little wider than a twin, covered with a quilted spread in a blue-flowered print. There was one blue-green chair, the same color as the carpet, and a short, built-in dresser with a mirror on the wall behind it. A proportionately small television was bolted to an extension of the dresser. The bathroom was about the only thing that was normal size.

Kicking off her flat shoes, Pet dropped her bag and the keycard on the bed, and started to move away. On second thought, she reached into her bag to take out a pack of snack crackers, then walked to the single chair. She turned and sank into the seat in a single fluid motion.

Peeling off the wrapper, she tossed it into the ashtray, then noticed that the maid had left a half-smoked cigarette in it. Ugh. No wonder the room smelled so stale. She glanced at the television, but didn't bother to turn it on. After munching the crackers without tasting them, she leaned back in the chair to reflect on the unlucky beginning of this gig.

If she had kept her mouth shut and resisted the urge to vent her opinion of Dane Kingston, he would never have overheard it. Chances were that he had probably forgotten the hostility of their previous meeting. Now she had resurrected it all again when it had been better off buried.

She didn't like him. But just because she didn't like him, she didn't have to tell him that to his face. If you didn't like people, you avoided them—or were

polite if you had to be around them. But you didn't
declare war, which was virtually what she had done.

A sigh broke from her throat. She was usually patient and in control. So why was it that Dane Kingston
had the ability to make her lose her temper?

The crumbs covered her lap. Being ridiculously
neat, she brushed them into her hand and tipped
them into the ashtray that still held the cigarette,
wishing she hadn't eaten the crackers. Her mouth
was dry. She opened the dresser drawer where she
had put her nightgown after unpacking, and laid it
on top.

There wasn't much point in staying up since it was
after ten. It would be a long day tomorrow, even if
Dane Kingston had reminded her of it. She began
unbuttoning her khaki top and tugging it out of the
waistband of her camo pants.

A knock at the door stopped her action with only
two buttons left to unfasten. "Who is it?" Pet called.

"Dane Kingston," was the muffled reply.

She didn't for one minute believe that the producer was standing there. Some members of the
crew had a weird sense of humor. It was more than
likely somebody's idea of an idiotic practical joke. Irritation surged through her in a quick rush.

"Oh, go away!" she grumbled.

But whoever it was simply knocked again. She had
started to tell him she wasn't in the mood for jokes
when she decided it would be much more fun to
turn the tables.

"I'm coming." She deliberately put an inviting lilt
in her voice and discreetly buttoned a couple of buttons, but left the top ones undone to permit a
provocative glimpse of the shadowy cleft between her

breasts. She sauntered to the door, not bothering with the safety chain as she turned the knob and pulled the door open. "Have you come to tuck me in, Dane?" she murmured sexily.

Crap. It *was* Dane Kingston. Standing right there in front of her.

Chapter Two

Stunned, Pet held the sultry pose she had unconsciously adopted, one hand on her hip and her forearm resting along the edge of the opened door. His dark gaze made a slow and insolent appraisal of her. It was only when he had finished that she recovered from the shock of finding him at her door. The blood rushed to her head, filling her senses with a hot awareness of the situation.

"I thought you were one of the boys—Lon or Charlie." She was instantly defensive.

"Were they coming to tuck you in?" He cocked his head to one side, a suggestive glint in the hard brown eyes, but the smile touching his mouth wasn't pleasant or amused.

Anger flared at the jab. "If that's why you're here, Mr. Kingston, I don't think it's funny and I'm not interested!" Pet stepped back to slam the door in his face.

But it was stopped short of the frame by a large hand moving swiftly to block it. For a fleeting second Pet leaned her weight against it, but she wasn't any match for his superior physical strength. As soon as she realized how undignified she must look, she straightened to simply block the opening.

"What do you want?" She let her exasperation show.

"I want to talk to you," he stated with a crispness that indicated the subject wasn't personal.

"You've talked to me. Now please leave. I want to get some sleep." She remembered the buttons she'd undone and hurriedly began to fasten the strategic pair over her breasts. "As you pointed out, we have to be up early and work long hours tomorrow."

"This will only take a few minutes of your time, I promise you." Dane Kingston seemed indifferent to her sudden show of concern for plenty of rest. "Are you going to invite me in? Or do we have this discussion in the hallway where anyone can overhear?"

The flat of his hand was still resting on the door. Pet guessed it would take only one push of that muscled arm to wrench it out of her hand. He could shove his way into her room if he wanted, and there was very little chance that she could prevent it.

"Aren't you worried that someone will see you come into my room at this hour of the night?" she taunted.

"Not really. All the rooms for the crew are down the other corridor." There was a humorless curve to his mouth. "Your reputation is safe."

Damn! He was making her look so foolish and prissy. "I was more concerned about yours," she retaliated, and spun away from the door, admitting him by moving away. "Ever heard of sexual harassment lawsuits and that kind of thing? They're messy. And expensive."

He only shrugged.

"What did you come to see me about?" She came quickly back to the point of his visit since she hadn't been able to get rid of him.

"Tonight—" he began, then stopped, glancing at the cigarette in the ashtray. "You smoke? Don't you know that's an unhealthy habit?" he criticized.

"Really? No one ever told me. Are you sure?" She didn't feel like she had to explain that the maid had left it there or anything else to him. Still, her sarcasm wasn't lost on Dane, but he kept his voice even.

"Yeah. I'm sure."

"I only do it when I want to keep someone at a distance. Guess I should have opened the door with a cigarette in my mouth," she snapped. "My mother always told me that didn't look ladylike."

"Do you think it looks *ladylike* to be one woman sitting in a bar at a table with a dozen men?" He put biting emphasis on her term.

Pet turned to stare at him, seeing the disgust in his expression. Although she was tall, he still had the height advantage, being easily another six inches taller. It was rare that she had to look so far up to anyone, so it was equally disconcerting to have it be Dane Kingston.

"I don't see that it's any concern of yours." She had managed to recover from her initial amazement.

"Maybe not," he said blandly.

"I work with those guys," Pet reminded him. "Most of them are married with families. Joe Wiles is a grandfather. Why is it a crime to sit around a table and have a beer with them?"

"Okay, it isn't." His eyes had narrowed. "I can't seem to say the right thing tonight."

Pet was still angry. "What am I supposed to do on my off hours? Sit alone in my hotel room while the boys are in the bar having a good time? If that's your idea, you'd better think again," she informed him in no uncertain terms. "I do what I want to."

"In case you haven't looked in a mirror lately"—he grabbed her by the elbow and turned her around to face the wall mirror—"you don't happen to be one of the boys!"

But it wasn't her own reflection that her turbulent sea-green eyes saw in the mirror. It was his, standing tall and dark beside her, overpoweringly masculine beside her willow-slim body. His obvious virility aroused raw feelings of femininity in her. Pet tugged her elbow free of his hold and took a quick step away. She was used to feeling strong and independent no matter what man she was with, not weak at the knees.

"So what do you expect me to do—remain cloistered for the next couple of weeks or however long it takes to finish this special?" she demanded. "I'm not a nun! I like to laugh and socialize and—wait a minute!"

She turned on him roundly, a thought suddenly occurring to her. "Is there some significance to the fact that my room is in this corridor while the guys all have rooms in the other one? Was this your idea? Or is it just because this is a single?"

"When the hotel reservations were made, attention was paid to the fact that you're the only female member of the crew outside of wardrobe and makeup," he admitted smoothly. "While we're talking sexual harassment, it didn't seem wise to put an unattached female in a room next door to a couple dozen men."

"Then you're responsible for my being separated

from the others," she said, feeling anger rather than appreciation for this thoughtfulness.

"The production assistant made the actual reservations."

"The assistant followed your orders," Pet challenged. "Do you have any idea how hard I've worked to be accepted by them? To be treated as their equal? Now I'm in a different wing. You're saying I shouldn't socialize with them at all. What's next? Do I eat at a different table?"

"Maybe you wouldn't have objected to sharing a room with 'one of the boys,'" Dane jeered.

"I suppose next you're going to insinuate that I wouldn't be safe if I spent a night in the same room with Joe Wiles. Come on, he's a grandfather!" Pet went a step further. "He's old enough to be *my* grandfather." She went to brush past him and escape from the narrow path between the bed and the dresser to the wider space near the chair, where there was breathing room. "You sure don't have a very high opinion of the crew on the production payroll. Or maybe you know something I don't."

Dane stopped her, catching her by the arm and turning her around to face him, the solidness of his brawny frame bringing her to an abrupt halt. The air left her lungs in a rush at the unexpected contact with his body. As she was not a lightweight herself, the impact rocked him slightly. His large hands spanned her waist to steady both of them, the imprint of his fingers pressing the khaki material into her flesh.

Conscious of the masculine power of his thighs and the steel band of muscles flexing in his arms, Pet tried to collect her scattered wits and slip out of this accidental embrace, but her limbs wouldn't respond to the signals her brain sent out. She felt her heart skipping beats in sheer sexual attraction. Her mind reeled from the possibility that she could be physically attracted to the man.

"You're gorgeous, Pet. An honest-to-God Amazon, but gorgeous."

"Why the *but*?"

His low voice had a huskiness to it. "Any red-blooded American male—regardless of his age—would get ideas in his head if he spent a night alone in the same room with you. Don't tell me you aren't aware of that."

The warmth of his breath fanned her face and hair like an intimate caress. His potent vibe was almost intoxicating. Fighting it, Pet abruptly turned her head to face him and make a retort. But in turning she discovered his head had been bent toward her, and in consequence her lips brushed the angle of his jaw. The resulting sensation was a shivery tingle that ran through her nerve ends, leaving them quivering for more. She twisted out of his arms as if she had been jolted by an electric prod.

"I'm quite aware of it. I didn't mean to imply that I wanted to share a room with one of—" That phrase "one of the boys" was becoming overused. "But I sure as hell don't have to be in a whole different wing of the hotel from them."

The phone rang, and Pet nearly jumped out of her skin at the sound. Dane, in a purely reflex action, took the one stride necessary to reach the phone on the stand beside her bed and picked up the receiver. He had barely said hello before Pet realized he was answering her phone.

"Give that to me! Who do you think you are, taking

my phone calls?" she demanded, and grabbed the phone out of his hand. "Hello?"

"Pet?" It was a very startled and confused Lon Baxter on the other end of the line. "What's Dane Kingston doing in your room?"

Oh, God, she thought. "He's lecturing me on the moral behavior proper for a young woman. I'm not even listening. " She vented her irritation toward the whole situation. "What did you want, Lon?"

"I . . . I wondered if . . . you wanted to join me for breakfast?" He sounded unsure whether he should even ask.

"Sure," Pet agreed, with total disregard for everything Dane Kingston had said. "What time do you want to meet? Is five too early? We have to be at the Garden State Arts Center at six."

"Yeah, five o'clock is all right," he said with a trace of uncertainty.

"Good night, Lon," she prompted him to hang up.

"Yeah, good night, Petra," he said absently.

She sighed as she hung up the phone. All the questions Lon hadn't found the nerve to ask tonight would be dumped on her in the morning. She did have an explanation—a true one. Whether Lon would prefer a more measured explanation of his own was another question. Men were impossible.

Turning, she saw Dane standing at the foot of the bed, watching her, his hands in the side pockets of his pants.

"Problems?" It was a one-word question with no apology for causing them.

"Nothing that I can't handle," Pet replied.

His dark gaze slid to the phone, then back to her. "So you've decided not to take my advice."

"About socializing with the boys? No, I'm not taking it." With space between the two of them she could think more clearly. She realized the way she had been manipulated, always in reaction to his statements and accusations, and she was thoroughly annoyed that she had allowed it to happen.

He seemed to be waiting for her to say something.

"You and I see things really differently, Dane. As far as my being in the bar tonight, well, there's safety in numbers. Before you came to my room I would have said no to Lon. Having breakfast with just him—geez, I would never hear the end of it. But I said yes because I knew you would disapprove."

"That's a stupid reason." The corners of his mouth turned down in a scowl.

"You bet it's a stupid reason," Pet agreed blandly. "But I can't be friendly to just one of the guys. If I do, the rest will assume that I'm taken and there goes the camaraderie I've struggled so hard to achieve. Why did you have to interfere? Nobody asked you to!"

"I don't need permission to interfere. This is my company, and my production. When I bring a crew on location I ultimately become responsible for aspects of the members' private lives—yours included, Petra," Dane snapped. "We're on location. The men are going to be away from their wives and girlfriends. The very first night I see you sitting in a bar, drinking with the whole lot of them, I can't help but think that it isn't a good idea."

"Now maybe we've come to the heart of the matter." Her temper rose in direct proportion to his cold anger. "The good old double standard. What do you plan to do? Make my life on the set so miserable that I'll quit?"

"I can't win—"

"You can't seem to decide between sexual discrimination or sexual harassment."

"Actually, I do know the difference. And neither applies," Dane informed her bluntly. "But if you"—he lifted a hand to point a finger at her—"can't be reasonable about discussing an issue that affects everyone, then you're not part of the team."

"Just stay out of my personal life, okay?" she flared, and began pointing back. "You can dictate to me on the set, Dane Kingston, but don't you dare give me one order outside of work!"

"How many location shoots have you been on, Pet?"

"Quite a few." Which wasn't exactly a complete answer.

"How old are you?" he demanded next.

"Twenty-six." She would be in September, which was only two months away. The extra year implied more experience.

"I top that by eight years. And I've seen happily married men make complete fools of themselves when they've been separated from their wives for a week. Why do you think Ruby Gale and her singers and dancers are staying in a different hotel?"

"I . . . assumed it was more luxurious than this one." Pet shrugged a shoulder uncertainly.

"It is. More importantly, it keeps my production crew separated from her cast so there won't be any socializing after hours. If it had been at all practical, you would have been staying in a different hotel, too. Unfortunately, it wasn't." His irritation with that showed in his tight-lipped expression. "You've got me all wrong. I'm trying to avoid trouble."

On that note he turned on his heel and let his

long, swinging strides carry him to the door. Pet's hands curled into fists. "Oh, really?" she called after him, but it was too late. Dane was pulling the door shut behind him as he stepped out into the hall.

Frustrated and dejected, Pet sank onto the squeaking mattress of her bed. She flopped backward to stare at the ceiling and rest the back of her hand on her forehead. This had not been her finest hour, she realized. Nor was the situation likely to improve unless she learned to control her temper around Dane Kingston. He was her boss, no less. The *big* boss. You couldn't go any higher in the company than Dane Kingston. Why hadn't she remembered that and behaved accordingly—regardless of the provocation?

Unable to answer that, Pet pushed herself off the bed and walked to the door. She flipped the security lock and the night latch and slipped the chain into place. Perhaps a shower and a good night's rest would put the whole thing in perspective

The next morning Pet was deliberately late to meet Lon for breakfast. Wearing the same khaki top and camo pants, she had braided her flaxen hair into a single plait down the center of her back. Few women could get away with such a severe style, but Pet could, thanks to her strongly defined features and well-shaped head.

As she had hoped, two members of the crew had joined Lon at his table. She walked to the empty chair. "You saved a place for me. Thanks." The sentence was deliberately chosen to show Lon how casually she had accepted the invitation for breakfast.

"Good morning." She greeted them all as she sat down and felt the curiosity in each of their glances despite the normal chorus of replies. "Is there coffee in the pot?" Pet asked, and reached for the thermal carafe in the center of the table to pour herself some. "I need something to open my eyes this morning."

"Don't drink it all," Charlie Sutton said.

"There's about a half a cup left," Pet answered after glancing inside the pot. The waitress stopped at the table to take her order, Lon and the others having already eaten. "I'm running late, so I'd better settle for toast and orange juice."

"Could we get a refill?" Joe Wiles handed the empty carafe to the waitress. "Thanks."

When the waitress had left, Pet leaned back in her chair, blowing on the hot coffee to cool it. Over the rim of the cup her gaze swept in an encompassing arc around the table, taking in her three companions. It was early in the morning, but their unnatural silence wasn't caused by sleepiness.

"Come on, guys." She sipped at the hot brew. "Isn't someone going to ask me what Dane Kingston was doing in my room last night? Or are you going to sit there eaten up with curiosity?" she teased. She had it all thought out, her explanation carefully rehearsed.

"That's our Pet." Joe Wiles shook his head and smiled wryly. "Straightforward and open."

"You said he lectured you?" Lon looked skeptical.

"Yeah. He's a piece of work," she declared with a grimace. "Only this time it wasn't about the way I dressed, but what I was doing. He didn't think it was ladylike to have a beer with you guys and he suggested I behave myself. Can you imagine?" she laughed, and took another sip of coffee.

"From now on, we'll make sure you order Shirley Temples—a proper drink for a proper girl," Joe teased.

"Dane seemed to be saying that I shouldn't associate with you at all." Pet blinked her deliberately rounded green eyes. "You guys are a bad influence on an innocent young thing like me." She made it all appear to be a huge joke that everyone could laugh about.

"We are bad to the bone. No doubt about it." Charlie twirled one end of an imaginary mustache.

"What did you tell Kingston?" Lon's eyes were gleaming with amusement. Maybe he was accepting her explanation without trying to turn it into something it was not.

"What do you think? I told him to mind his own business!" she declared with a twinkling look.

Her remark drew the expected chuckles and comments that suggested approval and encouragement for her stand. But Pet was careful not to mention Dane's threat about causing trouble or dissension among the crew. For the time being the men were on her side, and she didn't want to put ideas into their heads that might change their attitude.

Claude Rawlins, the floor director, stopped at their table when the waitress brought Pet's toast and orange juice, and the conversation was immediately shifted to a discussion of the day's schedule.

"When we're finished shooting here at the performing arts center, where do we go?" Pet asked. "As I understand it, the idea is to show Ruby performing in different settings—the concert stage, a casino theater, and so on."

"That's right," Claude nodded. "From here we'll move to some outdoor locations, then on to Atlantic City to tape her opening night at the casino."

"We're really going to be plugging New Jersey, aren't we?" Lon remarked on a less than enthusiastic note.

"This is Ruby's home state. She was born and raised here in New Jersey," Claude reminded them. "These backdrops will all be fresh and new to a viewing audience that's seen Las Vegas casinos and Madison Square Garden or the Kennedy Center hundreds of times."

"I agree," Pet nodded. "I think it's a good idea."

"Spoken like a Jersey girl," Charlie teased. Which she was.

"Your New York nose is in the air again," she countered.

Joe didn't take part in their playful feud, choosing to stick to the original subject. "It's fitting to tape the special in New Jersey. After all, Ruby Gale has been tagged as a female Bruce Springsteen."

"Boggles the mind," Pet said. "Not that I don't love the Boss."

"I assume you're not talking about Dale."

"You know I'm not."

Claude glanced at his wristwatch. "You'd better drink your coffee, dudes. It's getting late."

Pet quickly downed her last bite of toast and joined the others in line at the cash register. Everyone took it for granted that she would pay for her own meal, including Pet. The situation with the crew seemed to be back to normal.

Eight of them crowded into Charlie's van to make the ride to the Garden State Arts Center. The early morning sun cast a golden hue on the white building and its supporting pillars. The summer-green setting of grass, trees and bright patches of flowers was serene and pleasing to the eye. Charlie drove around back where the semi trailer filled with technical computers and control panels was parked. Several of the crew had already arrived, and others were driving in behind them.

Dane Kingston had just walked out the side door of the trailer rig and was coming down the set of metal steps shoved against the trailer door when Pet piled out of the van with the others. He noticed her immediately. His hard and narrowed look made her feel she was somehow responsible for their arriving late when in actual fact they were seven minutes early.

But there wasn't time to dwell on the injustice of his attitude. All the camera, lighting and sound equipment had to be set up and checked, which was an involved process. Everyone set to work at once. Pet, Lon, Charlie and Andy Turner entered the center to learn where the cameras would be positioned, and to what position each would be assigned.

In all, there were four large studio cameras. One would be kept in reserve in the event of a technical failure of one of the others. Pet was assigned to camera two, covering center stage. Andy was manning camera one on her right and Charlie had camera three on her left. Lon was assigned to the handheld, which allowed him the ability to move around to capture fast action and provide shots from in back of the stage, from the side, or below the footlights.

The first order of business was erecting the platforms to elevate the fixed studio cameras to a degree higher than stage level. Working as a team, they pitched in to help each other erect the scaffolding for the platforms one at a time. Pet worked right beside the men, not shirking any of the heavier work because she was female.

While they were busy with their work, other members of the production team were busy with theirs. It was controlled chaos, with two dozen people, sometimes more, hustling around and shouting orders amid general conversations. A web of cables was spun over the floor to relay power and feed into the main controls in the long trailer outside.

As soon as the platforms were finished they brought in the studio cameras, disassembled and packed in their metal traveling cases. It wasn't easy for Pet to handle the bulky and heavy pieces, but she had learned little tricks over the years that enabled her to compensate—and hey, she lifted big iron at the gym. It never occurred to her to ask for help. She would have refused it if it was offered.

"Petra, what do you think you're doing?" a voice barked behind her.

The suddenness of the demand forced Pet to ease the camera onto the platform floor after she had finally levered it a couple of inches off it. Still kneeling, she turned to look behind her. Dane Kingston was on the floor, glaring at her.

He wasn't dressed much differently from any of the other crew, except that his jeans were more expensive and his long-sleeved shirt was made of linen. The cuffs were rolled up to reveal his sun-bronzed and hair-roughened forearms. The modified work clothes emphasized his rugged male appeal, a factor that didn't make Pet feel any more at ease.

His gaze ripped from her to Charlie. "Get up there and get that camera mounted, Sutton," he ordered with an impatient wave of his hand.

"I can manage it!" she protested forcefully when Charlie started to vault onto the platform.

"I'm not interested in finding out whether you can or not," Dane retorted, and started to turn away.

"This doesn't happen to be the first camera I've ever assembled. I'm fully capable of doing it alone. I don't need any help," she insisted.

Dane swung back to face her with blazing dark eyes. "You can play superwoman another time. All the guys work in teams of two and you don't get to be the exception. That camera is an expensive piece of equipment. If it gets dropped, then we don't have a spare. Do I make myself clear?"

Just in time she remembered to hold her temper, although it flashed in her green eyes. "Very clear, Mr. Kingston," she said, clenching her teeth.

"Good. Make sure I don't have to tell you again," he warned.

He waited at the base of the platform until Pet had moved out of Charlie's way so he could hoist the camera into place on the rotating head of its stand. As Pet went to help Charlie fasten it into place, Dane walked away. She glared at his back

"Like I ever think of myself as Superwoman," she muttered angrily. "He's such a friggin' know-it-all."

Charlie's gaze flickered uncertainly over her. "You have to admit, Pet, the camera was a little heavier than you could handle."

"Who asked you?" she retorted, sarcastically, but Charlie didn't hear her as he turned to say something to Andy.

Chapter Three

By midmorning all three of the camera platforms were in place. One of the cameras was mounted and the crew was unpacking the second and getting it ready to assemble.

"Break time!" Claude shouted to make himself heard above the racket. "Coffee and carbs down front!"

"Sweeter words were never said," Pet murmured, and hopped down from the middle platform. "Those two slices of toast I had for breakfast disappeared about an hour ago. I'm starved!"

"Just direct me to the coffee," Andy declared as he followed her down the aisle. "I must be eight cups behind my normal quota of caffeine for the morning. I'm on the verge of getting the shakes."

A long table had been set up near the fire exit along the wall to the right of the stage. A huge stainless-steel coffee urn was perched in the center of it with paper cups stacked on one side and boxes of Danish pastry on the other. Pet joined the others who had already lined up to help themselves.

With her coffee and a pineapple pastry in hand, Pet wandered over to an empty area below center stage. Andy joined her there. Soon after Lon and Charlie came and a few of the other crew, to talk shop. Pet listened, but spent most of her time eating to quiet the hunger pains in her stomach. When it was gone, she licked the sticky frosting from her fingers.

Tired of standing, but intrigued by a technical explanation Andy was making, Pet set her cup of coffee on top of the stage. With her hands to lever her, she vaulted onto the stage, swinging around to sit on the edge, her long legs dangling. Between sips of her coffee she listened to Andy and asked questions when she wanted something clarified.

Her mouth still felt sticky. She reached for the pack of gum that she usually carried guy-style in a front pocket. Too late, she remembered they had fallen out when she was assembling the camera.

"Can I bum a stick of gum from somebody?" she asked. "I left mine somewhere."

"How about this?" Lon came up with a stick of plastic-wrapped beef jerky and handed it to her like it was something fabulous. "We're not supposed to eat in here. Chew fast."

"Ugh. Disgusting," Pet declared. She gave it back to him.

"Nice try, Lon," someone said, and everyone laughed in agreement, although Pet just smiled.

"How come you're starving this morning?" Lon noticed her silence and began to tease.

"Don't go there, Lon, okay? All I have is a teddy bear to snuggle up to at night," she joked. "It doesn't complain if I have a headache."

"Do you have headaches often?" Charlie asked with a laughing smile.

"Working with you guys, yeah." She wondered if she would seem greedy if she ate two pastries. There probably weren't any left.

"Want another cup of coffee, Pet?" Andy offered.

"I'd love one," she admitted. "But I can get it."

"I was just going to refill mine. There's no sense in both of us walking over there," he reasoned, and reached for her cup, which she surrendered to him.

"If the queen is through holding court"—Dane appeared at the fringe of the small group, withering Pet with a dry look—"let's get back to work."

A few of the men murmured "Right," and "You bet," as glances were darted at Pet sitting rigidly on the edge of the stage. Over the heads of her colleagues her gaze locked with Dane's. Holding court indeed, she thought angrily. Up until a few seconds ago they had been giving her a hard time. And Dane tried to make it sound as though all the guys had been dancing attendance on her. She was furious, but she held her tongue.

As the group around her began to disperse, a pathway cleared between her and Dane. When he moved to approach her, Pet stayed where she was. The stage gave her a height advantage. She would enjoy looking down on him for a change. No matter what he said to her, she was determined not to lose her temper.

Stopping in front of her, Dane peered at her through spiky male lashes as dark as his eyes. The powerful line of his jaw was hard and unyielding. An awesome mingling of danger and excitement danced along her nerves and she found that she couldn't maintain the silence.

"I wasn't 'holding court,'" she insisted stiffly.

In one smooth motion he came a step closer and spanned her slender waist with his large hands. Instinctively Pet clasped his bare forearms with the intention of fending off his hands, but he was already lifting her off the stage and setting her feet on the few inches of floor left in front of him.

His hands stayed on her waist, as if he knew that the minute he took them away she would move out of his reach. She was forced to stay where she was, their tall bodies almost, but not quite, touching. His nearness was unnerving.

"Don't deny you were the center of attention," Dane stated, a muscle working in his hard jaw.

"Maybe when you walked up, but not before." Her gaze moved restlessly over his shirtfront, looking anywhere but into his implacable features.

She watched the steady rise and fall of his chest, noticed the curling, golden brown hairs peeping out through the opening made by an unbuttoned collar, and saw the brawny muscles beneath the shirt sleeves over his upper arms. He was just too masculine for her comfort.

"They were clustered around you like bees around honey." His voice was low, but that didn't lessen its cutting edge.

"That isn't true," Pet denied. "They'd gathered around the stage because it gave them something to lean against."

"They leaned against the stage rather than sit in those seats out there," Dane mocked. "In case you haven't noticed, there are several rows of comfy, cushioned, empty seats out there."

"Quit it," she hissed. "I am not the object of their

lust. They have the Internet for that. Why do you think they stay up so late? Believe me, not all of them are checking their e-mail. Check his browser history for long-legged Nordic—" She almost pointed at Lon and thought better of it.

"Which one? I thought you said they were all family men."

"You know who is and who isn't."

"Whatever. That's their business."

"Just stay out of mine."

"Will you listen to me?" His fingers dug into her waist. If his intention had been to make Pet finally look at him, he succeeded. "I have a pretty good understanding of the fantasies a man could come up with when he looks at you."

"Such as?" Pet challenged, goaded by his superior attitude.

An eyebrow flicked upward in aloof amusement. Dane paused. "Do you really want me to answer that question? Because I can, very easily."

"No." Her voice was all choked. She had to swallow to breathe easily. He had made it clear what he thought when he looked at her without saying one specific word. For a few seconds she had allowed herself to be carried away by the possibility that he was attracted to her. "Some men might fantasize like that, but not Andy, Charlie or the others. They know me."

"They work with you, but that doesn't mean it never crosses their mind to wonder. Men tend to think along those lines," he said. "Women probably do, too, but they're reluctant to admit it even to themselves."

"I wouldn't know," she replied huskily. "I can only speak for myself."

"No? You've never wondered what it would be like if—" Dane asked, tilting his head to one side.

"No. Never." Pet rejected whatever the hell he was getting at with a rushed answer and pushed at his forearms. "Now let me go. I have to get to work. I can't keep standing around here talking to you."

"Or the boys might start to think I was in your room last night for a reason other than the one you told them," he suggested complacently.

"They wouldn't." But she turned to look toward the middle platform where Charlie and the others had gone to finish assembling the camera. As she watched them, Andy glanced over his shoulder toward the stage. The object of his attention was obviously her and Dane.

"They would enjoy thinking it," Dane insisted dryly.

"Well, they would be wrong." Seriously annoyed that he had placed her in another awkward situation, Pet wrenched out of his hands with a twist. "So just stay away from me from now on!" With a quick pivot she whirled away from him, her long braid flying out behind her and nearly slapping his face.

Her mixed feelings about him gave her a surplus of energy. She burned a portion of it walking up the aisle to the platform and hopping onto the planks. The rest she immediately put to use helping the others, aware of their speculative glances and telling silence.

Finally Andy teased, "Did you quarrel?"

She turned on him with a vengeance. "If you think for one minute that I'm interested in that muscle-bound, know-it-all tyrant, then you're no friend of mine. If he'd been anyone other than Dane Kingston—my boss—I would have told him where to get off! He accused me of holding court. And all because you offered to get my coffee!"

"Are you saying it's my fault?" His look was incredulous.

"Yes, yours! And his"—she waved a hand toward the stage where Dane was talking with the lighting director—"overactive imagination!"

"Do you want us to help you find it?" Lon asked.

Pet turned to glare at him. "Find what?" she demanded.

"You've obviously lost your temper. I thought you might want us to help you look for it," he suggested. The other three were wise enough not to smile in front of her.

"Yuck, yuck. No, thanks. I'll find it myself," she said tightly, realizing that she was unfairly venting her anger on them. "I just need to cool down a little bit."

"Let's speed up the process." Charlie picked up the piece of white cardboard and began fanning her with it.

"Very funny." But there wasn't any amusement in her expression. She never fully recovered her sense of humor. By the time they broke for lunch, Pet had succeeded in pushing the disturbing incident to the back of her mind. The others had either forgotten or were careful not to bring it up.

In the afternoon, the impression of chaos was increased when the cast of entertainers arrived to practice their songs and dance routines. To an outsider, it had to look as though no one knew what was going on, but it was all very well organized.

Wearing her headset to communicate with the control booth in the semi trailer, Pet was checking out her camera to make certain it was functioning properly and transmitting a clear picture to the monitors in the control booth. Invariably when a sophisticated and sensitive piece of equipment like this was transported any distance, something needed adjustment.

Digital taping and computerized post-production hadn't changed that. Although generally the adjustments were minor, they could be time-consuming, which was why a day was set aside more or less for the sole purpose of assembling and checking out the equipment, including the spare camera. Barnes was the name of the technician in the control booth with whom Pet and her co-cameramen were working.

"She's here. She just walked in the door." It was Lon's voice that came over Pet's headset. "Wow! She's sexier in person, if that's possible."

"You mean Ruby Gale? Where is she?" Charlie questioned.

Pet had the feeling she was listening in on a sound-snatcher as the headset hummed with the intercommunication of the cameramen. The star of the television special had arrived and all thought of the technical checklist to be completed had been temporarily forgotten. Admittedly Pet was a little curious to see what Ruby Gale actually looked like in the flesh after having heard and seen her perform on TV.

"She's coming down the center aisle," Lon answered Charlie's question.

Turning her head, Pet saw the titian-haired starlet skirting the camera platform. Her first thought was how small Ruby looked, then she realized she was guilty of carrying a larger-than-life screen image in her head. Instead of being as tall as Pet was, Ruby Gale was probably two inches shorter, but her shapely legs provided that illusion of extra height.

Glimpses of those famous legs clad in tights were provided by the side splits in her skirt each time she took a step. She had a flaming mass of red hair that cascaded in thick, glowing curls around her shoulders. Unfortunately, Pet's only view was of the star's backside as she walked down the aisle toward the stage, so she wasn't able to see if Ruby Gale was as naturally beautiful as she appeared on screen and in photographs. Soon even that view was blocked by two people following Ruby, no doubt part of her personal entourage.

Then Pet noticed Dane coming at right angles to intercept the star. A wide, lazy smile added a potent charm to a man she regarded as being already too ruggedly appealing. Irritation made her press her lips into a thin line as she watched him greet the redhead with a kiss, even though she knew perfectly well that kissing was as much a part of an everyday greeting as a handshake in the entertainment business.

"Do you see the way she's cuddling up to Dane?" Charlie murmured. His voice coming over her earphones was an unneeded verification of the scene Pet was witnessing.

"Kissy kissy. I wish she'd press against me like that," said Lon, and imitated the sound of a growling tiger.

"Dane's enjoying it," Andy observed dryly.

"There would have to be something drastically wrong with him if he didn't," Lon retorted. "Hey, you're sorta quiet, Pet. Isn't there any comment you want to make?"

It took her a second to find her voice. "About what?" With the pencil-thin microphone directly in front of her lips, it didn't take much above a whisper to make herself heard. "She's an absolutely gorgeous woman, but you can't expect me to be turned on by her the way you guys are."

Ruby Gale was very beautiful. Pet could see that now as the redhead turned toward the audience seats. Her features were sultry and exotic. Her dark eyebrows were perfectly arched, winging to her temple. Full, sensuous lips parted as she breathed, as if silently inviting her invisible fans to join her in some forbidden pleasure. Although Pet was too far away actually to see the color of her eyes, she remembered from the tabloid covers of Ruby Gale that they were a startling peacock blue.

"A word of warning, fellas," Andy inserted. "She has a temper to match the color of her hair."

"I don't care," Lon declared. "All I know is that these next few days it's going to be a treat having to look at her all the time. I'd be willing to pay for the privilege."

"Better not let the union hear you say that," Charlie suggested.

Barnes from the control booth spoke up. "Don't you think we'd better get back to the job at hand, guys?"

"Killjoy!" Lon grumbled.

Fortunately Ruby Gale disappeared behind stage with Dane and the distraction was eliminated. Not for long, however. Fifteen minutes later she was on stage to rehearse with the dancers. The skirt and blouse had been taken off in favor of a dancer's leotard and a skintight body shirt that revealed every curve and contour of her breasts. Pet had to suffer through more male slobbering over the redhead's beauty and silicone-enhanced figure. Maybe those boobs were real, though. She was heartily sick of the entire subject when a halt was finally called for the day.

Back at the hotel, Pet showered away the day's tiredness. The khaki outfit was cast aside in favor of a pair of pants and a blazer over a sleeveless top. She walked alone to the dining room, certain there would be somebody from the crew with whom she could share dinner. There were three tables' worth, with an empty place setting at each table. Pet avoided the one at which Lon and Charlie were sitting since they had been so, uh, vocal in their praise of Ruby Gale, and she had already had her fill of that subject.

She proved to be a minority of one. All through dinner every other sentence contained some reference to the star of the television special. It seemed everyone had some anecdote to relate or gossip to add. At the conclusion of her meal, Pet stayed at the table to have coffee with the guys.

When the exodus began toward the lounge, she decided that she couldn't endure another minute of Ruby Gale and opted to return to her room. No one seemed to notice that she wasn't coming with them, which kind of bruised her ego.

Perhaps that was why she didn't notice Dane Kingston standing near the exit of the restaurant until she was almost level with him. Her steps faltered for a brief instant.

"Hello," she murmured, and would have walked on.

"Aren't you going into the lounge with the others?" His dark eyes moved over her with interest.

"Not tonight. It's been a long day and I'm tired."

She explained only because she didn't want him to think her decision had been based on his admonition not to socialize with the men in the crew.

"It never crossed my mind that you would listen to my advice," Dane assured her. "But I can't say that you look tired, either."

Pet took a deep breath and released it in an exasperated sigh. "The truth is I'm bored with the subject of Ruby Gale. It's all I've heard for the last several hours."

"You don't like playing second fiddle, is that it?" he mocked.

"Think what you like." She refused to argue about it. "You may find her to be a scintillating topic of conversation, but I don't. Good night."

"Good night," he returned. Before she had taken a step past him, he asked, "By the way, is Pet a nickname?"

She was surprised by the personal question, or perhaps by the genuine interest in his voice. "In a way, it is. It's a shortened version of Petra, my given name." She tipped her head curiously to one side and frowned. "Why?"

"No special reason. I just wondered," he shrugged. "There's a meeting at seven o'clock in the morning."

"Yes, I know," Pet nodded, and glanced over her shoulder toward the restaurant. "Were you just going in for dinner?"

"No. As a matter of fact, I was on my way out of the hotel." The glint in his eye seemed a little bit wicked, although his expression was impassively bland. "I'm dining with Ruby this evening."

His announcement seemed almost the last straw. First the crew, many of whom she had numbered as her friends, had talked of nothing but Ruby Gale. Now Dane Kingston was having dinner with her. The defection of a man Pet really didn't like was the hardest to take.

Her gaze swept over him, noting that he hadn't changed out of his jeans and shirt. "You're going in that?" she questioned icily.

"It's informal." A smile tugged at the corners of his mouth without really showing itself. "We're just having some sandwiches in her suite."

"What? No champagne and caviar?" There was an acid edge to her murmured question.

"That's being saved to celebrate the completion of the special," Dane responded easily.

"How nice. Enjoy your evening," she said, and hurried on her way before he could stop her again.

It was too early to go to bed. After twenty minutes in the small hotel room the walls began to close in on her. Jamming her writing pad and paperback book in her large shoulder bag, Pet left the room and went out of the hotel through a side door leading to the pool area.

There were two families with children swimming in the pool, but few of the deck chairs were occupied. Pet chose one with a small wrought-iron table beside it. It was nearly a full hour before sundown on this warm summer evening—not that it mattered, since the pool area was lighted.

Shedding her blazer, Pet settled into the deck chair and got out her writing pad. She had barely written "Dear Rudy" when a shadow was cast across the paper. She looked up to find Joe Wiles's wide bulk standing beside her chair.

"Writing love letters?" he smiled.

"It's to my brother. He's in the coast guard. Right now he's stationed in Texas on the Gulf Coast," she explained. "Are you taking an evening stroll?"

"Yeah, I'm taking my nightly constitutional before turning in," he grinned, and pulled up a chair to sit beside her. "Do you have any other brothers or sisters?"

"An older brother, Hugh. He lives in Connecticut, married with three kids—all boys. His wife, Marjorie, is a total sweetie. We all love her. Do you want to see some pictures of my nephews?" she asked.

At his nod, she reached in her bag and took out the small photo album to show him the trio of boys with the Wallis blond hair and green eyes. Then Joe took his billfold out of his hip pocket and showed her pictures of his grandchildren, all seven of them.

"How come you aren't married, Pet? You should have pictures of your own kids to show off, instead of your brother's. I hope you don't have something against settling down," Joe said with a wink.

"You sound like my dad! I get his lecture every weekend about the blissful state of matrimony." There was a laughing twinkle in her eyes. "I can't seem to convince him or mom that I'd get married in a minute if the right man asked."

"Somebody must have asked you before now," he insisted. "You're a goddess."

"Thanks. I have been asked," Pet admitted. "I was even engaged for a year, but it didn't work out."

"That can hurt." Joe could get a lot into three little words.

"You know, it didn't," she remembered. "I really liked Brad. As a matter of fact, we're still very good friends. When we mutually decided to call off the engagement, I was sorry—disappointed that it hadn't worked for us but my heart wasn't broken. It wasn't even cracked or bruised. Which proves it would have been a mistake to marry him."

"I guess so," he agreed with regret.

"I think I'll have a Coke. Would you like one, Joe?" she offered, and reached in her purse to get change for the drink machine standing against the exterior wall of the hotel.

"No, thanks," he refused, and pressed a hand against his big belly. "The carbonation gives me heartburn."

There was a definite golden cast to the western sky. Pet noticed it when she walked back to her chair after getting the cold can of soda. For a fleeting second she allowed herself to wonder whether Dane and Ruby were admiring the sunset together in her suite.

"Why do you suppose Dane Kingston has never married, Joe?" she asked idly. "Or has he been?"

"Not that I know about," he answered her last question first. "Could be his reason is the same as yours—never met the right person. He's certainly had more than his share of beautiful women hanging on his arm over the years."

"And probably hopping into his bed, too," Pet added on a note of disgust. "I'll bet no one has ever said yes to him, because he's too bossy and obnoxious. A woman can't tolerate that for long."

Joe shook his head in disagreement. "In this life you have to go after what you want. Nobody's gonna hand it to you. I admire the way Dane never lets anything stand in the way of what he wants. He knows what it is and goes for it. I like that."

"That's heartening," Pet murmured dryly.

"I'm not going to argue with you about him," Joe declared, and pushed to his feet. "I'd better finish my stroll and let you finish that letter to your brother. G'night, Pet."

"Good night." But it was several minutes before she reached for her pen and resumed the letter to Rudy.

Chapter Four

The orchestra was positioned to the rear of the stage, the pianist running through a few quick chords to loosen his fingers. Dancers in leotards were posed around Ruby Gale, standing at front center stage. Beyond them the backup vocal group was fanned out.

This was a practice session, a dry run before tomorrow's dress rehearsal and the following night's concert. Each one of the songs and dance routines would be performed so camera angles could be corrected and the lighting adjusted. The cameras were warmed up. Everyone on stage was waiting for the cue from Claude, the floor director. Dane Kingston was in the control booth in the van parked outside. It was his instructions and directions that were coming over Pet's headset.

"Camera two, we'll be opening with you," he informed Pet. "I want a close-up shot of Ruby Gale, widening on my order. We'll be coming to you next, camera three. All right, we've been through this number twice already. I want no retakes on this one."

Pet nibbled at her lower lip, tension building as

she rechecked her focus. She knew the procedure. Everything they shot would be reviewed later that night for any final changes in angle or lighting. All of tomorrow's dress rehearsal would be taped, since the concert show was a one-time event. There were a dozen things that could ruin a song at a live show. In that case, the dress-rehearsal recording would serve as backup that could be edited into the final product.

"Action," Dane stated.

"Let's have it quiet!" Claude instructed the cast, and absolute silence descended on the center.

From this point on, the only voice would be Dane's as he communicated with the cameras, Claude, the soundman and the lights. Mentally Pet blocked out everything else. Someone else would be responsible for the quality of the sound, the tempo of the music and the volume of the singer on stage.

"All right, two." Dane's voice was calm, and Pet relaxed, too, now that the taping had begun. She didn't notice the signal Claude gave, nor hear the heavy beat of the bass drum begin the song. Ruby Gale's face filled her camera lens, her heavily made-up but beguiling blue eyes staring straight at the camera.

As she began to sing the first lyric, Dane ordered, "Widen the shot, two! *Slowly*," he emphasized, then a little sternly as she began to reverse the zoom, "Don't lose focus, Petra! Camera three, get ready. We're coming to you. *Now!*"

Pet didn't need to consult the paper clipped to her camera, listing the various angles of her coverage in this song. The next one was to be an overall shot of the entire stage, including the orchestra and performers, then narrowing in to isolate the star singing within the circle of male dancers.

"Hold the shot, two. We're on you," Dane advised. "When she moves stage left, go with her." Pet tried, not very successfully, as Dane's angry voice informed her, "You're letting her get behind a dancer. Three, take it on the turn—quick! You blew that shot, Petra."

She gritted her teeth, not convinced the fault had been entirely hers. She suspected the dancer had been out of position, although no one was ever precisely where he was supposed to be. Either way, there wasn't time to dwell on who had been in error. She had to be in position for her next shot.

Meanwhile, she listened to Dane heaping praise on Andy. "Great shot, one." The even pitch of his voice didn't change, although a level of amusement entered it. "I didn't know you had it in you, Turner. You'd better make sure you can do that again." Then, crisply, "You're off center, Petra. I can't come to you until you have Ruby in the middle. You've got it!"

Concentrating, Pet followed the star through her next sequence of steps and its accompanying song lyrics. Her coverage was flawless. But she didn't receive the deserved praise from the control booth; Dane's attention was occupied elsewhere.

"Baxter, you're in three's picture. Duck behind the reed section," he ordered the cameraman on stage with the handheld camera. "Okay, three, it's yours."

As the song drew to an end, Pet's was the last shot. It was to be a close-up on the star while she belted out the last line, then opening to full length and finally widening to full stage. The first Pet executed perfectly but she faltered on the second.

On the third, Dane was barking in her ear, "Loosen

it up, two! I said, loosen it up," he complained. "Hold it!" The song was finished. There was a mental count-down ticking in everyone's head. Then Dane gave the order, "Stop."

"Good job!" Claude called to the performers on stage.

His voice unfroze them from their positions. There was an instant gabble of voices and movement everywhere. Pet released an unconscious sigh and turned off her camera. The tension of needing to be as soundless as possible had been lifted.

A public-address system had been connected be-tween the stage and the control van to extend Dane's communication link to the performers. It was switched on now and his voice filled the theater.

"That was a great number. You were sensational, Ruby," he praised her.

The compliment brought a radiant smile to the star's face. She blew a kiss in the direction of the loudspeaker over which his voice had been pro-jected, and glided into the wings. Just as quickly, the PA system was switched off and Dane's voice was again restricted to the headsets of the crew.

"Claude, get the group set up for the next number," he advised the floor director.

But it was Lon Baxter's voice that dominated the earphones, "Hot damn! Did you guys watch her strutting through that number? My blood pressure went through the roof!" His next comments bor-dered on revolting, Pet thought. Men!

"Shut up!" Dane snapped. "This isn't a locker room!"

"It isn't?" Lon questioned, then hooted, "Oh, you mean Pet's listening."

"That's exactly what I mean!" was Dane's angry and silencing retort.

In the past, Pet had ignored crude language rather than inhibit her male co-workers. If they weren't able to talk freely, she had always felt she would be driving a wedge between herself and them. So she didn't welcome this interference from Dane Kingston.

"Don't worry about it, fellas," she said into her microphone. "I have special earphones that automatically censor any words that might shock my virgin ears. All I hear is a confusing set of bleeps."

"Petra"—Dane's voice came low and threatening over the headset—"I give the orders around here. I don't care whether you would be offended or not. As long as I'm running this show, these guys aren't going to act like nut-scratching Neanderthals. Is that clear?"

"Perfectly." She ground the response through her teeth, crimsoning at his sharp reproof.

"Now that we all understand one another, let's get ready for the next number. Ruby is doing a solo on stage. You shouldn't have any trouble this time, Petra, in making sure no one else blocks the star out of your shot," he suggested.

Pet seethed at that totally unjustified slur on her ability, and clamped her teeth down hard to hold back a sassing reply. She had already been the recipient of several rebukes from him and she didn't intend to invite another.

But it seemed nothing went right after that. One major production number went continuously wrong. Either a dancer missed a cue, or Ruby Gale muffed the lyrics, or the assigned camera lost the shot—usually Pet, it seemed. Finally Claude murmured to

Dane that maybe it was time for a midafternoon break since their star was showing signs of screaming.

The minute Dane voiced a reluctant agreement, Pet tugged her headset off and hopped down from the platform. Her long blond ponytail was swinging back and forth like a cat's tail lashing in anger as she walked swiftly down the aisle for a tall cup of iced tea.

Without saying a word or waiting to see if anyone wanted to join her, she pushed out of an exit door and walked outside. Frustrated by her own apparent inability to do her job right and angered by the way Dane kept pointing it out to her, she needed to escape the tense and stifling atmosphere inside the building.

It was a hot July afternoon, but the air was fresh, circulated by a gentle breeze. She found a shady place to sit where the breeze reached her, and flopped down, hoping the position would calm her jangled nerves. Some of the others wandered outside, as well. When Charlie walked over to enjoy the shade she had found, Lon and two others followed him.

"It may be hotter out here, but it's a lot more peaceful," Charlie sighed.

"Good thing Claude suggested a fifteen-minute break," Lon remarked. "We came very close to seeing that temper Andy has been telling us our star has. You should have heard some of the things she said to that poor dancer who forgot the routine! If Dane thought my language was out of line, he should have heard some of the words Ruby Gale used."

Pet wished he hadn't brought up that earlier matter. As if he realized what he had said, Lon glanced at her, noting her strained and downcast expression. A rueful grimace twisted his mouth.

"I guess I do owe you an apology, Pet. Some of the things I said were really off color. I forget sometimes that you're actually not one of the boys. I'm sorry," he offered.

"Forget it. I have." She closed her eyes.

"I agree with you, Lon," Charlie inserted. "Dane was right to keep us in line. Things get out of hand."

"Listen, I've never asked for any special treatment from you guys," she reminded them.

"If you think I'm going to open a door for you, you're crazy," Lon joked, trying to make Pet see the situation with a little humor.

"Sorry, I'm a little touchy. It's been a rotten day what with Kingston constantly harassing me," Pet explained with a genuine effort to contain her irritation. "I can't seem to do anything right."

"Maybe you're trying too hard," Charlie suggested.

"It sure sounded like Dane was singling Pet out for more than her share of criticism. Of course, that's just my opinion," Lon shrugged. "I don't know how it looked on the monitors. Maybe you had it coming."

"I just wish he'd quit picking on me in general," Pet sighed. "I can take criticism, but I'd like a pat on the head every now and then."

"Aww. Don't let him get to you," Charlie urged, and rubbed a comforting hand on her shoulder. "You're good at what you do. Just remember that."

"Hey!" Claude stuck his head out of the exit door. "Everybody back inside. Let's get to work!"

Pet followed the crew inside and took one last drink of her iced tea before throwing the cup in the wastebasket. Then it was back on the platform to warm the camera up and try the same number just "one more time."

The short break didn't seem to improve anything. By the end of the day her nerves were stretched thin and coiled tight. As always, the ride back to the hotel was noisy, which didn't help. The crew tended to make up for so many hours of enforced silence by laughing and joking at a fever pitch of excitement. Usually making a racket was the ideal means of relieving their stress, but it didn't work for Pet this time.

At the hotel she didn't dawdle in the lobby or corridor with everyone, but went straight to her room and almost directly into the shower. She didn't take the time to dry her long hair. Instead she wound it into a golden brown bun on top of her head, crisscrossing a pair of jade pokes through it for an Oriental look. Her jade silk blouse buttoned up the front with a mandarin collar and a hand-embroidered water lily on the left side. The top was complemented by a pair of mother-of-pearl slacks. It was usually a morale-boosting outfit that enhanced her proud carriage, but she didn't feel any better when she studied her reflection in the mirror. It was over the top for someone who was definitely not Chinese, she decided, but there wasn't time to change.

Sighing, Pet left her hotel room. Too on edge to have dinner yet, she decided to stop in the lounge and have a relaxing before-dinner cocktail with the boys. Her plans went awry when she walked into the dimly lit bar and didn't see Charlie, Andy or any of the regular group. At a table near the bar she noticed Claude, Joe Wiles, Dane Kingston and the audio man, Greg Coopster, all seated together.

She started to leave, then decided to have a quiet drink by herself. After all, that was the reason she had come into the lounge. When Joe spoke and the others glanced around, Pet just nodded. She didn't approach their table as she made her way to a secluded booth in the corner. The barmaid came to take her order.

"A glass of sherry, please." Why on earth had she ordered that, Pet wondered when the miniskirted girl had walked away. Respectable grandmas drank sherry. She wasn't one.

Reaching for the bowl of snack mix, she picked out a tiny pretzel and nibbled on it. Then a shadow blocked what little light reached the corner booth. Her hand began to shake even before she looked to see who was there.

Because she had already guessed it was Dane Kingston. Lowering the hand holding the pretzel to the table to hide its trembling, she slowly turned her head to meet his gaze. His set mouth didn't make her feel any more comfortable. He bent forward to lean a hand on the table. It was an action that struck her as threatening despite his attempt at a smile.

"Would you care to join us, Petra?"

"No." She didn't temper the flat refusal and looked away to take another pretzel, like they were just the most irresistibly tasty little things in the world. She was pretending to ignore him. Which was an impossibility.

"I insist," Dane commanded firmly. "You shouldn't sit alone in a strange bar."

"You're impossible, do you know that?" Pet flared, unleashing the anger she had kept bottled up inside her all day. "First you criticize me for being the sole female drinking with a group of men I happen to work with, saying that it didn't look—what was that word?—ladylike. Now you're upset because I'm here alone. Why don't you make up your mind?"

"I have."

She didn't like the sudden flash of amusement that glittered in his dark eyes. Agitated, she looked away again. "Nothing I do ever pleases you," she complained bitterly.

The barmaid came back with her glass of sherry. Dane had to move to one side so she could serve it. After the girl had left, instead of resuming his former position, he slid onto the booth seat beside Pet. Initially she was too startled to offer a protest. Once she felt the contact of his hard thigh alongside hers, she couldn't seem to breathe, let alone speak.

Aware that his head was turned so he could watch her, Pet stared at the glass of sherry sitting on the cocktail napkin. His gaze was making a slow inspection of her profile; she could feel it as certainly as if he were touching her.

"Do you want to please me?" The drawled question suggested an intimacy she really didn't want.

His implication sent her imagination off on a forbidden tangent. If he could affect her this deeply just by sitting next to her and hinting at familiarity, how would she feel if he made love to her? Her heart knocked against her ribs.

"I couldn't care less," she lied, impatient with herself for being physically stirred by him. She reached for the sherry glass. "Why don't you go away and leave me alone? I was doing fine before you came along."

"A woman alone in a bar is a target for any man

who walks in. You can't sit here by yourself," Dane insisted, gently this time.

But it only increased his attraction and made her all the more determined to resist it. "Did it ever occur to you that maybe I wanted to be picked up by some—some traveling salesman?" she said angrily.

"Do they still exist?"

She nodded. "I think so, on your planet. Where they hit on unladylike chicks who don't have big, strong men to protect them."

"Really." His gaze narrowed to bore relentlessly all the way to her soul. "Is that what you want?"

Bravado failed her, but she managed to hold on to her poise. "All I wanted was a quiet drink before dinner and a chance to relax. If you're finally satisfied, will you please leave?"

"I'm not going to let you sit here by yourself. Bring your sherry over to our table. We're going over tomorrow's schedule," Dane told her.

Sighing, Pet could see that she had about as much chance of persuading him to leave as she did of moving a mountain. If she couldn't move the mountain, the only alternative was to remove herself.

"You obviously didn't hear me. I said I wanted a quiet drink and a chance to relax. Neither would be possible in the middle of a technical discussion," she retorted, and opened her purse to take out the money for her drink and leave it on the table. "Would you please get out of my way so I can leave?"

"But you haven't had your drink." His gaze roamed over her face, stubbornly not moving until he found out her intentions.

"I'm taking it into the restaurant with me. Is that a crime?"

"It might be a shame, but I don't think it's a crime," he agreed, the corners of his mouth twitching slightly in amusement.

"Then would you mind getting up so I can leave?" she demanded in a voice that was growing steadily thinner with the strain of his nearness.

With the suggestion of a smile still playing at his mouth, Dane slid his brawny frame out of the booth and rolled effortlessly to his feet. The touch of his hand was pleasantly firm as he helped her out.

"We'll be playing today's tapes about an hour from now in one of the meeting rooms to make any last-minute changes. If you're through with dinner by then, you can join us." He didn't release his hold of her elbow even though she was standing and didn't require his assistance anymore.

His fingers transmitted the natural warmth generated by his body and sent it spreading up her arm. It made her flesh tingle quite pleasurably. Briefly, she was tempted by the prospect of spending more time in his company until she remembered the tapes they would be viewing. She had endured enough of his criticism for one day.

"Is that an order?" she questioned, turning to pick up her drink and thus forcing him to release her arm.

"No, you aren't required to attend." Something flickered in his look—displeasure, maybe.

"Then I respectfully decline," Pet replied with faint mockery. "Excuse me."

Pausing long enough to inform the barmaid that she was taking her drink into the restaurant, she entered the dining room through the connecting door to the lounge. She did eat alone. It wasn't until the waiter brought her coffee that any of the crew arrived. Pet could have joined them, but there wasn't any point.

Too restless to return to her room, she wasn't in the mood for the kind of shoptalk the group would be having in the lounge, so she wandered outside to stroll around the pool area and watch the sunset from a lounge chair. Reentering the hotel, she stopped by the small gift shop and newsstand to look around.

Ruby Gale's face stared at her from the cover of a celebrity tabloid. Curious, Pet leafed through the pages to find the article about the star. Several photographs of Ruby accompanied the write-up. One of them was a picture of the redhead and Dane Kingston lying side by side on a beach mat. Ruby Gale was wearing the skimpiest bikini Pet had ever seen, but it wasn't the woman that riveted her attention.

It was Dane in his dark swimming trunks. Lean and powerful muscles rippled across his chest and shoulders and held his stomach flat. The implied strength in the sinewed columns of his legs reminded Pet of a Greek god. Drenched, the material of his swimming trunks molded his narrow hips, adding emphasis in just the right place. Wow, was he virile.

She quickly studied his expression. He wasn't smiling, but there was a self-satisfied look about him that indicated just as plainly that he was enjoying himself. And the lazy way his eyes were lingering on the woman beside him indicated that she was the cause of his pleasure.

Cross with herself for becoming so absorbed in the photograph of him, Pet abruptly closed the magazine and set it back on the shelf. She no longer allowed herself to have pointless crushes on men who were unattainable. But was he unattainable, a little voice argued. She ignored the question. That kind of thinking would ultimately bring her grief. Before leaving, she bought a pack of gum and stuck three sticks at once in her mouth, chewing fiercely.

Crossing the lobby, she turned down the main corridor of the hotel. Joe Wiles walked out of a meeting room, leaving the door ajar, and started down the hall ahead of her. Pet glanced in the room as she went by, but there was only a member of the hotel staff inside, carrying away the coffee cups. She stole a little napkin and rolled up the wad of her chomped gum in it, then quickened her steps to catch up with the heavyset man.

"How did the meeting go?" she asked.

The carpeted hallway had muffled her footsteps. Joe's balding head turned with a jerk at her question.

"You startled me. Hey, Petra."

"Sorry. Did you make many changes after you saw the tapes?" She walked with him. For the time being, they were both going in the same direction.

"Nope, very few. And most of those were minor," he replied. "Audio has some problems that they have to correct, but Dane was satisfied with the video. He's going to experiment with the switcher tomorrow, try for some different effects on the solo numbers."

"But it looked good?" Pet persisted. It didn't seem possible that Dane was as satisfied with the results as Joe implied.

"Of course. Did you think it wouldn't?" His smile was a little confused. "It'll be even better tomorrow. Having everyone in costume will really make a difference in the finished product."

"Yes, I know it will," she agreed absently.

"What time does the dining room close?" Joe glanced at his watch. "I haven't eaten yet and I'm starved."

"I think they stop serving at eleven."

"I'd better hurry." He raised an eyebrow. "I'd like at least to wash and change my shirt before I eat."

They reached the point where the corridor branched into two separate halls. Pet turned left. "I'll see you in the morning, Joe."

"Good night." He waved and ambled off.

Arriving at the door to her room, she searched through the bottom of her bag for the key. Just as she found it, the door opened in the room directly opposite the hall from hers, and Dane stepped out.

"Is that your room?" Pet blurted in surprise.

"Yes, conveniently located to keep an eye on you." The corners of his eyes crinkled with a smile.

She hadn't expected him to admit such a thing. His frankness baffled her. She turned to unlock her door.

"As you can see, I'm retiring for the night—all alone—without any of the bad boys tagging after me. Or the good ones. You don't have to worry about checking on me tonight."

"I'm not checking on you," Dane chuckled. "It's purely coincidence that my room is across the hall."

Instead of feeling better, she felt worse. She had been foolish to believe he was so concerned about her that he was virtually standing guard over her. To add to her difficulties, the lock was being its usual stubborn self and resisting her attempts to insert the keycard. Dane was watching her struggle with it, which made Pet even more uncomfortable. She tried to urge him on his way. "If you're going to the dining room to eat, you'd better hurry. I think they stop serving at eleven."

"I'm not on my way to the restaurant." He crossed the hall. "Give me the keycard. There's a trick to these. They're a little different—the magnetic stripe is at an angle."

It was simpler to hand him the keycard than to argue, so she did. "Have you had dinner already?" she frowned. "I thought the meeting finished only a little while ago. I just met Joe in the hall."

"It just broke up," he said, and inserted the keycard in the lock again. "And no, I haven't had dinner."

She studied his bent head and the curling thickness of his dark brown hair, and wondered what it would feel like to run her fingers through it. She was shaken by the force of that romantic little idea. She clenched her hands tightly around her bag in case she unconsciously gave in to it.

"You have to eat." She tried to concentrate on the subject. "It isn't healthy to skip meals."

With a deft twist of his wrist he slid the keycard out of the lock and pushed her door open. "Don't worry. I'll have room service send a sandwich or something up to the suite," he promised smoothly as he turned to face her.

"The suite?" she repeated. Separated from him by only a few feet, she noticed the shadows along his cheeks. The lights overhead were bright, clearly illuminating his rugged features. The darkness was obviously caused by fast-growing, rather nice stubble. Another distraction. Her thoughts returned to the implication of his statement. "Then you're on your way to Ruby Gale's hotel."

"Yes," he nodded, and moved out of her doorway.

"At this hour?" She said exactly what was on her mind and instantly regretted it. "I'm sorry, it's really none of my business."

"No, it isn't," Dane agreed, but he regarded her with indulgence rather than anger. "After viewing the tapes tonight, I have a couple of things I want to suggest to her before tomorrow's dress rehearsal and taping."

"You don't have to explain to me." Pet didn't want him lying and making up excuses. Surely he realized that she had heard the gossip about the torrid affair he was having with Ruby Gale.

She had taken one step across the threshold into her room when his finger touched her chin and turned her head to look at him.

"Don't I?" he asked softly.

He was suddenly very close. His rough male features seemed to fill her vision, leaving room for nothing else. Alarm fluttered her pulse, sending danger signals through her veins. She didn't dare believe what her senses were saying. Dane was on his way to see Ruby Gale. She couldn't forget that, or that candid shot of the two of them in the tabloid.

"Don't you think you should shave first?" she suggested with an admirable degree of calm.

His hand was removed from her chin to rub his cheek. The action produced a faint rasping sound of beard stubble scraping across his skin. He seemed to have been unaware of the growth until she called his attention to it.

"Does it bother you if a man shows up to see you with a five o'clock shadow?" he asked.

"It doesn't bother me," she shrugged. "But I'm not Ruby Gale."

"No, you aren't." When he took a step forward, Pet took one backwards and bumped against the door. "Here's your keycard."

She felt foolish for retreating like a timid school-girl before her first kiss when she saw the card in his hand. Her fingers loosened their death grip on her handbag to reach for it but she didn't get the chance to take it from him, because the keycard was forgotten entirely as he lowered his mouth onto hers.

A pleasurable shock held her motionless until the warm taste of his mouth melted her stiffness. She responded easily to the persuasive ardor of his kiss, a glow spreading through her veins. There was even pleasure in the light scrape of his beard against her soft skin. Desire grew within her for him to deepen the kiss . . . and go farther than that.

Something cold and flat slipped inside her blouse where the top set of buttons was unfastened. Her skin shrank from the contact, but couldn't elude it. It took her a dazed second to identify the object as the keycard. The discovery was followed close on the heels by the realization that Dane's fingers were guiding it under the left strap of her bra.

"You don't want to lose that, Petra."

Before she could protest his flagrantly intimate action, Dane was lifting his head and withdrawing his hand from inside her blouse. She tried to look indignant, but she wasn't very successful—the smoldering gleam in his dark eyes told her so.

As if to prove how completely within his spell she was, he circled her left breast with his large hand. The possession was light, in no way forcing her to endure his caress, while claiming his desire to do so.

"Do you know what you do to me, Pet?" he murmured

in a voice that nearly melted her knees. "Maybe you don't. Whatever. Get a good night's sleep, hmm?"

While she was still trying to surface, he was moving away from her and striding down the hall. In a wonderful kind of daze she stepped the rest of the way into her room and closed the door, trying to figure out how it had all happened and what it meant.

The first was easy, because she recalled vividly the comment she had made in the bar that she couldn't please him. She remembered that Dane had asked if she wanted to. If that kiss was a sample, she definitely wanted to please him.

But why had he kissed her? Because she was all dolled up and willing to be kissed? There was nothing wrong with that: it was a typically male reaction. Except that Pet hoped it was more than that. She didn't like to consider the possibility that it might never happen again.

Sighing, she turned to bolt and latch the door. The action caused the keycard's edge to press into the soft curve of her breast. She reached inside her blouse to take it out and return it to its rightful place in her handbag.

Chapter Five

The next morning it was work as usual, with a meeting scheduled first thing to go over the few changes. Other than a vague smile and nod in her direction, Dane paid no more attention to Pet than to any other member of the crew. She tried to tell herself that she wasn't disappointed, that she hadn't really expected anything different.

In an effort to show she didn't give a damn, Pet threw herself into her job and worked to establish the usual camaraderie with the boys. She had kissed men before without it meaning anything and forgotten it the next day. She could do so again.

It was later in the morning before they were ready to actually begin taping the dress rehearsal. The production crew had plenty to do to keep busy while the cast spent their time with the makeup and wardrobe people.

All the performers were finally on stage for the opening number except for the star, Ruby Gale. When she walked out to take her position, Pet gave an audible gasp at the gown the redhead was wearing.

At first glance it didn't appear to have any sides. She stared to see why it didn't flap open and that was when she noticed the flesh-colored netting at the sides.

An assortment of reactions came over her headset from the male members of the production crew. They ranged from a breathless "Wow!" to "Sweet momma!"

Amusement deepened the corners of her mouth and sent a sparkle of laughter into her green eyes. "If I didn't know better, gang," Pet murmured teasingly into the small microphone, "I'd swear I was receiving an obscene phone call, what with all this heavy breathing."

"What's keeping that dress on?" Lon groaned.

"It must be glued." Charlie made a choked guess.

"It's sheer willpower, fellas," Pet teased, not explaining that the three-inch-wide strip of skin they saw on either side was not bare flesh but covered with netting.

Dane's voice came through. "Cut the chatter," he ordered, "Get the white boards up. I want color checks on these cameras again. Joe, I'm getting a hot spot on the vocal group. What's wrong?"

His briskness snapped them into action. But it didn't end the speculation or the avid interest in the unbelievably sexy gown and the woman wearing it. Amazed comments continued to find their way into the otherwise technical communication over the headset.

"If it's glued on, what do you suppose is going to happen if she starts sweating?" Charlie wondered. "Do you think it will stay on? Will the glue hold?"

"Oh, Joe, turn up the lights and bake this stage," Lon pleaded. "Turn this into a sweat bath."

"Then bring in the fans," Andy said.

"All this panting is going to melt my earphones, guys," Pet warned impishly.

"I said cut the chatter!" Dane barked in her ear.

It didn't matter that he was out in the trailer where she couldn't see him. A mental image of him sprang into her mind—his mouth tight-lipped and his dark eyes blazing. Pet was stung by the injustice of being singled out.

"Why pick on me?" she griped to herself, but forgot to push the highly sensitive microphone away from her lips. "I'm just about the only one who doesn't care. The guys' eyes are popping out of their heads and they're drooling."

Since she hadn't intended her comment to be heard by anyone, she visibly jerked when Dane answered her question. "That is exactly the reason. The others are a lost cause, but you can set an example, Petra. So straighten up!"

"Yes, sir! Anything you say, *sir!*" She masked her angry defiance with exaggerated obedience that left no one in doubt of her temper.

Any question about what last night's kiss might have meant no longer existed. As far as Pet was concerned, the meaning was clear: it had been nothing more than a passing whim. Dane was going to be hard on her today to make sure she understood that and didn't get any ideas. The message was loud and clear. Pet wasn't deaf or stupid. After all, she hadn't really thought she could successfully compete with that red-haired sex machine on stage. And she hadn't forgotten that Dane had been with Ruby Gale after he had left her.

It was another ten minutes before the floor director told the performers to take their positions on stage for the opening number. When Dane informed the crew that the tape was rolling, Claude asked for quiet and began the countdown: "Ten, nine, eight, seven, six . . ." He stopped there and continued it with his fingers, so his voice wouldn't be picked up on tape.

All that was mainly for the performers' benefit. Dane was issuing his own instructions prior to that. "Do you remember the sequence of the opening number, Petra? A close-up frame of Ruby. Open it *when* I tell you and the *way* I tell you or I'll do something dire," he warned, and began counting. "Ten, nine, eight . . ." It was his countdown that the floor director repeated.

So it began. If Pet thought Dane had been demanding the day before, it was mild compared to the relentless way he drove the crew today. The slightest flaw or imperfection in a shot drew sharp and immediate criticism. Although everyone felt the razor edge of his tongue at some point, the majority of his criticism seemed to go to Pet.

Take after take, number after number, Dane pushed them. Even when the fault was with the star, Ruby Gale, for missing her spot on stage or going beyond it out of camera range, it was the crew he blamed over the loudspeaker system. A couple of times Ruby flubbed the song lyrics.

Over the PA speaker Dane's voice was benevolent and forgiving as it filled the theater. "Don't worry about it, Ruby. After all the mistakes we've made, you're entitled to blow one now and then. You're perfect. You're doing great."

Silently Pet seethed at this preferential treatment for the star. Nothing remotely resembling a critical word was ever directed at Ruby Gale. Why couldn't Dane snap at her the way he did everyone else? In his eyes Ruby Gale could do no wrong, while Pet couldn't seem to do anything right. She felt raw, suffering from a thousand needling remarks, oversensitized by a barrage of pinpricks.

She had the closing shot on another production number. "Hold that frame, camera two," Dane's voice advised sternly in her ear. "Hold it. Hold it!" Impatience inched into his tone and scraped at her nerves. "Okay, stop tape."

At the statement, Pet immediately closed her eyes and lowered her chin in wary relief. Her long blond ponytail swung forward to brush the top of her left shoulder. Releasing her grip on the control handles of the camera, she wiped her sweaty palms on the legs of her faded denims. She straightened to glance across the rows of seats to Andy's camera position and he gave her a crooked smile and a thumbs-up signal.

"We made it through that one," his voice murmured through her earphones.

Before she could reply, Dane's voice came over the public-address system. "Good job, gang, I think we've earned a twenty-minute break."

The richly resonant pitch of his voice vibrated over Pet. "Ah, a voice from above," Charlie joked, and lifted his hands in mock awe.

"Regardless of what he thinks, he isn't related to God Almighty," Pet muttered, assuming that Dane

had already removed his headset after announcing
the break.

Her mistake was quickly pointed out to her by
Dane himself. "If I was, Petra, I would use my influence to do something about you," he said curtly.
"And the next time I tell you to hold a shot, that
doesn't mean you should move."

She wanted to scream at him to stop criticizing
everything she did and to tell him that she had read
between the lines and knew he wasn't romantically
interested in her. Some perverse streak made her do
just the opposite.

"Oh, angel pie, it won't work," she cooed over the
headset mike. "Everyone's guessed that you're madly
in love with me. Trying to hide it by yelling at me all
the time isn't fooling anybody. We can't keep it a
secret anymore."

There was an incredulous laugh from someone,
but it wasn't Dane. Pet knew she had invited his
wrath upon her and grimly tugged off her headset.
Then she hopped off the platform into the aisle.

Charlie called to her, still wearing his headset.
"Hey, Pet! Dane wants to talk to you!"

Holding her head at a proudly defiant angle, she
didn't slow her strides as she yelled back, "Tell him
that's tough! I'm on my break!"

At the refreshment table set up for the crew, Pet
skipped the insulated container of iced tea in favor
of the coffee urn. It was left over from the morning
break, which made it strong and inky black. Pet felt
in need of its strength.

"What got into you, Pet?" Charlie came up to stand
beside her. The smile on his face seemed to be there
in spite of his better judgment. It was as if he ad-

mired her for talking back while he thought she was crazy for doing so.

Lon was there, shaking his head. "You really believe in flying in the face of danger, don't you?"

"I just want him off my back," she grumbled, and swore under her breath when she tried to take a drink of the scalding black coffee and burned her tongue.

The explosion of a door being forcefully slammed open thundered through the cavernous theater and echoed in shock waves. A quick glance over her shoulder saw Dane striding toward them. Squaring around, Pet kept her back to him and hooked a thumb through the belt loop of her jeans, trying to adopt an attitude of nonchalance while studying the black liquid in her cup.

"Looks like you're in for it, Pet," Andy murmured, glancing at her over the rim of his drink.

With an exaggerated blink of her eyes, she pretended she didn't care. The skin along the back of her neck prickled a warning. Out of her side vision she saw Dane stop on her right, but she wouldn't look at him.

"You didn't really think you were going to get away with that, did you?" Dane sounded remarkably calm as he made the low challenge.

She didn't try to answer. To cover her silence, she started to raise the cup of coffee to her mouth, but Dane reached out to take it from her.

"Hey! That's my coffee." When she tried to hold onto it, the hot coffee sloshed over the side. At least it burned his hand but he didn't let go. What a man.

"Hold this." Dane handed the cup to Andy, then turned back to her. She was wary of the glint in his eye and the hint of a smile on his mouth. "How wonderful that everyone knows and I don't have to hide it," he taunted softly.

In the next second his hand had clamped itself on her arm to pull her toward him. Her protesting outcry was choked off by shock at what he was doing. She tried to ward off his chest with her hands, but she was no match for his sheer strength. His palm cupped the back of her head to hold it still, his fingers tangling in the length of her hair, while his mouth came down onto hers.

The encircling band of his arm held her fast, arching her waist to bring her more fully against him. He dominated her lips, moving over them as if satisfying a very male need to sample their softness. Her senses were filled with the sensation of his hard length bent protectively over hers, the thrust of his hips, and the solid muscles of his torso flattening her small breasts.

Aware of the fascinated spectators watching the embrace, Pet pushed at him, but it was an ineffectual attempt that gained nothing at all. Not that she really minded; the things his kiss was doing to her rivaled her imagination. The wild singing in her veins was a hot, sweet thrill. He could convince her she was floating on a cloud, no problem. She stopped resisting and began kissing him back, her hunger matching his appetite.

Before her hands could begin their final, submissive curve around his middle, Dane pulled away. There was a roughness to his breathing and the smoldering darkness of passion in his eyes. Yet the clearest impression Pet had was the scattered cheers and applause of those around them.

The crew regarded the kiss as a huge joke, thinking

that Dane had deftly turned the tables on her. And it was true. The heat of embarrassment rushed into her face, staining her cheeks scarlet. Pet couldn't remember ever blushing in her life, but she had never made such a fool of herself. For a few seconds she had forgotten all that had gone before the kiss.

She lowered her gaze to the hollow of his throat, his arms still containing her within their circle.

"Why did you do that?" she asked huskily. Had she really deserved it? Or had she wanted it?

Dane crooked a finger under her chin and made her look at him before he would answer her question. "It seemed the most effective way of shutting up a smart mouth." The lazy glint in his dark eyes seemed to hold only amusement at her discomfort. "Don't do it again." He tipped his head back and to one side, as if to get a better angle of her face. "Truce?"

Before she could answer, someone called to him from the stage. "Ruby Gale would like to see you in her dressing room, Dane."

With a sigh he loosened his hold and let Pet stand free. "I'll be right there," he replied. Reaching around, he took the cup of coffee from Andy and gave it back to Pet. As he walked past the refreshment table on his way backstage, he stopped to take two sugar cubes out of their box and tossed them to her. "Put some sugar in your coffee—it might sweeten your disposition."

Sheer reflex enabled her to catch them. "I haven't been the one snapping at everybody all day." She tossed them back, surprised she could move or speak.

"You're right." Dane turned away with a wry shake of his head, not bothering to catch the cubes.

Pet had the feeling he had just turned the tables yet again. She didn't know if she was coming or going. Warily, her gaze flashed around the semicircle of men, almost daring them to make a comment.

Joe Wiles was the only brave one. "If you're going to dish it out, Pet, you'd better learn to take it," he advised.

"I can take it," she insisted, and gulped down a swallow of tepid coffee.

But the crew was careful not to tease her about the kiss. Ten minutes later Claude was summoning them back to work.

The next day was Friday. Ruby Gale's concert was scheduled for that evening at nine o'clock. Since they were taping it before the live audience, the production crew had the morning and the bulk of the afternoon off.

Dressing for the taping that evening, Pet chose dressier pants and a crepe-de-chine blouse and wrapped a slender belt around her waist. Her everyday work clothes were too casual to wear in front of the public, and a dress or skirt was out of the question since she still had to climb off and on the platform.

The audience began arriving at the Garden State Arts Center half an hour before the performance was scheduled to begin. Perched on her platform in the center aisle, Pet became the cynosure of many eyes that had nothing better to do than look around while waiting for the show to start. It was amusing to listen to some of the comments.

A young brunette about her own age pointed Pet

out to her date. "Look, there's a woman operating that camera."

Her date looked like a jerk. "She's probably only a helper," he said. Yep, he was a certified, card-carrying, sexist jerk.

A few stopped to ask questions, most of them concerned about when the show would be seen on television. "I don't know the air date," was Pet's stock answer. "Probably in the fall or winter."

Sometimes they asked where she had learned to operate the camera. "I went to college and took courses in it."

In a way, the most difficult question to answer was why she wanted to be a camera operator. "It's what I always wanted to do," rarely satisfied them.

As the time drew closer to nine o'clock, Dane's voice came over her headset. She had barely seen him at all since yesterday's episode. The few times she had, he had been in conversation with someone else and she didn't receive any more than a preoccupied glance. In the interim, Pet thought she had got things back in their proper perspective—until she heard his voice and her pulse went skittering all over the place.

His initial comments were instructions to the crew in general, then he was directing a remark solely to her. "What about you, camera two? Do you think you have the sequence of the opening number down pat?"

"If I don't, I'm sure you'll tell me about it," she replied with surprising ease.

"You can bet on it," he chuckled softly.

"I would, but nobody will give me odds," Pet returned, joking with him.

"Watch your mouth, girl, unless you want another lesson in keeping it shut." It was a fake threat, issued with a smile in his voice that made light of yesterday's incident as if it had been all in good fun.

"Promises, promises," she heaved a sigh. "That's all you men ever do—promise and forget to follow through."

"I'll remember that," he warned. Then it was back to business. "Claude, how are things moving backstage?"

"We'll be on time," the floor director promised.

"Baxter, I want you to get me plenty of audience shots," Dane instructed Lon, who had the hand-held camera. "You shouldn't have any trouble when the house lights are up. The rest of the time there should be enough light falling back on the first two or three rows to give me reaction shots, not just applause."

"Gotcha, boss."

Precisely at nine the curtain went up. Right from the opening number the first half of the show went without a hitch. The mistakes by both crew and performers were so few and minor they were practically nonexistent. It seemed that all the rehearsing, the countless takes, the endless criticisms had paid off to achieve near perfection.

Ruby Gale's performance had been electric, charged by the applauding audience. She was sexy, stunning, scintillating, alive as Pet had never seen her before. Everything flowed with such magic that when intermission arrived Pet couldn't help wondering what would happen when the clock struck twelve and the coach became a pumpkin again. Would the spell wear off?

"Excuse me, miss." An elderly man was standing beside her platform. Pet had noticed him before since he was sitting in one of the aisle seats near her position.

She shifted the mike wand of her headset away from her lips. "Yes?" She thought he probably wanted direction to the men's room. She supposed she could always ask Andy or Charlie.

"I've been watching you and I just wanted to say that you're a very beautiful woman," he said, smiling quite benignly. "You belong in front of the camera instead of behind it."

"Thank you." Her smile was wide and wholly natural.

"I know you're busy, but I just wanted to tell you that." He nodded in a gesture of apology and turned to go back to his seat.

"What did the old guy want?" Charlie asked, having seen him stop to talk to her from his camera position. "Did he ask you to go out with him?"

"He was very sweet," she insisted. "He told me I was beautiful and belonged in front of the camera."

Dane joined the conversation to state unequivocally, "Well, you don't. You belong behind the camera."

"That's a pleasant switch," she drawled.

"Why?" he demanded.

"I had the feeling you think women belong in a kitchen either in front of a stove or behind a sink full of dirty dishes," Pet explained in wry amusement.

"Better you than me," Dane said. "Okay, gang, we have five minutes. Five minutes!"

As Pet had feared, the second half of the show didn't run as smoothly as the first. Midway through the second number, camera three went out. They had to do some fast improvisations of camera angles to cover the shots assigned to Charlie. When the problem defied immediate correction, the spare camera was hurriedly carted in and mounted.

In all, camera three was out for three songs, an amazingly short period. Yet that frantic race for time had thrown everyone off tempo and they were never able to regain that effortless coordination that had made the first half of the show so flawless.

It was a relief when the concert was over and the tape stopped rolling. While the audience filed out, the crew began shutting down the equipment. It was twenty minutes after the last curtain call before Pet had finished.

"Are you driving back to the hotel with me?" Charlie called to her from across the seats.

"Yeah! But I left my bag in the van," she explained. "I'll run out and get it now. Wait for me!"

The seventy-foot-long semi trailer had seemed the safest place to leave her bag during the taping. She couldn't have kept it with her on the platform since it could have been stolen too easily. Nor had it seemed wise to leave it backstage with so many people coming and going all the time.

As she walked in front of the stage, a woman stepped out from behind the curtains. Pet had seen her before. She was usually a part of Ruby Gale's personal entourage. Pet suspected she was an assistant publicist or something.

"Excuse me," the woman requested Pet's attention with an uplifted finger. "Could you tell me where I could find Mr. Kingston?"

"I"—Pet glanced around the theater—"haven't seen him. He might still be in the trailer outside. I'm on my way out there. Shall I send him in?"

The woman considered that, then said, "Could you give him a message?"

"Sure," Pet nodded.

"Ruby Gale is leaving now for her hotel. She wanted to remind him about the party she's having in her suite tonight. Would you mention it to him? She really wants him to come," the woman added.

"I'll remind him," Pet promised.

"Hurry up, Pet!" Charlie shouted.

With a quick wave to acknowledge that she had heard him, she hurried out through a side exit to where the trailer was parked. Its long white-painted sides gleamed in the moonlight, emblazoned with the Kingston crest and the letters spelling out Kingston Productions. A bare light bulb illuminated the metal steps leading to the side door.

As Pet reached for the railing to climb them, the door opened and Dane stepped out. He frowned in surprise when he saw her, his gaze narrowing at her haste.

"Is something wrong?" He was down the steps and grabbing her shoulders almost before she could catch her breath. "Has something happened?"

"No, I . . ." She was momentarily flustered by his touch. "I left my handbag in there and Charlie's waiting to give me a lift to the hotel."

"Oh." He seemed to smile at his overreaction, and let his hands fall from her shoulders. "You'd better hurry then. If he's ready to leave, he's probably getting impatient."

"He is." She started up the steps, brushing past him, before she remembered the message she had promised to deliver. "Oh, Dane, I forgot." She stopped and half turned.

"What did you forget?" He moved back within the circle of light cast by the bare bulb. There was something warm and velvety in his look that tugged at her heart.

"Ruby Gale's assistant publicist—I think that's who she was. She asked me to remind you about the party in her suite tonight," Pet explained.

"Damn!" He released a long, tired breath and rubbed his forehead. Both his sound and his action made it plain he wasn't overjoyed by the message.

Pet watched him, feeling a little glad that he didn't look happy about going. "She also said Ruby really wanted you to come," she added.

"I don't have any choice," Dane said wryly. "It's more or less obligatory on both sides. Ruby has invited some local celebrities and the press over for drinks. It's good public relations—and good publicity. It's good for her, and for this television special of mine," he explained. "So it's a business affair masquerading as a social event."

Pet wasn't exactly sure why he was telling her this. It wasn't really any of her business what this party was for or why he felt obligated to attend. But the fact that he had made her feel . . . well, a little important.

"That's entertainment," she offered lightly.

"Have you ever been to one of these parties?" Dane asked.

"Hell, no!" she laughed.

"Why don't you come with me tonight?" he suggested. "Then you'll always know what you're not missing."

For a minute she thought he was serious, then she wasn't sure. "You don't want me along." She shook her head, her long blond hair swinging loose about her shoulders, and started to climb the last steps to the van door.

"I wouldn't have asked if I didn't want you come with me, Pet." His voice was low and serious.

Startled, she looked back. There wasn't a hint of mockery or amusement in his face. His look was silently questioning as he patiently waited for her answer.

"But I'm not dressed for a party . . ." Pet managed a faint protest to give him a chance to back out of the invitation if he wanted to.

"As you can see, neither am I." He lifted his hands in a gesture to indicate the casualness of what he had on. "But I'm going like this. And they can hardly turn you away when you're with me. Are you coming? It will be a new experience for you. I can't say it will be one you'll want to repeat, but—"

"I'll never know, though—" she began.

"That's right," he agreed.

"Okay," Pet accepted, and shrugged, trying to be as offhand about the invitation as he was. "Why not?"

But she knew precisely why she was accepting. She wasn't at all curious about what the party might be like, nor the experience of it. It was the chance to spend a couple of hours with him that she was accepting. It was crazy, and probably foolish, but that was the truth.

"Go get your bag, I'll wait here for you," Dane said, and rested an arm on the railing at the bottom step.

That reminded her. "Charlie's waiting for me. He thinks I'm going back to the hotel."

"I'll tell him to leave without you, that you'll be with me. The gang will really be confused then," he grinned. "I'll meet you here."

"Okay," she agreed.

When she opened the trailer door, Dane had disappeared into the semidarkness. Pet didn't understand this spell he had cast over her. One minute she was infuriated with him, and in the next he could have her melting in his arms. It didn't make sense, but she wasn't sure if it had to.

Her bag was right where she had left it, tucked under the bench seat inside the door. She glanced once at the multitude of television monitors across the control panel, the screens glassy and gray, all the little lights out. Behind the panel, out of sight behind the partition, was the sophisticated computer that controlled everything and turned the semi trailer into a portable television studio, complete with all the latest electronic gear. Pet shuddered to think how much it cost, or how wealthy that made Dane, since he owned it. He was way out of her league.

Chapter Six

Riding in a powerful, low-slung Jaguar was the best part of the drive to the star's hotel. Pet was surprised at how easy it had been to talk shop with Dane, as easy as it was to chat with the boys in the crew. Of course, his knowledge was much more encompassing than hers. Perhaps that was what had made his comments all the more interesting and thought-provoking.

Things she'd previously regarded only from the production side, she now began to consider from the management and executive side. She had learned a lot in a very short time. She was almost sorry when Dane guided her out of the elevator and down the hallway to Ruby Gale's suite, because it meant their private conversation was coming to an end.

Gradually she realized the reason for her regret was more subtle than that. Discussing television kept her from thinking about Dane as if he were her date. He wasn't. She had been using the talk as a defense mechanism to keep that sense of physical attraction at bay.

In another few minutes they were standing in the hallway at the door to the suite, waiting for Dane's knock to be answered. His hand had found the curve of her waist, his palm covering her hipbone. The warmth of his touch was melting through her clothes to her skin, heating her flesh with an awareness of him.

Under the sweep of her lashes she slid him a look out of the corner of her eye. His good looks made her breath catch. She was struck again by his height, something she didn't notice about most men since they generally weren't so much taller than she was.

As if he felt her eyes upon him, Dane's gaze swept over her in a way that upset her heartbeat. She quivered all over inside with the desire to have him make love to her. It was fun but kind of shocking to be so completely aroused by just a look. She averted her gaze to the door, her ivory-smooth composure not giving away at her pleasurable agitation. Dane's hand applied slight pressure on her hipbone as if he wanted to pull her closer. "You look great," he murmured.

A simple thing to say, but it got to her. "Thank you." It was a breathy answer, barely audible.

With excellent timing, the door was opened to the suite by the same woman who'd given Pet the message for Dane. The eager smile she gave Dane faltered when she saw Pet with him. "Hello, Mr. Kingston. Ruby will be so glad you could come."

"Hello, Clancy." There was a ghost of mockery in the look he gave the brunette. "You can call me Dane. You remember Petra Wallis, don't you?" he prompted as he swept Pet along with him inside the suite.

"Of course." Behind the polite nod, it was obvious the woman was trying to figure out what Pet was doing with Dane. "Ruby is—" The woman took a step, obviously intending to take them to their hostess.

"I see her, Clancy," Dane interrupted, glancing across the room.

Ruby Gale's red hair was a beacon, standing out in the crowd, which was mostly men. Pet had spotted her almost instantly, too, but mostly she was staring at the decor of the suite. It boggled the imagination.

Pink. Everywhere there were shades of pink from the thick, powder-puff carpet to the rose velvet sofas and chairs. On nearly every other antiqued-white tabletop there were vases of flowers, mainly dark pink roses. White woodwork outlined the pastel print silk covering the walls. Even the caterers were wearing dark rose red jackets over black trousers. Pet felt as if she was gawking as Dane guided her into the main room of the suite.

Removing two glasses of champagne from a proffered tray, he put one into her hand, and her gaze flickered to his face in surprise. Amusement gleamed in his eyes at her stunned reaction to the room. She looked around it again before lifting the glass to sip the bubbling wine.

"I thought hotel suites like this existed only in Hollywood movies," she commented.

"It's horrendous, isn't it?" he agreed, keeping his voice low, too. "You should see the main bedroom. It has a round bed with a red velvet canopy draped into a rose design. I think I prefer mirrors to staring at giant red roses above my head."

A sick feeling weighted Pet's stomach. Was he speaking from experience? Of course he was. She was angry with herself for even questioning it. How else would he have known about the bed unless he'd been in it? Only a naive idiot would believe he had only been testing the mattress for firmness. And she wasn't naive. She had always suspected—known—that he and Ruby were lovers, so why had she accepted his invitation to this party? The answer was so plain. She had a stupid crush on this sexy, exciting man who could infuriate or arouse her by turns.

Her inability to resist him made her feel spineless. She took another sip of champagne, but the constricting muscles in her throat rejected it with a tiny choking cough.

"I'm surprised the champagne isn't pink," she managed at last, her long fingers delicately covering her lips.

"Ruby probably didn't think of it." A smile twitched the corners of Dane's mouth as his gaze ran interestedly over her face, a little aloof. "I told you this would be an experience. You don't like it, do you?"

There were many things she didn't like. Above all, the discovery that she was envious of Ruby Gale for getting to roll around with Dane in that round bed with the rose canopy. Although she was determined not to reveal her feelings, her expressive sea-green eyes obviously showed them.

"This suite, everything—it's all so phony." Pet shrugged to show her dislike of it, lowering her gaze to the sparkling liquid in the crystal wineglass.

Dane's fingers touched her cheek to turn her face to him, then moved away. "And you aren't, are you?" He studied her more closely as if discovering something he hadn't noticed before.

Pet became uneasy under his scrutiny and immediately Dane ended it, shifting his gaze to the room of people, buzzing with hearty conversations that rang false.

"This is all part of the image," he said, a sweeping glance taking it all in. "These people would have been disappointed and disillusioned if this suite had turned out to be no different from any they could have rented for one night. Ruby Gale is a star. Nothing ordinary would suit her in their eyes. A star has to be surrounded by a spectacle. Ruby's smart. She gives them what they want and keeps them coming back for more."

He looked back to Pet. She wondered if that explanation was true for him as well, but she wasn't going to ask.

"It's fake," he went on, "a fantasy world of red-hots and candy canes—sugar and spice wrapped up in glitter and sequins. It's called packaging the product."

"I suppose that's true," Pet conceded with a trace of his cynicism.

"You haven't been formally introduced to the 'product,' have you?" Dane closed a hand on her elbow. "We'd better do that before Ruby starts throwing real poison darts instead of invisible ones."

Following the direction of his amused glance, Pet saw their hostess through a gap in the cluster of guests. Her long hair tumbled over her white shoulders in a mass of titian curls. The low-cut spangled gown was the same peacock-blue shade as her eyes—eyes that glittered possessively whenever they rested on Dane, which was often.

When Dane and Pet finally got through the crowd to the star's side, Ruby Gale gave Dane one of her radiantly provocative smiles. "I wondered when you were going to show up, honey." She curved a scarlet-nailed hand along the back of his neck when he bent to greet her with a kiss.

Their lips clung together a few seconds longer than it would take for a casual smooch. Pet wasn't prepared for the surge of jealousy that shook her. She stood motionless, her face frozen into blankness, while the three men Ruby had been speaking to exchanged knowing glances.

When Dane lifted his head, the star wiped the traces of lipstick from his mouth with her fingers. The gesture, more than the kiss, implied a long-standing familiarity and intimacy between them. It was also territorial. Pet was rigidly aware that Dane didn't protest it.

Then the redhead was linking both her arms though the crook of his elbow, further staking her claim to him while turning to the trio she was with. "You all know Dane Kingston—my producer, my director, my"—Ruby paused deliberately, sweeping him a look through her long lashes as if exchanging a secret—"dear friend."

The phrase got only the slightest smile from Dane, which made a total mockery of it. Pet would have slipped away, but he chose that moment to remember she was with him and turned to take her hand, drawing her within the circle. She half expected a blue-eyed glare from Ruby, but it didn't happen. The singer's glossy red lips were parted in a welcoming smile of interest.

"I don't believe I know her, do I, Dane?" she asked, and extended an open hand to Pet.

Pet let her hand be clasped warmly by the star and

even managed a stiff smile. Pride kept her head high while defensiveness masked her gaze.

"Hello." The single word from Petra was infused with wary coolness.

"You haven't actually met her before, Ruby," Dane explained. "But you've spent the last few days looking at her without knowing it. This is Petra Wallis. She's been operating the number-two camera."

"The center one?" Now the star's gaze became sharp, slicing Pet into unimportant pieces. "You actually have a woman in sole charge of a camera? That's not like you, Dane."

"It isn't?" he replied, turning aside the comment.

"Are you the token female, Petra?" the star inquired archly. "My, my. What big muscles you have."

In other words, not feminine. Petra wanted to smack her.

"I wouldn't want to look like that. I love being dominated by a big, strong man." Ruby's glance at Dane made it obvious who that "big, strong man" was.

Pet seethed with jealousy and the sensation of betrayal by one of her own kind. What Ruby Gale was insinuating was insulting and demeaning to her. Worse, the three men with their glasses of champagne and lascivious looks were nodding agreement with Ruby Gale's girly-girl nonsense.

"Petra was the best person for the job," Dane said easily.

His support didn't bring the reassurance that it should have. Instead, one of the younger men—a reporter by the cynical look of him—gave Pet an assessing look that made her feel stripped naked. Anger flashed in her eyes, the turbulent green of storm-tossed seas.

"Hey, she looks like she could throw me over her shoulder," the reporter remarked suggestively. "Any time." He smirked and everyone chuckled in total agreement.

Pet struggled to contain her anger. Usually she could ignore stupid comments like that from men, dismissing them as small remarks from small minds. Yet she was bristling now.

"I'm not so sure." Ruby Gale was talking like Petra wasn't even there. She turned to Dane. "Just look at all the delays and technical problems we encountered taping this concert because of one or two unskilled crew members."

"As a professional, Ruby, you know there are always problems of one kind or another," Dane stated with a hard glint in his eyes. "But you certainly can't blame Petra. She's the best technician in the company—that's why I put her on camera two. When you're on center stage you deserve to have the best covering you, so I made sure you did. You'll see for yourself when we review the tapes of tonight's performance."

"My, my!" The redhead blinked her startling blue eyes and teased him with a smile. "High praise coming from you, Dane." Her gaze shifted to Pet, who had been stunned and skeptical of his assertive defense. "You must be very flattered."

"I am," she admitted, since flattery also implied exaggeration.

"Is that why you brought her to the party? As a reward for all her hard work?" Ruby questioned, and rose on tiptoe to kiss his cheek. "How sweet of you, honey! You really are very thoughtful."

The conclusion Ruby had reached sent Pet's mind racing. Was that the explanation for this unexpected invitation? Was she supposed to be at this party as a bonus for a job well done? She'd liked it better when she believed it was just a friendly invitation.

"I don't think Pet would agree with you, Ruby." Dane commented, and sent a meaningful glance in her direction. "I think she's convinced I'm a cross between an ogre and a tyrant."

"You neglected to mention an obnoxious jerk," Pet reminded him smoothly.

"So I did," he agreed, and lifted his champagne glass in wry acknowledgment of the omission.

"What's this all about?" Ruby glanced from one to the other, suspicion shimmering in her hard blue eyes.

"A minor rebellion in the ranks against authority." Dane dismissed their previous skirmishes with an indifferent shrug of a shoulder and sipped at his champagne. "I neglected to tell you how sensational you were this evening, Ruby. You had the audience in the palm of your beautiful hand all the time."

Diverted by his compliment, the redhead beamed, "Thank you, Dane."

"Hear, hear," one of the men murmured in agreement, and lifted his glass in a toast to her successful performance.

"Yes, to a very triumphant performance by our own, uh, Jersey Lily." A second man seemed pleased by his own eloquence.

"In case you men haven't noticed it, Ruby is a tiger lily—a wild, exotic flower," Dane remarked with an admiring glance at the self-absorbed entertainer.

Pet could almost see the reporter making a mental note of the phrase. She was sure it would show up somewhere in the post-performance publicity.

"You know all the right things to say to make a woman feel special, Dane," Ruby purred, and let her hand glide along his arm to curl her fingers through his. "I should be upset with you for bringing a blonde to my private party, but I'm not. I let you get away with everything."

"Really?" he asked, as if he didn't care what her answer would be.

Her laugh was a low, throaty sound. "Oh, yes. You can be so bad. I never know whether to believe you. I guess that's part of your dangerous charm," the star suggested.

Pet silently agreed with that assessment of Dale Kingston's character. Ruby slipped her hand out of the loose clasp of his fingers. "Gotta go walk around, Dane. You're making me neglect my guests. Be sure to introduce . . . Petra to everyone."

"I will," he replied smoothly.

Pet had the distinct impression that Ruby Gale had given him permission to escort her. It would have proved more bolstering to her self-esteem if the star had resented Dane's accompanying her. This way the woman obviously didn't regard her as representing a serious threat.

The three men introduced themselves, but Pet didn't make an effort to remember their names. Dane chatted with them a few minutes, then took Pet by the arm to wander to another group. The procedure was repeated several times, and Pet realized that Dane was doing his own brand of circulating, advertising his product and making himself known to those who were important. A necessary part of any business was socializing.

But she found it impossible to relax in his company. She could talk quite naturally with others, yet managed only a stiff nod or some stilted reply when Dane addressed a remark to her. Tension began drumming at her temples, demanding a respite from the constant strain of his presence.

A particularly garrulous guest had trapped Dane into a conversation about the merits of television programming, and Pet took the opportunity to touch his arm lightly and claim his attention.

"Excuse me, I'm going to fix my face. I'll only be a minute," she murmured as his gaze wandered over her mouth to assess the need.

Without waiting for his permission, Pet moved away. The brunette assistant or whatever she was, whom Dane had addressed as Clancy, showed her where the ladies' room was located in the suite, and Pet sank onto the strawberry velvet stool in front of the lighted mirror and gazed at her reflection.

A pair of plain gold studs gleamed on the lobes of her ears. The sides of her long hair were pulled high on the crown of her head and secured with a wide gold barrette. Her strong features were sculpted in clean lines of classical symmetry rather than prettiness. With her jade eyes, she would probably age well, Pet thought dismally.

She looked blah. Washed out. Noting the pallor of her lips, she removed the tube of gloss from her bag and outlined her mouth with the burgundy stick. She ran a comb through the ends of her hair and flipped it down the center of her back. With a sigh she accepted the fact that being athletic and naturally blond was no competition for Ruby's many charms, two of the biggest in particular.

Entering the spacious main room of the suite, she

saw Dane with a state politician, and the independent streak in her asserted itself. Instead of making her way to his side, she wandered over to the hors d'oeuvres table, sampled some caviar, which she loved, and stuffed mushroom buttons, then accepted another glass of champagne.

"Fancy party, huh?" a cynical male voice remarked to the right of her elbow.

Turning her head, Pet glanced down at a man easily three inches shorter than she was. She resisted the conditioned impulse to hunch her shoulders and stood up even straighter. The man was familiar, but it was second before she remembered he was one of the three who had been talking to Ruby Gale when she and Dane had joined them. At the time she had decided he was a reporter.

"Yes." She continued to stand straight and tall.

"Petra Wallis, isn't it?"

He remembered her name. What a thrill. "Either you have an excellent memory or else you know everyone else here," Pet replied with a wry look over the rim of her champagne glass.

"It's a combination," he admitted. "I know most of the people who are here and remembering names is part of my trade. But a man would be a fool to forget yours."

He smiled in a real way for the first time. In his late thirties, he wasn't unattractive—when he didn't have that expression of bored superiority. Plain brown hair and shrewd brown eyes went with his unassuming features. As his gaze made a thorough study of her, it didn't contain the suggestive stripping quality that he had subjected her to before. Pet didn't feel any of the initial hostility he had generated in their earlier meeting.

"I know you've probably forgotten. The name is Nick Brewster." He wasn't offended that she had.

"You're with the newspaper, right?" She wasn't sure if she had been told or if it was only a guess.

"Yeah, I'm doing a feature article on the 'Tiger Lily' for the entertainment section. I'll probably post it online in my blog, maybe syndicate it to a few other papers." He shrugged to hide the boasting tone, then studied her again. "You might've given me an idea on a different angle."

"Me?" Pet was startled.

"Yeah. See the star through the eyes of a television camera." He made an imaginary frame with his hands.

"I'm not sure that I understand what you mean." She shook her head, a little confused.

"I'd be writing it from your viewpoint," the journalist explained. "What Ruby Gale is like to work with, that kind of thing. You've seen her in rehearsal and in concert. How is she different?"

"That's easy. Before an audience she's electric. When she's rehearsing, she's concentrating on technique, delivery, the routine." Pet didn't see how that was particularly interesting or new.

"But what about her temperament? Is she easy to work with? Demanding?"

She began to see where his questions were leading. "Of course she's demanding—of herself and everyone else."

"Come on, Petra, you can tell me." The reporter gave her a trust-me look. "It's common knowledge that she can be a temperamental bitch, throwing tantrums, walking off the stage. From some of the things I've overheard, this last session hasn't been without its problems."

"Well, yeah, we've had some problems," Pet admitted. "But I haven't seen any evidence of this terrible temper you're describing."

He raised a skeptical eyebrow. "Dane must have her eating out of his hand." When Pet showed signs of becoming aloof, he chided her, "Everyone knows that the two of them are having an affair. They aren't trying to hide it, even if he did drag you here."

"I'm not going to discuss Dane Kingston's private life with you," she retorted. "I work for him."

"Such loyalty," he mocked her, his gaze sliding sideways. "It should be rewarded. But I forgot," he said as Pet turned to find Dane standing near her elbow, "this invitation to the party was by way of a reward."

"You should ask who's being rewarded, Brewster." Dane smiled pleasantly and laced his fingers through hers. "Maybe the pleasure of Petra's company is my compensation for a week of hard work and long hours."

"I wouldn't be surprised," the reporter laughed. "Some people can have their cake and eat it, too."

"Then you won't mind if I don't share. Excuse us."

Dane led Pet away. The smile faded from his expression, if it had ever really been there at all, and his dark gaze was sharp as it examined her. "I'm sorry. I hope Brewster didn't subject you to too much of his dirty digging."

"He didn't." She was curt as she pulled her hand free from him. She disliked being used as a decoy. "Not that it matters. I'm not in the habit of backstabbing, no matter what you think—and I don't really know anything about you worth sharing."

"What's that supposed to mean?" Impatience clipped his voice.

"It means that I didn't have any 'dirt' to give him." Pet refused to meet his gaze.

"He did upset you," he concluded grimly.

"He didn't," she insisted. If she was upset, it was because of the round bed with the rose canopy, Dane's insincere praise of her skill, the non-threat she was to Ruby Gale and the pointless invitation to this party. "I've been around television and news reporters before. I didn't need to be rescued."

"I can't win with you, can I?" Dane sighed. "I try to do a good deed and it doesn't work."

"Is that my fault?" Pet countered defensively.

"Hey, I'd hoped for a pleasant evening, not more bickering." The reply was underlined with tautness.

On that, Pet agreed. "Maybe we're both tired. And tense." She was thinking of more than the taping.

"Yeah, I guess so." But there was a grim reluctance in his acceptance of her explanation. "We'd better make our apologies to Ruby and leave."

Without waiting for her reply, he cupped a hand under her elbow and guided her to the corner of the room where the flame-haired woman was flirting with one of the several politicians in attendance.

"Honeybunch!" When Ruby Gale saw Dane, she must have read his intention in his face. "You're not leaving so soon?"

"We really have to," he said firmly, and shot an apologetic glance to the others for having interrupted them. Smoothly, he bent forward to kiss a blushed and powdered cheek.

"I suppose you must," Ruby sighed, and let her glittering blue eyes wander to Pet, "After all, Petra is a working girl." The tone was meant to shrivel an inferior. "Call me tomorrow, Dane, okay? But not too early."

"It probably won't be until the afternoon. I'll be busy in the morning," Dane replied.

"I enjoyed the party, Ruby," Pet said, so she wouldn't be ignored or treated as if she weren't there.

"Glad to hear it." The singer turned away a little too quickly.

Then Dane's hand was on Petra's waist, guiding her away toward the door. When the ever-hovering brunette appeared Dane dismissed her with a brisk, "We can find our own way out. Good night, Clancy."

"Good night, Mr. Kingston."

Chapter Seven

The silence between them was almost tangible, charging the air with crackling undercurrents. Not a word had been spoken since they had left Ruby Gale's hotel. Pet sat motionless in the bucket seat, an arm resting on the padded upholstery covering the door, a hand covering her mouth while she stared out of the side window of the car.

She ached inside—ached for the pleasure that could have been. The evening had been a disastrous experience. She would rather not have discovered how deeply attracted she was to Dane Kingston, how jealous she could be and how easily hurt. The one consolation was that such intensity couldn't last; it would burn itself out. She had only to wait. In the meantime it was agony to be sitting beside Dane and forcing herself to ignore him.

In an empty parking space next to the side entrance of the hotel, Dane braked the Jaguar to a stop and switched off the powerful engine. Feeling his gaze on her, Pet collected the leather handbag from her lap and reached for the door handle, but Dane was quicker, leaning over to take her wrist and discourage her escape. His arm was a strong band running diagonally across her, the sensitive nerve ends in her breast aware of the muscles beneath the silken material of his shirtsleeve.

"What's bothering you, Pet?" His voice was low and taut with command.

Her head turned away from the door to bring him into her side vision, but she didn't look at him. She was conscious of the hard cast of his features, the determined set of his jaw, and the weary lines around his mouth.

"Nothing's bothering me," she insisted in cool dismissal.

"Something is," Dane persisted, not relaxing his hold so she could open the door. "And I don't believe it had anything to do with that reporter. You were acting like this before Brewster cornered you."

"I don't know what you're talking about," Pet lied. "I'm tired, so will you please let go of my hand? I'd like to go to my room and get some rest."

For a long second she didn't think Dane was going to release her. A barrage of overwhelming sensations closed in on her. The warm air held the male scent unique to him, spiced with a whiff of his aftershave. Under his muscled arm her heart was drumming its panic, while her flesh quivered beneath his touch.

Then he set her free. She sensed the reluctance in his action, just as if he knew he could have gotten a truthful answer if he had pursued it. She was grateful he hadn't as she climbed out of the sports car. Simultaneously the door was slammed on the driver's side.

The summer night was refreshingly cool. Her face

was hot. Dane was waiting on the sidewalk to walk with her to the side entrance of the hotel, his eyes never leaving her until she was at his side. Pet held her head unnaturally high, keeping her face expressionless.

Dane made no attempt to touch her; no guiding hand touched her arm or waist as they walked. There was something aloof in the way he held the door open for her to enter the building first, but there was a smoldering look in his brown eyes.

When they reached her room door, Pet already had the keycard out of her bag but, before she could make a move to unlock the door, Dane was taking it from her hand and turning coldly to insert it in the lock. Her pulse was racing with the memory of the last time he'd done it, and the result.

At the click of the lock, Dane pushed the door open and stepped aside. The keycard was in his hand, yet he seemed hesitant to return it to her, as if he, too, was remembering the last time he'd had it. She held her breath for those few seconds. When he started to hand it to her, she knew she had to say something to him before going inside.

"Thank you for a lovely evening," she coolly recited the meaningless phrase that was intended to dismiss him.

Annoyance flashed in his eyes. "It was no fun from start to finish and we both know it."

"True enough, " Pet said sharply, reacting out of self-defense. She forgot about the keycard in her need to get inside the room and shut the door on him. Before she could succeed, his outstretched arm had stiffened to keep the door jammed open.

"I want to know why you were so unhappy," he demanded.

The hollow wood door seemed an inadequate shield against the man filling its frame and bracing it open with an arm. Yet Pet stood halfway behind it, taking advantage of whatever protection it offered. As usual, he gave the impression of contained strength.

"Maybe I don't like being patronized, Dane. Did that ever occur to you?"

"You know, it did."

She glared at him. "Then come on in and listen to me rant."

"Okay. I will. I could use an explanation."

He pushed the door shut but it didn't quite latch. Even though she'd invited him in, his stance seemed challenging. Still and all, Pet intended to confront him with all the many wounds to her pride she'd endured that night.

"For starters, I didn't appreciate those stupidly flattering things you told Ruby Gale about me," she retorted.

"What things?" He looked taken aback.

"You know very well what things!" Pet stormed. "All that stuff about how I was the best camera operator in the group! If you felt you had to defend me and rationalize my presence for her benefit, you could have simply said I was good. You didn't have to heap false praise on me!"

Her voice was choking on the last. Conscious of the bitter tears pricking her eyes, she pivoted before he noticed, intending to put distance between them, but Dane took her arm and turned her around. "That happened to be the truth."

"Oh, come on now!" Pet mocked him. "I should have recorded the cross talk." She used the term for the communication over the headsets so he wouldn't misunderstand what she was angry about. "Some of your comments were really choice!"

When she tried to walk away, Dane got in front of her. "My turn, okay? Will you listen to me?"

"I'm not interested, Dane." But she didn't have any choice. His arms were the bars trapping her between the wall and his towering frame.

"Then listen to reason," he demanded, and brought his face close to hers, his features etched with fierce determination. "You must have some idea of how much money I have wrapped up in this special. Do you think that I chose this production crew at random? Every member I personally hand-picked, because I wanted the best! And that includes you! I've reviewed everything you've done. I knew I was asking for trouble by bringing a single woman on location—a *beautiful* single woman, I might add. But trouble or not, I wanted the best. That's why you're here, so what I told Ruby wasn't a lie."

His explanation made sense, but Pet couldn't relate it to the way he'd treated her these past few days. She eyed him warily, not trusting her ability to sort fact from fiction where he was concerned. He simply had too much influence over her ability to reason.

"Is that what made you angry, Pet?" he questioned in a gentler tone as his gaze roamed over her face, then paused to linger on her mouth.

"You don't know when to stop." That was an easy shot, so she took it. "You're always saying something to irritate me."

"The next time I do," he murmured, moving closer, "Why don't you try kissing me? I guarantee it will shut me up."

Bending his head, he took her lips. Pet stood very still, inwardly shaking with the desire to put her arms around him, but she permitted her hands to go no farther than his chest, resting lightly on his shirt and feeling the heat of his body warm her palms. His mouth moved powerfully against her own, parting her lips and invading them with sensual tenderness.

A whirl of confused sensation began taking over her body, spinning a fine web of dazzling brilliance. His hands pulled her from the wall and into the support of his arms. When his mouth grazed a path across her cheek to the lobe of her ear, Pet dipped her head against his shoulder in somewhat unwilling surrender. But she clung to him . . . it felt so good.

"Why did you say those things?" she murmured, still not understanding that part. "Why did you make me think you believed I was incompetent?"

"I never intended you to think that." His voice was soft against her ear, his mouth brushing the gold stud earring. "I couldn't tolerate anything but the best from you because I knew you could give it to me. You could always give it to me."

There was the heady implication that he was referring to more than her work. His hands glided slowly over her spine to press her against his hard, lithe body. Her head was spinning as he kissed her throat and followed the wildly pulsing vein in her neck to the sensitive hollow below her ear. Then he was seeking her lips again, consuming her with his hunger. Pet struggled for some semblance of control before he undermined it completely.

"That party—" Her lips were against his cheek,

their moist softness scraped by the rough stubble of his beard, increasing their sensitivity. He kissed her again but she made him stop. "Was it a reward for doing a good job?" With each breath she inhaled the intoxicating smell of him, all too aware of its potency. "Is that why you invited me?"

"That damned party was the last place I wanted to go tonight," he muttered, lifting his head to satisfy himself that she did look kissed and aroused. "But-I had to go. It was as necessary for me to attend as it was for Ruby to give it. And I knew the crew would be whooping it up on their own. If you weren't with me, you'd be with them."

"So you were just keeping me out of trouble again." Hurt, she flattened her hands against his chest, resisting, yet aware of the heavy beat of his heart.

"I wasn't looking after you." Dane shook his head wryly. "I was looking after myself. You get to me, Pet. I thought I had a chance of enduring that insufferable chatter if you were with me, but it all went sour within minutes after we arrived, and I couldn't understand why. I thought you wanted to be with me as much as I wanted to be with you."

"Did you really?" She wanted to believe him, but she was afraid to. Her self-doubt put a troubled look in her green eyes.

"How can you even ask that?" he demanded, and suddenly covered her lips with his mouth, devouring them with sensual passion that left her breathless and dazed.

The pressure of the hand at the small of her back was fiercely possessive. She was hardly conscious of his other hand moving to stroke her hair. His fingers found the gold barrette that secured the top and sides in a single clasp at the crown. With a deft snap he unfastened it to let the silken length tumble free, and a muffled groan rippled from his throat as he tunneled his hand beneath the golden mass.

"I've wanted to do that for so long." His mouth formed the words against hers, roughly moving over her lips with uncontained urgency.

Desire flooded her mind and body, sweeping her high on a tide of emotion that was dizzying. In Dane's arms, held close to his hard shape, Pet forgot about the round bed and the rose canopy, and his ongoing affair with Ruby Gale. His dominating kiss could make her forget everything but this aching need to be possessed by him.

His shirt became a barrier, keeping her from the closeness she sought. Her eager fingers found the row of buttons and began unfastening them one by one until the buckle of his belt stopped them. Unable to resist any longer, she slid her hands inside his shirt and over his hard, flat stomach to caress his bare skin. His hand took the same license, slipping off her belt to glide under her blouse onto the bare skin of her back. When it moved to the front to enclose a firm breast in its palm, an erotic joy quivered through her.

She barely heard the loud voice singing in the hallway at first. Then she remembered. The crew guys, making merry.

"Hey, Pet!" A loud, slurring voice resembling Lon Baxter's called her name. "Wake up! You gotta come to the party!"

The first hand to pound on the unlatched door swung it open while the combination of noise and movement made them stop kissing and turn their heads. But there wasn't any way they could untangle their hands from inside each other's clothes. In cold shock, Pet stared at Lon and the handful of other crew members clustered around her door.

Dane recovered a shade more quickly than she did, withdrawing his hand from under her blouse to let it rest reassuringly on her arm. His action drew her glance, and she shuddered at the grimness in his features and the accusing silence from her co-workers.

"The door was open," someone mumbled in a lame attempt at an apology.

"Yeah," Lon agreed, swaying belligerently in the opening. "We wanted to invite you to our party, but you were having a little private one of your own, weren't you, Pet?"

The color that had receded from her cheeks came flooding back. She looked away from the door, pushing at the rumpled length of hair near her ear. Vaguely she was conscious of someone urging Lon to get the hell out of there, then Dane was letting her go to button his shirt.

"*All* the parties are over, boys," he stressed in a tired voice. "It's time we all called it a night. We have to break down the equipment and pack it all up first thing in the morning."

A few embarrassed mumbles of agreement followed his statement. The quiet shuffling of feet was a vast contrast to their exuberant arrival as the men retreated down the hallway.

"Pet?" His quiet use of her name lifted her head. Dane was near the open door, half-turned to study her.

"You'd better leave," she said. "They'll hang around to see if you go."

"I'm aware of that," he replied dryly.

Staying close to the wall, she moved to the door and wrapped her fingers on the latch to close it while keeping a distance from him. Aftershock had started her thinking about the round bed with its giant rose canopy and a red-haired woman in his arms.

"Good night." She accompanied the words with a proud toss of her head.

Frowning, Dane took a half step toward her, then stopped. "Okay. Good night."

As soon as he was in the hall, Pet closed the door and locked it. She leaned against it, her knees shaking in reaction. Across the hall she heard his door open and close, then nothing. The silence hurt.

She managed to keep her mind blank as she undressed and slipped on her nightgown. Switching off the light, she crawled under the covers of her empty bed. A few minutes earlier she wouldn't have been lying there alone, she realized, and tightly closed her eyes. The thought started a war between regret and gratitude. There wasn't a clear-cut victor by the time she fell asleep.

Firm and warm, a mouth eased itself onto her lips, gently moving over them to explore their curves. It coaxed them into a sensual pliancy, masterfully persuading a response. A masculine fragrance tingled her nose, clean, fresh and divinely heady.

What a delicious way to wake up, Pet thought as that warm mouth drifted kisses over her cheek and jaw. She arched her neck to allow access to the sensitive skin along its curve, and the mouth nibbled a slow path to the base of her throat and returned up the other side.

A soft, sensuously contented sound came from her throat, inviting that pair of masculine lips back to hers to urge a further response. Arms that had been flung above her head in sleep lifted to find the one who was causing all these wonderful sensations. Her languorous hands encountered wide, muscular shoulders encased in some smooth material that allowed her to feel the contoured outline of his hard flesh.

A forearm rested on the mattress alongside her to position him above her while his other hand caressed the bare skin near the curve of her opposite shoulder. It was all so beautiful, so enchanted—like a dream that had come to life. Dane felt so solid and real, his thick, springing hair curling around her fingers as she curved them to the back of his neck.

Gradually it dawned on her that the dream was real. It was all the better when she slowly lifted her lashes and saw that rugged face poised an inch above her own. Finding him sitting on her bed and kissing her awake was much too pleasant a surprise for Pet to be shocked. Her initial reaction was curiosity. She shifted her head on the pillow to get a better look at him, her gaze wandering to the lazy half curve of his mouth and her hands sliding from his back to his arms.

"How did you get in here?" she murmured with a flicker of a curious frown.

"I forgot to return your keycard last night. Evidently I slipped it in my pocket," he explained absently while his fingers stroked the delicate curve of her neck.

"This morning I found it when I was transferring my change from my brown pants to these."

"What time is it?" she wondered, rousing a bit from her delicious lethargy.

"Seven-thirty," Dane admitted, and bent his head to let his tongue trace the hollow of her throat.

For an instant Pet surrendered to the provocative sensation. Then his answer awakened alarm bells in her head. She shrank against the mattress to end the distraction of his caress.

"Is it that late?" Pet protested. "I have to be at the center by eight to help pack up the equipment."

"I know," he sighed, and lifted his head. "I stopped at the desk to leave your keycard. That's when I realized you'd probably forgotten to leave a wake-up call. I checked with the clerk but he wouldn't verify it, so I used the key to do it personally."

"You could have used the house phone," she pointed out impishly.

"This is much more rewarding." He was so close, his mouth brushed her lips when he spoke. "I fully intended to wake up with you this morning until we were so rudely interrupted. This is the next best thing."

Pet wished he hadn't brought that up. It reminded her of the stunned expressions on the faces of the guys when they had accidentally barged in on her and Dane. She knew it wasn't because they had caught her in the arms of a man. No, it was worse than that. She had been in the arms of their boss.

"You'd better let me up." She nudged him with her hands in a gentle reproof to move. "I still have to get dressed."

"I have a better idea," Dane murmured, settling

more firmly into place. "Instead of you getting up, why don't I climb into bed?"

"No!" Her refusal was too quick and too weak, because she had never been exposed to a sweeter temptation in her life.

"Why not?" It wasn't a question to which he expected an answer as his mouth traveled onto her lips and the probing tip of his tongue traced their outline.

His fingers slid the strap of her nightgown off her shoulders. It immediately loosened the dark lace of the gown's bodice, allowing his hand to slide inside and cup her breast. Pet breathed in blissfully. With masterful ease Dane explored and caressed its sensitive point into pebble hardness.

It took a concerted effort to turn her mouth away from his tantalizing kiss. "Dane, I have to go to work," she insisted tremulously.

"Have you forgotten?" He laughed softly against her throat, confident and male. "I'm the boss. I'm giving you the morning off."

"A special assignment?" She resented the use of his authority.

"If you want to call it that." He missed the hint of trouble in her tone. "I want you, Pet. I want to make love to you." An element of urgency entered the rough pressure of his mouth against her cheek, rubbing closer to the edge of her lips. "I'll see that you're satisfied, too—I've been told I'm a good lover. But with you, Pet, I'll be even better."

He should have known it was the wrong thing to say. With a muffled cry Pet twisted from beneath him and rolled to the opposite side of the bed from where he was seated. She came quickly to her feet, grabbing the thin cotton robe draped over the end of the bed. A dark frown of confusion clouded his face.

"Who said you were good?" Pet stormed. "Ruby Gale? While you were lying in her round bed with the giant roses and all that crazy crap?"

"What the hell are you talking about?" he demanded, coming to his feet to glare at her across the width of the bed.

She hurriedly tugged the robe on. "This hotel room doesn't come equipped with mirrors on the ceiling. You'd better find yourself another place!"

"Will you make sense?" Dane exploded.

"I am making sense!" Pet cried. "That's what makes it so . . . awful!" She choked on the last and turned away, blinking at the tears filling her eyes.

"We aren't going to start this again," he warned.

The knock on the door was a welcome interruption. "Yes? Who is it?" Her voice was strained. She quickly wiped at the trickle of tears on her cheek.

"It's me, Lon. Aren't you awake yet?"

"Damn!" she cursed softly. Of all people, why did it have to be him? Or was he checking up on her because of last night? Behind her there was a faint sound from Dane that suggested similar irritation, but Pet wouldn't turn around to look.

"Yes, I'm awake," she answered back, her voice growing steadier in its volume.

"When you didn't show up for breakfast, I thought I'd better check," Lon replied in explanation of his presence. "What did you do? Oversleep?"

"Yes," Pet admitted. "Thanks for checking."

"I've brought you some coffee."

Which meant she had to open the door. She threw

an anxious glance over her shoulder at Dane. His mouth was compressed in a tight, hard line, a resigned expression on his features. She pushed her tousled hair away from her ear and walked reluctantly to the door, holding the front of her robe shut.

Behind her, Dane made no attempt to conceal himself from view. Lon saw him standing at the end of the bed the instant she opened the door and his gaze flashed over Pet in silent condemnation.

"I should have known," he jeered.

"It isn't like that at all," Pet said in a weary voice.

"Like you, I also noticed she wasn't around," Dane inserted. "I brought her coffee, too. One cup." He lifted a Styrofoam cup to show the cameraman. "So you can get your imagination out of the gutter."

"Listen, you may be Dane Kingston, the big man around here"—Lon stabbed an angry finger in the air to make his jealous point—"but you want to crawl in bed with her the same as I do!"

Pet shivered at the cold rage that flashed across Dane's face. "I'm going to forget you said that, Baxter. Now get out!" he snapped.

"Like hell" Lon took a step forward.

"No, please." Pet half lifted a hand to stop him. "Both of you leave. Dane was just going anyway. " She cast a challenging look at Dane, her heart hammering at her ribs. The last thing she wanted was an ugly scene.

He held her gaze for a fraction of a second, then strode forward. His hard glance flicked over her as he brushed past her into the hallway occupied by Lon Baxter. There had been a promise in his look that their discussion wasn't over, merely postponed.

"I'll wait for you in the lobby, Pet," Lon stated.

She simply nodded and closed the door. Her gaze strayed to the bed and the rumpled covers. A weakness attacked her legs, but she made them support her. What had begun as a blissful awakening had ended in such turmoil that she felt torn apart.

Pet released her tense frustration in a flurry of activity, going to the closet and dragging out her faded jeans. She grabbed a soft chamois blouse as well and tossed them both on the bed.

Chapter Eight

Pet dressed in a hurry, taking time only to put on some lipgloss and tie a green scarf into a knot that gathered her hair at the nape of her neck. Leaving the room, she mentally braced herself for Lon's inquisition, but he wasn't in the lobby when she reached it.

Dane was, however, looking out a window in a relaxed stance. But when he turned to meet her, she realized he wasn't relaxed at all. He was a coiled spring, poised to unleash that contained energy.

"Where's Lon?" Pet glanced around, knowing she wouldn't find him, but the action provided her with a few seconds to readjust her defenses.

Dane's impatience showed in his dark eyes. "I imagine he's at the center by now."

"He said he'd wait for me," she reminded him.

"I changed his mind." Dane stated what she had already guessed.

"I really hope that you intend to give me a ride, otherwise I'll be without transportation to work." There was the right trace of humor in her cool voice to make it a casual remark. Her raw nerves hadn't betrayed her.

"I don't need to be reminded that you prefer work to a morning in bed with me. You've already made that clear." His smoothness held a noticeable edge. She paled a little at its steeliness. "My car is out front."

"Shall we go?" Pet walked to the door without waiting for him.

Outside, she had to wait beside the Jaguar while he unlocked it. Anger was in every controlled move he made, from the severely polite way he opened the car door for her to the deadly quiet way he shut it. She doubted that she would come away unscathed from the inevitable argument.

An unearthly silence reigned until Dane turned the car onto the main road. "What was that idiotic remark about roses and mirrored ceilings all about?" He gave her no more than a glance, his features hard and uncompromising.

Pet continued to look straight ahead. "It should be self-explanatory."

"Then I must be incredibly dense, because I can't make head or tail of it," Dane replied in a edgy voice.

"I've heard that's a problem when you sleep in a round bed. It's impossible to tell the head of the bed from the foot." Pet forced the casual response.

A muscle played along the edge of his strong jaw. "I should have known this was all tied up with Ruby." He released a heavy breath that held anger and impatience. "You're jealous of her."

"You're mistaken," she said calmly while a hot pain twisted her stomach. "I'm not interested in anything she has."

"And you think she has me?" The corners of his mouth deepened with derision.

"Haven't you heard?" Pet cast him a look of false surprise. "It's common knowledge."

"And you believe it." Dane challenged with a hard glance.

"Do you deny it?" she countered.

"I didn't think I had to." On that note, he pressed his foot on the accelerator to send the Jaguar shooting past the slower car in front of them. It was an awesome display of power and agility that Pet found somehow characteristic of him.

"I'm sure you didn't. There are probably plenty of women who would be glad to go to bed with you without caring who else you might be sleeping with, but I'm not one of them," Pet stated when the burst of speed was over.

"And what was last night? A momentary lapse of moral principles?" Dane asked.

"I didn't go to bed with you." It was a moot point but the only defense she had.

"No, but you damned well were willing to!" he reminded her. "Or are you forgetting that you were undressing me?"

Her cheeks flamed with the memory of it. "I'm trying very hard to forget that."

But Dane didn't pay attention to her tightly worded reply. "In another fifteen minutes the boys would have walked in on something much more intimate than a simple embrace."

"That's something we'll never know, because they didn't walk in fifteen minutes later," she retorted, her hands clenched tightly in her lap.

"Are you going to deny—" he began angrily.

"Physically . . . sexually, you excite me, so I'm not going to deny your ability to make me feel aroused," she interrupted, since he wouldn't believe her if she tried. "But I don't want to get involved with you. Their arrival was a mixed blessing. It saved me from making a stupid mistake."

There were two long beats of tense silence, then Dane prompted, "And? If it was a mixed blessing, there must be something you regret."

"There are two things. One, that it happened in the first place, and second, that they had to see me with you at all." She stared out the window, sitting rigidly in the seat. "I've worked so hard to get them to accept me as an equal. Now," she laughed bitterly, "I can just imagine what some of them are thinking. That I thought they weren't good enough, so I went after the boss." Just as quickly as the anger had surfaced, it vanished on a sigh. Pet brushed a limp hand over her face. "I should have had my head examined for going to that party with you last night. I was crazy to let myself in for all this."

"If you're so concerned about their opinion, you should have yelled 'Rape!' last night," he taunted.

"I wish I'd thought of it," she lied.

When they reached the turn to the center, Dane took the corner fast, the low-slung sports car hugging the curb as it whipped around it with a squeal of tires. He braked abruptly near a side entrance where men were entering and exiting to get all the gear loaded.

As Pet reached for the door handle, Dane said, "You can tell them I'm docking your pay for being late this morning. I know you won't want them to think I'm showing you any favoritism." There was a sarcastic curve to his mouth.

"Thanks." She matched his tone as she climbed out of the car and slammed the door.

She had one foot on the curb when he leaned across the seat to add, "By the way, I haven't slept with Ruby since a green-eyed blonde invited me into her room to tuck her in. So you might give me credit for some degree of fidelity." He gunned the motor before accelerating away.

Momentarily stunned, Pet couldn't get herself to move. She stared after the fast-moving car and its driver. What exactly had he said? She knew the words, but what did they mean? *No, no,* she admonished herself, *don't get your hopes up. Don't be a fool. You were right—it's just a physical thing, and the last complication you need in your life is an involvement with your boss.*

Heads turned when she entered the building. Self-conscious, she paused, aware of the hushing of voices. Squaring her shoulders, she walked to the partially dismantled studio camera at the number-two position.

"We wondered if you were going to show up for work this morning." Charlie said what was on everyone's mind, but with a teasing gentleness.

"Why not?" Pet shrugged, and hopped onto the platform. "I'm a working girl."

"But what are you working at?" Lon said softly.

She guessed that his sarcasm came from plain old jealousy that Dane had succeeded where he had failed. She understood the fragility of his male ego, but that didn't prevent her from defending herself.

"I know how it looked last night." There was a hint of pink in her cheeks, but she didn't hang her head.

"I don't blame any of you for what you thought. I'm just as much of a sucker for a good line as the next person. You're going to believe what you want to regardless of what I say, so let's just drop the subject."

"Pet's right," Andy agreed. "We've got a lot of work to do."

By the middle of the afternoon all the equipment had been packed and loaded up, and after a stop at the hotel to pick up their luggage, the production crew went out for the next location. The majority of the technicians and equipment would head for Atlantic City. Pet was among the group destined for Batsto; the outdoor segments were to be taped there.

Riding in the passenger seat of Charlie's snub-nosed van, Pet incuriously watched the Sunday traffic on the Garden State Parkway. Rick Benton, one of the soundmen, and Ted, a lighting technician, were sitting on the black fake-fur bedspread in the back, part of the skeleton crew that would be needed.

"Don't forget to watch for the exit," Charlie reminded her, not for the first time. "We'll probably get lost before we get there."

"I doubt it," Pet offered dryly.

"I'd like to know whose harebrained idea this was," he muttered. "Location shots in New Jersey of all places!"

"New Jersey is more than a place to drive through between New York and Pennsylvania." Her state pride insisted that she couldn't let that remark go unchallenged. "I know that's all most people see as they zoom through on their way someplace else. No one wants to believe we have farms, forests, lakes, marshes, and miles of beach. If they can't see it from the highway, it isn't there."

"This must have been your idea, then," Charlie declared with a laughing glance.

"Why do you think it's called the Garden State?" she retorted, ignoring his remark.

"Because it has gardens of concrete," he joked. "That's all I've ever seen. Hey!" He smiled broadly. "I just thought of something. Ruby Gale is the lily of the Garden State. That's a pretty good slogan, isn't it? Why don't you mention that to Dane?"

"Why me?" Pet stiffened because she knew precisely why. Charlie believed she was on very friendly terms with Dane. She could have been, but she wasn't going to go into a long, detailed explanation of why she wasn't anymore. "It was your idea. You tell him."

"He'd be more apt to listen to you, wouldn't he?" Charlie probed for information.

"I seriously doubt it," she replied indifferently.

At that moment a midnight-blue Jaguar swept past them. Her heart did a somersault at the sight of the familiar car. It was highly unlikely that there would be two identical cars on the road. When she saw Ruby Gale's red head in the passenger seat, she knew she hadn't made a mistake about the car's owner.

"That was Ruby Gale, wasn't it?" Charlie frowned.

"Yes, with Dane," she added briskly, and sent him a cool look. "Do you still think he would listen to me?"

Charlie took one look at her strained face and let the conversation die a natural death. Confusion tore at Pet. Dane had indicated that his interest in Ruby Gale had waned since meeting her. But Ruby had been riding with him. Was it because of the television special—purely business? Or, because Pet herself had turned him down, had Dane turned to Ruby again?

Why were the answers so important? Her heart was becoming involved, that was why, a little voice warned. Pet sighed dejectedly and gazed out the window. The Jaguar was far out of sight. She grabbed a brochure someone had left in the van and read it to distract herself.

> Located on the fringes of Wharton State Forest, Batsto Village is a restored Revolutionary War town. Growing up around an early bog-iron furnace, it was a major supplier of munitions to the colonists. There are tours of old houses, coach rides and demonstrations of an operating water-powered sawmill. Weekend fare also includes craft displays and flea markets. The picturesque colonial town sits on the bank of the Batsto River with shaded streets and the verdant backdrop of the forest.

She put it down. There was no work to be done on their arrival. All the location shots would be set up the following morning, which left Pet and the small crew free to wander through the village on the late and lazy summer afternoon.

Pet would have been content to stroll along the streets and browse through the curio shops, but the men would be bored fast with such passive entertainment. Someone produced a Frisbee, and before Pet knew what was happening, she was engaged in a lively game of catch in a park square. It was boisterous fun, leaping high to catch the soaring disk and trying difficult catches behind the back or under the leg. It was exactly the kind of distraction her tense nerves needed.

The Frisbee came sailing in her direction, but just as she got set to catch it, the wind caught it to change its trajectory. The disk drifted backward, and Pet realized at the last minute that it was going to be high and to her right. She turned to make a diving leap for it and rammed right into a solid object.

Her height and weight staggered Dane backward, but she managed to keep them both upright. Pet wasn't sure if it was the impact or the shock of finding herself in his arms that stole the breath from her lungs. She stayed there, unable to breathe for several seconds while her fingers were spread across his chest and her head was thrown back as she stared into his vitally male face.

Her hair had long ago escaped the confining knot of the scarf and was a windblown mass of gold. Dane's hands were on her waist, holding her hips against the support of his. Desire flamed through her when his gaze drifted down to linger on her mouth.

Her lips parted, wanting his kiss, inviting it, and there was an answering tightness in the grip of his hands to let her know the message had been received and understood.

"You really should watch where you're going," a musically female voice chided.

Pet's startled eyes clashed with a pair of vivid blue ones that studied her with a calculating coldness. The sight of Ruby Gale standing near Dane brought her quickly to her senses. Pet pushed out of his hold, nervously brushing her palms over the terrycloth material of her shorts, the blue jeans abandoned earlier in the day in favor of something cooler.

"Excuse me," she apologized to Dane on a breathless note.

"No harm done," he assured her.

"Hey, Pet! Are you going to get the Frisbee or not?" Charlie shouted from across the way.

Glancing around, Pet saw that it had landed a few feet behind Dane. Before she could retrieve it, Dane was there bending, over to pick it up. His gaze raked her as he straightened. She was conscious of the sweat shining wetly on the skin of her neck, beads gathering in the hollows of her collar bone to start a trickle running down between her breasts. The thin cotton knit of her tank top was clinging to her damp skin. Dane made her aware of just how revealing it was before he returned the Frisbee.

"Thank you," she murmured awkwardly, and turned away. He couldn't know how much he had contributed to the color in her hotly flushed cheeks.

Taking a few quick steps, she sailed the Frisbee back to Charlie with a flick of her wrist. But it took a nosedive short of its target, and a shirtless Charlie came trotting forward to retrieve it.

"You're welcome to join us if you like, Miss Gale," Charlie invited, puffing slightly behind his wide grin.

"No, thank you," the redhead refused, making a face at the mere thought. She sent a coy glance at Dane and slipped a hand under his arm. "Dane would hate it if I looked as hot and dirty as she does," she declared with a pointed glance at Pet.

Pet had been conscious of her appearance before, but that remark made her doubly uncomfortable. Which was just what the star wanted. Ruby looked as if she had just stepped out of an advertisement for teenage couture in her snow-white skirt and candy-pink blouse. She was a little old to get away with it, Pet thought uncharitably.

Rather than stay, Pet decided to switch with one of the others. "Let me have the shady side for a while, Rick." If she looked like a mess, there wasn't any point in quitting. Besides, she didn't want to give Ruby Gale the satisfaction of knowing she made her feel self-conscious and unattractive.

After she had traded places with the soundman, she saw Dane and Ruby strolling away arm in arm. It hurt, really hurt, because she wanted to be the one walking with Dane. If she had stayed in bed, it was entirely possible she could have been. She shook her head to rid it of that tantalizing thought.

Monday morning meant a return to the work schedule, rising early to get the equipment ready and the outdoor shots set up. The weather cooperated with a clear sunny day, a warm temperature and hardly any breeze to muss the star's coiffure.

There was no need for headsets or lights. The smaller and lighter weight handheld camera took the place of the fixed studio models, although it meant a helper was needed to carry the recorder. Someone was walking through Ruby's positions so it could be decided where the shiny reflectors were needed to alleviate facial shadows.

Dane had already explained the setup to Pet in crisp, strictly businesslike tones. She was strapping on the battery packs that powered the camera and the shoulder pad to cushion its weight. The equipment had all been tested to make sure it was working properly. Now they were waiting for Ruby Gale to emerge from the motor home that served for her private dressing room. Pet cast another glance in its direction, acutely aware that Dane was with the red-haired entertainer.

When they came out together, she quickly veiled her glance. But she noticed his arm affectionately around the woman's shoulders, the warmth and charm in his look, and the easy way he responded to Ruby's provocative glances. He was going over the precise sequence of this taping and reiterating the effect he planned to achieve.

Pet hoisted the camera onto her shoulder and adjusted it to a relatively comfortable position. While Dane walked Ruby to her starting point, Pet began lining up her opening frame. Her long hair was swept on top of her head, secured on the sides with combs and on top with a leather hair clasp. With it loose there was too much risk of catching a strand on a part of the camera or between the pad and her shoulder, which often resulted in a sudden and painful yank on her scalp when she moved or altered position.

Dane's gaze made an absent inspection of her hairstyle as he approached her, but it was the only recognition of her that he made. His rugged features were impassive, all his attention focused on the business at hand. Damn him. The fluttering of her pulse revealed that she was far from calm.

"Ready, Pet?" His gaze centered on her for a piercing second, long enough to see her positive nod. When he turned away, he gave Ruby a big smile. "We can begin whenever you say, Ruby."

If he had wanted to make the difference in his attitude toward the two women any clearer, he had succeeded. Pet felt almost chilled by his lack of interest.

Instead of being enchanted by the warmth Dane had shown the star, Ruby Gale appeared anything but pleased.

"What's *she* doing here?" she demanded, and pointed a scarlet fingernail at Pet.

"She's operating the camera, of course," Dane smiled.

"How can I possibly flirt with the camera the way you want when I'm looking at her?" Ruby protested with an angry gesture of her hands.

"Flirt with the lens, girl, and think of the men in the audience that will ultimately be watching you," he replied easily, using that smile again.

But Ruby wasn't easy to persuade. "That's impossible! I want a man on that camera. Get rid of her!" She flung an impatient wave in Pet's direction. "I want her off the set."

"Ruby, you aren't being reasonable." Dane moved toward the star.

"Do you want to know how unreasonable I can be?" the redhead flashed, exhibiting the temper Pet had heard so much about. "Either she goes or I do. Take your pick, Dane. You can't have us both."

There was silence all around. The ultimatum seemed to have a dual meaning. Pet was well aware which one would go even before she heard the low chuckle from Dane.

"Ruby, I'm not arguing with you," he insisted calmly, amused by her outburst. "There's no need to make an issue of it. If you're more comfortable with someone else operating the camera, then I'll just replace Petra. As sexy as you are when you're angry, I think you should conserve all that volatile energy for your performance."

Ruby Gale was instantly and provocatively contrite. "Honey, I'm sorry for making a horrible scene. Will you forgive me?"

"Naturally I forgive you." He bent to brush a kiss across her cheek and turned to dismiss Pet. "Sutton will handle the camera today, Petra. We won't need you."

"Okay." Her voice was barely above a whisper as she acknowledged his order. As she shifted the camera off her shoulder to set it on the ground, Charlie moved over to help her. His eyebrows were raised in a sympathetic look. She managed a grim smile and a supposedly uncaring shrug, then began unstrapping the bulky packs from around her waist.

"It will take us a few minutes to switch the equipment," Dane explained to Ruby. "Why don't you relax and have another cup of coffee while you're waiting? There's no need for you to stand around."

"Are you sure you don't mind, Dane, about using a camera *man*?" the redhead persisted. "I'd hate to think I was interfering with your job."

"If I thought she was irreplaceable, I would argue with you. So don't think that you've upset me," he assured her.

As soon as Pet had removed all the gear and given it to Charlie, she slipped self-consciously away from the location set. She was aware that Dane had observed her departure without comment. By getting rid of her, he'd averted a scene and a possible delay. It had been the sensible thing to do, she knew that, but it did hurt. In fact, it stung like hell.

Chapter Nine

Sitting beneath the shade of a tree with the trunk for a backrest, Pet set the paperback book aside. It didn't hold her interest, or else she wasn't concentrating. She sighed and plucked a long blade of grass to twirl it between her fingers. Eyeing the sun, she wondered if its lengthening shadows had called a halt to the day's shooting yet. In a little while she would wander over to Charlie's van and wait, but it was cooler here and more peaceful, although her surroundings didn't seem to soothe her.

A bird flitted in the branches overhead. Drawing her knees up, she pulled the blade of grass apart and discarded the pieces. It was worse having nothing to do. Finally she pushed to her feet and absently dusted the seat of her pants. The soft rustle of footsteps on the grass turned her head toward the sound.

A breath stopped in her throat. Dane was walking toward her. His gaze never ceased its study of her while he approached, gauging her reaction to his arrival. Pet knew her eyes could be much too expressive, so she made a casual move to pick up her book.

"Hey, Dane. Finished for the day?" She was able to ask the question without having to look at him.

"We wrapped it up about twenty minutes ago. Too many shadows, even with digital equipment." He leaned a hand on the rough bark of the tree trunk and let his gaze roam the surroundings. "It's peaceful here."

"Yes," she agreed. Her glance slid away before it actually met his. "Charlie will be waiting for me, I guess."

"He was packing the equipment up when I left. I told him I'd find you and send you along to his van." Dane continued to study her with disconcerting directness.

"He'd probably like some help. I'd better go." But she didn't want to leave.

"Pet, about this morning, it wasn't by choice that I ordered you off the set." His dark eyes were grave as they searched her face, waiting for her response.

"I know." She looked across the green grass to the village center, liking its quaintness. "You did it because you had to keep Ruby happy for the sake of the production."

"Yes." He reached out to take hold of her forearm and force her to look at him. "But who's going to keep *me* happy? Will you?"

Unable to answer, Pet could only gaze into the masculine face, loving his angular features. But the longing to be the one who could keep him happy was written in her jade eyes. She heard his sharply indrawn breath, then his mouth was coming down over hers.

His arm hooked her waist to haul her against his length. The contact with the muscular columns of his thighs and hard flatness of his stomach made her

weak. Her hands clutched his waist, hanging on while
the world spun at a dizzying speed. Nothing seemed
to exist as her mouth opened under his, passionately
returning the hungry kiss. Then his hand moved
onto her breast, circling it, cupping it, flattening it,
and fighting the restriction of her blouse. When she
felt his fingers tugging at the buttons, she returned to
her senses a little and pulled breathlessly away, half
wriggling out of his arms while she had the strength.

"Don't!" There was a catch in her voice, a deep,
tearing desire interfering with the protest.

"Don't what?" Dane yanked her around, keeping
her in his strong grip while his ardent gaze roamed
over her. "Don't touch you! Don't hold you! Don't kiss
you! Don't what? Don't want you? That's impossible!"
he raged in a low voice. "I've tried. I've tried it all—
working till all hours of the night, cold showers, and
beating myself up for getting mixed up with someone
who works for me! It hasn't changed a damned thing.
Dealing with Ruby is a nightmare when I want you."

Pet was shaken by the ferocity of his emotional response. This intensity was more than she had bar-
gained for. She didn't know how to cope with it, any
more than she knew how to handle her own abandonment of common sense.

"That's over, Pet," he said at last. "It was over long
ago."

When he slackened his hold, she didn't try to escape
him. There was no resistance as his hands moved to
her hair to release it from the confinement of the
combs and leather clasp. His fingers slipped through
its length and gathered it into silken handfuls.

"You have beautiful hair, Pet," he groaned, and
rubbed his mouth across her cheekbone, drawing

closer to her lips. His breath was warm and moist, caressing on its own. "I keep seeing it this way—the way it was yesterday morning, like a cloud on your pillow. I never should have used that keycard," he sighed. "Or else I should have thrown Baxter out."

"Why didn't you tell me you weren't . . . involved with Ruby anymore?" Her voice throbbed as her arms curved around his middle.

"Why didn't you ask me?" Dane countered. "God, I thought I'd made it obvious. Do you actually believe I would invite another woman to a party given by my girlfriend if she and I were still lovers?"

"You . . . you could have been having your cake and eating it, too." Pet recalled the phrase the reporter had used. It had sounded so plausible at the time.

"I could have." He held her hair and kept her face turned to his, keeping the emotional connection between them. His gaze seemed to go deep into her. "But I'm not the type. What are you doubting now? I can see it in your soulful eyes."

"I was just wondering how you knew about the rose canopy above her bed," Pet admitted, because the question would plague her until she knew. "You said you hadn't slept with her lately, but—"

"I haven't." Irritation put a harsh edge on his voice. "All entertainers are big babies and they have to be babied. She happens to like going over new arrangements while sitting in bed. In order to have a discussion of them, it seems logical to join her on the bed. I suppose I could have pulled a chair up, but I don't happen to be bashful or easily embarrassed."

"But you and she were lovers."

"Yes, we were lovers, for the lack of a better term."

His scowl revealed his dislike of Pet's continued pursuit of the subject. "Did you expect me to be a virgin?"

Pet attempted a negative shake of her head, and succeeded as much as his grip on her hair would allow. "I just wondered if you were always so quick to dump a woman once you grew tired of her." Because she wasn't sure how well she would take it if he dropped her as quickly as he had seemed to abandon Ruby Gale. "Everyone still believes the two of you are having an affair," she reminded him when she saw the darkening anger in his eyes. "You act like it when you're together."

"As you pointed out earlier, I have to keep her happy. Dammit, Pet," he muttered in exasperation, "you know how costly delays can be. No other producer would touch Ruby with a ten-foot pole. Her reputation for walking off a production and demanding endless changes has thrown a hundred budgets out the window. A television special with her can be a gold mine if it doesn't cost you two gold mines to get it. I'm walking a tightrope with her. Why do you think I'm personally handling this project?"

"How far would you go to keep her happy, Dane?" Pet hated herself for asking, because it wasn't fair. She had no right to ask that kind of question.

"Do you have to ask?" He stared at her, an incredulous frown narrowing his gaze.

"Dane, I'm not sure about anything," Pet whispered. "I'm unsure of how I feel, what I think, what I do. Every ounce of sense I have tells me I shouldn't want you, but I do."

With a muffled groan he pulled her forward against the hard warmth of his mouth. The hand at the nape of her neck began stroking it softly and sensuously, sending shivers tingling down her spine. A faint, hungry sound rolled from her throat as she arched against him, surrendering to the wild joy that flamed from his embrace.

When she wound her arms around his neck, his mouth parted in an irresistible invitation to deepen the kiss, and Pet accepted it eagerly. In direct response, his hand curved around on her hip, shaping her more firmly to him to give her potent evidence of his need, and she trembled uncontrollably.

Abruptly Dane dragged his mouth from hers, the hand at the back of her head applying pressure to bury her face against his neck while shudders racked his torso. She could feel the hard, uneven thud of his heart. The rate of her own pulse would have rivaled the speed of his car. Happiness was such a fragile thing. Her eyes filled with unshed tears. How could she ever contemplate denying this ecstasy that she was a kiss away from discovering?

Her hands spread across the broad muscles of his back to hold him closer while her lips began exploring his throat, savoring the taste of his skin and absorbing the heat of his flesh. In a slow, roundabout way she reached his ear, her tongue delighting in the shape of it. A raw sound of desire came from his throat before he turned his head to stop the arousing caress, his mouth rough against her cheek and his breathing heavy.

"Don't," he ordered in a low, thickened voice.

"Don't what?" she whispered, and teased him with his words while her fingertips sensuously traced the strong column of his neck. "Don't want you? Don't kiss you? Don't—"

He silenced her with a wildly passionate kiss. Then

he growled against her skin, "Half the time I never know whether you even want me to kiss you!"

"Right now I do," Pet murmured, careless of the provocation in her reply. The world had stopped its frenzied spinning, but she was still giddy.

His hands firmly created a space between them, the support of his hard length denied her as he held her a few inches away. Her gaze ran warmly over the rough planes of his essentially male features, aware of the determined set of his mouth.

"We've got to come to an understanding," he insisted, "These next few days aren't going to be easy." Under his breath he added, "And that's an understatement!" Then he turned his hard gaze away from her for an instant.

"I think you could be right," Pet sighed, because it was hard staying out of his arms. It was always like that when she was near him.

"I know I am. Pet"—he spoke more softly—"I have to leave now for Atlantic City. There are a few details I have to iron out with the management at the casino. Then I have to be back here for the taping tomorrow. We aren't going to have any time to be together."

"I see." She didn't ask if she could go with him. If Dane had wanted her along, he would have invited her. He had to know she would accept.

"I still have a company to run, so my schedule is going to be like this until this damned special is done," he said, revealing his impatience with the circumstances, which offered some consolation. "I want you to understand that isn't the way I want it. I don't want you getting any crazy notions in your head that because I'm not with you, I don't want to be. No more of that imagination of yours working overtime about her bed of roses, and being patronized, or whatever ridiculous molehill you can make into a mountain."

"No more." Pet shook her head in promise.

"There's another thing you'd better know. I don't give a damn what the crew thinks about us. You can keep on trying to be one of the boys if you want. But if I get a chance to touch you or kiss you, you don't have to scoot away from me because one of them might be watching," Dane warned. "I'll be discreet. There won't be any passionate clinches in front of them, but I'm not going to guard my every look and action. If they want to accuse you of receiving special treatment, you can tell them for me that you damn well *are* special! Any objections?"

"None. Half of them think we've already slept together anyway," she admitted, a little thrilled by his possessiveness.

"I wish we had. Maybe I wouldn't be so twisted up inside." His gaze raked her, smoldering with the frustration of unsatisfied desire. Pet saw the effort he was making to get a grip on himself and bank the fires that burned in his eyes. "Okay. Getting back to Ruby."

"Dane, I—" Pet began.

"Listen to me," he insisted. "She has to be the center of attention all the time. She won't share the spotlight with anyone. So when I'm around her, it's going to seem like I'm totally indifferent to you. You saw what happened this morning the second she suspected my attention wasn't wholly devoted to her. She immediately made a scene. It doesn't matter to Ruby whether the attention she receives is genuine or not, just so long as she can command it. Now I'm going to repeat myself. Until this taping is wrapped up, she will *seem* to have my undivided attention. Do you accept that?"

"Yes," she nodded, beginning to understand Ruby's spoiled and self-centered temperament a little better. Pet didn't have to like it, but she did have to understand. At least she knew why Dane had been so incredibly attentive to Ruby.

"You know she isn't going to let you work at the taping tomorrow." Dane eyed her with grim resignation. "She's going to keep you off the studio cameras at the casino, too, which means you'll be working the handheld, providing she doesn't demand that you leave the production altogether."

"Maybe it would be best if I did. I don't want to cause problems. You can get someone to replace me," she suggested. "I can go back—"

"No." He rejected that idea out of hand. "You aren't going back, not even if I have to replace you. You're going to stay with the crew. You aren't going back until we all go home. I know I'll be working all the time and maybe I'll only get to see you five—ten minutes, half an hour at a time. But I'll know you're there and if I get the chance to be with you, I will."

Keeping her at a distance, he kissed her, his mouth clinging to her lips for a sensual instant before he lifted his head. The ache of longing made his expression bleak. Pet wanted to smooth away the hardness in his face with her hand, but he wouldn't let her touch him, as if not trusting his reaction.

"You said before that you were unsure," Dane said tightly. "Maybe you can appreciate the way I feel. The times I've been with you haven't been among my more rational moments. It's like being trapped between two battling weather fronts—one hot and the other cold. I never know which it's going to be with you."

"You pick a lot of the fights yourself." Pet wasn't about to accept full responsibility for their arguments. He had been at fault too. "You shouldn't say things you know will irritate me."

"Maybe I have." He granted that it was possible without admitting it, which peeved her a little. "But from now on, understand the pressure I'm under. If I'm sharp with you, be tolerant . . . at least until this taping is done. I'd sell my soul to have it finished right now." Then Dane laughed, a wry sound. "Some say I made a pact with the devil when I signed the contract with Ruby."

"Don't laugh!" A sudden pain brought a quick frown to her forehead. "It isn't funny."

Dane stared at her, his eyes narrowing. "I don't want to know what you're thinking right now. I haven't got time to correct whatever's going on in that mind of yours." He raised an arm to glance at his watch. "I'm already five minutes late. Ruby will be wondering where I am."

"Ruby?" Pet stiffened. "I thought you said you were driving to Atlantic City."

"I am," he said tightly, and released her.

"She's going with you." Her voice sounded flat, even to her.

"Yes, she's going with me. She wants to check on the dressing rooms backstage. God help us if they aren't up to her standards," Dane grumbled, and irritatedly ran a hand over his hair.

"I'm sure you'll make it right, Dane." Pet managed a smile, an attempt at reassurance, yet the words had an ominous ring to them.

"I have to leave," he said as if needing to impress her with the inevitability of it.

"I know. Go ahead." This time she really worked at the smile and it felt more natural. "Tell Charlie I'll be along in a minute. I just have to gather up my things." The combs and the hair holder were still scattered on the ground, as well as her handbag and the book she'd been trying to read.

Dane took a step away. "I probably won't see you until tomorrow."

"Drive carefully." A sarcastic little voice wanted to add a few last words. *The star of the show will be riding with you and nothing can happen to her.* But Pet didn't let that voice speak.

Although Pet wasn't present during the next morning's taping, she gathered from what Charlie had hinted at lunch that it wasn't going well. Ruby Gale was being difficult and demanding, and Dane wasn't satisfied with the results they were getting. Only the crew knew of his displeasure, from what Pet could tell. Not a shadow of blame was ever cast on the star.

Professional curiosity got the better of her. Bored, with nothing else to do, she wandered over to the mobile television unit parked some distance from the shooting site. The snub-nosed van was no bigger than Charlie's. She tried the door and found it was unlocked. Even though the van was parked in the shade, it was stuffy and hot inside. She left the sliding door open to let the fresh air in.

The interior was equipped with a monitor and a small plasma TV, both hooked up to a CD player, among other goodies. Those interested Pet the most, along with the CDs she found on top of the player. Charlie's handwriting on the shiny discs identified what was on them as part of this location's taping. She slid them into the player and adjusted the monitor screen, sitting back on the little stool to see what had been taped and what might be wrong with it.

Twice she played them through, nagged by something she knew wasn't right yet unable to fault the performer or the cameraman. The lighting was perfect and so was the background. She took the discs out and examined them for scratches or sticky spots. Nothing. Sliding a CD in for the third time, she kept asking herself how they could be improved.

Halfway through watching it, Pet got an idea. She stopped the disc, backed up for a few sequences and studied it again. In her mind she made the changes and additions, and checked them mentally to see if they would work. The elation grew with each passing second.

"No one's allowed in there!" Dane snapped the order before he saw it was Pet inside the van. "Hey, what are you doing?"

"I know what's wrong!" She stopped the CD player and looked at him eagerly.

"You know what's wrong, do you?" he mocked. "What's wrong is you haven't kissed me hello."

"I was talking about the rough cut on these CDs." But she quickly brushed her lips across his mouth and grabbed hold of the hand that reached out for her. She pulled him inside, too excited by her discovery to be put off by his impatient look.

"What about it? There weren't any problems with the taping." He crouched to keep from bumping his head on the van's low ceiling.

"Charlie mentioned at lunch that you weren't pleased with what you had, but you couldn't find anything wrong with it. I got curious, and since I didn't have anything to do anyway—"

"You decided to snoop," he concluded.

"It isn't snooping," she protested. "I work on the production, too. There's nothing wrong with wanting to see the results." She was kneeled in front of the CD player, tapping the eject button to take out the one that was in it and put in the one with the scene she thought needed work.

"I've looked at them fifty times. I'm taking what we've got, Pet. Let's not waste time looking at them again." Dane slid his hand across her stomach to circle her waist and attempt to draw her back to where he was sitting on the stool.

She pushed his hand away. "But I know how you can improve it." She looked at the monitor, listening to the faint whirring of the CD player, which could be cranky about booting up discs when they were changed too fast.

"I happen to be an experienced director. Are you trying to tell me how to do my job?" There was a thin thread of exasperation in his incredulous question.

"Give me a break. And skip the manly pride for now." Pet flashed him an irritated glance. "You could listen and give me a chance to explain my idea."

"I'll listen." He sat back on the stool, folding his arms in front of him and looking anything but open-minded.

"You could give me credit for knowing a little about what I'm talking about, instead of acting so damned superior," she retorted.

His mouth twitched. "Didn't I tell you once how to shut me up if I was making you angry?"

"The problem is that you've made me too angry to do it. If I kissed you, you'd like it, then it wouldn't be a punishment," Pet reasoned. At least it qualified as reasoning when she was pissed off. Which she was.

Scambling on her knees, she turned to watch the screen, which put her back to Dane. His hands closed firmly on her shoulders to draw her back to rest against his legs. Lifting the weight of her hair, he gently draped it over her shoulder.

"Then sit next to me. I won't do anything and it will serve me right," he gently mocked. When she turned her head to look up at him, regret for her sharpness flashing in her green eyes, his finger touched her chin and moved her face toward the screen. "Show me what you found."

"You were experimenting with camera angles," she began as the first take was being played, minus the sound since it hadn't been mixed and added. "But it's the elevation that's wrong."

"The elevation?" By his tone she could tell that it hadn't occurred to him and his mind was racing the same way hers had.

"Yes. Charlie should be up high and shooting down—up about five feet, I would say. Maybe smear some gel around the circumference of the lens so the outer edges of the picture will be in a kind of dreamy focus. And here"—she drew attention to the particular sequence—"where Ruby does that half turn to the right, Charlie should make a half turn to the left, sort of a sweeping arc with the camera to give that illusion," she explained with growing enthusiasm. "It's tricky, but you could use some sort of ladder or scaffolding."

"I wonder where I can get a crane," Dane mused.

"That would be best, but there's the time factor, and the delay it would entail. I think you can rig something up—Charlie's good at that kind of thing. And here"—another part came up that she had an idea for—"the camera could swing a little bit in tempo with the music."

Turning, she found Dane was leaning forward to watch another take, visualizing her ideas in place of the ones that had been used. His expression was a study of concentration and inward reflection. She nibbled at her lip, anxious for his reaction and certain it had to be positive.

But there was only silence that lasted through two more takes. Unable to wait any longer, Pet unconsciously swayed against him and laid a hand on his thigh, her fingers just brushing the hard flesh. She immediately had his full attention. "What do you think?" she asked.

"I think you pick the damnedest times to touch me." His eyes glinted with a wicked, dancing light before directing a glance out the open door to a crew member approaching the van. "And I think you do it deliberately." His hand closed warmly over hers and moved it to a more discreet location near his knee.

A hot wave of color flooded her cheeks, but he wouldn't let her look away from him, holding her gaze with some invisible thread. Pet was jolted by the intimacy of the moment—an intimacy that didn't rely on a kiss or a caress, but could be accomplished with a look.

"In answer to your question, you've come up with the solution," Dane admitted. "But I doubt we can get that pirouette shot unless Charlie is directly above her."

"We're all set up for the next number, Dane," Rick announced, pausing at the open door of the van. "Are you coming? I'll bring the new gizmo Charlie wanted. The camera stabilizer."

"I'll be there in a minute." He opened the storage cabinet to take out a small device that could have been anything. "Here." He tossed it to the man, then began to maneuver himself out of the cramped quarters of the van.

Pet followed him out, hopping the last foot to the ground, a hand on the door frame for balance. "Do you admit that I did know what I was talking about?" she asked, her green eyes sparkling with challenge.

Dane paused, looking at her with dry amusement. "I admit it. Now why don't you suggest how I'm going to convince Princess Ruby to do that number again without arousing her imperial temper?"

"Keeping her happy is strictly your department," she retorted, conscious that Rick was dawdling on his way back to the location, remaining within sight of them.

Dane was aware of him, too. His hand stroked her hair, then traced the clean line of her jaw to her chin, where his fingers outlined her lips. The sensual caress started her trembling.

"Aren't you sorry you didn't kiss me when you had the chance?" He tapped the end of her nose with a finger, an affectionate reprimand for her stubbornness. Without waiting for a reply, he walked after Rick.

Pet sighed.

Chapter Ten

The constant din of electronic beeps and buzzes floating through the casino was hypnotic, but an occasional explosion of joyful noise when someone got lucky cut through it. At the tables, the voices of the gamblers and dealers seemed almost muted in comparison to the surround-sound effect of the slots. Pet followed Charlie as he elbowed his way through the crowd of guests eager to part with their money. Coins clattered into a metal tray and a woman shouted excitedly to her husband.

"It's really something, isn't it?" Charlie shook his head, casting a disapproving look around.

Pet laughed at his seeming disdain. "Five minutes after you put your things in your room, you'll be down here and you know it!"

He grinned suddenly and let his hand find her elbow where the crowd thinned, enabling them to walk together. "Don't tell Sandy. She'll have my hide," he said, referring to his wife.

"I won't," she promised.

"I'm hoping she'll be so glad to see me that she

won't even know I'm not as rich as when I left. Rich being a relative term." He pushed the up arrow on the elevator. "I need some relaxation after these last three days. I thought Ruby was going to make the whole hotel collapse with that screaming fit she threw when Dane told her we were going to reshoot that first segment. That was a terrific idea you had, Pet. It worked like a charm once Kingston talked her into it."

"I saw the tapes. I'd have to say they looked great." She didn't comment on the star's outrage over being asked to do the number again. Nor did she want to know too much about Dane's role in changing Ruby's mind.

"What are you going to do after you get settled?" Charlie stepped aside when the elevator doors opened, and let Pet walk in ahead of him.

"Shower, then probably grab a sandwich." She supposed Dane would be busy that evening. She had seen practically nothing of him the past two days.

"I'm hungry, too. We could eat together, if you want. It would keep my money in my pockets a little while longer." He grinned, and pushed the floor number for his room. "What floor for you?"

"The next one." One floor above him—Dane's travel arrangements always kept her apart from the male members of the crew.

"The place was probably too crowded for all of us to be together," Charlie offered his own explanation. "I'm surprised we're even booked into the same hotel, especially since it has a casino."

"Dane probably didn't want to provide us with any excuses for being late," she shrugged.

"How about that sandwich?"

"Sure, Charlie, we can eat together." It was better than eating alone. "Where do you want to meet?"

The elevator stopped at his floor. "Why don't I just swing by your room in half an hour?" he suggested. "It'll be easier than trying to find each other in that madhouse downstairs."

"Okay, but make it forty-five minutes. I want to wash my hair," Pet explained hurriedly, and he waved an acknowledgement before the elevator doors closed.

At the next floor Pet got off the elevator and found her room. She heard a phone ringing as she set her weekender bag down to unlock the door. Pet dipped her keycard in the slot, sure that the caller was Dane, but she wasn't quick enough. The phone was silent when she stepped into the room. She wasn't even sure if it had been her phone that was ringing. She did know it wasn't her cell.

Opening her suitcase, she shook out the uncrush-able dress she had brought with her, the only one, and laid it on the bed. The taupe and beige dress was simple almost to the point of plainness, with button-tab roll-up sleeves, deep side pockets and a tie belt. After more than a week of tops and jeans, it would be kinda fun to wear a dress, Pet decided.

She unpacked her makeup and shampoo from her cosmetic case and carried them into the bathroom. Forty-five minutes wasn't much time to shower, dry her hair and dress, so she left the rest of her things to unpack later, stripped and stepped into the shower.

Her hair was lathered with shampoo when she re-alized the phone was ringing, the sound muffled by the running water of the shower. Grabbing a towel, she made a quick dash for the phone in the bedroom, leaving a trail of water and shampoo bubbles on the carpet. It stopped ringing as she reached it. She waited a few dripping seconds before returning to the shower to rinse her hair.

It happened again when she was drying her hair with the blow dryer, the hum of the dryer blocking out the ring of the phone. Again the caller hung up before Pet reached the phone. If it was Dane, she was becoming thoroughly frustrated. She returned to the bathroom and finished drying her hair, shutting the dryer off every few minutes to listen for the phone. Only it didn't ring again.

Not until she was brushing her teeth.

With a mouthful of toothpaste she ran into the bedroom and stubbed her toe on the end of the bed, yelping at the shaft of pain that stabbed her injured toe. She hopped the last six steps to the phone. This time she heard the line click dead before she could get the receiver to her ear.

"Damn you, Dane Kingston," she cursed tearfully, then noticed the clock. It could have been Charlie, checking to see if she was ready early, she realized.

The thought made her speed up some. Five minutes before she was supposed to be ready, she buckled the strap of her beige sandals and reached for the tie belt to knot it around her waist. At the knock on her door, she glanced at the phone. She would positively scream if Dane called her after she had gone. But how would she know if she wasn't there?

The knock sounded more impatient. Sighing, she walked to the door while making the first loop in the knot of her belt. She was adjusting the trailing ends to hang smoothly down her side as she opened the door.

"Where the hell have you been?" Dane demanded,

striding inside the room and slamming the door shut. "I've been trying to reach you for the last forty-five minutes!"

Pet's surprise at the way he was dressed—evening suit and tie—turned to indignation at his demanding tone.

"But—"

"I've called three times without an answer. The desk verified that you checked in more than a half hour ago. I finally called Charlie to find out where the hell you were and he told me you were on your way up here when he left you. Why didn't you answer the phone?"

"Why didn't you let the damned thing ring long enough to let the room voicemail pick up? You didn't give me a chance," she hurled back at him with equal heat. "The first time I was just walking into the room. Then I was in the shower. And then I stubbed my toe trying to get in here because I knew it was you! How dare you yell at me, you pigheaded—"

"No." The one low word cut across her retort. He wasn't in a mood to concede. "We aren't going to have another shouting match, not this time. I've waited too long."

Seizing her shoulders, he got her against his lean, hard length. Pet struggled, resisting the temptation of the sensual mouth so close to hers, but not very effectively. She couldn't escape and she wasn't sure she wanted to. But rather than let him think it was that easy to get around her, she twisted within the steel circle of his arms and pummeled him.

The sheer absurdity of her actions finally struck her, keeping her motionless for an instant. This was what she wanted, where she wanted to be. Her arms went around his neck, her body becoming pliant to his hands.

The kiss that she'd been fighting began to happen . . . and it became deeply sensuous. Pet returned it with equal passion, arching closer to him under the guidance of his shaping hands. His roaming caress excited her flesh, filling her with the completeness of her love, the totally sweet impossibility of it.

When breathing was permitted again, she whispered achingly, "I missed you so much, Dane." He nipped very gently at her throat in a way that caused a shiver of desire.

"I can't believe how upset you can get me." He lifted his head to frame her face in his hands, his fingers in the just-washed fullness of her hair. "When I walked through that door I wasn't exactly thinking anymore. That's not your fault, though." Weary lines were etched in his tanned skin, the strain of long hours leaving their mark. A gentleness shone in his dark eyes as a smile touched the corners of his mouth. "Do you know this is the first time I've seen you in a dress?"

"Is it?" she murmured. What she wore was just never all that important to her.

"Yeah. You look good—like a woman. But then you always do look good, even in camo pants and workboots. And God knows you're *all* woman." He slid a hand down to cover her breast, letting its round contour fill his palm. "But I get a kick out of seeing you in a skirt just the same. Were you going somewhere?"

"Didn't Charlie tell you?" Pet couldn't seem to drag her eyes away from his mouth. His lips had just a trace of her lipstick. He could kiss her like that anytime. What he did to her was electrifying. "We were going to have a sandwich together."

"He's married," Dane said.

"As far as I know, a meatball sub in mixed company doesn't count as adultery."

He took a deep breath, obviously trying to control his jealousy. "You're sure about that?" He slid her a rueful look.

"Yes. He's just a friend," she explained in case he wondered. "I didn't want to eat alone." She felt hopeful— if he could laugh at himself, things weren't so bad. "Are you free? I can tell Charlie—" But Dane was already shaking his head.

"No, I'm busy this evening." He didn't volunteer any specific information as to who he was going to be with or why he was dressed the way he was. "I just wanted to be sure you'd arrived safely. I expected you an hour ago."

"Charlie doesn't drive as fast as you do," Pet smiled, and tried not to wonder about his plans for the evening.

His light kiss seemed to be a reward for not asking. "I want you to have dinner with me tomorrow night, after the taping is finished. No one else. Just the two of us," he invited.

"I accept." She let her lips tease his, "On condition that you don't take me anyplace that's really dressy. This is the only one I brought."

"You got it." Dane returned the torment, rubbing his lips against hers while his fingers found her nipple beneath the bodice of her dress and teased it into erectness. "I'll take you somewhere that you have to *un*dress."

"You would!" Pet accused him.

"You bet." His mouth closed on hers, parting her lips to drink in her sweetness.

A knock at the door brought the kiss to a lingering end. "It's probably Charlie," she whispered against his mouth.

Reluctantly Dane let her go. "You'd better answer it. I have to leave anyway."

Pet moved unwillingly out of his arms to walk to the door. Remembering, she turned to warn him, "You have lipstick on your mouth."

When she opened the door, she saw that Charlie had brought Lon Baxter with him. "I bumped into Lon in the elevator, so I invited him to join us if that's all right," he explained, and glanced past her to see Dane. "Hey, there. Hi, Dane."

Pet glanced over her shoulder to see Dane returning his handkerchief to the inside pocket of his suit jacket. She supposed it would take about a second for the two men to figure out why he needed to wipe his mouth. She would have been less than honest if she didn't admit she was a little self-conscious.

"Hello, Charlie, Lon." Dane nodded to both men, but his gaze narrowed dangerously on the latter. Then he was moving alongside her, touching her shoulder lightly in farewell and smiling. "I'll see you tomorrow." An oblique reference to their dinner engagement.

"Tomorrow," she promised, saying more with her eyes.

The two men stepped to one side to let Dane pass, then Charlie raised a questioning eyebrow. "Ready?"

"Just let me get my bag," Pet nodded, and went to retrieve it from the dresser.

Nothing was said initially about Dane's being in

her room, although Lon's gaze was sulky when it met hers. The conversation during their meal centered on the production, with Lon filling them in on what had gone on here while they were in Batsto. After the waitress had cleared their plates and served coffee, Pet ripped open a couple of sugar packets, dumped them in, and enjoyed the sweet result.

"Dane was all worried when you didn't answer your phone." Charlie finally brought up the subject that had occupied both men's minds. "Where were you?"

"Taking a shower." She didn't go into the rest of the details.

"Don't make a fool of yourself, Pet," Lon said irritably. "All he wants to do is to sleep with you."

"I do seem to be popular, don't I?" Pet took another packet of sugar and ripped it open a little too fast, dumping the paper part into her coffee by accident. She took the spoon and fished it out.

"Maybe it is." Lon reddened, but he wasn't deterred. "But it doesn't change the facts."

"And those facts are?" Her voice was as cool as her glance.

"The only advantage to having an affair with him is get promoted or something. Even then, you might be out of a job when it ends and you two start throwing things at each other. Why would somebody like Dane Kingston want an ex-girlfriend working for him?" He leaned forward to stress his arguments.

Annoying as it was to be taken to task like this, it was twice as annoying because Charlie was right there. But that didn't stop her from defending herself.

"I haven't slept with him, and I'm not becoming involved with him because I want a promotion, a raise or anything like that." Pet sipped at her hot coffee, trying to appear indifferent despite Lon's blunt appraisal of her motive.

"Then the only thing you're going to get out of this affair is a lot of painful memories and regret. It isn't going to last," he insisted.

"Aww. I'm really touched by your show of concern. Why won't it?" she said.

"Give it a rest, Lon," Charlie urged. "It's none of our business."

But Lon ignored him. "He's Dane Kingston and you're Petra Wallis, that's why it won't last. You're a babe, but his world is full of babes. You can't compete with the fabulous Ruby Gale. Maybe he's through with her now, but there'll be someone else like her down the line. What are you—little Pet Wallis—going to do then?"

He shook his head as if despairing that he could get through to her. But he was. Every word that came out of Lon's mouth made her feel worse, much worse.

"If you want to fool around, then do it with an average guy like me," he said. "If not with me, then with someone like me. At least you'd stand a chance of having something that might last."

"I appreciate the advice," she said stiffly.

He sighed. "I know you aren't going to believe this, coming from me, but I like you, Pet. I don't want to see you get hurt."

"I like you, too, Lon," was the only reply she could make.

It was hectic getting ready for the last taping. Because another performer had done an hour of encores the night before they weren't able to set up the bulk of their equipment until the day of the taping. An hour before everything was supposed to be ready, Pet was helping Andy secure a cable that had worked loose from the duct tape holding it to the floor.

"Hey, Pet!" Rick called to her from the stage and motioned. "Dane wants to talk to you."

"Tell him I'll have a headset on in a few minutes."

"No. He's backstage," Rick explained.

Andy glanced at her. "Go see what he wants. I'll finish up here."

Wiping her sweaty palms on the hips of her brown slacks, Pet left him—but none too eagerly. Yesterday she would have raced for the chance to speak to Dane. However, Lon's warning had forced her to take a long, hard look at where she was going.

She didn't question anything Dane had told her or his desire for her. It was the things there hadn't been time to say—things she wasn't even sure he would have said if there had been the time. She was getting nervous about having dinner with him after the show because she knew where it would lead, and she wasn't sure anymore if that was where she wanted to go.

Backstage was total confusion as singers, dancers and stagehands arrived and mixed with the production crew. Pet hesitated, glancing around for the familiar sight of Dane's tall, muscular body. But she didn't see him. Female instinct guided her in the direction of Ruby Gale's private dressing room.

He was standing outside the door, half-turned away from her. Pet stopped when she glimpsed the red-haired woman with him. She didn't want to approach him while he was with Ruby and provoke the star's temper somehow. Since neither of them had noticed her in the midst of all the commotion, Pet stayed where she was until he was finished.

With a punishing kind of fascination, she noticed the way Dane's hands rested on Ruby's hips with such familiar ease. Her fingers were stroking his shirt front and fiddling with a button as if she was about to pop it open and stroke his skin next. Something plummeted to the pit of Pet's stomach when she realized her hearing had become attuned to their voices.

"Honey, I feel so badly about tonight," Ruby was saying. "We were going to celebrate with champagne and caviar, and now I can't make it."

Ruby couldn't make it? Pet had thought the date was off because Dane had canceled to have dinner with the singer. Uh-huh. She understood now. And no, she wasn't going to think of herself as a substitute. Dane had said whatever he'd had with Ruby was over, so what did it matter?

"Okay. I'm disappointed," Dane replied, and didn't mention anything about having another engagement.

It wasn't necessary that he should, Pet thought.

"I shouldn't be celebrating now anyway," he was saying. "My work is just beginning. The editing process always takes twice as long as you think it will and I want to get it all together into a smooth, fast-paced show. It's just as well that we have to postpone it."

"Wow. Thanks for understanding, Dane." Ruby beamed and stretched up on her toes to kiss him.

"I understand that my favorite superstar has a show to get ready for and she's letting me detain her." The kiss he gave back was little more than a peck. He turned her around and gave her a gentle push toward her door. "Go and make yourself beautiful."

With a husky laugh, Ruby Gale slipped into her dressing room. As Dane turned to leave, his gaze immediately fell on Pet. She started forward quickly, so he wouldn't guess she had been standing there watching and waiting, a bright smile fixed on her expression. His features softened at her approach.

"Rick said you wanted to talk to me," she explained.

"Always . . . yeah, I do. Wish I could get you alone more," he murmured, caressing her with his voice and his velvet dark eyes. Then he seemed to catch himself and took a deep, regretful breath. It was strange, because Pet couldn't breathe at all. "It's strictly business right now, though. I want you to get some behind-the-scenes action before the show starts—dressing rooms, makeup, wardrobe, musicians, stagehands. You know the kind of color I want. And concentrate on what goes on in the wings during a performance. You should be able to pick up some audience shots in the background."

"Sure." Pet continued to stand there, looking at him, loving him, and struggling to seem cool and professional.

"Then you'd better get a move on," Dane urged with a dancing look, "before I take you behind that curtain and make love to you."

Her pulse beat super-fast, losing any semblance of normality. Behind that glint of amusement in his dark eyes was hot desire. It was unmistakable.

"Yes, sir." Breathless, she snapped off a pretty good salute and turned to hurry away.

By the time she got the handheld camera strapped

on with all its paraphernalia and commandeered a helper named Tom to carry the recorder and keep the attached wires and cords out of the way, it was half an hour before show time. Preparations for the performance were in full swing backstage. She noticed Dane standing on center stage in consultation with her three co-workers who would be manning the cameras out front. They were going over his detailed notes on each number.

Her gaze lingered on his brawny build for an aching second, but her task had already been assigned, so she set to work. Tom tagged along after her like a faithful dog carrying its master's newspaper, only in this case he carried the recorder.

As she was setting up to get a shot of the general hubbub around the dressing rooms, a florist arrived with a huge standing bouquet of blood-red roses. Pet quickly seized on this piece of glamorous backstage color and followed him to the star's dressing room, the tape rolling. She was standing some ten feet away when the door opened at the florist's knock. Luck gave her the perfect angle over the shoulder of the florist into the dressing room.

Clancy, personal assistant to Ruby Gale, answered the door. Beyond her, Ruby was sitting in front of a mirror with her back to the camera and the door, dressed in a lavender robe. The mirror's reflection gave Pet a view of the star's face. If it had all been rehearsed, it couldn't have been more perfect.

Evidently the florist had added some flattering comment of his own to the delivery of the roses, because the red-haired entertainer half turned to give him one of her sexy smiles. Her blue gaze flickered past him to the camera and Pet. She was instantly livid, coming to her feet and storming out of her room in a volcanic fury as flaming as her hair.

"You snooping little bitch!" she screamed at Pet. "What are you doing sneaking around out here? Like the freakin' paparazzi aren't bad enough?"

"I'm sorry." Pet tried to apologize and explain about the flowers, but her voice was drowned by the vicious abuse and accusations Ruby Gale hurled at her. She attempted to retreat, backing away, but she was relentlessly pursued. Too stunned by the vitriolic attack, Pet understood only half of the insults.

"What were you hoping—that I'd be half-naked so you could sell the tapes to a tabloid? I know how you got your job—on your back! How many men did you have to sleep with?" Ruby raged.

Pet's face was scarlet. Everyone backstage was witnessing this disgusting scene. She couldn't think of a thing to say.

"You aren't on this production because of your skill with the camera!" Ruby went on. "It's what you can do in bed, as in keeping the rest of the crew happy while they're away from home! You're a—"

"What's going on here?" Dane's angry voice was the most wonderful sound Pet had ever heard. She turned as he came striding forward, relief cooling her hot cheeks.

"This blond slut was snooping outside my door!" His arrival did not abate the redhead's abusive tongue. "She—"

Pet interrupted quickly, "The florist delivered some roses and I was—"

"You were stalking me!"

"No more." Dane intervened to lay soothing hands on Ruby's shoulders, which trembled with the force

of her wrath. "I don't want you getting upset. I'll take
care of it. You can leave it to me now."

Pet stared at him incredulously, shock giving way
to indignation. She was aware of the calming effect
he was having on the star, but she really didn't care
if Ruby couldn't be pacified. In fact, jamming a paci-
fier in Ruby's mouth could be the way to go.

"I won't tolerate anyone sneaking around me," the
redhead insisted. Some of the venom had leached
out of her tone although it remained imperious.

"I promise you she won't bother you anymore." He
curved an arm around the lavender-covered shoulders and turned Ruby toward her dressing room.
"Don't worry about it."

Tears scalded Pet's green eyes. She furiously blinked
them away, turning to see Tom staring at her, wordless
in profound sympathy. Aching with righteous anger
and raw pain, she couldn't respond to his look. She
didn't need to communicate her desire to move away
from the star's dressing room as Tom picked up the
recorder to walk with her. Pride kept Pet's shoulders
squared and her head high, but she was trembling
inside from Dane's abandonment of her. She was
determined not to let it show how deeply she was hurt.

That resolve flew out of the window when Dane
came in search of her a short few minutes later. The
welling tears in her eyes kept her from seeing him too
clearly, but she had a blurred image of his tight-lipped
countenance, which was all her temper needed.

"How could you let her talk to me like that?" Her
angry voice scraped her throat to make the accusa-
tion hoarse. "How could you let her get away with it?"

"It's only twenty minutes before the show starts!"
Dane flared. "What did you expect me to do? Try to

defend you and have her do one of her exit scenes? Then where the hell would I be with all this equipment and crew and a half-finished special?"

"I don't care who she is or how important she is, nobody has a right to talk to anybody like that—not to me! Not to Tom! Not to anybody!" Pet retorted in a husky protest.

"And what about the show?" he challenged.

"Oh, God, yes. The show!" Her voice was breaking, cracking under the strain. "You said you'd sold your soul for it and you were right. You'll get your show, Mr. Kingston. And I hope it keeps you happy, because I won't!"

"Of all the damned time and places to pick—" he began in exasperation.

"You'd better leave. You've got work to do before the show starts." She turned away from him, pretending to adjust something with the equipment while she choked on a sob. It felt like an eternity, but it was only seconds before she heard him walk away. She closed her eyes at the shattering pain in her chest.

"Are you all right?" Tom murmured anxiously.

"I'm fine," she sniffed, and wiped at her nose before lifting her chin. "We'll do his damned show."

The decision created a strange detachment that permitted her to get through the taping of the performance, functioning mechanically, completely emotionless. From the wings she got a shot of Ruby Gale accepting the final ovation from the crowd, an applauding audience in the background, and exiting to the opposite side of the stage to receive the congratulations of her personal entourage.

The minute it was over Pet set the camera down and began unstrapping all the gear. "Take care of this stuff for me, Tom," she said tightly, and started to walk away. "I'm leaving."

"But what if Kingston—"

"Tell him he has his show. And tell him he can't fire me, because I quit."

Chapter Eleven

Moonlight silvered the foamy caps of the waves rushing onto the sandy shore. Pet lifted her face to the ocean breeze, closing her eyes to the pain that hadn't found a release. Her hair had long ago been freed from its confining pins as if loose and falling free it would somehow allow the hurt to tumble from her. But it hadn't.

Turning parallel to the ocean, Pet began to walk again along the stretch of beach. To her left was the boardwalk, the towering buildings and hotels of Atlantic City etched in lights against the night sky. She didn't know how far she had walked since she had bolted from the casino theater to wander aimlessly up and down the quiet beach, avoiding the piers with their noisy rides and bright lights. She wasn't the only one walking along the oceanfront. A few others were strolling its expanses, mostly couples.

A wave came rushing in to lap the firmly packed sand near her feet, but she ignored its mild threat. Her gaze wandered ahead, studying the strip of glistening wet sand that marked the extent of the tide's encroachment onto the beach. The dark figure of a man was standing ten yards in front of her by the water's edge, but facing her and not the sea. Her heart gave a painful thump in her chest as she recognized Dane and paused.

Refusing to run or walk up to him, Pet took a few steps into the soft sand beyond the reach of the waves and sat down. Her hands shook and she squeezed them into fists to control it as she stared out to sea. Drawing her knees up, she rested her forearms on them. The sand crunched under Dane's approaching footsteps, but she didn't look up when he stopped beside her.

"I'd just about given up hope." His voice was low and husky. "I looked everywhere—the hotel, the casino, up and down the boardwalk. If it hadn't been for all that golden hair shining in the moonlight, I would probably have gone on looking all night for you."

Pet made no reply, not even acknowledging his presence with a look. She stayed calm, but inside she was dying.

"Don't you know you shouldn't be walking alone at night?" But when his question was met by her continued silence, Dane sighed heavily. "I can't even make you angry, can I?"

There was an agonizing tightness in her throat. The paralyzing numbness that had kept everything dammed up inside was wearing off. She started shaking and had to trap her hands between her knees to control the shaking that had started again.

"You were right, Pet," he said with a throbbing hoarseness. "I sold my soul for that show."

A tiny, agonized sound slipped through the constricted muscles of her throat.

He continued to tower motionless above her. "Pet, you're the only one who can buy it back for me."

The husky appeal in his voice finally pulled her head up. She searched his shadowed face. The pride and strength remained carved into his features, but his dark eyes were haunted.

"When the show was over and I found out you'd walked out, I didn't try to find you right away. I went back to the control van and sat there, going over in my mind what had happened and what you'd said." Turning, Dane sat down on the sand beside her, adopting her position and letting handfuls of sand run through his fingers.

She didn't say anything and he sighed.

"I thought I had the thing that was most important to me right there in front of me—the show tapes. And then, not in so many words, you told me what an arrogant, selfish bastard I was. I've been called that before, but coming from you . . ." He sighed heavily and clasped his hands between his spread knees, studying his linked fingers. "What I'm trying to say, Pet, is that what's important to me is your love and respect. Nothing else means anything."

"You don't really mean that, Dane," she whispered sadly. "You just want me to forgive you so you'll feel better. You don't care whether or not I love you. We haven't even known each other long enough to fall in love."

"Maybe you haven't, but I've been waiting for you all my life." His gaze locked onto hers and refused to let it go. "I love you, Pet. I realized it the morning that I came into your room to wake you up, and I knew that I wanted to wake you up every morning for the rest of my life. It was too soon. I couldn't tell you then. You would have thought I was handing you some line to persuade you to sleep with me. So I waited, knowing you were attracted to me and hoping that after this show was finished I'd have the time to make you fall in love with me, too."

"You don't even know me." She shook her head for a moment, breaking the spell he was casting.

"I know you. After our run-in a year ago, I made it my business to know about you. At the time I told myself my interest was purely professional," he said with a humorless laugh. "I personally reviewed everything you did, every project you were on, your past employment, your education, your family, everything. If you weren't any good, I was going to get rid of you—the green-eyed blond who told me to shut up."

"You've succeeded. I quit." She wouldn't let herself be swayed by his revelations. He had hurt her too deeply tonight. It wasn't something that could be easily forgiven or forgotten.

"Pet, I erased the show tapes—all of them."

"What?" She jerked around to stare at him, wary and frowning.

"It wasn't an impulse. I thought it over very hard before I did it. You can call it a noble gesture if you want, but it was the only way I could prove that you were more important to me than the special."

"You shouldn't have done that!" She was stunned, incredulous.

"Why not?" Now he was watching her, his gaze searching every nuance of her expression.

"Because . . . all that work . . . all that time . . ." It was impossible to think of all the reasons when there were so many. "You've spent a lot of money."

"A lot of money," Dane agreed. "But it's worth every dime if you finally believe me."

"I believe you." After that kind of sacrifice, how could she doubt him?

"Do you forgive me?'"

"Of course," Pet breathed, just beginning to realize the fulfillment this meant. "Dane, I fell in love with you, too. I was the most miserable person in the world when I thought the man I loved could care so little about me that—"

But she was never allowed to complete the sentence as his hand reached to pull her off balance and into his arms. He was kissing her and murmuring love words that she would cherish in her heart forever.

When Dane finally allowed her to breathe a little, she was lying on the sand, her head pillowed on his sinewy forearm while he leaned over her. She drank in the sight of his compelling face above hers, passion in his eyes.

"When will you marry me?" he demanded.

An old fear returned. "Do you really think I can keep you happy?" she whispered with a catch in her voice.

"No one else can. Haven't you accepted that yet?" he said gently. "No one else can rile me up quicker than you can, because you're invariably right. And no one else can touch me and set me on fire like you do. You're perfect, that's your problem—or mine. Oh hell. I'm not saying this the way I planned."

"Keep going. So far I like what I'm hearing."

Dane scowled. "I never knew a woman could make me happy with just a smile. But you do."

"Ruby Gale—" Pet began.

His mouth thinned. "Once and for all, let's settle

that. It was always business between Ruby and me. The physical side of our relationship—okay, that happened. She had needs and so did I. Emotions were never involved on either side. I can't say that I'm particularly proud of it, but she's gorgeous and sexy. I am just a man."

"That's exactly it, Dane," Pet tried to explain again. "In your business there will always be women like Ruby Gale."

"I know!" he muttered.

"Please, I'm serious," Pet insisted.

"But none of them will be you, Pet! Can't I get it through your head that I love you? It isn't just desire or physical gratification. It's love."

His mouth closed onto hers to convince her of the difference. Pet surrendered, not wanting to even think as his weight pressed her onto the soft bed of sand. She was breathless and aroused when he finally transferred his attention to the hollow of her throat. She ran her fingers through his dark hair, quivering as his hands worked deftly at the buttons on her blouse.

"Do you think this is a proper behavior for a lady?" she whispered with a trace of teasing amusement. "Letting a man make love to her on a public beach? After all your lectures, Dane Kingston, what will people think if they see me?"

"Dammit, Pet!" He started to get angry, then laughed. "I have champagne chilling in my room." He kissed her hard. "And if you say a lady wouldn't go to a man's hotel room, I'll carry you there. Like the hero of a romance."

She linked her fingers around his neck and gazed at him impishly. "Who ever said I was a lady?"